Lockdown Tales II

Lockdown Tales II

Neal Asher

NewCon Press
England

First edition, published in the UK February 2023
by NewCon Press
41 Wheatsheaf Road, Alconbury Weston, Cambs, PE28 4LF, UK

NCP297 (hardback)
NCP298 (softback)

10 9 8 7 6 5 4 3 2 1

ISBN: 978-1-914953-42-2 (hardback)
978-1-914953-43-9 (softback)

Cover Art and front cover titles by Vincent Sammy
Editing and typesetting by Ian Whates

Contents

LOCKDOWN TALES II
An Introduction

I would have preferred not to have a Lockdown Tales II, rather some other collection with the necessity for another title, but it was not to be. Frightened politicians who want all the power without the responsibility deferring to 'experts' who, like many before them, continued predicting catastrophe so as to maintain their position in the limelight and their 'importance', have kept the lockdowns going. And, of course, as with all these ersatz catastrophes, big vested interests have put their weight behind this one, and the corporatist money-trousering circuit has kicked in. But enough of that – we are here to enjoy stories.

I continued with my attempts to write short stories that (mostly) transitioned into something longer. Here are some more of them including a few I mentioned in the first Lockdown Tales as being published in various magazines. I also have one, or maybe two, stories that appeared prior to lockdowns but this collection is as good a vehicle as any for them and I would argue that their publication year extended into lockdowns. Anyway, the title of the collection is almost immaterial – I'm pretty sure you reading this would be annoyed that I didn't include a recent material because I got OCD about dates.

In some of these stories I stepped out of the Polity and in others I went to places in it where few have ventured, or show aspects of that realm that haven't appeared in my books. Stepping back and looking at the list I see that some kinda cover more recent interests of mine. One arises from my reading in longevity and the efforts made in that direction in the growing biotech industry (Longevity Averaging) and a quite possible near future. Four stories have sprung from my life on Crete. The obvious one here is An Alien on Crete which contains scenes and personal encounters straight out of my life here Aanother three are Polity stories, so how do they arise from Crete?

When I first bought a house here my understanding of the language was enough for me to order a beer, say good morning and goodnight. I spent many years acquiring some new words and phrases but, as many expats here have discovered, it's very easy to be lazy about what is a difficult language. Go into any bar, restaurant or shop and you'll find someone who speaks English. Attempt to speak Greek and, more interested in selling you something than teaching you, they'll immediately figure out your nationality and reply in English. It's easy to be lazy. However, since my wife died (now eight years ago) I made a concerted effort to learn the language. I took lessons from a woman in my local village, went on to make copious notes which, at one time, I spent an hour a day reading out loud, watched videos, avoided the shortcut of apps, and stubbornly spoke Greek whenever possible. I also took the view that as well as learning a language useful to me, this would be great mental exercise – it is, apparently, one of the best. Arising out of this interest are three linked stories that run in this chronological order: The Translator, The Host and Moral Biology. That order is not the order in which I wrote them and titles swapped around too, but more on that in the introduction to each story.

Other stuff arose out of, well, whatever the answer is to that perennial question, 'Where do you get your ideas from?' I also have two novellas written in the time of lockdown I haven't included. One got instigated by a dream in which I used an old style asthma inhaler (the kind that punctured a capsule so one could inhale the dust inside) whose capsules contained dead flies, and grew in the telling. I've agonised over that because its structure just isn't right, and I am also beginning to wonder if I need to deconstruct it and thereafter turn it into a book. The thing is set in the dystopian Owner universe and is called Fly Pills. Another arose out of a picture someone showed on Facebook of her holding a large insect, while in the background was a picture of a trapdoor spider. Jenny Trapdoor also has structural issues. Perhaps it will appear in another collection, but hopefully not Lockdown Tales III. Enjoy!

Neal Asher,
June 2022

When I started out writing short stories I was still under the influence of all the stuff I'd read before so threw in everything. While transitioning from Fantasy to Science Fiction I still included psychic powers. In fact a very early story (which I can't find at the moment) concerned a telepath travelling by runcible to triangulate the position of an alien psychic scream. Later on I dropped that stuff because, though I don't mind 'technology indistinguishable from magic', psychic powers began to strike me as simply magic. They seemed like a copout. In retrospect I see that they, and magic, are perfectly doable so long as they have a logical foundation. Suspension of disbelief in the end arises from how the story is told. Anyway, after that ramble, here's a Polity story where I've ventured back into that territory. The discerning fan will recognise some aspects of Weaponised first arising here.

XENOVORE

The creature looked vaguely humanoid, but also like one of those bipedal robots that acted as mobile platforms for complicated guns. It was big – standing three metres tall at full stretch. Jutting forwards from the body the head resembled a stretched-out bird's skull, though underneath the beak, which was in fact a tube measuring a couple of inches across, it sported a large set of mandibles. Or maybe they were arms. Sometimes they looked like the former when folded up underneath that skull, and at other times, when spreading out seemingly for balance, the latter. These limbs terminated in stunted hands, but the utile parts of them were hooked barbs running down their inner face for grasping prey.

The thing moved fast – faster than a man could run. But it also moved faster even than that, as Tupolek… no, Cranston, with his long legs and ropy muscle giving him an inhuman turn of speed, soon found out. Anstor blinked in confusion at a surge of déjà vu. No, definitely Cranston. Yet now he had a memory of Tupolek running like this, and maybe there had been others? He shook his head and returned his attention to the present.

The creature dashed after *Cranston* with a long loping gait that seemed almost comedic and, drawing close, it sent him sprawling with a flip of one of those mandible limbs and bore down on him. It grasped him about the hips as, yelling and swearing, he managed to get to his knees. He tried to struggle forwards, but it had him now. What the files described as its wet feeding tube went in at about the position of his left kidney. He bellowed in disbelief, then struggled in ferocious silence. The digestive fluid went in fast – so fast that the skin of the creature's bloated torso sank back against internal skeleton. Cranston began shrieking in horrified agony as his body abruptly began to inflate. His overalls popped open at the front, his belly bulged enormously under a white T-shirt. His limbs and neck inflated and where his skin could be seen it turned green, veined with red. One sleeve split over an arm grown grotesquely fat above a hand disappearing in swelling. His screams became liquid and turned to gurgling. Finally that ended as the digestive fluid jetted from his mouth and nostrils and, after a moment, his eyes.

Cranston's struggles ceased and he slumped in the creature's grip. Anstor, crouching down behind the boulder, wondered if he was dead now, or simply incapable of screaming or moving. Certainly he must be drowning with the digestive fluid flooding his lungs. No, he had to be dead. The stuff worked quickly to liquefy all internal soft tissue. The appearance of maybe life stemmed from an evolutionary quirk of the fluid. It formed a membrane as it neared skin – something to do with contact with a pheromone the creature also emitted into the air – as it was now forming membranes over his mouth, nostrils, eyes and probably anus. The creature's body then began to pump like bellows and Cranston rapidly deflated. Within just a few minutes he returned to normal size, with just a few areas still bulging. The creature's body had now expanded and its belly hung pendulous and gurgling. It stripped off Cranston's flimsy overalls and undergarments and discarded them, then stabbed its feeding tube into other parts of him to get to other liquefied internals. Finally, when he looked like just a skeleton wrapped in skin, it discarded him.

Anstor had wondered at this feeding method when first reading about it in the files the Nok allowed them to access. He wasn't sure when that had been, but yes, he remembered thinking that nature here seemed particularly cruel. But then again no, this method was little different from that of many insects on Earth – a creature called a shield bug being one example. The files went into more elaborate detail. The xenovores here used a variety of pre-digestion phases to allow them to process alien meat and other matter before full ingestion. They were capable of eating just about any life form found across the galaxy no matter their biology which, now he thought about it and remembered thinking it about it before, rather negated the idea of 'nature'. Creatures could not evolve naturally to eat other creatures from other worlds.

The xenovore rose up now and searched its surroundings with two black eyes. Anstor crouched lower behind the boulder and prayed he had not been seen. He heard it hissing and clicking as it moved about, and then the sounds beginning to die. He rose up into a squat and peered out to see it moving off into the landscape lying beyond: rolling hillocks of mud and stone of a purple cast from the clouded red sky. As usual drizzle filled the air, but seeing the darkening above and hearing the grumble of thunder he knew heavy rain would soon arrive.

What were his chances now of reaching the two hundred miles distant Polity base? That's where they had been running to, wasn't it? He could feel the tension of rope muscle in his body. His eyesight and hearing had improved, too – his eyes now unnaturally large with that secondary pupil growing and nictitating membranes working, and his ears larger, cupped forwards and growing an addition inside that looked like a starfish. He hesitated, undecided. Surely he was a brave man? Damn it, he recollected being a Polity commando and having trained for and been involved in some serious fights. Yes, that had been… some time ago, but surely he still had that courage? He frowned into the past – days and nights here an endless blur. If he returned now, his adaptations would have a chance to reach Cranston's level or beyond and he could try again when he was faster, when his senses were more attuned, and maybe having acquired something new introduced into the program. He grimaced, vaguely remembering something about Cranston being a newer inductee… a much newer one. He also thought of the danger that remained back there, for he might at some point be designated a *failure*, and he began to fall back into indecision.

No, damn it!

The situation back at the Facility would not have changed. The perimeter would allow them out but would not allow the creatures in. The Nok would remain apparently indifferent to escape attempts, though it did enquire about the efforts of those who returned. It apparently considered escape would signify the success of its project – a confusing attitude since escape should result in this place swarming with Polity soldiers come to free the prisoners, and the Nok being shut down.

Still, the possibility of escape remained, while bravery could also be stupidity and surely he was not a stupid man?

Without further thought, he found himself moving back away from the boulder and towards the Facility. He was strong and fast – surely more so than he had been with his Polity enhancements, though he had little recollection of what they were – but he was not ready yet. The second xenovore arrived almost as confirmation of that.

Humanoid again like many others he had studied in the Nok's files, this monster came out of the ground ahead. springing upright on ostrich legs, squat squarish body above and long arms terminating in three-fingered hands. He recognised it as a stripper and one of the cruellest. When he first read about it he doubted the Nok's contention that this was all about feeding on alien flesh. This creature, whose head bore some similarity to the one that had killed Cranston, or Tupolek, extruded a skein of tubes. Once it captured its prey, it injected those tubes, in some places attaching them to maintain the function of organs and in other places feeding. It ate those things non-essential to the maintenance of life first, starting with fat, then eating out the limbs from the inside, then the digestive system and finally the organs whose loss killed its victim. It reminded Anstor of the hooders of Masada – devolved biotech war machines that kept their victims alive while feeding on them – though he did not know if he had ever seen one of those.

'It is part of the process,' he remembered the Nok saying. 'It learns its prey at a biochemical level while feeding on it and it cannot learn as much from something no longer functioning.'

The Nok seemed very adept at these explanations, in its didactic and sometimes urbane manner.

Anstor leapt aside, a three-fingered hand grabbing for his arm but getting only a torn-off sleeve from his flimsy overalls. He ran, energy surging through his body, and did not have to look round to know the thing was right behind him and catching up fast. The acuteness of his senses amazed him sometimes, for he seemed to know its position just from the thump of its clawed toes and the weird keening issuing from it. It seemed as if he could see it perfectly behind him – its image clear in his mind. When it drew close enough to reach out and grab him he dodged – that hand whipping through the point he had been just a moment before, but then the other hand sweeping in. It had him. It would get him. He felt a surge of panic and the world seemed to judder around him. Suddenly he found himself further from the xenovore than he had thought. All he could think was that in terror he had misjudged the distance, despite his acute senses.

To add unpredictability he dodged again and leapt a rain-glistening boulder. But now with the heavy rain arriving to add to his difficulties, he stumbled slightly in glutinous mud. Something snakelike writhed from his path and he recognised one of the numerous scavengers. Instinctively he threw himself forwards into a roll and heard, and *saw*, those hands grabbing air above him, then he was up and changing direction again, but at no point losing his sense of direction. He was close now and looking ahead could see the sections of wall that had ringed the Facility before the perimeter guns went up.

A glance back showed him a hand reaching for his shoulder, a writhing mass of those tubes following along its course. He ducked aside, but felt something loop around his ankle and send him stumbling. The other thing – the scavenger – had intervened in hope of a portion of the bounty. As he shouldered the ground he felt a surge of disbelief. This could not be happening! But, even as the thought passed through his mind, he knew Cranston and so many others had probably thought the same as the tubes went into them. He rolled, struggling to get back upright, saw the stripper looming over him. If only he had got a few yards further he would have been in range of the perimeter guns. He could see one of them clear in his mind, could feel the mechanism of it turning and aiming and the intense need for it to fire, and then just a *push*...

Bright white light flashed and momentarily took his vision away. It returned a second later with shadow spots blocking the intense glare so he could see the electric discharges of the pulse cannon running down the stripper's body in shades of red and umber. It stood frozen, its mass of tubes in spasm, spread like the tentacles of a squid. Anstor gaped. Again he must have misjudged distances. Surely? A thing like a large white flatworm rose up out of the mud by his leg, derailing that train of thought. He grabbed and squeezed, relishing the strength of his hand as he crushed and discarded the scavenger, bounced to his feet and ran inside the perimeter. To one side he saw the weapon there up on its tripod and it still looked too far to have fired that warning shot, but maybe the heavy rain had confused him.

Once firmly inside the perimeter, he looked back at the xenovore. The pulse shot had been just to scare it off – enough to hurt it but not enough to kill. If it advanced any further the energy levels would ramp up and the next shots would kill it. He felt an utter hatred of the thing and wished and prayed for those other shots. In a moment of madness he shouted at it and then capered in a circle. It hesitated, last static discharges running down its legs, but when he picked up a rock and threw it, accurately hitting that mass of tubes, it surged forwards a few paces, but then halted.

'Come on you fucker! Come and get me!' he shouted.

The thing squatted down and observed him.

'Come on!'

He grabbed at the air and looked over at the nearest pulse cannon, his imagining of its workings expanding as a complex schematic in his mind. But the thing remained static, its barrel pointed in along the line of the perimeter, which didn't make sense because it had already fired a warning shot. A sudden sharp pain speared through his skull. Lines of bright flashes punctuated the air, as if the cannons on either side had opened fire. These punched into the monster's body, burned in and passed out through its back in explosions of steam and embers. It came upright, staggered and finally crashed down, smoke and steam issuing from it, one hand grasping at the ground. Anstor shrugged himself, made some attempt to straighten his raggety overall, turned and strode back towards the Facility. The ache in his skull continued as he tried to make sense of what had happened.

Twenty metres in from the ring of perimeter guns he reached the remains of the original wall, and headed towards where he and Cranston had come through at a point where it had fallen down. The pain in his skull receded and his confusion cleared. He had mixed things up, as he often did. A perimeter gun had fired a warning shot just as it should, and when he had taunted the thing to come after him, they had killed it at the perimeter. But now, as so often happened after one of his headaches, time and memory swirled in his mind.

He could not remember how long he had been here. His far past as a Polity commando and as a traveller was a bright segment buried in the endless red rainy days and nights here. Sometimes he thought himself trapped in a nightmare virtuality and might wake up at any time. All the stuff that did not make sense reinforced this conjecture. The Nok had implanted something inside them. He was sure he had seen that thing once, but the memory escaped him now. The Nok's experiments were changing them. Their ability to survive the hostile life out there appeared to be a signifier of that, yet the *failures* did not back that up. He had seen the Nok take people who had become inordinately strong and fast and designate them as failed. He had seen others whose changes had left them weak and sick and sometimes immobile, yet it did not consider them failures.

Other things did not make sense either Chunks of memory slid up for his inspection. He saw one inductee spontaneously erupting into flame, run burning from a Facility building to stand in the rain, burning down to a twisted atomy and laughing crazily all the while. Objects sometimes disappeared and then reappeared. He remembered finding himself lying in his bed outside in the rain, then spending some time afterwards trying to find out who had performed this prank, and getting nowhere. When other objects disappeared and reappeared in the same manner, he had accepted it as part of the twisted logic of this place. One time he remembered walking through the Facility and everyone standing as still as statues. No response from Indira even when he threatened to poke her in the eye, and when he touched her she had felt as smooth as glass. Maybe that had been a dream or a nightmare – sometimes it was difficult to tell. His memory had been faulty for a long time and he often mixed up the order of events. He often did not know what was real. And here, on the exterior of the old wall, which, he was sure he could remember at one time being new, was another example.

The front of a skull protruded from the wall. Lower down wrist bones stuck out – the bones of that hand once lying on the ground below, but now long gone. And further down, a knee protruded. What had her name been? Pearson, Preston, Parapsinge? She had disappeared and they had all thought she'd tried to get past the xenovores to the halcyon Polity base. Someone else venturing over the wall – there had been no break then – had found her and come back to tell them. She had not even begun to decay at that point and Anstor remembered gazing at her face – mouth open in a scream, or in laughter. And though his memory was faulty, he knew for sure he had seen her well after the wall had been built, in the Facility, walking round in a seeming perpetual dream. She

15

could not possibly have become imbedded in the plasticrete wall during its construction.

He moved on round and through the break, over the rubble pile. He recollected earthquakes, or explosions, and seeing these breaks the next day, or maybe the next week. Four inductees had gone missing, but fragmented human remains were found, some spattered across the ground in the Facility, others plastered against the Nok's ship, later to be absorbed. Some escape attempt using homemade explosives? He had no idea, and it seemed pointless to blow holes in a wall that could be easily climbed. He moved on in.

The Facility consisted of a mass of buildings like gas storage tanks scattered on a large flat rock. Beyond it, and still within the perimeter, lay another flat rock upon which rested the Nok's ship. A low circular fence like a pipe supported just off the stone encircled the vessel. He had no idea what defences were in that pipe but, if you tried to cross it, you died, instantly. In fact two skeletons and a new corpse lay over it even now – yet to be completely stripped down by scavengers the perimeter guns didn't respond to.

The strange ship resembled detritus washed up on the tide line of a beach on Earth – the egg case of some fish or mollusc. From below it looked vaguely rectangular with protrusions from the corners stretching to the fore at one end and curving in, but trailing like twin tails at the other end. It had blisters and pockets strewn over its surface that had to be drive systems, instrumentation and maybe weapons. Pale yellow like old bone, it somehow seemed soft, fleshy. It clung to the ground with those fore and aft protrusions and, when seen out of the corner of the eye, seemed to be moving. Anstor had once stared at it for hours trying to see that movement directly but never did, however he was damned sure when he looked at it another time, that some of those things on its surface had changed position. But why did he think it strange when numerous radically different designs of ship could be found in the Polity? It was fully organic for one thing – he was sure of that. Yes, some biotech worlds produced semi-organic ships but always with many of the necessities of space travel grafted on. A hull and a life support system might be grown, but Polity science had yet to find a way to grow fusion engines or a U-space drive. However these anomalies did not account for its strangeness which, in a way he found difficult to nail down, was because he knew it to be alien.

Just like the Nok.

Anstor approached the steps leading up the side of the Facility slab and climbed them. Reaching the top he paused. For those who had been here some time, like him, and who had learned how things ran here, there were no fences. However, one of the buildings did have a fenced compound around it. In there, Anstor saw, new prisoners clustered. The Nok kept them enclosed throughout their 'induction' as it stripped them of any belongings, along with their Polity enhancements. They were told their location, and how they could try to escape but would likely die horribly. The Nok had graphic educational films for them to watch. They were then told they were part of an experiment in a special form of organic human enhancement. Anstor remembered, vaguely, waking up in that building when previously he had been on an in-system passenger transport. Had the Nok taken his enhancements then? And when had he known there was something inside him and that the experiment had already begun? It didn't matter. The order of events didn't matter – just the reality of now.

The Nok went amongst the captives while they occupied the compound, and always they tried to attack it, and always they failed. It didn't deliberately hurt anyone – generally just swatting them away as irritations. The hurting only happened during upgrades or, briefly, when it decided one of the recipients of the gamosphore had 'failed'. Finally, when it considered their induction complete, it allowed them out into the general population. Many tried to escape then and never got as far even as Cranston.

'What is it doing? What does it want?' he remembered a woman asking him querulously. Was he in the compound then or out of it?

'If you ever figure that out, please let me know,' he had replied.

As he walked towards the buildings now, he saw a group of inductees, of about his level, out in the rain. Indira, Packam, Leach and Troisier. They all had adaptations or alterations at variance to those of him and Cranston. Indira had been a woman with the kind of hourglass figure Anstor favoured, but she had lost that now. She looked brutally muscular and parts of her skin had taken on a stony appearance – hardening up like carapace. Her head had a ridge under the hair, like she was growing a crest, and two strange looking nodes protruded from her temples. She said she could sense the pheromone output of the xenovores.

Packam, a thin man when he arrived here, had grown even thinner and taller. He could move faster than any of them but seemed disinclined to use this ability to escape. His intelligence seemed to have dropped through the floor and when they discussed their situation here he often looked on in bafflement. Perhaps his head growing tall and thin had done something to his brain? Anstor often wondered if he would be failed, but it seemed intelligence was not a prerequisite of success. In fact, he had no certainty of the Nok's actual aims.

Troisier had the same brutish appearance as Indira, but his head had sunk lower and his eyes seemed to be developing facets. He did not know what senses he was developing, only that he could crush rocks with his hands.

Leach had a brutish upper body but long thin legs. One eye had developed facets and the other a double pupil. It seemed that his gamosphore could not decide what to do with him. Occasionally he had fits and had bitten off the end of his tongue. He didn't talk much now. Occasionally crevices opened on his body and leaked a clear fluid that turned to jelly on contact with air. Of them all, if physical organic enhancement was the aim, he should have been a failure, but he persisted.

'What happened,' asked Indira.

'Couple of miles out a 003 xenovore got Tupolek,' Anstor replied. 'He was faster than me, so I turned back.'

'Cranston you mean,' said Indira. She grimaced for a moment, then nodded her head affirmatively. 'Yes, Cranston.'

'Chicken shit,' said Troisier, but without much heat.

'So… what plan now?' asked Packam, showing that he did have at least a few brain cells still functional.

'Unchanged from last time,' said Indira. 'We talked about this.' She stared at Anstor with a contemptuous twist to her mouth. 'It was only Cranston's overblown confidence that he had achieved some kind of peak that allowed this last stupidity.'

Anstor dipped his head, annoyed with himself for going along with the other man. Indira had been right all along. In fact he could not enumerate the number of times she had been right about something, nor could he remember how long he had known her.

'It has to be coordinated and it has to be a large group of us and, damn it, we need weapons beyond what the Nok provides.' She gestured down at her body. 'Now I suggest you all think about that, talk to the others, get information, ideas.' She abruptly turned away and marched off.

'Don't sweat it, son,' said Troisier, patting him on the shoulder. 'I nearly went with you but I can't run so fast.'

'Me 'either,' said Leach, short-tongued. He closed his eyes and concentrated. 'Bu' I 'eed go tsoon.'

Anstor had no words to acknowledge that. He felt oddly resentful that Leach had not yet been designated a failure, thus going some way to prove that physical enhancement was the aim. Then he felt ashamed to feel that way.

The buildings were always uncomfortably warm inside. Everything here was of Polity manufacture: the beds in the alcove rooms, the communal showers and toilet facilities, the food fabricator standing like a pillar in the centre of each building. Things might have been different inside the Nok's building, Anstor had no idea – he had never been in there and did not want to be one of those the Nok took there – either as a failure or for upgrade.

He climbed out of his bed as he had numerous times before, but still dressed this time. He went to take a shower, discarding his torn and soiled overalls and undergarments on the floor, and saw that Abdulla was in there. The man liked to get the shower to himself ever since his body had absorbed his testicles. His skin had a metallic sheen and his irises had turned white. As he soaped himself, the shower water splashing from his body formed spirals in the air that slowly settled to the floor. When he became aware of Anstor, this stopped and Abdulla turned his back. Some kind of electrostatic manipulation of his environment? Abdulla had no explanations when asked and didn't talk much anyhow.

Anstor showered, inspecting his body as he did do. His limbs were knotted with rope muscle and the little toe on each foot had moved further towards the back while the division between the other toes had grown deeper. Eventually he would have the birdlike feet of Tupolek… or Cranston. His kneecaps were also disappearing and he could now bend the joints much further in the opposite direction than intended. Once washed, he dried himself on a disposable towel then wrapped it round himself, grabbed up his old clothes and went out to throw them in the recycler attached to the fabricator. There he got a new set of overalls and undergarments. There was no choice – these were the only clothing the fabricator would make. Back in his alcove he dressed, then, not feeling particularly hungry, he headed outside. Something had occurred to him last night concerning what Indira had said and, unusually having retained it, he was going to check it out.

Anstor walked over to the lesson, as they had come to call it. He glanced over at the nearest building where a hole in the wall let the rain in, then peered down at the shattered stone and metal lying in a hole in the slab of rock the buildings stood upon.

'I am the Nok,' it said the first time Anstor and the others saw it. 'I have few instructions for you, but you will obey them.' It then gave its spiel about how they were experimental subjects. The other stuff came via screens playing the same scenes over and over, and through the information it allowed them access to through a scattering of consoles. It looked the same then as it did now. Was it a machine? Anstor had no idea.

Precisely humanoid, it stood a head and shoulders above the biggest man. Its body seemed androgynous. It wore a helmet that covered its eyes with a skirt at the back of the neck, knee-length shorts, thick wrist bands and a short-sleeved tunic. All, clothing and skin, were of a uniform pale grey. Closer inspection revealed no actual separation between the items it apparently wore and its skin. It seemed to have been cast as a whole from a single mould. In the Polity this could have been a cosmetic choice for either a human or a Golem android, so why did Anstor and the others get the sense of the completely alien forced into a familiar shape? Whenever it came near it made his skin creep – an utter wrongness about it seeming to distort the reality he knew.

He had a surprisingly clear recollection of that first day when ten prisoners, including him, decided to bring it down. Six of them were Polity military – four serving and two who had served. At that point they still had physical augmentations and felt sure, even if the Nok was a Golem, that they could at least disable it. They convinced themselves of that. They formed a plan. Two would go for the legs and tip it over. The others would go for the arms and the head. Damn it, they had to try something to get out of this place. When the Nok arrived they were ready and attacked. Anstor remembered trying to pull a leg out from underneath it and the thing seeming rooted to the ground like a ceramal post set in concrete. The others attacked too and did their best – two of them going for its face with rocks they had unearthed in the compound. They might as well have attacked a mountain.

After a brief pause, the Nok continued walking in until reaching the middle of the compound. They just bounced off of it and fell away. They could not even divert its course or unbalance it. In the end the attack just died away to nothing and they came away with broken hands and, in one case, a foot. The next thing Anstor knew was waking up lying in the mud, his broken fingers fixed. He'd pushed himself upright and noticed at once how light he felt, and how weak. It had taken away his boosting, and his skin hung loose over previously inflated and augmented muscle.

In later days Anstor saw this as a reason for hope: the Nok had removed their augmentations because it feared they might overpower it. Later still he conceded that it didn't want them damaging themselves against it and thus that damage interfering with its experimentation. And the Golem brought home the reality. He wondered if, when the Nok seized its subjects from the Polity, it had pretended to mistakenly include a Golem android so as to demonstrate their futility in attacking it.

His name had been Grantis and Anstor had known there was something about him from the start. By now Anstor had understood their situation and could feel the thing growing inside and steadily changing him. He could feel his muscles shifting, writhing, odd cravings, moments of weird clarity and the skull-splitting headaches. But now he could not remember if he had been inside the compound at the time or speaking to Grantis through the fence.

'So tell me – everything you know,' said Grantis.

'There is something about you,' said Anstor.

'Yes, I noticed that you noticed. I need to act before this Nok realises what I am.'

Anstor told all he knew.

Grantis nodded, seeing the Nok walking over from its building.

'Now is the time,' he said.

Grantis shot across the compound and leaped. Seeing that, Anstor wondered why he hadn't tried that since, when he had been boosted, he could have managed it. Psychology, he guessed – nobody with augmentations thought about escape until it was too late to do so. Grantis the Golem cleared the ten foot fence with balletic ease, came down running and hammered straight across, head down, into the Nok. Anstor was sure he felt the impact judder through the ground at his feet. The Nok stood as completely unmoved as a rock, while Grantis fell away, sprawled backwards, then came upright. Something looked utterly wrong about him until, with a clattering sucking sound his head jerked back up out of his upper chest. He surged forwards to deliver a sweeping kick to the Nok's head, which actually turned that head slightly. A series of other blows followed, too fast to see, their sounds like gunshots. The Nok took a step backwards, seemed to consider the matter for a moment and then, when Grantis got close enough, backhanded the Golem with speed that made a crack as its hand exceeded the sound barrier. Grantis left the ground in a flat trajectory and smashed into the wall of a nearby building. But the Golem was tough. He peeled himself out and staggered a couple of steps.

By now much of Grantis's syntheflesh covering had split to expose his composite and ceramal interior. Watching from somewhere, maybe as close to the wire as he dared, along with all the others, Anstor felt his guts tightening up. There seemed inevitability here.

'Run, get the hell out of here!' someone shouted. 'Get help!' Had he been the one who shouted? He could not remember.

Maybe he, or whoever, shouldn't have shouted that. Grantis glanced round, perhaps acknowledging that might be a good idea. And Anstor felt that the Nok had seen this as a danger too. Now the Nok moved. One moment it stood as rigid as a post and the next it was on Grantis, hand closed in the ceramal ribs of his chest, lifting him up and then slamming him down on the stone. Once twice, three times, so hard that shards of rock flew away, steaming in the damp air. Next it began stamping on Grantis as one would on a poisonous bug, breaking him completely and mashing him down into stone.

Anstor scrabbled away at shattered stone, shifted aside split syntheflesh and fully revealed the remains of the Golem Grantis. An hour later he returned to his alcove where Indira and the others joined him.

'We're going to need something better than those,' she said.

The two ceramal thigh bones made excellent clubs, he felt, and certainly Cranston would have stood a much better chance against that xenovore wielding one of them. Anstor shrugged, pulled back a blanket to show what else he had got, let them take it in, then covered the items with the blanket again. They all saw the various s-con wires, optics and other electronic gear, along with a sphere the size of a bowling ball. He had the Golem's fusion power supply.

'We've all thought about those barrier weapons,' he said. 'You checked on them.' He indicated Leach with a nod.'

'The power supply is a buried cable from back here somewhere,' said Leach. His expression looked pained and twisted, and it took Anstor a moment to realise the man was smiling, because he had never seen it before, and Leach's changes had altered the shape of his face. Leach understood: they had a power supply with which they could run a pulse-cannon, if they could only dismount one and get it connected up.

'Okay, now we're getting there,' said Indira. 'Leach?'

Leach opened the sack he had brought, to expose a good collection of napped flint blades. He had also collected thigh bones, but human ones made out of actual bone. He had already bound a piece of flint into the end of one of the bones to make a stabbing weapon. Anstor suspected he had used ligament, though had no idea how the man had made the resin layered on top of that.

Another four joined them as word spread. These all revealed items they had collected that could be used as weapons. The primitive hoard looked straight out of the Stone Age.

'What about you?' Anstor asked Indira.

'I've been thinking along your lines,' she replied. 'I know that in the end we need some serious weaponry and it's only available at the perimeter. She opened her blanket bag and showed them what lay inside.

'Well that's a surprise,' said Leach.

Indira had tools: a memoform screwdriver, a multispanner and a weld debonder. She had also collected optical fibre, superconductor, glue, binding tape and numerous other items.

'Where the hell did you get those?' asked Anstor.

'The Nok took everything else from us when it took away our enhancements, but it only took what we had in our clothing or had left lying around in the compound building. Some people concealed things. Some things were just left and picked up by others passing through induction. Things have made their way into the Facility over the years.' She frowned at that – her recollection of how many years as vague as Anstor's. She turned to a new recruit to their escape attempt. 'Is this enough, Jaden?'

The woman nodded. 'They're standard compact pulse cannons. In fact you shouldn't need tools to dismount them as they are made to be easily disconnected.' She nodded in satisfaction. 'I'd thought this a waste of time until I saw that.' She gestured to Anstor's folded over blanket. 'The rest will be tinkering with connections and there should be enough here.'

Others visited the alcove as the day progressed. A wide assortment of weapons had been made or collected, but mostly they were primitive. The best addition of these had been from a woman called Zearel, who many had thought was turning to alcohol with the amount she had been taking from the fabricator, but she'd been putting the high grade spirit into disposable coffee beakers and come up with passable Molotov cocktails. She had even fashioned a primitive lighter using flint, and then seemed miffed when one of the others produced a short-beam laser lighter for cigarettes.

By the time night fell, Anstor wondered if they were ready. Indira said she would go and inspect one of the perimeter cannons with Jaden. She returned with a grim smile. Jaden had climbed up onto the cannon and it had not reacted to her. After inspecting it for a while, the woman had gone to sort through the tools and make preparations.

The Nok's presence seemed a blister in a reality, a sore point in his perception of the world, and he could feel it even before it became visible, and he just *knew* it was coming for him and not simply heading in his direction. He stepped out of his alcove, away from his haul from the remains of Grantis and went outside. He considered running, but surmised the creature wanted one of those little talks it always had with those who had attempted to escape and had returned.

He moved out into the open and watched the Nok's building, saw the door open and the creature come out and begin striding directly towards him. How had he known? How could he possibly put this down to enhanced human senses? It halted abruptly a few paces away. Glancing round he could see others watching. Indira simply looked angry, while Leach, standing a few paces away from her, was handling one of the weapons he had fashioned out of flint and a human leg bone.

Please keep out of this, he thought. *Even if I am taken the escape attempt must not be jeopardised.*

Leach turned away and headed back into a nearby building, and Indira nodded agreement but kept on watching. A second later he realised he had not spoken out loud, but decided they must have understood his attitude anyway. What else could it have been?

'Tell me about your escape attempt with Cranston,' said the Nok.

'Cranston thought he could move faster than the xenovores and convinced me that I could too. An 003 caught him and I returned. A stripper tried to get me but I got to the perimeter in time. The pulse cannons killed it.'

The Nok stepped forwards and laid a hand on his shoulder. It seemed almost a friendly gesture, but that hand felt as solid as stone, if not more so, and could crush his shoulder to pulp.

'Now tell me again, in detail, everything that happened from the moment you left the old defensive wall.'

Anstor shrugged, then winced at the tightening of that grip on his shoulder. 'What is there to tell – this same scenario has played out many times.'

'But you don't really remember them, do you. Give me that detail.'

Anstor sighed and went through it all, how the xenovore had come after them both and how he had somehow lost Cranston and found himself crouching behind a boulder, how Cranston had died. He then detailed his own return to the Facility, missing out nothing he could remember, including the scavenger tripping him.

'Your memory fails too much for required clarity,' said the Nok. 'The perimeter guns did not fire.'

The grip on his shoulder became agonising as the creature lifted him off the ground then tucked him under one arm. He struggled against the iron wrap of the arm as the Nok turned and marched back towards its building. Again he felt what he had felt out beyond the perimeter. How could this be happening? This cannot be happening!

'I'm not a failure!' he yelled as he struggled. 'I'm not a failure!' And he felt ashamed to be crying out like this. He tried to fling himself away and the world seemed to judder as he did so. Unbelievably he found himself out of the Nok's grip and lying in the mud a few yards away, but it was on him in a second, its big hand closed around his skull. Agony seared through his mind and he thought it might be crushing his head, but it took its hand away and it seemed his skull remained intact. Thoughts now, however, had become severely disjointed and any intention to escape, escaped him. He found himself being carried again, glimpsed a flint weapon bouncing off the Nok's back, heard yelling and saw a club hammering repeatedly at its knee but to no effect. A door opened and then it carried him into the dreaded building.

Anstor began to return to himself, lying on a slab, paralysed. Unbelievable pain washed through him and though he could not move his head, he could see that a series of probes from stands all around had pinned him like a bug in some entomologist's collection. With this, despite the pain, he felt something akin to relief. He was not being vivisected but upgraded. This had been described to him by others who had experienced it, then faulty memory accrued some fragments that told him this had happened to him before. He *had* been in here before.

The Nok stood unmoving over to one side. Anstor's vision, which went beyond the focus of his eyes, gave him a view of one of the probes retracting. It did not look mechanical at all, but rather like a spike-nosed eel as it reared back then coiled down to a floor covered with coils like that of its own body. As each of these withdrew the pain in his torso receded. He could see that somehow they closed the wounds as they retracted. But the pain in his skull steadily increased, only relieved when something at the back cracked as if taking off pressure.

'You will no longer alter external detail to fit your internal narrative,' said the Nok. 'Human mental capacity will restore and then we will talk again.'

Ignoring his yell of pain, it heaved him up off the slab by his biceps and took him along an oval corridor like something found in the hive of a social insect, took him to a Polity format door, opened it and cast him outside.

'What did it do to you?' Indira asked, as she and others clustered around him.

'Some kind of upgrade,' he replied. 'I don't know what it is.'

But he did. Detail had now become clear: the guns had not been pointing at the xenovore and had not fired at all, and yet, pulse gun fire had hit the thing. He had seen the shots materialise out of thin air. He remembered something of the internal mechanism of the weapons but, if he had made them fire, surely the shots would have come from them? He also remembered clearly being about to be captured, and then fleeing by a route he could not trace in his mind, and ending up some distance away. Just as he had fled the Nok's grip.

'Did… something to your head,' said Packam. 'Bigger. At the back.'

Anstor could not remember how long he had been out of the compound when he saw his first failure. Her name was Mila — a very attractive woman upon arrival, but steadily looking more and more ragged as time progressed. Her skin turned pale and sickly and she complained of stomach cramps. By the time they walked out of the compound her skin had taken on a scaly appearance and often chunks of it fell away to expose open sores. She frequently had nose bleeds and her belly began to swell up as if she was pregnant. It was the memory of her that connected 'failure' to physical disability in Anstor's mind, though later failures had destroyed that hypothesis.

They established themselves in their alcove rooms and learned what they could. Three, upon learning of the Polity base from Sharp Tagon, disappeared on the first dark rainy night. Instructive recordings of their demise, just beyond the perimeter, arrived in the files the next day. Anstor felt perpetually stunned to be trapped inside this nightmare, and then it got worse.

They were outside discussing their situation. Indira and others had formed their own subgroup from the whole which Anstor had joined. Mila had joined them later, though her attention seemed more focused on her growing bump. The day was an unusually clear one with hints of red sky showing between clouds cast into umber silhouette. They were sitting on rocks discussing the recordings they had witnessed. Those creatures, damn it, they'd read the reports on them and pondered on the name 'xenovore', but how was it they existed?

'You need to talk to Tagon,' said Mila, but seemed to run out of energy and said no more.

Leach took up the baton: 'He's an original, I'm told — one of the first captured by the Nok. A taxonomist or something.' He looked at Anstor. 'You should know.'

Anstor didn't understand what he meant, but let it pass because he knew there were things he had forgotten.

'Right, we need to talk to him,' said Indira. She too gave Anstor a querying look and when he could find no response she shook her head in frustration and turned away.

But they didn't get to talk with Tagon then. Packam pointed and they looked over to see the Nok standing outside its building, with its head tilted back to look up at the sky. Eventually it shrugged into motion and strode out. Around them, people who had been here longer began disappearing from sight. Anstor felt the same urge. He knew that on these occasions some of them risked going just beyond the perimeter while others kept moving around and hiding to keep away from the Nok. This never worked, for the Nok always found the failures.

It walked directly towards them, came to a halt, swung its head from side to side as if it were operating like some kind of scanner.

'Disappointing,' it said. 'You have failed.'

It stepped forwards horribly fast, swept up Mila under one arm and marched away with her yelling and struggling. After a stunned moment they acted as one and went after it. They tried to stop the Nok, tried to pull Mila from its grasp or tried to block its path, but all to no avail. The Nok went to its door, swept those ahead to one side, and entered, the door slamming shut behind.

'You'll see her again in about an hour or so,' said one of the earlier inductees who, with others, had now come out of cover.

The man pointed off to one side of the Nok's building. Anstor recollected a pile of refuse over there. He always got a bad feeling when he looked towards it and felt no great urge to inspect it. Faulty mind or otherwise, he knew there was something about it he didn't like or didn't want to remember. However, he did go over with Indira this time, wincing at the smell of putrefaction and gazing at distorted human remains caught in some slimy green weed with scavenger worms writhing between. An hour later Mila's remains shot out of a side chute in the building and landed with a thump amidst the rest. Anstor gazed at the chute and knew he had seen it operate many times. Too many times.

She'd been opened up from neck to crotch, and her legs and arms had been split open too, but then she had been stapled back together again. He could see burns, disposable instruments made of some grey composite lying around her, the sockets for fluid tubes in her body too. He stared, taking it all in, and vague haunted memory affirmed that this had not been the autopsy of a corpse, but vivisection.

Three further failures occurred in ensuing days. They could have seen the reality with Mila, but it was the last of the three that Sharp Tagon took them to see – the two prior ones having been eaten by scavengers. They finally got to him in his alcove where he had been holding court with new inductees out of the compound.

'The place was here when I arrived, but everything was new and untouched – a long time ago,' Tagon looked at Anstor. 'Do you remember?'

Anstor stared at him in bafflement. He hadn't been here that long, surely?

'Of course you don't,' said Tagon.

The man was all whorled stony skin, a bit like a krodorman but hard and unyielding. Anstor doubted most of the predators out there could get their feeding implements through that skin, but others spat acid like a droon, and still others had carapace-saw mandibles like a sleer, and Tagon was painfully slow.

'Where did the Nok capture you?' asked Indira.

'A few hundred miles that way,' Tagon replied. 'We put down a tagreb to study the creatures here. I work taxonomy. I was out on a grav platform gathering data and then bam, I woke up here.'

Anstor remembered a tagreb being a study base that could be dropped on a world to fold out and establish itself before the researchers arrived to occupy it.

'So what is it with the creatures here? The Nok calls them xenovores,' said Packam – this was before his extending and narrowing head compressed his brain.

'That's what we called them at the tagreb and, judging by the files here, the Nok stole them from us. Alien experimentation we think – probably the Atheter. We reckon they were making soldiers that could survive in any conditions and on any food supply. Since the Atheter lobotomised themselves the experiment has had two million years to run riot here.'

Three other researchers had been grabbed from the tagreb but, with the Nok's experiments seemingly in their initial stages, only Sharp Tagon had survived. At the time, Anstor suspected the Nok kept Sharp around to deliver his wisdom to the new inductees, since in many respects he must be one of the failures. That was when he thought failure a physical thing related to surviving the xenovores.

'What has it done to us?' Anstor asked at one point. 'I know there is something inside me. I know there is something inside us all.'

'You need to be told again and again,' said Tagon.

Anstor felt suddenly angry. 'I'm not stupid, you know!'

'No, never that.' Tagon turned to the others, who were all watching Anstor with expressions ranging from bafflement to irritating sympathy.

'I've told others, and him.' Tagon waved a hand at Anstor. 'And they've taken a look. But I'll show you since it's time I reminded myself and shook up my growing complacency.' He heaved himself to his feet and at a slow walk, creaking like old leather, he led them outside.

'Where did you get the knife?' Indira asked.

Tagon was dressed in numerous sets of overalls, subsequent sets covering the dilapidation of the ones before. Around his waist he had a belt braided from the same material and from that hung a sheathed knife. He drew it and held it up. The handle was bone, almost certainly human bone, and the blade looked like napped flint. He put it away again.

'You can find the stone around here, but it won't do you much good,' he told them. 'This is my second one – I broke the first trying to push it into the Nok's throat.'

He led them over to the trash pile beside the Nok's building. Mila was almost gone now – just bones and skin and a knot of worms where her guts had been. Tagon stepped over to the fresh corpse – a young man whose eyes had disappeared and whose feet and hands had turned into club-like lumps. He dragged the corpse from the pile and flipped it over onto its back. The man had been opened up just like Mila, and stapled back together again. Tagon drew his knife and stooped down. He sliced down from neck to crotch beside the staples, cut across top and bottom where the man had been stapled there too. After jabbing his knife into gritty mud, he reached down, pushed in stony fingers and heaved the man's ribcage open.

Lungs guts and liver lay exposed, soon glistening with beaded moisture. Anstor took a step backwards and looked around at Indira, seeing his horror reflected in her expression. But they both knew what Tagon was doing, for they both knew they had something inside them. Tagon took up the knife again, made some cuts and began discarding internal organs to one side. He grunted as he worked, then finally stepped back.

'Take a look,' he said, then went to clean his knife and his hands in a puddle.

They all stepped forwards and peered down into the corpse. Tagon had removed just about everything to leave a cavity right back to the spine, but something still remained. It looked vaguely like a foetus, but green and black. The long body was melded into the spine below while, stretching out from that, arms and legs branched and branched again, spreading into the surrounding body. It had a thin neck and a perfectly formed foetal head. The mouth moved and the head whipped from side to side. It opened evil little red eyes and made a hissing gargle.

After he had stumbled away and vomited his last meal from the fabricator, Anstor wondered about that 'You have failed'. When it said that, was the Nok addressing the human being, or the thing sitting inside? Later still he wondered if he had truly seen that thing, or if it had been another nightmare. Because, when he thought about it, he saw a whole series of *things* clinging to the spines of corpses, all wildly different. He saw Tagon slicing with a different knife, again and again, then again with the knife he had now. And now a further disparity in memory came to him. Yes, he had seen corpses coming out of that chute, but they had only been a small portion of the failures the Nok had taken into its building, so what had happened to the rest?

'There's a coastline over there,' said Sharp Tagon. 'You go to the sunrise and eventually you hit it. If you come to cliffs you're too far to the right and have to head left. You'll reach the start of some beaches of flaked stone and have to go another three or four miles and turn inward along the course of a river...' Thereafter his instructions became increasingly complicated.

'You know the area well,' said Indira. 'Come with us.'

Tagon shook his head. 'I'm slow – slower than all of you.'

'There are twenty of us going and we're not all fast. Many can only move as fast as a normal human being. You're not much slower than that. And you are, as we have all seen, very strong. Those pulse cannons are heavy. Do you think you could carry one alone?'

Tagon shrugged, stood up, reached out with both hands and put them around Indira's waist. She was no lightweight now, but he picked her up and held her out straight-armed.

'Okay, I think you can,' she opined and he put her down again.

He shrugged and sat back down. 'Everything seems to be made of aerolite to me now. I wonder sometimes if I could go and pick up that.' He gestured towards the Nok's ship.

The number increased to twenty-eight of them. The more the better, Indira said. Anstor wasn't sure. If there were more of them might that not draw in more predators? They had all been busy over the last week making back packs out of their blankets and taking more food from the fabricator than they needed – food that wouldn't spoil too quickly. Under Indira's instructions their actions were mostly concealed. The Nok had not reacted to previous escape attempts but those had not been so organised. They could not rely on it ignoring them. They had made too many preparations, constructed weapons and gathered together the meagre supply of tools. They could not lose all that now, for they might never have a chance to garner so much useful stuff again.

When they trudged out into red darkness, some peaked out to see them off but remained at the Facility. They hoped for success, and then subsequent rescue by the Polity, and Anstor could not help but feel contempt for them. As the escapees moved through the Facility, laden with packs and makeshift weapons, the Nok did not show itself. It was drizzling as they left but later that lifted and they got a rare glimpse of the orange moon, like a blister in the face of the reddened and veined sky. Finally they reached the perimeter where tripod-mounted particle cannons curved back from them in a line to either side. Jaden clambered up on the nearest, lit up a torch and set to work.

Anstor gazed out across the bleak moonlit landscape. For a while he could see no movement, then he spotted a xenovore like the one that had killed Cranston. It came closer, now clearly visible, paused to rise up high on its two legs and tilt its head back as if sniffing the sky. It next sped towards them but, twenty metres out, came to an abrupt halt. Obviously it was aware of the danger here, so must have been singed by the pulse flash.

'Power's down,' said Jaden. 'If that fucker comes in there'll be no warning shots.'

'Fuck,' said Indira. She stood below the cannon, accepting items Jaden passed down. Tagon climbed up with the slow strength of a sloth to lift the side of the cannon's main body so Jaden could set to work on something underneath. As he watched, a brief flash of the internal workings of the weapon, passed through Anstor's mind.

The xenovore began edging closer – perhaps so many lunch items being too much of a temptation. Leach stepped forwards.

'I might as well try this now.' He held up one of the weapons he had fashioned. The thigh bone now had a flint point and trailing from the back end were long shreds of blanket turning it into a dart. Though his changes had done badly for him, his upper body was unreasonably strong. He drew back his arm and threw, as hard as he could. The dart shot across and thumped into the creature's body, burying itself deep inside. The xenovore squealed, staggered back and went down on its rump. Anstor stepped forwards, the others around him doing the same, a concerted growl arising from them. They could not hurt the main agent of their misery – the Nok – but these things, which had been killing them for an age, could be hurt. In a moment they were on the creature. Anstor's Golem leg bone club rose and fell. Other clubs crashed into the thing's body and flint hatchets chopped. It whipped its head round sending someone tumbling, tried to rise but failed.

Then, with an odd crump, its body collapsed and its head carapace cracked open. They continued their attack, beating it into the ground, but it was already dying. Anstor stepped back and glanced round. Troisier had been the one thrown clear. He stood now with his spadelike hand held out from his body, inspecting it in bafflement.

'I did it,' he said to Anstor.

Adrenaline running hard through his body, Anstor's thinking accelerated. The back of his head, where it had grown out since his upgrade, was throbbing. He thought about all the weird things that had happened in the Facility and at last they began to drop into place. He knew, in that instant, that Troisier had crushed the xenovore, somehow. Perhaps some ability to generate hardfields? Perhaps some manipulation of U-space? All in a rush he extrapolated and realised what 'failure' meant. The Nok wasn't seeking physical enhancement through these extreme mutations, but this. But then, as his mind began to slow, a series of recollections arose for his inspection and he understood that he had realised this before, many times, and forgotten. He now felt a dread of losing this memory.

'Okay, we're good,' said Indira.

He turned and saw the three walking from the tripod. Tagon balanced the pulse cannon on one shoulder, wires and feed tubes running into his backpack. He grinned and it was fearsome.

'We'll have to limit shots,' said Jaden. 'I've attached the fusion power supply to laminar storage from the tripod and we have a cylinder of particulate. The storage holds enough power for fifty shots and it takes the fuser an hour to recharge each shot – I've set it for single shots and not bursts – and the particulate will only last for about a thousand.'

'Indira!' said Anstor.

She gazed at him curiously.

'I know what the Nok wants! It's other abilities... to manipulate things beyond our bodies. The things moved around. Her in the wall.' He gestured back to the wall encircling the Facility. 'Abdulla –' he gestured to the man '– creating those water swirls.'

She clapped him on the shoulder. 'You've remembered again, that's good.' She shook her head and moved on. 'That mind of yours.'

As they set out – Tagon leading the way – Anstor remembered telling her this many times. They soon passed where Cranston had died. The man's skin-wrapped skeleton remained intact, draped over a rock but was a marker for the furthest Anstor had been... that he remembered. Ahead the landscape was ever as if had been and they kept going. He paused to club a scavenger worm that rose out of mud beside him and noted others doing the same. Movement all around indicated other worms, waiting for their portion of the feast. Gradually the landscape began to change with hillocks and gullies appearing, large pools and occasional fast-moving streams.

Perhaps it was the excitement, the change of circumstance, or more likely it was the Nok's upgrade, but Anstor found himself retaining memory and others arising. He considered Packam with his small narrow head and loss of intelligence, and could see that reflected in him. A growing function of his brain had compressed the rest of it and displaced memory, but now, with his skull expanded behind, it was coming back. Many other strange events at the Facility, and what he had heretofore thought of as nightmares, became firm memories of reality.

'You will no longer alter external detail to fit your internal narrative,' the Nok had said, and now he understood what that meant.

Yes, it had been Gregon who had destroyed the wall because in anger once he had turned another inductee to an explosion of red slush and shattered bone. He had this power and he had gone to turn it against the Nok. Had he been a success and thereafter taken somewhere else? Or had the Nok killed him?

And what about Anstor himself? He now remembered being one of the first inductees, walking out of the compound to find Sharp Tagon and just a few others. He knew now he had passed years of not being a 'failure' so in what ways was he a success? He gradually began to put it all together. That time he had found himself outside in his bed, his narrow escape from the xenovore and escaping the Nok's grip and now, with his thinking increasingly clear, he remembered other such events. Many of them. He had no idea how to do it, but it was apparent he could move himself instantly to other locations. An old word surfaced in his mind: teleport. But what else? Oh yes, the conversations when people had heard his unspoken questions and when he had replied to theirs, and so another word: telepath. Other oddities of his existence at the Facility surfaced, but they all meshed with those two words. He then thought about the pulse cannon firing but not firing and his vision of its internal workings. Teleportation again? He had moved his bed so could he also move energy? What else? He remembered that one time when everyone had frozen about him and he had walked around the compound baffled and confused by the statue figures there. Time, he thought, something to do with time.

Frenetic excitement arose as all this passed through his mind. He gazed at a spot far ahead and visualised being in that spot. Nothing happened. He tried many different approaches – tried to push whatever lay in his mind, but to no avail. He tried reading the thoughts of those around him, tried to pick up the mutter of their minds but came up blank. He tried sending thoughts to the man walking beside him, a tall fellow with bat ears, a face sans nose and with protruding fangs. Traster was his name. When Traster turned towards him he thought he was getting somewhere.

'Do you need to take a shit or something, Anstor?' Traster asked.

Anstor grimaced, turned away, and tried to stop time. But he got no further than another series of grimaces when, as they rounded a deep pool, the xenovores rose up out of it and attacked.

Three strippers surfaced from the water and leapt straight in amongst them. Anstor fell and he saw Packam snatched screaming up off the ground. The man blurred briefly in its grip and broke free, shot away a hundred yards and went down on his knees. An explosion lit the dull day and one of the strippers, wreathed in flame, shrieked and whistled amongst them. One of the Molotov cocktails had worked. Where the hell was Tagon? Another stripper was going down under concerted attack and Tagon made his presence known with a pulse shot straight through its head. It died, instantly. But the one that had attacked Packam was still up.

Anstor leapt up and ran in, club raised. He smashed it into the creature's back and it stumbled forwards. Ahead of it he saw Troisier, holding out his hand and then closing it. Nothing happened. The creature grabbed him around the neck and with a sick crunch threw him aside. Another pulse shot took it high in the back and it went down, and they piled onto it and beat it into the dirt. The burning stripper stumbled back into the pool and submerged, but Anstor could see it still had someone struggling in its grip.

'We lost seven. Fuck it. We lost seven,' said Indira.

Anstor wanted to cry. Where was his ability to teleport – his ability to summon pulse shots out of the air? Where was his ability to manipulate time, if it existed at all? He wished he could take time back and not see Troisier lying with vertebrae jutting out of his thick neck, or see Packam kneeling with blood pouring out of numerous holes punched in his body. The man had muttered something about being so fast, then keeled over on his side and died.

'You need to react quicker with that thing,' Indira said to Tagon.

The man dipped his head in shame, but it wasn't his fault – they all knew he was slow.

They had stopped atop a slab similar to the one upon which the Facility had been mounted. Others had managed to get here, Anstor saw, their remains lay at the foot of the slab. It seemed a common sight. Throughout the day's travel he had seen many bones jutting from the earth, and occasional slews of human skin. How had that survived for so long, he wondered. Perhaps the xenovore feeding method preserved it and made it unappetising for the scavengers, and maybe the bacteria to do the job did not exist here.

They paused to eat and rest while Tagon sat on the highest point of the rock and kept watch. A group of four xenovores appeared and drew closer. These were ones Anstor had only seen in the files. They moved like apes on four limbs but rose up on two to scan their surroundings. From small heads two saucer-like eyes jutted out, almost on stalks, while their forelimbs sported large clawed hands. Below the heads and down as far as the chest was the vertical slot of a mouth. They were called Slow Eaters. Human prey they inserted legs first into that mouth, closing the lips about the necks so the head remained protruding. They then slowly digested this prey while still alive and the head kept screaming. Again, Anstor disbelieved the Nok's contention that these creatures used such techniques to digest alien meat. It was all far too cruel and seemed simply torture.

Tagon lowered himself to prop the cannon against rock and allowed them to draw close. His first shot hit the lead creature straight in its mouth, blowing smoking debris out of its back. His second shot blew the leg off another and his third sent the remaining creature running with its back smoking. They all cheered with each shot, but with muted joy. After eating, then drinking water collected from a nearby pool while others stood guard, they moved on. They had travelled for most of a night but no one was tired, and now they headed towards the dim glow of the rising sun.

The day progressed, growing steadily lighter. At one point they paused when cloud broke and the red sun glared through. It was as if they were walking out from a permanent dark and depressing cloud that hung over the Facility. It raised their mood and now conversation started amidst their group.

'We've seen none all morning,' said Anstor. 'Perhaps we've scared them off?'

Indira shook her head. 'More likely they gather close around the Facility for that ready source of food and there are fewer out here.'

'Still, a good thing?'

She nodded cautious agreement.

'How far do you think we've come?' he asked.

'Negal?' she enquired of a man walking with them. Negal turned. He had one large double pupil eye in the centre of his forehead over a nose and mouth that had turned into a raptor's beak. He had short feathers running down the outsides of his arms and the joints in his thin legs had shifted so he walked with the legs of a bird on clawed feet. Anstor felt a moment of fierce victory when he remembered that this man had once jumped and sailed up onto the roof of the Facility. It had been a real event and no dream or nightmare, but another of the abilities the long-termers had developed. He now understood that Negal could not actually fly like a bird, though, of course, all referred to him as Negal the Eagle. Did he have some sort of antigrav mechanism growing inside him? Or was it another of those old defunct and ridiculed words: telekinesis.

Negal reached into one of the many pockets sewn into his overalls and took out a device like a wrist watch but with one side of the strap missing. He inspected it, the two pupils in his eye drawing closer together. After putting it away again he used sign language to communicate with Indira and, again, Anstor felt victory because he could understand that language – had learned it long ago when Negal's growing beak rendered him incapable of human speech.

'Thirty-five miles,' Anstor said, before Indira could tell him.

'Yes,' she replied, but that was all. Yes, they had travelled a good distance, but still they had lost seven of their number.

As the day progressed, the landscape retained its rolling aspect and its streams and pools, but now they began to see plant life. Why, he wondered, had it been so barren about the Facility? Because of the continuous tramp of clawed feet? No, he realised, it was just a dull wet spot while here, on this morning, the sun had broken through on three occasions and he had felt warm outside for the first time in an age.

First were the fungi: rings of toadstools that bore all the appearance of those of Earth. At one point the group filed past the slimy head-high trunk of a tree with bracket fungi jutting but also buds of dark green from a few straggling branches. Anstor felt a painful nostalgia because the only green he had seen at the Facility had been artificial. As the sun reached its zenith, the cloud cover broke up enough to reveal separate clouds – again something he had not seen in an age. Here too the ground had become drier, areas of gritty mud were hard and other pale areas were free of moisture. The long day progressed, however, and the cloud began to close up again. Anstor felt weary because he had never walked so far, others were starting to stumble.

'We need somewhere defensible,' Indira opined. 'And that looks perfect.'

She pointed to another slab. This one had steep edges rising ten feet from the ground. Over to one side of it stood a copse of twiggy shrubs which, when they drew closer, they saw sported bunches of green needles and cones like clenched fists of gnarled walnut wood.

'I keep thinking of spring,' said someone.

'It's like we are walking out of night,' said another, 'though night comes.'

At the base of this slab there seemed other growth, but as they drew closer it revealed itself as a ragged slew of human skin, brown as old leather, and numerous bones. They paused there.

'Perhaps not a good place to stay,' suggested Jaden.

'We are far from the Facility here,' said Leach. The man looked quite ill and a split had opened down one arm to ooze clear fluid. His legs shook with weariness.

Anstor understood his point. How had others come so far? And, in retrospect, how was it that they had seen so many human remains during their journey? But now memory provided perspective on the years. He had seen new people in the compound so very often. He'd seen the Nok's ship rising into the sky time and again and returning with fresh meat for induction. And now he wished his memory had not returned so well, because the Facility generally had only fifty or so people in it, yet thousands had passed through.

'Look,' Negal signed, stooping amidst the mass and picking up a flint axe made from a human thigh bone. Seeing this, others began searching through the remains. They found similar weapons but most were rotten and falling apart, though retaining useful chunks of flint. One person even found an old gas-system pulse handgun, but it was dead. He handed it over to Jaden because perhaps she could do something with it.

'There is danger everywhere,' said Indira. 'And even if whatever killed these is still here, the best place for us is still up on that slab. And remember, we have a pulse cannon.'

No one disagreed. They were all accustomed to seeing human remains. They moved on round the slab to finally find a place easier to climb up. Human remains scattered the top of the slab. They kicked them over the side.

'Okay, we get organised,' said Indira. 'We'll sleep in shifts of six hours. I suggest seven sleeping while the other fourteen guard. Every watch must have in it those with night vision and other useful senses.' She pointed to those protrusions with which she, apparently, sensed xenovore pheromones. 'Tagon, take a position there. Have two people with you ready to wake you when you sleep.' She gestured to a high point.

Tagon glanced round at her. 'Sleep?'

'If you need sleep,' she said, briefly as confused as Anstor felt. Memory revealed that he had never seen Tagon asleep. Other curiosities about the man arose too. He took food from the fabricator and Anstor had seen him chewing on some, but most of it went back into recycling. It was as if he ate food to fit in and be one of them, but also as if it wasn't something that bothered him greatly.

Tagon positioned himself on the high point. Seven made themselves comfortable at the centre of the slab while the rest spread out in a ring around them, Anstor including himself in that number. He sat with legs akimbo, his metal thigh bone ready within reach, and ate some of his food supply. One of the others came by with water, collected from a stream along their route in a sewn up bag. He drank gratefully, then felt a little bit nauseated when he saw the tattoo on the bag, and handed it back. The red moon turned the night bloody. The landscape darkened and others kept calling alerts to movement. When Anstor looked he saw nothing, except on one occasion a scavenger worm rearing out of the soil.

'Just a worm,' he said.

The beam from one of their precious torches speared out, finally catching the worm as it disappeared back into the ground.

'How the fuck did you see that?' someone asked.

Anstor felt unreasonably happy. At least something seemed to be working.

Indira did her rounds – constantly on the move.

'We should see anything long before it gets here,' she said. Later, on a second walk around, she said, 'I sense something. There is a pheromone in the air but I don't recognise it.'

In the second case she was right, and perhaps her warning helped, but in the first case she was completely wrong, because they came from the sky.

At first he thought a squall starting that being the only time he felt wind against his skin. He felt something creeping down his spine and in an instant his perception, which had thus far been concentrated on the landscape ahead, seemed to flash out from his skull in every direction.

'Flying creatures above!' he shouted.

A booming sound ensued as of sailcloth thwacking in a wind. Shapes mottled the red sky. He could see them distinctly now – hundreds of them.

'They are on us!' Indira shrieked, but by then two of the sleepers had been snatched yelling into the air. Anstor rose to his feet with a ceramal thigh bone ready, but his acute senses had him duck as a claw snatched at him from above. He came up and swung, connecting solidly with a scaly leg and the creature cawed like a crow and rose higher. Ahead he could see huge flapping wings and crested heads, vicious raptor beaks stabbing down. He ran towards them in time to see one of the creatures launching. It seemed a by-blow of pterodactyl and man and held its prey close to its chest with strange folded up legs that branched like roots. It pecked down and ripped out a collarbone, then protruded a long segmented tongue with pincers at the end and jabbed it in through the hole. It rose higher with its victim struggling and screaming.

With a blinding flash the ion cannon lit the night and burning, one of the creatures fell. Tagon fired again and again. Anstor stood with his club ready and gazed in frustration at an enemy he could not reach. An explosion lit the sky as one of the Molotovs hit one of the creatures. In the glare below Anstor could see Abdulla holding up his hands as if to warm them from the heat. The fire there swirled and snaked out from one burning form to wrap around another, and then another, but then it began to flicker out perhaps because of lack of fuel. Anstor ran over to Zearal as with shaking hands she tried to light up another bomb.

'Just throw them!' he shouted.

She looked at him in puzzlement for one interminable moment, then understood and threw. Abdulla took up the slack, swirling splashed alcohol into the fire of one falling creature and taking it onto the next. Someone else joined them – Indira – and threw more of the Molotovs.

'Yes!' Anstor yelled. He dropped his club. 'Bring the fuckers down!' He reached up as if to snatch at one and pull it from the sky as it tore out the bones of a victim it carried upwards. The creature jerked and folded up, then dropped faster than the pull of gravity and smashed into the stone, shedding its dismembered prey. Anstor stared at his hand in amazement, something crackling in the back of his skull. Suddenly it was there; it was all there. He reached up again, tentatively, and like Troisier, crushed another of the creatures in the sky, and it fell in a more natural manner. He reached again and again, and saw Indira staring at him with her mouth open. He could feel something from his ears and his nose and his overall sense told him blood was running out. But he could not stop, not now. He had killed some of the creatures, but there were hundreds and they were not going away. Each one was like plucking a leaf from a tree.

Sharp Tagon...

He looked over to the man steadily firing the cannon, tracked its mechanism inside and *pulled*. Forty pulse shots flared into the sky and found nearly as many targets in the horde, but now Tagon's cannon died. It was energy, just energy, and the dust of the pulse cannon's particulate. Anstor reached out and around, everything so utterly clear to him. He raised dust from the dirt surrounding them and sought for energy nearby. Numerous sources were available but he managed to halt the urge to feed off them, because he knew them to be his fellows. There was another way. He let the dust drop and instead reached up for the energy sources clustering above and began pulling it out and grounding it below him. The stone underfoot grew warm and began to steam, and then the raptor creatures began raining from the sky, crashing down all around, icy and sometimes breaking, so deep was their cold. He felt Indira crash into him then and take him off the side of the slab as the bodies shattered above and around. They sheltered under a jut of stone until finally the rain ended.

'There. I did it,' said Anstor, knowing he had blood on his teeth.

Then a hammer seemed to hit him in the back of his skull, and all he knew was darkness.

Anstor returned to consciousness, reminded of some of the worst hangovers he had ever experienced. He felt nauseated, his head hurt, his mood had dropped into a dark well and he wished he had never woken up. The mood aspect he understood as chemical imbalances in his brain, and the terrible reality of the rest of his condition. His body felt like lead and when he tried to move an arm or a leg, he got no response. He couldn't even open his eyes and his mouth hung open, dry and sore. He was in motion, he knew that, whatever he lay upon dragging over stony ground.

Paralysis? He didn't think so. The idea terrified him and yet it seemed just a side effect of changes in his skull. The lights were off. The abilities, the almost godlike power he had felt bringing down those fliers, his omniscient vision, his telepathy and whatever other nameless talents had expanded in his mind, no longer functioned. He could feel them there – structures that seemed to extend well beyond his skull to some other place, but they felt as dead and empty as the sucked out remains they had seen during their journey.

'Take a break,' someone said, and it took him a moment recognise Indira's voice. The object he lay on changed direction for a second then went down on something, holding him propped up at an angle. He could hear movement all around and it gladdened him that at least he hadn't lost his hearing. A hard object touched his lips and slid into his mouth. Panic arose for just a second until water flowed in. It thawed the dryness there and small flashes of light passed through the darkness of his mind. It was as if he could see a network activating, or a system coming online. He closed his mouth around the spout of the water bag and drank greedily.

'I think he's awake!' someone called.

The spout came out of his mouth. He made a gagging sound, his mouth gaping. It seemed the only way to express his need.

'Give him more,' said Indira.

The spout went back in and he drank more, and more. He didn't feel nauseated when he remembered the water bag was made of human skin. The fluid filled up his stomach and flowed out into his body as if into a dry sponge. Another circuit engaged and his hand came up to grab hold of the thing and keep it at his mouth. Like oil into a seized machine it began to free up other things and his eyes, breaking some crusty accumulation, opened. Everything was blurred. Finally, he released the water skin and it was taken away. He could see a figure standing before him with hands on hips. Only by her bulk, general shape, and long dark hair did he recognise Indira.

'You're back with us,' she said.

He tried to speak but only a dry rasping came out. He tried to see her clearly but his eyes would not focus. A flash of further pain stabbed through his skull and, briefly, as if a malfunctioning power source had put out a few Watts, one of those structures seeming to extend beyond his skull, ignited. He saw his surroundings, all of them, above and below and 360 degrees around out to about ten metres. They had propped him at an angle against a rock, strapped on travois fashioned of those shrubs they had seen back at the slab, and veined skin he suspected to be from the wings of the flying attackers. A few people were standing around, lugging packs. He recognised Tagon, Leach and others, but there seemed far too few of them. One he did not recognise brought a protein bar to his mouth. He bit, raised a shaky hand and took it, gobbled it down quickly, then choked until given more water. Even as he drank the light went out again and all he could see was the blurred form of Indira. He cleared his throat, tried to speak but only squeaked at first, but then finally got the words out, 'How many did I kill?'

'Hundreds of the fuckers,' Indira replied with satisfaction.

He shook his head and wished he hadn't when sharp pains stabbed his neck. 'No, I mean our people.' He still recollected those frozen or semi-frozen bodies falling from the sky.

'The fliers killed thirteen of our people. You killed no one, though of course there were some injuries.' She grimaced – his vision had cleared enough for him to see that. 'The fliers were bird-boned and light.'

'Ah, good.'

The food sat lump-like in his stomach, sucking away his energy. His eyes drifted closed and sleep came down on him like hundreds of winged black shapes.

When he next woke he felt very much better. His skull didn't hurt so badly and his body did not feel so leaden. The function of his mind seemed a tight ball of activity in wide open spaces of consciousness, centred amidst those structures extending beyond him. The travois was on the move again and he had no sense of how much time had passed. He opened his eyes. Vision was still blurred but not so badly as before. He began testing things in his skull – began reaching into those structures. Each flickered with life in turn but sent warning nauseating pain back to him. Only one seemed to be viable at the moment, perhaps because it was not one he had strained to the limit.

Omniscient vision returned, extending out maybe twenty metres. It was quite odd really because he could see in great detail everything within that sphere, but, beyond, it seemed that everything had ceased to exist. He studied the eight walking along around him. Tagon led, with Indira walking a few steps back from him. Negal and Jaden were pulling the travois. The other four he now recognised easily. They were the Plester twins who had arrived at the Facility indistinguishable from each other, but now they looked like no relation at all. Acram Plester had taken on some of the aspect of Negal, though a heavier form with head jutting forward and extended as if more like a vulture than a raptor. Setram Plester had tall rabbit-like ears and a face similarly changing to that end. Then there was Eva Salter – still retaining her lissom human form but now with huge violet eyes and pointed ears. People were jealous of how she had transformed. Then Gaunt Chapter – a man with the bulk and armouring of Sharp Tagon.

Such perfect recall of these, and of the others, surprised him. He knew all their names and all his interactions with them. Tagon was the earliest inductee, Negal and Eva had come in with the same group as him. Indira, Leach and Gaunt arrived some years after that and the rest much later still. His memory was as clear as it could be, though the constant red days and nights could confuse even someone with perfect recall.

Anstor lay thinking about them, and considered letting Indira know he was awake again, but he still felt utterly exhausted. He closed his eyes to concentrate on the function of his mind. He needed to get it back. He needed to get it all back and he felt the first to test should be that omniscient vision, which seemed to extend from the centre of his being. He continued to observe those around him, with his eyes closed, remembering detail about them. He found a delight in that, but it distracted him from his purpose. He pushed and worried at the relevant structure. Headaches flashed in his skull and drained away. It felt as if the structure drew on what little energy he possessed and quickly burned it up each time. But of course that made no sense because the simple human body could not provide the kind of energy he had deployed back at the slab, so it had to come from somewhere else. And then, in some deep recess in his being, he found it.

Everything flashed whole and complete around him and he could see to the horizon. He still had that sense of distance of normal vision, but only beyond a hundred metres. Within that boundary he found he could inspect things as if they were right in front of him and then, with a little effort, look inside them. Further exploration of the talent enabled him to relocate his centre point a few miles away, and from there he could inspect things closely. He drew back again and studied his companions, saw the fibrous structures spread throughout their bodies, inspected himself and saw the same there. He then ranged out and out until he finally found the slab with its piles of flier corpses and now swarms of scavenger worms.

Anstor delighted in this. He lay strapped to a travois almost too exhausted to move, yet it seemed he could fling his perception anywhere. He came back to the travelling group and spiralled out from them, looking for xenovores. He found six of the kind that had killed Cranston – and yes it was Cranston and not Tupolek who he had last accompanied out of the Facility. The time with Tupolek had been not long after he came out of the compound. The man had been convinced they were being fed lies about the creatures out there, and had died just like Cranston. The xenovores were in a huddled group, the heads of five of them pointed up at the sky, while another crouched low, spiked beak resting against the ground. He watched them for a while and saw the five abruptly turn on the other one, grabbing it and driving in their feeding tubes. It struggled but simply had no chance. He saw it inflate rapidly and then collapse just as rapidly – the skin taut over its bones and revealing the shape of the skeleton which, Anstor noted, seemed a distorted version of a human skeleton. He absorbed that datum and moved on, speculating on these creatures. There were many of them here, yet he had seen no prey beyond the humans on this world.

His perception flew into twilight under an almost permanent cloud layer and he came at last to the Facility. He entered and saw the familiar faces of those they had left behind with new ones amidst them, recently released from the compound. But his interest lay elsewhere. He searched for the Nok but could find it nowhere outside or in human quarters and so, with indoctrinated reluctance, slid towards its building. Always, an inductee entering that place faced pain and or death. But he needed to see inside to dispel that demon in his skull, and he needed to find out something related to the xenovores. His perception shot over the ground to the door, and simply bounced off it. Baffled, he circled the thing and tried to go through the walls, through the roof, but he simply could not enter.

He backed off and considered this. That he had this omniscient vision and those other talents, which he hoped were merely exhausted and somnolent and not damaged in some way, was due to what the Nok had done to him. He had become what it had been trying to create with some form of organic technology, so it must understand, at least to a degree, what it was doing. He should not be surprised therefore that it had other technology related to those talents – to block them in this case it would seem. He must keep that at the forefront of his mind for the future. He hovered over the building contemplatively, then felt it briefly open to him. In a flash he glimpsed an interior he had seen before – the building filled with pipe-like tunnels and cyst-like rooms as of some kind of hive. He fell inside to expand within the constraints of the walls and tried to see it all. In some of those cyst-like rooms he found blisters on the walls

– hundreds of them and, peering inside one that looked new and fresh, he saw an altered human being knotted up foetal, fed by tubes from an attached yolk, changing: head extended and arms ridden up below it, mouth turning into a feeding tube. Despite these radical changes he recognised one of the Nok's recent failures.

Then the perception blinked to the outside and he saw the Nok now standing just beyond the door it had closed. He peered down at the thing, drew closer and tried to see inside. The Nok felt slippery and he encountered some resistance, but not as much as from the building. Within, he saw nothing but the same solid matter as the Nok's exterior but, looking closer and closer still, he sensed it shifting and he sensed patterned matter stretching down and down like Mandelbrot sets as he probed. Order and structure were there and, delving as deep as he could, he expected to see a linked mass of nanomachines or the like. Nothing came distinct and then, abruptly, the Nok raised a hand and swung it, as if swatting a fly, and Anstor found himself tumbling away.

His perception ended up by the encircling wall. The thing had sensed him and pushed him away in some manner and, when he looked back towards it, it faced in his direction. He could see the danger now as the Nok turned away, almost dismissively, and headed towards its ship. He had felt, once his talents had returned, he would be strong enough to go up against the Nok and find some route to freedom. But he and the others were the product that creature was aiming for, so logically, and as had been demonstrated, the Nok had ways of handling such talents, nullifying them and... using them for whatever purpose it had engendered them for. He needed to prepare – he needed to be strong. He fled back across the landscape to return to his body.

Anstor found his fellows trudging along as before. He brought his perception back to his body and now got a more immediate sense of his condition. He still ached and felt exhausted, but did feel better.

'How far have we come?' he abruptly asked and, only as he did so, another structure lit up and he knew that, as well as speaking the words out loud, he had spoken them into their minds. It appeared this was another talent he had not overstrained, and so came back quickly.

Negal, over to one side, had paused to kick at some slew of bones and old skin. He took out the device he had looked at before, and was about to sign the answer, then looked round in confusion towards the travois.

'A hundred and three miles,' said Anstor.

The words had risen in Negal's mind before he reflexively turned them into sign language. Other thoughts below that were a chattering crowd, waiting for some input to get one member shouting loudest. It was the same with them all, but in everyone he read a melange of fear and hope, and wild speculations rising to be dismissed. Suspicion arose from the newer inductees because they knew Anstor had been around for a long time and they... wondered about him. They all halted and moved in to surround Anstor, Indira moving to stand directly before him.

'You spoke in my mind,' she said.

He nodded mutely and peered down at the straps holding him to the travois. He considered trying to remove them to some other location, but decided it best to recover more strength before pushing those other mental structures. He also felt a display of human weakness would be good for the nerves of the others.

'Can you help me up?' he asked. 'I think I might be able to walk.'

Tagon stepped over to untie the straps, the particle cannon on his back. Thinking back to the flier attack, Anstor understood he had teleported both energy and particulate from the cannon to make those shots into the sky, thus draining its storage. Now, with the same sense he had just ranged out with, he peered inside the weapon and saw that fusion had topped it up again. He analysed that. He had understood the mechanism and bypassed it, created a facsimile of it in the ether – simply used the power of his mind to form it. What was the limit of this power should it return? Did it have one? He then turned his attention to Tagon himself, brushing over the man's thoughts only... there were none. He tried again, dreading that this ability was failing, and simply could find nothing to key into. He then really looked at the man – inside him – and now found himself in familiar territory for Tagon's insides resembled the mechanism of the pulse cannon. He didn't react to that as he shakily stood up. There were far too many questions to be resolved that were better resolved with thought and the surreptitious exercising of his new powers *when* they returned – he had to work on that premise else all would be failure. The answer to Sharp Tagon he felt would come along with the answers to the Nok, what it was doing here, and why.

'So what have you got?' Indira finally asked.

They left the travois propped against a boulder and continued on, Tagon leading the way to the supposed Polity base. Senses ranging out again, he could find no danger as yet, though strippers and 003s were within ten miles. He ranged out further and further to reach the coast Tagon had told them about. He searched there and saw, in the end, Tagon had not lied about the Polity base, that tagreb, but he had been a little parsimonious with the truth.

'They are words that moved into the territory of myth because we have known that telepathy, telekinesis and teleportation have always been the products of fiction. But here, apparently, they are real.' He gestured to Abdulla who he was glad to see still alive and then to Negal. 'They both have some form of telekinesis.'

'I guess,' she nodded her head. 'And you?'

'I have very little at the moment.' He shook his head. 'I can feel the talents in my skull but they are like lights with the power turned off.'

The conversation occupied just one small part of his mind. He told Indira about the things he might be able to do and his speculations on that. He talked of possible limitations because of what had happened after he brought down the fliers. In truth, even as he spoke, he felt an exciting breadth of something within him, and knew his limitations had been stretched and pushed far away. His excitement reflected in his mind, causing brief ignitions in the structures there – like the equipment in a house coming on for a second, as work is being done to restore the power.

Meanwhile, he probed his companions – he began to look into them as he had looked into the pulse cannon and Sharp Tagon. He studied closely the fibrous growths throughout their bodies and knotted up in their skulls, and found no sign of any foetal heads with glowing red eyes. That, in fact, had been a nightmare that had slid into apparent real memory as a side effect of his malfunctioning mind.

He made comparisons with himself and could see the differences. He went deeper, into their physical structure, into the structure of their minds and into that territory that lay close to the telepathy he had used, but did not quite reach it. Deeper and deeper he went, integrating information and making logical inferences in a mental capacity that seemed to grow with the more demand he put upon it. He saw into the fibres then, and their function, saw where reality pushed to the edge of something else, for the fibres were cases around mechanisms not of baryonic matter. Dark matter? Argument continued about this particular hole in some theories, but no one had ever discovered the stuff. Exotic matter perhaps – formed by processes as far beyond Polity technology as it lay beyond the Stone Age.

'I see some of the shape of it now,' he said.

'The shape of what?' Indira asked.

'This is speculation only.' He looked at her and shrugged. 'What was put inside us creates a plasticity of being. By our will we can change ourselves and of course the pressure of that will, the need, increases when survival is at stake. We wanted to move fast to get to the Polity base and freedom, we became faster. Negal wanted escape, freedom, and so takes on the aspects of a bird. Abdulla wanted control of his immediate environment, with the result you see.'

'And me?' she asked.

'To understand the enemy and to be strong, perhaps?' He shook his head. 'I wonder if you do not sense their pheromones, but are dully sensing their minds.'

'Dully,' she said, obviously annoyed.

'But the intention was to force us to acquire what I can only describe as psychic powers.'

They were all close around now and listening.

'Why does the Nok want this?' signed Negal.

'I don't know,' Anstor replied. 'But it has processed thousands of human beings to try and come up with us, so there must be a payoff. We are a product and you can be damned sure we are to serve a purpose not our own. We will need to be ready.'

'Ready?' asked Jaden.

He knew danger loomed and they were not ready. Yet, he could see the alterations inside them he could make from comparisons with his own mind and the ball of fibres penetrating it. But of course, only once he had his telekinesis back.

'Can we stop for a while?' he asked, indicating a nearby slew of rocks about which low bushes grew scattered with red berries.

'Okay, we have a way to go yet,' said Indira.

They settled themselves on the rocks and passed around food and drink. Tagon demurred, but of course he would. Anstor told them about his omniscient perception as the talents flickered and shifted in his skull. He ate with shaking hands and at one point dropped a food bar.

Reaching to catch it, pain flashed in his head, a whole structure lighting up and then settling to a dim glow. He had caught the food bar without using his hands and it floated in the air just a foot off the ground. They all stared at this in silence.

'They're coming back,' he said, and plucked the bar out of the air.

'Could you… stop the Nok?' asked Leach.

'I don't know.' He told them about what had happened when he had shifted that perception far back to the Facility.

'So it has ways of dealing with the product it is producing,' said Jaden bitterly.

'So it would seem.' Anstor ate and drank and every moment felt better. But he knew it could not be the food and drink. The merely organic – the calories of food bars – could never be enough to transfer the energy from hundreds of fliers into the ground and to freeze them in the sky. He looked internally again, concentrating on that fibrous network and felt the schism between matter and that core of something that was not. He pushed and probed and felt things naturally mating up. His skull began to fill with light and he felt a savage joy. The lights then dimmed as his internal perception shifted, and those structures became working engines no longer wasting their energy on light.

'Xenovores coming,' said Indira.

Anstor switched his perception outwards again and saw that two 003s were heading rapidly towards them. He moved close to the creatures and looked inside at degrading fibres and the simplified though familiar function of their minds. He turned to Indira and saw what was working in her and now what he could move, what linkages he could make – how he could firm the connection between matter and non-matter. Maybe he couldn't bring her to his level, but he could certainly fully express her nascent abilities.

'Do you want your power in full?' he asked her. 'Do you all want this?' he asked.

They leaned in towards him, curious and hopeful because what sensible person denies an offer of power?

'Yes, I want mine,' said Indira.

She looked around at the others and got cautious nods of agreement.

'But how?' asked Leach. 'And what do I have?'

Anstor again looked into Leach to be certain of what he had seen before. 'You, Leach, are all potential, confused by your attachment to the physical with the physical results we see. It could be that you will gain everything I have, but that will require more work than the others.'

'But how?' Leach repeated.

'I have the ability to teleport myself and other things, telekinesis too and perception of matter down to the nanoscopic level. Running comparisons with myself I can alter you – I can correct what the Nok probably saw as faults it hoped would resolve themselves.' He gestured to Abdulla. 'In you, for example, they are resolving and you can feel it. It's not just fluids you can manipulate with your telekinesis now.'

'Yes, I can feel that,' said Abdulla, and by way of demonstration gestured with one hand at the ground. Gritty soil rose up and swirled into a long spiral snake-like form, then after a moment collapsed.

Anstor nodded and then concentrated on Indira. She looked suddenly startled as he began to probe at those fibres in her mind and throughout her body. It wasn't quite enough, he realised – proximity gave him more connection and finesse. He stood, walked over to her, reached out and put his hand on her skull. He mapped across and made alterations, saw the stunted forms of her other talents shifting too and knew that eventually she, and they, could all be like him, but he suspected he would not be given the time.

Indira groaned as her telepathy kicked in and her telekinesis flashed intermittently. She bowed her head out of his hand and now he could see the process continuing within her. He tried to disentangle himself from her but found fibres or threads routing through some unseen continuum to her – that a connection had been formed. He stepped back and watched as she raised her head and looked round at them all. She was seeing the function of their minds and the slew of surface thoughts – the debating society of the unconscious and primary thoughts arising from it. He could see this as she was seeing it – through the connection. As she looked from each to each in turn he spoke directly into her mind.

'You will find nothing in Tagon – we will deal with that soon.'

In reply to a wordless question he routed over images of what Sharp Tagon looked like inside. He expected argument, since she had been their leader from the beginning, but found only acquiescence. He did not like it, but it seemed she had just become subject to his will.

Out loud he said, 'I didn't tell you all about what I saw back at the Facility.' He studied them all. 'Remember that the number of failures we see ejected from the Nok's building is much lower than the number that goes in. Remember too how the Nok often lands its ship on that building for some purpose.' He focused on Indira. 'Now look into the minds of those approaching xenovores.'

She turned to face in that direction. The xenovores were now visible about a mile away heading towards them. She blinked, frowned and struggled with her new talent. Then her eyes grew wide in shock.

'You understand?' he asked.

She nodded sharply.

'I needed confirmation,' he said. 'It seems that the corpses we see ejected from the building are only the failures the Nok finds unsuitable for another purpose.' He pointed to the xenovores. 'Those are ones that were suitable.'

It took a moment for them to absorb that as they came to their feet.

'They're human,' said Leach, looking sick.

'Are, were – semantics,' said Anstor.

'But what about the tagreb data?' said Tagon.

'Indeed,' said Anstor, 'what about it?'

He gazed out at the xenovores, sickened by his knowledge, enjoying the power surging inside him, but still utterly certain it wasn't enough. The Nok made them and it would use them. It had no human morality and, if it was prepared to turn 'failures' into horrific monsters, what might it have in store for them? Time to get proactive, he felt. He could not keep on speculating. They needed to garner as much power as possible before they faced that creature, for he was sure that face it they would. Perhaps the distance would help. He didn't know but he had to try.

'It is time for us to stop walking and resolve a more immediate matter,' he said

'What do you mean?' Negal signed.

'This,' said Anstor, without moving his lips but speaking directly into their minds. He reached out and encompassed the fibrous growths throughout them, the substance of their bodies clinging, entangled, and sure to be dragged along. He reached out then to the location of that Polity base and chose a location outside it. A dull warning throb resounded in his skull, but then faded. He included all their belongings and the pulse cannon – mere material and almost a subtext to the act. Sharp Tagon too. And he teleported them.

'Mother of God!' Indira exclaimed, stumbling through knee-high grass and weeds. Leach fell, then abruptly scrabbled to his feet. Negal appeared just above the ground and rose up higher, floating in the air. Anstor could see that teleporting the man this distance had shifted things inside him and his power to levitate himself had now become subject to his will. However, he had further to go, for he had the potential to shift or levitate other objects too. Abdulla smiled and dipped his head. His telekinesis had taken a step up and now he had acquired inward vision and could see how to change himself. Anstor suspected his testicles would be returning sometime hence. The Plesters, who had the potential to teleport, were now much closer to it. Gaunt Chapter pushed towards heavy telekinesis while Eva Salter's mind slanted towards omniscient vision and telepathy. Tagon landed with a heavy thump and looked around in bewilderment. Of course he had no awareness of the teleportation – the energies involved had not affected him internally and he had not perceived them.

'And here is the Polity base,' said Anstor. He looked over at Tagon, 'A tagreb, just like you said.'

It lay amidst trees at the edge of a forest ahead, bright in red sunlight – the cloud a great grey bank far back in the direction they had come. When tagrebs landed they folded out like opening flowers, with a central 'bud' building that housed the AI and control systems, while living quarters folded up from the petals. Little of this whole lay visible, for all they saw were ruined and overgrown buildings.

'You never asked what your potential is, Jaden,' said Anstor, turning to her.

'It is connected to my profession before – that's all I know,' she replied.

Anstor nodded. 'Yes, it's very specific. You had an almost instinctive Facility with technology and it has grown from that. Your potential is to see into technological items and manipulate them at the macroscopic and microscopic level. It's a version of the telekinesis and omniscient vision that I have.'

'Wow,' she said, smiling.

'It must have been abandoned while I was at the Facility,' said Tagon, staring at the ruined base. 'I'm sorry. I thought there was a way out for us here.'

Anstor walked over to Jaden, reached out with his power and froze her to the spot. He could feel the growth inside her fighting against him and knew that given time it would reorder and she would break free. He placed a hand on her skull – the closer proximity of what he had inside him to what lay in her giving him finesse of control once again. He began making alterations even as he turned his head to look at Tagon.

'The Polity base – the idea of the Polity base – was merely to give us something to strive for. The Nok understood that merely subjecting us to survival pressures was not enough. We needed the possibility of escape, or freedom, else with our changes we would simply destroy ourselves – turn ourselves into organic mechanisms to that end. Psychic abilities would not have developed. We would all have been on the failure pile or turned into xenovores.'

'What do you mean?' Tagon turned to him.

Within Jaden's body and mind he could feel the fibres shifting and falling into new shapes. The sensory parts of her brain were connecting up and her eyes grew wide. She ceased to struggle against him and in a clumsy fashion began to assist.

'I mean that the Nok deliberately established the myth of some halcyon escape for us, but then of course put in our way all the horrors it could conjure for us to survive to reach that escape.'

'But I was here,' said Tagon.

Anstor pulled his hand away from Jaden and she staggered back.

'Do you have it now?' Anstor asked her.

She nodded mutely. Yes, she had it, and with the same entanglement as with Indira he had her. Why did he not feel so bad about it this time? *Power corrupts*, he thought.

'Take a look at the Polity base.'

She turned towards it, suddenly seemed weak and went down on one knee. She dipped her head and scrubbed at her face with her hands, then looked again. She pointed. 'The fold out platforms are supposed to be made of layered composites that little can penetrate. Plants have penetrated these. They are simple foamstone that has degraded and cracked.' She shook her head then continued. 'A tagreb has all the necessities inside – a fusion reactor, power systems, a controlling AI, drills and connected systems to find groundwater… there is nothing here. It's a mock-up.'

Anstor turned back to Sharp Tagon. 'You were already at the Facility when the first of us arrived.' He shrugged. 'You were always there.' He reached out and snatched. With a sucking whoomph the particle cannon and its connected gear disappeared from his back and reappeared at Anstor's feet. Tagon staggered forwards looking bewildered.

'Jaden, now look at Tagon.'

She glanced at Anstor then turned to the man, squinting and puzzled. After a moment her expression cleared. 'The fucker.'

Anstor turned to the others. 'It has always been difficult to distinguish genuine AI from machines that can emulate life. It's a debate that still rages in the Polity. But in this case we have a mechanism with a vast bank of various responses that could fool most Turing tests.' He raised a hand and with it Tagon rose from the ground.

'What is this?' Tagon said. 'What are you doing!'

'It doesn't know,' said Jaden.

Anstor shrugged. 'It has no self awareness at all.'

He brought his hands together as if gripping some fruit between them, then wrenched them apart. Tagon shuddered in the air and with a ripping sound, and a crackling as of wine glass stems breaking, his head parted in the middle. The split traversed his body from there down to his crotch and when Anstor opened his hands the two halves crashed to the ground spilling shiny metallic components and skeins of sparking wires. Anstor walked over, now identifying electromuscle, cog wheels and joint motors. He stooped and using physical strength combined with telekinesis ripped out a cube from which numerous wires trailed.

'Not even AI crystal – just an organo-metal processing substrate. I would guess that he wasn't made from the Nok's technology because some of us can sense that.' He discarded the cube over to one side and turned to them again. 'We must prepare. The Nok will be coming for us now.'

Anstor studied the group, now realising it had been a mistake to tear Tagon apart like that. He had frightened them and now they had become very wary of him, all, that is, apart from Indira and Jaden. They needed to be together on this. He had no idea what powers the Nok might bring to bear and how they could react, but they definitely needed to be together.

'It's a bad choice of word, considering how it was at the Facility, but who wants to upgrade next. Make your decisions fast – time is running out.'

'How do you know that time is running out?' asked Gaunt.

'I can see the Nok's ship coming this way,' Anstor replied, only briefly unhappy with the lie because flashing his perception back to the Facility he saw that the creature's ship still there. It had moved from its landing area to the top of the Nok's building, doubtless loading up a new batch of xenovores to distribute in the surrounding lands. 'We can stand here debating, or we can try to be as ready as we can be.'

'I agree,' said Indira. 'When you look at the xenovores, look inside, and see that they were once human, who knows what plans the Nok has for us? It has no sympathy, no empathy and is just fashioning us into tools.'

Anstor glanced at her. Such agreement was uncharacteristic, for in the past she would always argue things through – looking for holes in any plan. The way she had spoken could almost have been him speaking, and that made him uneasy. Yet it did not make him so uneasy as to doubt what they must do. He briefly studied Gaunt's surface thoughts, his doubts and fears, and how they stemmed from the fact that Sharp Tagon had supposedly been his friend. They had talked a great deal. Chapter Gaunt was finding it difficult to accept Tagon as a non-conscious machine, despite the evidence lying scattered on the ground before him. But thoughts could be changed, as he had seen with Indira, and underneath that conscious swirl lay Gaunt's huge attraction to a power he could almost taste.

'You're telekinetic,' Anstor said, walking over to the man. 'From what I can sense, your strength is huge. Tagon once said that he wondered if he could lift the Nok's ship with his physical strength. You might be able to do the same but with your mind.' Anstor stepped closer, apparently putting everything he could into persuading Gaunt. He slapped a hand on the man's shoulder 'Listen man, wouldn't you like the power to smash that damned ship into the ground?'

Connection.

Gaunt was stronger than Jaden so it took physical contact to freeze him to the spot. But he did manage to talk as Anstor delved into his mind and to that matter/non-matter connection.

'He said things like that,' said Gaunt. 'He spoke like he was puzzled about what he could do. Maybe he was a man... before...'

Gaunt's words trailed away and his eyes went glassy. It required only a tweak here and a tweak there and everything within him went into cascade. As Anstor withdrew his hand it was as if he could see it trailing sticky threads – his control over the man now the same as with Indira and Jaden. He looked round and saw the look on Abdulla's face. The man knew what had happened and seemed ready to run. Abdulla's power had almost completed and it would be a fight to subdue him. Could he cross the intervening ground before Abdulla tried to defend himself? He mentally reached for him, trying to form a connection, and found his mind slick and difficult. But now the other three were with him and he found himself drawing on them. Already Gaunt's telekinesis had increased and Anstor had him slam down on the man and freeze him. He drew on Indira's telepathy and found Jaden's precision with matter a great advantage. Dust began swirling up around Abdulla but then he grunted, staggered and went down on his backside. His powers ramped up as his mind and intertwining fibres formed into a new shape, but Anstor's threads of connection were in there, and the man belonged to him.

Leach looked on angrily. He too knew what was happening, but he did nothing apsrt from raising a hand as Anstor went into him and set things in motion. All the talents lit up in the man's mind, but weak and undeveloped. He lowered his hand, frowned, and Anstor could feel his awareness of those controlling threads of connection.

The Plester twins... they had turned and were running towards the fake Polity base. Negal rose into the air, panic writ across his features, but Eva Salter walked towards Anstor and put a hand on his shoulder. He took her in an instant, felt her reasoning. She knew he was seizing control of them, but the alternative was the Nok. She felt the clarity of her mind and even as he drew on her resources he apologised mentally. And through the lens of her perception felt ashamed yet determined. Gaunt pulled Negal down to the ground and Anstor took control of the man too, the upgrade in his mind almost instantaneous, and then with his power complemented by Gaunt's he brought the Plester's to a staggering halt. With a combination of psychic talents from the others Anstor had the twins turn round and walk back, and by the time they stood with the group again, they were his.

Anstor surveyed them all. Rebellion and fear were there, disgust and alarm, but all suppressed with consciousness acceding to his will. But he found he could not be unaffected by their underlying thoughts, nor especially by the clarity he still found in Eva Salter. If he kept them so utterly subject to his will they would simply be resources to throw against the Nok and he would have little of their intelligent input – slaves and not compatriots. However, the linkage of them all together provided power he found synergistic rather than cumulative. If he sacrificed his control over them – and he was not sure if he could at that moment – he sacrificed that power. However, he could loosen the reins. He could have their input and did not need to keep them completely suppressed.

'I only understood this when I gave Indira her full ability,' he said, slackening control, allowing their unconscious access to the upper levels of their minds.

'You fucker,' said Gaunt, and others expressed similar sentiments.

'Divided we fall… etc,' he said, but also sent his reasoning to them all as a bloc transfer of information.

'Have you ever considered that this is precisely what the Nok wants?' asked Indira.

'No, not until you just said it, which is why I don't want to fully control you all.'

'But you still want control,' said Leach bitterly.

'The Nok comes,' he replied.

'You lied about that,' said one of the Plester twins. Yes, he had access to and control of their minds, but they also had access to his. He wondered how it would run as their powers grew. Would he end up being displaced by Leach perhaps? He did not know. All he knew was the exigencies of the moment.

'But I am not lying now,' he said, and showed them the image of the Nok's ship rising from its building, crackling through the sky and now already halfway to their location.

Anstor allowed a conference, fast and telepathic, for it now seemed they all had that talent. They formulated their strategy which, in the end, was to hit the Nok with everything they had from the first moment they could. It wasn't coming to negotiate, they were sure of that. Indira suggested that the ship probably had weapons. Leach suggested they use the fake Polity base for cover, but Jaden surmised that the weak structure would come crashing down on them if the Nok used even a simple missile.

'The boulders,' said Gaunt.

Anstor allowed it and, drawing on the rest of them, Gaunt turned to a nearby boulder. He reached out with one hand, his expression wild, clawed his fingers as if gripping and heaved. With a sucking crump the boulder came out of the ground, more of it having been underneath than above. He brought it down ahead of them then reached out to claw up another. Anstor could feel the forces transferring through them all. When he actually began to feel it physically and his feet began sinking into the ground, he twisted the energy away into a new form and had damp earth steaming all around them. Gaunt piled the boulders in a rough curved wall standing ten feet high, its convex side facing the approaching ship. By the time he was done they were all sweating, but whether from the effort or from the heat it generated around them, Anstor could not say. Even as the last boulder crunched into place the Nok's ship appeared on the horizon and they quickly moved to cover behind the wall.

'We bring it down,' said Anstor.

He gave Gaunt free rein again, and routed through power from the others, meanwhile sucking up more from the surrounding hot earth. He was like the control in the circuit, the rheostat, the man at the console. He could feel Gaunt reaching out with all the power at his disposal to slam that ship into the ground, but the thing was slippery. It juddered and swayed in the sky as if hitting hard cross winds. Finally it dropped and ploughed into the ground half a mile ahead of them, throwing up a wave of earth and stone. It did not seem damaged, however, and knowing the durability of the Nok, Anstor doubted the creature had been hurt.

'So what now?' was the general question.

The Nok replied. The side of its ship split lengthways and hordes of xenovores poured out like baby spiders from their cocoon, and swarmed across the ground towards them. Anstor glanced round and with a thought transported the pulse cannon up on to the boulders. It had its fifty shots and operating just mentally he aimed it and fired, but not at the xenovores, instead straight into that split in the side of the ship. He could see detonations inside until the ship zipped closed and the pulse shots just splashed on its hull to leave marks like a rapidly fading bruises.

'The creatures,' Leach pointed out.

Anstor tried to draw out their energy and route it into the ground. Knowing they had once been human, he preferred this method, though it would kill them just as effectively as pulse shots. But he found himself struggling. The ground to either side of the approaching horde began smoking but not one of them dropped frozen. He tried to see it – to grasp what was happening – and finally surmised, on a level of perception that stretched across the electromagnetic spectrum from human vision, that the ship was somehow feeding them power. Reluctantly he reached out and squeezed and, now concentrating on his own powers, relaxed his hold on the others. Two 003s collapsed in bloody wreckage. Over to one side he saw a series of the creatures explode into bloody mist – Gaunt's telekinesis. He saw others turning to fight each other and knew that Indira was in their simple minds. Now freed up, the others began borrowing techniques from each other and soon xenovores were crashing to the ground with some part of their inner working ground to slurry. Negal, standing up on top of a boulder began lifting some up and dropping them on the others. Within minutes the charge was breaking up, and whatever had first driven them released its grip and they began running off in different directions. Was that it? Was it going to be as easy as that? Anstor thought not.

The ship unzipped again and the Nok stepped out. Nobody did anything for a long moment, until Gaunt sent a small boulder arcing over perfectly on target. It crashed into the ground, but by the time it did that the Nok had moved quickly to one side. Anstor tried throwing the creature, but it just kept sliding from his grasp. He tried to suck the energy out of it, but though he set the ground to one side smoking, the Nok just kept on walking.

'It's assessing us. It's just fucking assessing us!' spat Indira.

'Well let it damn well assess this,' said Abdulla.

He leapt up onto the top of the wall and like a wizard conjuring a storm drew dust clouds in all around the Nok. They swirled, turning faster and faster, building into a small tornado centred on the creature. Gaunt moved to back that up, and then Negal and the others, linking together to make something highly destructive. Anstor fed in energy and lightning strikes crackled down. The dust began to glow and tighten around the creature, which they could only now see, still walking towards them, through Anstor's omniscient vision.

He felt a sinking dread. Did this creature actually possess the same powers as did they? Why not? It seemed highly likely. As he fed in every force he could think of to cause the thing damage, he watched it, and it seemed to be smiling as it raised its hand. With a thud that he felt in his bones, something appeared. Standing atop one of the boulders was an object like one of the cysts out of bladder wrack seaweed, but the bone-yellow of the Nok's ship. This object, standing ten feet high, tumbled down off the boulder. Only as it thumped to the ground did Anstor feel Abdulla completely taken out of their circuit. He was inside the thing that had materialised there, and now the tornado began to die.

'Move locations!' Anstor bellowed.

He teleported to the end of the wall and watched others shift too. Gaunt did not possess that ability and could not seem to manage to draw it from the rest of them. One of the Plesters tried to shift him but her effort came too late. Another thump and Gaunt was enclosed, the wrack-form tumbling over and Gaunt's huge power gone from their synergy.

Was all this from the Nok? Anstor looked towards the ship then over to the pulse cannon. The small fuser was topping up its power supply once again and, with a massive effort of will, drawing so hard on Jaden she went down on her knees, he inspected and encompassed it. Yes, it could be done – he had an effective weapon. Something sizzled in the air about him and he teleported again – one of those wrack's appearing behind him and collapsing. He grasped the pulse cannon and its power supply and transported it, his perspective going with it. The thing went in through the split in the side of the Nok's ship and in the fuser he pushed the process to detonation. The blast lit up the inside of the ship like a flash bulb, blasting debris out of the split to send the vessel tumbling. The Nok, stepping out of the storm, paused to look back. Anstor saw energy lines blinking out, the connection dying but not completely dead yet. He drew on his remaining companions, sucked energy from the burning ship and focused it, concentrated it on one point right in the middle of the Nok's chest, but he could not get it inside so instead concentrated on the ground at the creature's feet. Another bright flash lit up underneath the creature and encompassed it. A fraction of a second later it tumbled out of the top of this, its legs missing below the knees, its right arm gone and the rest of the body shedding embers.

Had he killed it? Anstor looked round at the others. The Plester twins and Leach had sprawled on the ground. Eva was on her knees clutching at her head. Only Indira and Negal still stood, but they felt like empty vessels to him. He had to finish this himself – he had to be sure. Tracking the course of the Nok through the air to where it crashed down, flames issuing from the impact, he teleported to it. As he arrived he felt resistance, as if some wall had risen in the unseen continuum he travelled through, but it parted like a rotten skin and he stepped through to stand over the creature and peer down at it.

Deep burns had etched into its body, with glowing cinders at their bottoms. Where the legs and arm had been blown off he could see no bones, blood vessels or even mechanical and electrical components as in Tagon. Instead, the breaks exposed the same substance as the Nok's surface. It seemed a figure cast of grey-white clay – in fact a golem for real. He thought it dead until it tilted its head up at him, then raised its hand to clench it into a fist. He thought it must be trying to use some power against him but, after a moment it lowered that fist.

'What the fuck are you?' he asked.

'I am the Nok,' it replied succinctly.

'What is your purpose here?'

'You.' The Nok smiled and it was the first time he had ever seen that.

He surmised it must be dying and that it would fend him off with these half answers until it did so. He tried to push into it again with his extraordinary senses, and this time, because of the damage or because it allowed it, he found no barrier. Scanning its interior he again found some form of smart matter with organisation that dropped down and down, ever smaller, until it went below what he could perceive. Large areas in it were disrupted – losing their organisation – and that was spreading. This confirmed it was dying – if that was the correct term for such a thing. He next probed it telepathically, seeking out some mind he could probe, and immediate high bandwidth connection established with such force it knocked him from his feet onto his backside.

Information and memory flowed, giving him incredibly complex multiple perspectives. Out of this he had to pick coherent threads because it was like looking at events through a million eyes. He fined it down and found images of a similar kind to those that could be found in the Polity, on its war with the alien prador. He saw vast explosions eating up weirdly distorted cities, seas boiling and tsunamis swamping landscapes, high-energy beams cutting through atmosphere or vacuum, ships of multiple design in combat, worlds burning – they were snapshots all of interstellar war. He hunted through this melange of imagery and saw armies of beings clashing in all those scenarios. None of these creatures were human. Some weren't even individuals but flowing masses like plants that had been partially mechanised. Others were huge crustaceans guided by parasitic riders that bore some resemblance to cephalopods. Then he saw the grey soldiers. These came in multiple forms suited to whatever combat they were in, but all of them, he could see, were of the same substance as the Nok. Further battles arose for his inspection and he could not quite see what weapons were being deployed to create so much carnage. Then he realised: psychic powers.

But the images began fading as more and more of the Nok disrupted. Anstor pushed himself to his feet and walked over. The fires in the Nok's body had gone out, but the cavities had grown deeper, in some places cutting right through to the ground. The grey substance of it was turning black and leaking out everywhere.

'You were a soldier,' said Anstor, trying for at least some fellow feeling. 'There is a war you are in, or were in. What do you want with us?'

The Nok's smile was a calm upward tilt of the lips.

'We are the Nok. We are recruiting,' it said, and died.

Stupid stupid stupid…

As Anstor headed back to the others he cursed his blindness and assumptions, and sent his perception up and up. Shortly he had a view of the continent whose east coast he stood upon, but his vision was not really 'omniscient' and from this distance all he could make out was mountain chains, the flare of a volcano which somehow caused a weather phenomenon that put a large area under cloud – where the Facility lay – a collection of circular lakes and the silver veins of rivers. He began shifting his perception along the spectrum, one way then the other. Infra red was no help because the continent came to him then with a rash of spots. He brought his perception down to check a number of these and found thermal springs and vents everywhere. However, ultraviolet revealed a different scattering of spots, and he brought his perception down again to inspect one of these on the west coast.

Here he found another version of the Facility, and when he drew closer he saw people there, and the circle of pulse cannons. He shifted to another of these, and then another, and found the scenario repeated. At one of these he paused, seeing a grey head tilted up towards him. Another Nok was looking at him. Or was it the case that they were all one being? That might account for *his* Nok's lack of concern about dying.

Rounding the wall Gaunt had built he found the others now up and about, though moving like survivors of catastrophe. His connection to them was weak now – as weak as their powers had become after exhausting themselves against the Nok. Telepathically he acknowledged what they were doing. They had dragged the two bladders together and were now cutting one of them open – hard work getting through the thick rubbery layer with flint tools. He peered into one of the bladders and saw Gaunt folded up foetal like those who were being turned into xenovores, intubated with organic pipes, and with other objects attached to his body here and there. He was unconscious – put into some kind of hypersleep ready for transportation to that war of the Nok's. Then came a flash.

Anstor pulled his perception away and across the continent. Here at another Facility he saw a Nok ship rising – something about Nok technology radiated into the ultra violet. He tracked it, fearing it was coming for them, but it continued up and up. He brought his perception close to it and felt a slight tug of strain as he followed it out of atmosphere and into vacuum. Was it heading off to grab more humans for the Nok recruitment campaign? Only then, as he thought about how many hundreds of such ships must be on the planet, did he think to turn his perception outwards. And he felt his guts tightening up upon seeing the awful truth.

The mother ship hung in orbit above the world. When he saw it, Anstor thought, *bones.* The thing looked like a great mass of giant bones tangled together into a long mass, bloated in the middle. Even what might have been the fore of the thing resembled the stretched out skull of a snake. As he drew his perception closer he understood that the thing was huge, but only by making comparisons with the Nok *shuttles* attached to it, did he understand it had to be the best part of a hundred miles long. Closer still and he found resistance, his perception sliding off of those bones and again some sense of the utterly alien. He realised, in that instant, that the thing must be fashioned of the same stuff as the Nok they had killed. And he understood on a visceral level that the whole of this substance was in fact the thing called the Nok.

He encompassed it and searched for access. It arrived in the form of that Nok shuttle he had followed up coming in to dock – attaching like a leech to the behemoth. This created a brief psychic window and Anstor went through that. Inside the ship he felt his perception contract as if he had injected a probe from his outer self connected by a fragile thread. Then everything greyed out for a period he could not measure for it seemed the brief opening had closed, yet his perception remained inside the ship. He could only see the interior of the vessel just as a human in one place. But he could travel fast – he could move his perception swiftly through the interior.

He travelled along inside one 'bone'. It seemed an endless hall ribbed on the inside like a reptile's gullet. He tried to go through one of its walls but found it resisted him as the whole of the ship had, and that he could only travel through the open spaces. Eventually he started to find doors, oval and larger than a human might require, sitting between the rib bones. One of these opened from a centre point like a sphincter. A Nok propelled itself out, for there was no gravity here, and headed off down the bone.

Anstor went through the door into a cavernous chamber. At the centre of this hung a sphere of the same substance as the Nok and of this ship. Below it he recognised technology of Polity manufacture. Steel coffins on a conveyor, injector mechanisms attached all around with pipes leading back to a tank, robotic arms at the present stationary, paraphernalia of computing, optic connections and other items. He tracked it all back. The sphere trailed an umbilicus that entered an open port on the top of the feed tank. He watched and waited as injectors and optic feeds disconnected from one of those coffins and it shifted forwards on the conveyor into the chamber of a flash oven for the fast manufacture of ceramic components. The door closed and the oven briefly emitted bright light from chainglass ports. The door on the other side of the oven popped open and the coffin drifted out to where those robotic arms seized it. They stabilised and then opened it. Inside, perfectly matching the interior of what now turned out to be a mould, lay a Nok. It sat up and pushed itself free, drifted towards the door. The robotic arms closed the mould and moved it back round to the start of the conveyor.

Here then the singular Noks were produced, though the necessity of Polity technology baffled him. Perhaps this equipment had been made to fashion some form of Golem and so suited their purpose? He followed the newly moulded Nok out and explored further. Another opening gave him access to other 'bones' and cysts. He saw Noks everywhere, and in one part of the ship he saw them in battle form – monstrosities with multiple limbs terminating in hooked blades or manipulators for specialised weapons, complex sensory arrays – some of which turned to watch him as he drifted past – and bodies on which the grey substance of Nok had turned dark and hard to form armour. But only when he paused to try and push his perception harder did he start to sense what he now wanted to find.

Eventually, he entered a long cyst all around the walls of which were attached those bladder wrack cases – hundreds of thousands of them. He drew closer to study them and found the sizes of the cases varied in different areas. He managed to focus inside some of these and found forms wildly at variance from human. Only when he found the mutated prador did he realise that much of what he had seen before had not been at variance from human, but was truly alien. Mutated humans, when he found them, numbered just a few thousand, with a wide area of wall nearby yet to be occupied by further recruits of that kind.

Anstor's extrapolation of all this appalled him. How many races and how many star systems had the Nok visited during their or, perhaps more correctly, *its* recruitment campaign? How long had this been going on? A likely horrible truth here was of a war that had ended long ago, and the Nok just continued its program. But what could he possibly do? He was a lone soldier of the Polity and now of the kind the Nok was quite used to handling. What could even the Polity do if it found out? The Nok had been stealing people from there for a long time undiscovered, and evidently its technology lay far beyond that of the AIs. The AIs, in fact, dismissed psychic powers with the same contempt as did most humans in the Polity.

Finally, he'd had enough, but trying to leave the Nok ship he found himself blocked in every direction. He made his way to the hull through its Byzantine tubeways and there waited, trying to think of a way he and the others could get clear of all this. Could they steal a Nok shuttle and escape? Were the shuttles even capable of jumping through U-space? He moved round and round the hull, at one point entering a shuttle firmly attached to the ship so not allowing him any psychic exit. He studied the interior and could understand nothing. The thing consisted of smart matter without recognisable controls. Did the Nok aboard even pilot it? Leaving the shuttle he moved on to find Polity technology imbedded in the ship. Here were two long cylinders of normal matter that could not block him. He entered one and found himself surrounded by thousands of circular hatches. Another awful truth now dawned on him, for these cylinders were massive zero-freezers. Driving his perception into the walls he saw the rank upon rank of cold coffins containing Polity citizens. Obviously he, and the others, weren't brought directly to the planet after being kidnapped in the Polity, but came from here. And out of this arose thoughts about time.

A human being could remain alive and in stasis in a cold coffin for hundreds of years. How long had actually passed since the Nok grabbed him from the Polity? He probed these sleeping forms looking for some clue and finally managed to penetrate an offline aug one of them wore. From this he obtained a date fifty-six years after he was taken. This would be correct because the internal clock would not have stopped. However, augs always updated Polity time from the AI network to keep on track – correcting for relativity and the time-dilation of interstellar travel – and he had no idea how far they were from the Polity now. It was all moot. His most immediate concern must be to drag his perception out of here and back down to the planet because hours must have passed down there by now.

Only as he moved beyond the zero freezers did the illogic of his position now occur to him. If Nok technology blocked psychic access, how could his perception be in here while his body remained down on the planet? When he had entered the Nok's building at the Facility, the moment it had closed the door he had been shunted out – his psychic probe had been cut off. Why had it not happened this time? He moved mentally into the realm of his powers, examining processes he had no name for and little with which to compare them. He then remembered an ancient idea from fantasy virtuality called 'astral projection', whereby the human soul ventured out of the body to explore its surroundings, but remained attached by a long silver thread. It had felt like that and he had already made that mental comparison. The thread had been severed when the Nok closed the door to its building, and so it should have been here when the shuttle docked, briefly giving him access but then closing it.

Anstor explored that, translating perception and trying to visualise things he felt with unhuman senses. Memory did give him a thread, and memory also gave him the moment when the access closed. He had greyed out for a time and afterwards... millions of finer threads connected into the smart matter all around him and thence to his body down on the planet. It made sense, of course. He had Nok technology inside him and, by its evident interconnection, he must be in that circuit too. This gave him pause because now he could see possibilities – some of them frightening. It seemed in the end this might be an ultimate route for the Nok to control him and others of his kind, for they could become naught but subsidiary mechanism of the Nok entire. But maybe this connection could be a route into it; a way to subvert it?

He pushed his perception, trying to divide it as the dying Nok's perception had been down on the planet, with its memories seen through a million eyes. He now slid easily into the smart matter of the ship, as if he had liquefied his being to pass through its sieve rather than force himself through whole. And then he was in it.

In the vast and complex architecture of the thing he surfed a billion memories of a war that never seemed to end. Through the utterly terrifying violence he found himself being drawn into the purpose of something – that being to bring this all to an end. The Nok just needed to be stronger. It needed more soldiers to throw against the enemy and to that end it commissioned a war mind to hunt down such recruits. Drawn to the war mind in this ship, whose shape he could now see etched out of the complexity here, he explored, and found appalling reaches of time had passed. The thing had processed races for millennia until there were no more left to find. Then it had gone into the long dark, but with no change or relinquishment of its purpose, until it found new lights of consciousness and could begin again. And then that war mind focused its attention on Anstor and, in its alien regard, his attraction to its purpose died. Abruptly utterly repelled, he knew the technology within had drawn him in. Next, he found himself outside of the giant Nok ship. Briefly he thought he had found his way out along those multiple threads, but now he saw numerous shuttles detaching and pulling away – heading down towards the planet.

Anstor dropped down through atmosphere, passing the horde of shuttles. He felt no victory in having previous conjectures confirmed, for the confirmation was worse than he had imagined. The Nok war mind had denuded a galaxy to produce soldiers to feed into the meat grinder war. It had continued as worlds, civilisations and the war itself died. The long dark had been intergalactic space and those new lights of consciousness in the Milky Way Galaxy. And yet it continued recruiting because that was its purpose. And still he could see no resolution here, no way he or his compatriots or indeed perhaps millions or trillions of others could escape this. He fell, sucked of the power to think about this anymore, his thread winding him in, and arrived in his body with almost a physical thump.

'Anstor! Anstor!' The voice was of them all, shouting in his mind.

He blinked his eyes open on a bright day, yet it had been evening when he had been heading back to them. He sat up, logy as if from a long sleep. Everything he had perceived remained clear in his mind and darting his perception upwards he saw those shuttles still on the way down. He knew, because he had been inside it and understood it, that the war mind had perceived him and had now sent Noks to capture him and the others. What could they do? All they could do was fight and finally lose. He had half a mind not to tell the others about all this, but it was too late.

'Oh god in heaven!' said Indira, while similar exclamations arose from the rest. His connection with them had reaffirmed and now they could see what he had seen.

He held out his hands.

'What can we do?'

'We can fight the fuckers, and at least take some of them down before they kill us,' said Gaunt.

The others had freed him and Abdulla from their bladders, the remains of which lay over to one side. He felt strong to Anstor, as did all they all, and as did he as he stood up. He had expected exhaustion here, in them and in himself, but it seemed that having pushed themselves they had extended their boundaries. Also, he sensed with Gaunt and Abdulla that their sojourn in those bladders had given them some sort of boost. Perhaps that was part of the preparation to get them into fighting trim.

'Then that is what we must do,' he said. 'I can see no other way.'

Don't.

A grey presence invaded his skull. The word had not really been human language, just a negative; a denial. Along with it had arrived explanatory detail, but jumbled and connected up in ways alien to him. He sorted and reordered it, understanding his previous conjecture to be correct. The Nok were not individual beings but a whole – all that smart matter *was* the Nok. The Nok did not want a being as powerful as him to fight because in the end it might have to kill him. He was special – a rarity – a psychic being who could raise others to power and weld them together in synergy, for he could manipulate energy in ways the Nok had not seen before. He understood the Nok could not do this, or else the whole Darwinian scenario here would not have been necessary.

Just let us go, he replied.

I cannot – you are needed.

It seemed like the reply expected from the Nok's long term programming, but he felt a strange wistful need behind it that he struggled to identify. He also felt tempted to accede. They could not win against the many Nok units descending. Yet, in the end, being locked up in one of those bladders for an eternity, being prepared for a war they would never see, seemed no better than death. His links with the others strengthened with their agreement. They no longer resisted him in any way, and this created fluidity of connection and of thought, as they pulled closer together and seemed to think with one mind.

'We need energy,' Anstor opined.

They drew closer, standing in a ring, as Nok shuttles descended to their location. Anstor took hold of his fellows, their talents melding and mixing, and teleported them. In the instant of transition, his vision gave him the perfect spot at the location he had selected. They materialised in hellish twilight, fell through smoke flashed through with gleams of flying molten rock boiled from the caldera, and dropped to a slab jutting from the side of the volcano he had seen earlier. Cloud lay in a thick, brown and seemingly solid ceiling above, lit by rivers of magma running down the slopes – one of them beside their slab.

Hot flecks touched Anstor's face in the sauna hot temperature. Eva swore as a hot rock shattered into glowing pieces on the slab beside her. Abdulla, or perhaps Gaunt, or perhaps Anstor himself, it now being difficult to tell who did what, threw up a shield. *He* sucked heat out of the burning rain to power it, and the rain turned to fragile clinker breaking into pieces as it hit this and fell outside a ring around them. He gazed outwards and saw the Nok shuttles changing course to head to their new location. There seemed to be more of them than before and he now realised many had taken off from Facilities and some of those were now only tens of miles away. This gave him hope, for if the Nok thought it needed so many, perhaps they had some chance. Throwing his perception upwards, he saw more departing from the mother ship. How could there be so many? Then, on closer inspection, he saw the things budding from the surface of the vessel. It seemed likely the Nok could turn the entirety of its being into these vessels. He concentrated on the closest, and made a decision.

The volcano was a huge source of energy and particulate. He focused his powers, and those of the others, on the boiling column of fire, smoke and ash above. He pulled together heat and particulate into one spot and out of particulate in the air beyond the column, and pure energy, he formed the magnetic tube of a pulse cannon's barrel. The column formed an hour-glass waist with the bright spot growing at its narrowest point. Even the 'barrel' became visible, extending out from there – a ribbed structure of glowing gaseous matter. In his overall perception he saw the approaching Nok shuttle over a bed of cloud, adjusted to track it, and fired.

The bright point flared to a small sun, Anstor automatically darkening their shield to prevent its light burning out their eyes. It entered the throat of the barrel and accelerated instantly, becoming a brief streak of fire. He saw it rip up through cloud and smash into the shuttle, the blast cutting the thing in half in an explosion of burning smart matter. The two halves fell through the clouds. He followed them down and saw them hit the ground, the pieces spread with black veins that grew even as they bounced, and sprayed black liquid. He had killed it, yet he felt no satisfaction, for he could feel the subtextual pain of the war mind filtering through to him. Briefly, in passing, he noted the thing had come down just a few miles from their old Facility and that those still there would have seen it.

You cannot win, the war mind told him. *You do not have the power to draw upon there.*

'Who says I'm trying to win?' he replied out loud. 'This is payback for what you've been doing to us.' But even as he spoke the words, he again felt that strange hint of wistfulness in the thing's communication, as if it had left things unsaid, or could not say them.

He turned his attention to the next approaching shuttle, but then noted Gaunt down on his knees and panting, Eva clutching at her head, Abdulla looking resolute but in pain and the others seeming strained. He understood the circuit then. Yes he had his own powers singly, but like this – linked together and him in control – the others acted as psychic batteries for him. He did not feel the drain, but they certainly did. Exploring the network he saw the horrible truth. He could stand here throwing bolides at approaching Nok shuttles and one by one he would suck his companions dry… No, it was worse than that. The energies he had used were way beyond anything he had tried before. The weakest of them would go first, blown like fuse, and then the others in steadily increasing cascade. He would remain at the end, with them lying dead all around him.

'Do it anyway,' said Indira. Others agreed with her, but not all. The Plester twins now wondered if being an eternally sleeping soldier might be better than being dead, for at least that gave a chance of some change in the future. Eva agreed with them, but Negal remained undecided. Anstor could see how it would run. Those in agreement with Indira would start to reconsider their decision the moment the first of them died.

But now Anstor could see something else. The war mind – the Nok – had warned him of this, yet it had done so in a way that hinted at something else. There was no time. Even now another Nok shuttle slid in above and began to descend. Anstor grabbed his companions rigidly, and raised the barrel of the ghostly particle cannon into the sky. The caldera again provided the energy for the shot, but those standing around him provided the psychic capability of making it. The pulse-cannon bolide shot upwards and smashed into the second Nok shuttle. This one did not break apart but fell burning through the cloud within their sight and smashed into a lake of lava. There it transformed as it burned, into a form like a fast-moving amoeba trying to escape the heat. Screaming filled his mind but it took him a moment to realise it did not only arise from the pain of the Nok.

Anstor focused back on his immediate surroundings. Negal lay balled on the ground, his mind screaming. Anstor reached through his connection to the man, but it felt frayed and as burned as the Nok shuttle. He tried to give the man energy but that only seemed to accelerate what he felt there. The man's mind guttered out as he drew into a tighter ball. Anstor felt the horror of the mental connection to someone dying, and came out of it staggering. He could not do this. He could not kill them all like this.

Not enough there, said the Nok. *You will fail.*

The words came through painfully slow as if ripped from its consciousness. Even still in shock from Negal's death, Anstor understood the oddity of this. Instead of trying to push it away he reached for the war mind and there found massive internal conflict. It had run against its programming. Yes, it could speak to try to persuade him to give up and allow himself to be encysted within the ship, but it had been trying to communicate things it should not. Anstor gazed at his companions. They were all down now, all unable to stand under the terrible stress. As he had thought, those who had been in agreement about fighting to the death now doubted, especially after feeling Negal die. The Plesters remained utterly firm in their conviction that this was wrong. They had formed their own link and were now attempting to find some way out from under his control. His batteries were coming unlinked – he would lose power…

And then he saw what the Nok had been trying to tell him.

The nearest shuttles now lay twenty minutes away. Did he have the time? He again grabbed his companions rigidly, dismissing the Plester's attempt to break away from him, quelling Eva's pleading for rationality and quashing the doubts of those remaining. Drawing on their energy he threw his perception out under the cloud, and then down towards their original Facility. There he found a total of forty-eight people. They all stood outside, up on the old encircling wall, gazing out at the remains of the first Nok shuttle he had destroyed. He opened out his perception in the way he had learned – multiple perspectives – and assessed their minds. Could he do this from such a distance?

Anstor reached into the mind of a young man who showed a strong talent towards teleportation, even though newly arrived and with fibres yet to grow throughout his body. Anstor focused, saw the alterations he could make to bring that talent to fruition, and pushed. The man gasped and went down on his knees.

'Who are you?' he asked out loud, drawing the puzzled attention of those around him.

He resisted the change but then, as with those before him, on some deep unconscious level felt what it meant and began actively assisting. Time was passing and Anstor needed more than this single individual – much more. He pushed harder and the man shrieked. His talent exploded into life and he teleported back into his sleep alcove that being all he could see as a place of safety. Anstor withdrew from the man, the threads of connection made and his resources, his power, rising by the strength of one.

The next was a woman with nascent psychokinesis. He went into her fast and brutally, making changes she only assisted in the last fraction of a second. More powerful still he leapt to the next and the next. He could feel the extent of his mind expanding and now deployed that multiple perspective, raising three to functionality all at once, then six, and then ten. Others here, like the young man, were new arrivals with barely any talent expressing. He pushed them anyway and their talents began to grow. He knew they would continue to grow but that hardly mattered. He had his threads of connection and he had them as a psychic resource.

Fifteen minutes had passed and in another five, three Nok shuttles would arrive at the volcano. Searching memory he located the nearest next Facility and leapt to it. Here most were outside and, searching their memories, found the Nok unit here had left in a great hurry, and some had passed the news of other shuttles in the sky. He took fifteen of them all at once, and left them prostrate and shivering on the ground. Another twenty-five after that – two of them as their talents expressed teleporting to their alcoves, and another surrounding himself in a protective wall of fire. He took the remainder at that Facility even as those he had first knocked down began to rise and gaze around in baffled wonderment. He could feel those here and those at the previous Facility getting feedback from his mind, and slowly becoming aware of their part in a battle. But now the three Nok shuttles dropped through cloud.

Anstor reformed his ghostly particle cannon and fired it at once, the bolide blasting straight through one shuttle and hitting another to send it tumbling and trailing fire. Through his other mental connection – into the grey mechanistic thoughts of the war mind – he felt a shift and immediately responded to it. As he fed energy into the shield around them the particle cannon faded and blinked out. The volcano column expanded explosively and dropped boiling pyroclastic flows down the slopes. The remaining Nok shuttle contracted like a leech, dipped towards them and extended again, releasing a laser blast that glared bright green in the smoke filled air. It struck the shield and created a sun-bright hot spot. Anstor could feel intense heat on his skin, but that faded as he responded by ramping up the power to the shield. But he also felt two of those in the nearest Facility blink out like blown light bulbs.

No time to mourn…

He did not know from where the words had come, but it almost seemed they had filtered through from the part of the war mind still fighting its programming. The connection gave him a moment of inspiration. As he had found out aboard the mother ship the shuttles and the Nok entire could no longer block him. Dispersing his perception again he reached out for that remaining shuttle and penetrated it. Now he could use the same technique he had used against the fliers, and he sucked out its energy. The immediate entropic effect dropped the thing from the sky leaving a cold vapour trail. Where it struck the ground, five miles out, it shattered like porcelain.

No time…

Anstor brought the pulse cannon from the volcano back into being, maintaining it with a condign circuit of those in facilities he had visited, then leapt out again to another Facility. Here he took all those outside at once, then shifted into the nearest building. Some people there stood up abruptly and turned towards him. His 'astral projection' and teleportation blending, some of the substance of his being was here too. Through their eyes, as he took them, he saw his naked spectral form, wreathed in blue flames. Almost as an afterthought, while he viewed this strange vision of himself, he fired again from the volcano, bringing down another two shuttles. But he noted now that the rest were slowing and drawing together like a confusion of bees. He moved on.

At the next Facility he took them all at once. At the one after that he appeared on the ground outside and saw a Nok shuttle still on the ground here. The Nok itself appeared at a run from its building, changing as it did so. It stooped down, arms growing longer, becoming hound-like as it bounded towards him. Its head dished and he could feel something winding up in it, tightening. He recognised danger and began drawing energy at this spot, but then seeing people here collapsing as he sucked out their energy, he cut that at once and jumped away.

Seconds later, high up, he detected a nearby geothermal vent and tethered his energy draw there, and descended again. He dropped rapidly then slowed, just at the perimeter of this Facility. The Nok within sensed his presence and charged out towards him. It now had six legs and a sharp tail knifing through the ground, while its head had turned into a multiply dished protrusion. He could feel a build up of energy, and a linkage from it back to its shuttle. The air hazed before it in warning of an energy weapon discharge, but Anstor was quicker. Five perimeter particle cannons swung round and began firing, shot after shot slamming into the creature. It kept coming, a transparent sphere veined with fire appearing around it, but the fusillade was too much, the sphere collapsed and the Nok unit came to pieces as it ran, finally smearing across the ground in a mass of decohering smart matter.

Anstor breathed out a sigh. Now he had more understanding of his enemy's abilities. He reached out to the Facility and almost without thinking included the forty-three people there in his circuit, then he reached out to the grounded shuttle, which he could see moving, changing shape, and flowed into it to suck out the essence of the thing. It collapsed as if deflating, began to break apart and leak that black fluid as he leaped away onto the next Facility and then the next.

Meanwhile, other events were occurring. Rather than approach the volcano, the Nok shuttles dropped rapidly behind the horizon line. Even as they dropped they began coagulating into masses of tangled smart matter. He fired on them as they went down, and saw those spheres appearing around these masses and bouncing away his bolides. In the war mind he sensed a change in strategy, but now with its rebel component suppressed it became more opaque to him. He concentrated on those masses as they settled on the ground, but found it increasingly difficult to get close – something cutting his multiple threads of connection there.

More power...

He leapt from Facility to Facility, tracking from one to another in the map he held in his mind. Two more Nok units attacked him, but by now his resources were so high he simple incinerated them even as they transformed. The shuttles there he found difficult to penetrate, so could not draw their energy. Instead, he grabbed them with psychokinesis and flung them far from the facilities. One he smacked down into the sea and another he shoved down a geothermal vent into oven temperatures.

Whether that would be enough he did not know. It seemed almost irrelevant seeing as how many more of the things were still budding from the mother ship and descending. And then, at last, the final Facility: he had all the humans on the planet, connected to him, feeding him power.

The multitude was talking to him, questioning him, making demands and querulously begging, but with their unconscious minds while he bent their conscious minds to his will. He understood the danger of this – of being just the one active mind in the circuit – so separated out his original companions and gave them their will again. He returned a portion of his focus to them. They sat on the stone – their concentration in their skulls and through him. He sat too and gazed up at the covering dome. Clinker still fell from it and outside the weather was lava rain. The condign circuit he had created still maintained the particle cannon, so he shut it down and included those powering it in the whole of him. This brought down another pyroclastic flow to shroud them in dusty darkness shot through with red streaks of fire. He understood that if the dome failed, they would all be cooked in a matter of seconds. He acknowledged that. It would be quick.

'I don't know what it's doing, but I don't fucking like it,' said Gaunt.

'That it has felt the need to alter its response has to be a good thing at least,' Indira pointed out.

'But note,' said Acram Plester, 'that its response is now to try and kill us rather than capture us.'

'There was an alteration,' said Eva. 'That war mind switched over to some new setting. We all felt it.' She opened her eyes and looked around at them all. 'It doesn't quite make sense to have created such powerful soldiers and then so quickly decide to kill them.'

And she proved why one mind alone was not enough, Anstor felt. Eva had put her finger on something he had missed. Such haste to destroy something the war mind had been trying to create seemed utterly out of keeping. They sat in a trap and the thing had been in no real danger from them. Only by attacking them had it steadily raised their abilities to hurt it... And yet, still they could not. An entire ship up there of smart matter could be formed into the things that had been attacking them on the planet. Only roughly estimating, Anstor realised the vessels and creatures down here comprised only a fraction of a percent of the Nok entire. Some other game was being played – some other purpose being pursued. Was it all about making them into better soldiers? No, it had something to do with a smaller part of the mind.

Right from his first mental encounter with the war mind, Anstor had felt some hint that part of it had another agenda. It had, by an oblique route, given him the idea to grab the rest of the humans on the planet to act as his 'batteries'. It had been subtly poking him and prodding him in some direction. He needed to understand this and, rather than try directing energies available to him to events over the horizon, he reached into the thinking stratum of the Nok to find the grey thought processes that had reached out to him.

The war mind resisted but, because he and the other humans, by dint of the technology installed in them, were actually part of it, it could not completely block him. He pushed through memories of that long ago war, through strategies and logistics. As he did so he created a mirrored model of the thing, roughly sketched out in mental palaces. His thoughts moved with the breadth and power of an AI and, finally, he began to understand the shape of the thing. It had seemed completely unhuman to him, but now he saw the parallels. He traced thought processes to their beginnings and found an initiator of action presently partially suppressed. Examining it revealed calculations of cost in casualty rates and others concerning logistics and strategy. The aim for the least cost sat over something convoluted and for a moment quite strange. He pushed it for responses and it flashed out to make connection with the rest of the mind. In that moment he recognised it reflected in himself, in his guilt about Negal and others who had died, about his dislike of the necessity to control and suppress his human batteries. He had found the war mind's conscience.

But still he could not understand the sense of it. This portion of the mind had helped him to fight the whole, yet it had also initiated this total all-out attack on them. It had pushed the mind to switch over to a war footing – the war it had been fighting long ago had now come here while Anstor and the other humans on the planet were the enemy. Did this thing consider their deaths a preferable option to storing them as sleeping soldiers aboard the mother ship? That did not feel right at all.

No, said the war mind's conscience, straining against programming. *War has come and I come with it.*

Anstor did not quite understand that, yet he felt the hint of some opening. The thing could not tell him directly but had, in its way, given him a strong hint. He needed to solve this in the midst of battle, because even now the coagulated masses of shuttles began to release their army over the horizon towards them. Elsewhere he could see other Nok shuttles descending, and they weren't coming here, but settling towards the Facilities, doubtless to kill his power supply.

No human form Nok units in the horde. They came in their thousands, running on or brandishing multiple limbs – some for cutting or clubbing, some complex 'hands' for operating the strange weapons he had seen in memory, but which none of them brandished. Another tweak by that 'conscience'? They protruded dishes and spikes hazing with energy. Thick dark armour layered some while others, light and airy, emitted a glow from inside. A number of them rose into the air on sheets of smart matter that looked like the sails of hang gliders, but thick and disc-shaped and using some other mechanism for flight.

Anstor first reached out to the Facilities, because if he had learned anything as a Polity commando and from his penetration of the war mind, it was to protect supply lines. He chose lieutenants there with the required talents and linked them into circuits with those nearest to them so they could throw up protective hemispherical fields like the one over him. The moment it became necessary for them to use those fields the amount of power he could draw from them would drop, for if he drew too much the approaching Nok shuttles would be able to get through with their weapons. This zero sum game, he realised, with the sheer quantity of smart matter falling into atmosphere, he was bound to lose. People would die, thousands of people would die, burned out like those few before them. The prospect pained him, for his conscience made him aware that none of these had chosen to be part of the battle, while many had the same objections as the Plesters, Eva, and now weakly on the parts of Indira, Gaunt and Abdulla.

'They will kill us all anyway,' said Indira morosely.

She could be right. She knew as did he that the Nok was now in total war mode, but maybe, having won, its conscience would return it to some other mode? He searched for an answer in the vast complexity of the circuit he had made. It came via Abdulla and Gaunt. When the bladders had taken them they had shut down and now examining them closely he saw how that could be done. Essentially a circuit breaker sat between their human minds and the fibrous masses spread throughout their bodies. He measured energy levels and created a mental model of what was required. The thing needed to be protean so as to adjust to the various talents it found. A feedback loop from their talents was the answer. The moment those talents began to fail catastrophically, the connection would break, and they would be rendered unconscious. He transmitted it to them all and felt it steadily melding across the continent. The doubts of Indira, Gaunt and Abdulla vanished and, after a moment, even the Plesters and Eva were mollified.

Conscience satisfied, Anstor focused his attention on the approaching army. The pulse cannon had been right for the shuttles – heavy artillery as such. For these creatures he needed something else. Now scanning the rivers of lava running from the volcano he created energy draws. Out of rock and dust and memories of weapons he had used in the past he began to raise emplacements. They grew out of the ground – part matter and part energy – spectral glassy structures that began protruding those weapons. He formed railguns and began to draw iron from nearby deposits for ammo. He created gas lasers and instead of pulse cannons increased particulate feed and electromagnetic containment to create particle beam weapons. He felt amazed by the extent of his past knowledge in this, until he realised a maintained and constant connection with the war mind filled in detail. He was being assisted again – some data feed that should have been closed down still operating.

The weapons began firing. Railgun slugs hammered into the Nok, which raised those spherical force fields in defence. But he could see blasts of smart matter debris throughout this and creatures going down. He switched over to lasers – bright green in the smoky air – and saw Nok burning. In response dished heads emitted circular flat fields that thumped into some of his weapons and shattered them. He fed in more energy to reform those, and felt human batteries blinking out across the continent. Spikes of smart matter issued coherent lightning that burned through the thick boiling of the pyroclastic flow and splashed on the force field dome over them. He felt it weaken and grabbed more energy, felt more batteries fail, but knew they could not penetrate while the pyroclastic cloud blocked most of their energy. But the draw of energy to his weapons began dispersing that cloud. And the Nok army drew closer.

On multiple levels of perception Anstor gazed at the approaching creatures, searching for weaknesses. His weapons destroyed some while others, even severely damaged, pulled themselves together in new lethal forms. Meanwhile more flowed from those masses of ships, steadily decreasing their volume. All of their substance, he understood, could be turned into these soldiers. Then he saw something puzzling. Amidst the approaching horde a gap opened, a space out of which the other creatures stayed. As if oblivious to the destruction all around, a Nok unit in human form walked there. Anstor began to understand, and ensured his weapons did not fire on this one but, before he could take action on a hypothesis half-formed, Nok shuttles arrived at the Facilities.

One of them moved to station a mile up above one Facility, developed a split along its underside and out of this dropped a small sphere. It fell at normal gravity acceleration as those below put up their domed field. Just a few metres above the dome it detonated with a bright flash. He felt something rip in his mind as forty-six people dropped out of his circuit, and whether they had died he did not know. Through other eyes in the nearest Facility to that one, he saw a mushroom cloud rising. Thermo nuke. He was caught in a quandary. He should have provided weapons to hit those shuttles, but if he did that now the energy draw would simply put out many more minds. He did it anyway, routing through the technique to suck the energy out of the shuttles. Four of them fell and shattered, but hundreds of minds went out. Further shots brought down more, but in one place a whole Facility of people collapsed as a Nok shuttle approached. He watched in pained silence as around him he maintained a hold on the near battle. To his relief the shuttle simply turned away, and he now knew for certain he was being assisted.

The approaching human form Nok was the key. But now the surrounding cloud had cleared and such was the local energy draw that its fire had gone out. Nearby lava flows grew dull and sluggish as they hardened to rock and now, through falling dust spotting white with ice crystals, those coherent lightnings came. They hit the shield hard and. drawing more locally on a psychic level than he should have, caused Indira, Eva and Gaunt to collapse unconscious. More carefully he drew psychic energies from the Facilities, and saw more go down as he directed his weapons against those creatures with the spikes. Two more thermo nukes exploded taking out two more Facilities. He began to feel diminished – a small creature cowering under this onslaught. More of his weapons went down. He kept drawing on psychic and thermal gradient energy and could feel all of it waning. Entropy now exacted its price. The shield began to flicker as he found he could draw no more from the Facilities while they sucked the heat from Nok shuttles. More explosions. Abdulla collapsed and then shortly after him, both of the Plesters. Alone now he maintained the dome with what he could pull from the rest of the continent. He could feel his powers collapsing and saw that the circuit breaker existed in his own mind because it had copied to everyone. He looked out at the Nok horde, saw that the one in human form had drawn close, and had both a moment of epiphany and desperation.

Anstor shut down the shield, a white beam scoring across overhead and its heat singeing his hair. His weapons collapsed to dusty ruin, their inner lights going out as he garnered every resource he could to himself. The same draw knocked out more Facilities, and then more as he crashed their condign circuits and took away both their defences and their weapons. Then he teleported and, with utter accuracy, put his whole physical form inside the humanoid Nok.

At last…

He felt as if he had been turned to stone. Every organ simply stopped, except for his brain, which felt dull and slow for just a moment, and then sparked back into life. He felt his mind growing as its thought processes slid into the thinking substrate of the smart matter. He grew, the conscience of the Nok shaping itself around and inside his mind. Knowledge flowed, not as an addition but as if it had always been there. The Nok understood that its mission had ended but could not beat its programming. The things it had done to continue recruiting appalled its conscience, for a war that had ended over a million years ago.

But the Nok's creator or programmer had in some part become it. To change that programming required another will – separate from the Nok – and now Anstor had provided it. He continued to expand, now spreading tendrils of thought out into the overall war mind. Resistance was hard and the ocean of memory endlessly deep. The conscience guided him as best it could, but beyond a certain point it could not go. Anstor searched for places where he could shut down the program, but found it woven all the way through. He strived with growing desperation to stop the thing as it bombed two more facilities and its creatures swarmed in around the prostrate bodies of his companions. Teleportation crackled in the air and he saw them encysted in bladders.

Nok shuttles began landing at those facilities that were down. Nok war forms flowed out and once close to the unconscious inhabitants, encystment commenced there.

This last necessity for proximity for teleportation of the bladders brought some understanding. The Nok possessed only limited psychic powers. Instead of simply pushing his mentality through its smart matter structure he extended his powers. It felt familiar now, because he saw parallels to how he had taken over all the humans across the continent, only on a massive scale. Though it scared him to do what seemed contraindicated, he pushed at the Nok's psychic powers and felt them ramping up. The billion threads of connection strengthened and he was truly in, but fighting for control. He found a command sequence and wiped it out, physically, telekinetically spreading through the Nok entire. The ships down on the planet simply stopped, and then descended. Other sequences came into his grip and he had the creatures returning to their ships. But still he battled for control and the original program persisted.

You are we, the conscience managed.

He needed no more of a clue than that and searched multiple sequences. The protocol that shut down those installed in bladders applied to the Nok as a whole.

And finally found the off switch.

The Nok shuttle settled out of the sky next to the fourth Facility. The units that walked out were humanoid. They began collecting up the bladders scattered all around and loading them aboard the shuttle. In the chamber he had formed in the mother ship, Anstor watched this with omniscient vision, just as he watched the snaps and crackles in the air inside other shuttles at the facilities that had been bombed. Inside those shuttles bladders filled with victims of the bombings – teleportation no longer needing such proximity and able to run both ways. Thousands were unrecoverably dead, many severely injured and radiation burned. The sequences in the Nok mind that he had allowed, while he continued the long task of rooting out the original programming in the rest, assured him that the injured, no matter how severely damaged, would recover. They would not be quite so human as before, but they would recover. Still other shuttles were collecting up those that had survived undamaged, even conscious, and inserting them in bladders. He felt bad about that, but it was necessary.

'You trust what you have allowed to come back online?' Indira asked.

The chamber was now appointed with Polity technology taken from the Facilities, and more he had smart matter machines manufacture. He, and his recently arrived companions, had all the comforts of home. Indira, Gaunt, Abdulla, the Plesters and Eva were with him. They connected to his mind still, but he had suppressed his control of them to a minimum and now kept the sheer extent of his mind, spreading along the hundred miles of the Nok ship and in all the smart matter on the planet, hidden from them. He had not relinquished full control because some of them would find his plans unacceptable. He would have to put them back in bladders if that was the case. Others he would wake steadily, over the years, and assess. It would be a long task since the alien majority would be difficult to understand, and maybe races with integral hostility to other life, like the prador, would have to remain encysted.

'Yes, I trust it because it's clear of original recruitment programming and as under my command as you once were.'

'You can be so sure of that?' asked Acram Plester.

He nodded mutely and showed them just a little bit more of his mind.

They sat on sofas of smart matter. A Polity fabricator had provided drinks and food. Since he had woken them, and as their internal control began to finesse and connect to their body image, some were returning to their original human forms. Exceptions were Gaunt, who seemed to like his huge bulk, and Eva, who had retained her elfin look. Indira, he noticed, had a waist now, and a face once again attractive.

In a long silence they absorbed what he had displayed. The Plesters raised suspicions there must be more to see. Eva put her finger on the problem.

'So what now?' she asked.

'Yes,' said Setram Plester. 'We head back to the Polity?'

It surprised Anstor to sense the man's extreme doubts, and similar from the others. Perhaps this would not be as difficult as he had supposed.

'This ship contains hundreds of thousands of aliens, all with powerful psychic abilities. But put that aside for the moment.' He paused, grimaced. 'When I've finished collecting those down on the planet it will contain thousands of humans with such abilities, including us. Do you think the AIs will allow us to just return to our old lives? Will they allow us to freely roam the Polity? What do you think will happen?'

'They'll keep us somewhere – maybe one of those black research moons rumoured to exist,' said Acram Plester. 'They'll never stop studying us. They'll never release us to freely exercise our powers.'

Anstor nodded. 'And that really is the best scenario. I would be hardly surprised if some of us were "studied" to the point of destruction.'

'You are a cynical man,' said Eva.

'I fought for the Polity. I fought for the AIs. I know all about their cold calculations. Each us will be viewed as a dangerous spanner in the cogs of their utopia.'

'So again I must ask: what now?' she said.

'We cannot return to the Polity. I will not. And I have serious doubts about bringing others aboard this ship there. Yes, the AIs might lock us down and study them, but what if they broke loose. Can you imagine the possible devastation? What if the aliens broke loose? Can you imagine prador with psychic powers returning to their Kingdom?'

'Surely there is some way we can keep our freedom?' said Abdulla. 'You talk about the dangers, but what about the benefits we can bring?'

Anstor turned to him. 'The dangers are too great. I posit that the powers we have were developed through technology and are not really in some mystical realm. It's technology that has to develop slowly in a developing society.'

'And even then,' said Gaunt, flashing them images of the ancient war for which they were being recruited.

'Exactly,' said Anstor.

'So what do we do?' asked Eva. 'Just sit amidst all this, with the powers we have, and wait until we die?'

Anstor shook his head and waved a hand at the smart matter walls. 'This technology is way in advance of Polity technology. We'll only die through accident or because we choose to.'

'So we sit here for eternity?' asked Gaunt. The man really wanted to use his powers.

Time to tell them, Anstor thought.

'No, we don't sit here for eternity, because I have a suggestion.'

Telepathically they all queried that.

'We tidy things up here on this planet. We encyst the remaining xenovores and, by and by, see if we can do anything about them. We get all the smart matter back aboard and don't leave a trace. We will go back into Polity space to dump the zero freezers with their occupants and fire up beacons on them so they're collected.'

'That's a good start,' said Indira.

'And then,' Anstor said before anyone could interrupt, 'we have a very long journey to undertake to the Nok galaxy where many more ships like this are operating, and we shut them down. After that we search for others that have left that galaxy – their routes are in the programming here – and we shut them down too.'

The uncomfortable silence went on longer than Anstor liked, but he resisted the impulse to probe their minds.

'It's certainly something to do,' said Gaunt.

Anstor looked at the grim smiles all around him, and knew without reading their minds that he had their agreement.

Well, I spend half the year on this island so I felt beholden to write at least one story set here. The house, barring a few necessary alterations for the story, is mine. The scenery, the people, the heat and the olive groves are all around me. The cistern was something I also altered for the story because in reality most of them around me aren't that deep; then, the year after writing this, I found one that was. The story is set in the present day based on what ifs while walking through the mountains, with not a little of the power dreams we all have. It was published in Asimov's Magazine *Jan/Feb 2020 so just a month or so prior to the lockdowns kicking in.*

AN ALIEN ON CRETE

Erickson slipped his car out of gear and took the handbrake off to set it rolling down the road. The wheel felt leaden without power steering, but that kicked in when he started up the engine at the bottom of the hill and came to a stop at the junction. He wasn't sure why he was doing this now. Old Maria had died last year and would no longer be rushing out with her shopping list and endless complaints about her health, and endless detail about her feud with her neighbour Yannis. Maybe it reminded him of past stability and a life rooted in the prosaic.

At the junction he watched a big 4x4 trundle past, uniformed figures inside peering at him suspiciously. There were soldiers in the mountains. This wasn't exactly an astute observation since just a short drive from his village put him in sight of the 'No Photograph' signs, the chainlink fences and the radar installations sitting on some of the mountain tops. But now their presence had become overt. He had seen canvas-backed trucks loaded with them, jeeps driving uniformed bigwigs and once an armoured car sitting on a track leading up to one of the wind farms. He had also been turned back on the route to one of his favourite restaurants sitting above a cove on the east coast, and seen soldiers on foot walking in a line through the olive groves. Two had even turned up at the kazani some nights back to drink raki. They had been closed-mouthed about what was occurring, until they were on their second brizola, by which time the raki had done its work.

Erickson's Greek wasn't the best, at least then, but he did manage to catch some of it. Their search related to what all had seen in the skies three nights back. The object had streaked in from the south, lighting up the night, pieces breaking away, and had come down in the mountains to the northwest. Most assumed it was a meteor, though that hadn't stopped black-clad grannies crossing themselves and querulously calling for their god to protect them from this evil, while some feared that it had been something fired from Libya. He found the memory hilarious. Libya.

'Haven't they found it?' Yorgos had asked, well into his cups and sitting with the absolute rigidity of someone very drunk.

The soldiers told how they had found the impact site and some pieces, which had been collected up and taken away, but of the main object there was no sign. The army suspected locals had spirited it away for sale. When they had finished relating this they suddenly looked very worried, for they had told too much. The younger one caught his moustachioed companion by the shoulder and whispered urgently in his ear. They put down their glasses and quickly departed, their jeep weaving down the road.

Erickson grimaced, pulled out of the junction and accelerated, but not so fast as to catch up with the 4x4. He didn't want to be stopped and, apparently, that was happening now. Cars were being searched for pieces of the meteorite, which were now government property. Quite likely they *were* looking for those fragments, but it was no damned meteorite and hadn't come from Libya.

No one stopped him on the way down from the mountains, which he now gazed upon with a clarity he had lacked since first coming here, but police had parked at the turning into the coastal village of Makrigialos. Some were local, some were from the nearby town of Sitia, and others were those whose sum purpose was grabbing up illegals. Erickson wondered if the alien fell into the jurisdiction of the last, because certainly someone knew about it. The bullet holes told that tale.

They paused to watch him drive past. It struck him as likely that they had been told to search all cars, but right then it was time for frappe coffee and cigarettes. He drove into the town, the deep blue of the Libyan Sea glimpsed between the buildings to his left, finally pulled into the parking area before the butcher's and climbed out. Vegetables he had in plenty, he would also pick up some bread here, but most important was meat and plenty of it. Probably best would be multicellular stuff like liver and kidney. Yes, them and a good load of pork. The proprietors would assume he was stocking up for a kazani barbecue and attempt to sell him stuff on skewers again. Little did they know that none of the meat would get anywhere near hot coals.

Rationality was all.

The second day after the alleged meteorite came down, and after military vehicles began rushing about, he took a very long walk into the mountains. This time, rather than head up behind his house and through the wind farms, he had crossed the valley and headed up into wilder territory on the other side. The round trip was twenty miles. Before returning he walked a winding track through abandoned olive groves, feeling buoyant from the exercise. He strolled past the old iron pylon of an old water pump windmill, fragments of its canvas sails still attached, paused to study a mass of dictamus – the allegedly health-giving Cretan tea – growing in a ruin then, remembering the area, decided to pause for a rest on the wall of an old cistern that sat down at the bottom of a short track, hidden behind a stand of bamboo. The concrete tank was deep, he remembered, and during heavy rain it did fill up, but that tended to drain away quickly through cracks in the bottom. The only purpose it seemed to serve now in this deserted location was as a trap for unwary animals. One time he had stopped here and seen a small weasel running around in the bottom. He'd put in some lengths of bamboo in the hope it would have the sense climb up one of them to escape. It hadn't been there next time he looked.

Scrambling down the steep track he reached the flat slab of stone lying between the cistern and the stand of bamboo. It looked as if someone had forged a path through the bamboo but he couldn't figure out why. He shrugged, moved over to the edge of the cistern ready to sit down dangling his legs over the side. He'd spend many a happy interlude here contemplating his existence and reciting Greek verbs.

Something lay in the bottom of the cistern.

At first he thought someone had bundled bamboo and other debris, including electronic junk, in some black and purple fabric, rolled up the lot and dumped it down here. This perception lasted perhaps half a second as his mind put together the melange into a complete whole. No, he wasn't seeing bamboo and olive tree prunings, but big insect legs attached to a long segmented thorax terminating in a squat abdomen. And the head that turned towards him, extending on a ribbed neck, seemed that of a spider, with two binocular eyes of deep ruby, with smaller ones on either side of it.

He stood there utterly terrified, primordial horror freezing him to the spot. He'd never been particularly frightened of insects or spiders, or of the scorpions he sometimes found in his house, in fact he regarded them all with fascination, but this thing was bigger than a man. Next, slightly displacing the terror, he felt an odd twisting in his mind. It was as if he had shunted aside a filter of some kind; as if he had been seeing the world in sepia tones and now it hit him in full colour and clarity. Yet, when he tried to analyse the difference to his past perception, he could not find it. His mind suddenly working very fast, he realised it must be the surge of adrenaline driving a feeling of disconnection, dislocation of the kind people experienced when suffering from extreme anxiety. From where in his brain that particular knowledge arose he had no idea for a second, then remembered it had been in an article he had read three years ago.

The creature flexed out its legs, heaved itself up and scuttled to the far wall of the cistern. It tried to climb, got halfway up then slid down again, and slumped there panting. Erickson emitted a sound halfway between a gag and a yell and stumbled back from the edge, mind still twisting in his skull as if trying to fit itself around the utter implausibility of what he had stumbled upon. He wanted to turn and just run away from the thing but, more than that, he wanted to get away from the horrible sensations between his ears, and the bright bright clarity of his thoughts. He was almost back to the path before his mind seemed to shift into another gear.

Panting...

Rationality is all.

The thing was panting, yet insects and spiders did not have lungs. Now other facts began to impinge. It had not been after him because it had tried to climb out of the other side of the cistern. It was also leaking purple liquid from various holes so had been injured and, in the final analysis, it had *not* been able to get out of the cistern. He walked back.

The creature still lay where it had fallen, its nightmare head turned towards him. He stared at it, instinctive fear of the shape it bore fading, but a larger fear still current in his mind. He faced something completely outside his compass, he knew this at once, and it felt as if his mind might break as he struggled to incorporate it. After a moment he managed to suppress this weird feeling enough to note other anomalies beyond the size of the damned thing. He thought he had seen junk electronics when first looking in here, but now he saw stuff attached to its body. Inlaid in its segments were plates of metal and other materials, scribed with cubic patterns and protruding studs and glassy blisters. A shiny triangular plate sat in its head above its eyes. Tight bracelets of metal circled some of its limbs.

The twisting in his skull increased and Erickson knew now what he was seeing, but decided, in an attempt to quell his mental chaos, to run through other options to be sure. Could this be some escaped genetic experiment? No, he was an avid reader of science articles and knew for sure that no one was anywhere near producing anything like this. But perhaps the military? Certainly not the Greek military and why would any others do such experiments here? Remoteness might be a factor, but he seriously doubted it. Next he wondered if it could be a robot manufactured to appear alive. Certainly DARPA might be able to do something like that, and that might account for the tech he could see on its body. But again, this seemed a stretch, and he reluctantly returned to his original assessment. The light in the sky, the apparent meteor last night, and now this.

He was looking at an alien.

The mental twisting returned in force and he closed his eyes. His mind seemed to want to leap out of his control and he fought it. Coherent thought escaped him. Then, like exploded glass in reverse, the pieces began to fall back together and slot themselves in place. He gained enough coherence to tell himself, 'Accept it,' and 'Deal with it.' But even so, he knew, in the pit of his being, that his mind had not returned to its original shape.

Now he had come to a firm conclusion he did not allow himself to question it, for that way lay chaos again. He wondered what to do and, as he considered this, his mind returned to the prosaic. As a sensible citizen he should just walk away from here, go to the police or the soldiers, and tell them what he had found. But he had never been particularly sensible and had little trust in authority. He gazed at the thing, noting those leaking holes and it wasn't much of a stretch to come to the conclusion they were bullet holes. What would happen to this thing once he turned it over? Quite probably the military here would put more holes in it until it stopped moving, then drag it off for examination. The Greeks weren't exactly noted for their regard for anything that wasn't human, in fact their religion and culture tended to exclude it. Also, what would happen to him once he reported this thing? Quite likely they would want to keep it quiet, so would provide him with limited accommodation with a locked door.

Option dismissed. He continued studying the thing, thoughts swirling in his head. Abruptly he came to a decision – it arising without any previous conscious consideration. He was some hours from his house. This thing had not been discovered and might have been here for days, and he had seen no soldiers during his walk. He turned to go, then hesitated, turned back.

'I don't know if you can understand me, but I'm going to help you,' he said. 'I will be back in a few hours.'

Speaking seemed to root him back into some form of normality, yet still everything about him retained its clarity, its brightness while his thoughts seemed sharp edged, dangerous.

The head, watching him, tilted to one side for a moment, then back again. It then dipped down and up again. A nod? He turned away and bounded back up the path to the main track, setting out at a fast walk, but the buzz of adrenaline drove him into a run. He didn't think as he quickly ate up the distance, he just experienced his surroundings. When, after a few miles, exhaustion slowed him to a walk again he began to have some serious misgivings. He could be kidding himself that the thing had nodded at him. He should also bear in mind that his own kind had certainly shot it, so it might not be exactly friendly. Perhaps soldiers had shot it because it had attacked them? No, he had to stick to his rationality. If it was an alien it hadn't come from anywhere in the solar system because, surely, humans would have noticed an alien civilisation so close. It came from another star, which bespoke technology and intelligence way beyond any on Earth. But then, one had to wonder how the hell it had ended up trapped in a cistern in the Greek mountains?

During the ensuing walk he calmed to the steady hypnotic rhythm of his feet. He found himself noticing items around him he had never truly seen before, also recalling knowledge with odd precision; identifying plants and their uses, recognising minerals and geology, stopping by a broken down pickup truck and visualising the kind of engine it had and how it might have failed. Again he felt that clarity, but at a lower and more constant intensity. His surroundings came to utterly occupy him until, finally, he reached the track to his house, whereupon adrenaline surged again and he broke into a run again.

Finally, he entered his house, first chugging down a litre of water, then grabbing up some plastic sheeting, a large old blanket and the high stepladder he used to paint his ceilings. He headed out, put these all in his 4x4, the stepladder protruding out the side window, got in and drove. In just a few minutes he had reached the main road, took a turning into the mountains opposite his house, then another turning and another. He had only driven out here once, to collect some of that dictamus. Going by road, rather than along the tracks between olive groves, it had taken him ages to find the location of the plants, and then he did so more by chance than design. Subsequently lost on the way back, he had ended up taking a long route over the other side of the mountains, then down to the coast before recognising where he was and heading back to his house. This time he drove directly to the tracks leading to the cistern, remembering every turning and every dead end to avoid. Half an hour after leaving his house he parked by the rough short path leading down to the cistern.

Erickson sat in his vehicle. The walk and the drive had been a distraction but now he was back in the moment. The clarity remained but still the situation felt unreal. He forced himself into motion and got out. Before heading down he spread the plastic over the back seat, eyed the area wondering if there were room inside, then dropped the back seats down to give more. He threw the blanket over the backs of the front seats in readiness. Then he walked down with the ladder.

The creature had moved to the near side of the cistern, directly below him. Now further very serious misgivings kicked in. The thing might well be injured, but when it had tried to climb the far wall it had moved quite quickly and energetically. He might lower this ladder down and next thing he knew have the thing snipping off his head with those mandibles or sucking out his insides. He thought about going back to his car and fetching the club hammer from his toolbox, but then rejected the idea. He had to stay rational and believe in his primary assessment of the thing. Swallowing dryly, he lowered the ladder over the edge beside the alien and, rather than opening it, lodged it as firmly against the cistern wall as he could.

The creature moved – its limbs spiderlike but also flexing in a way somehow smoother. When it gripped the ladder with its forelimbs he noticed long 'hands' with rows of fingers running up their edges. The ladder shifted to one side and it paused, then abruptly came up in a fast scramble and over the top, the ladder crashing down in the cistern behind it. Erickson stepped back, ready for either flight or defence, eyeing a large rock lying over to his right, but the creature just stayed where it was, panting again. He stood upright. The thing sat on the rock slab between him and the track up. He gestured to the track.

'We go up there,' he said, reluctant to lead the way because that meant he would have to pass close by those long limbs and those mandibles.

It tilted its head again and made a sound, scraping and fluting, but did not move. Suppressing his fear he stepped forwards, his skin prickling. The creature froze as he walked past it, and he wondered if it might feel the same about him. He remembered telling an old girlfriend who had been hysterical about a spider in the house, 'It's more scared of you than you are of it!' How much that applied here he wasn't sure. He stepped on the path and gestured, scrambled up a little way and gestured again.

'Come on, it's not far.'

The thing hesitated, then slowly heaved itself into motion. He kept checking back with it as it climbed, panting all the way. Its efforts on the ladder must have used much of its strength. A human with that many bullet holes in it would have been dead by now, and perhaps it would yet die.

Reaching his vehicle, Erickson pulled open the rear door and waited. A minute later the creature reached the track and moved forwards. He gestured inside the car, then stubbornly, against the instinct to back off, remained by the door. Still panting, it moved right up close to him. He noted an acrid spicy smell and more leakage from its wounds. It began to climb inside then paused to turn its head towards him. Again that fluting sound, then it struggled inside, folding up its limbs to fit then slumping. Its squat abdomen still protruded. Erickson stooped, got hold of it as if lifting a sack of cement, and heaved it in. The creature made a grating sound and the fluting increased to a frequency that hurt the ears, then it heaved some more to get all of itself inside.

'I'm sorry,' he said, wiping his hands on his shirt 'I know that hurt.'

The abdomen had been hot and he wondered if that was usual.

It turned to look at him again, raised a forelimb and shook one of its hands. He leaned in and tossed the blanket across it. The creature immediately got the idea and pulled the blanket in all around it, its head protruding. He pointed at its head, then down.

'Underneath,' he said.

It ducked out of sight.

Erickson took it easy on the stony track, though he wanted to drive fast. As he accelerated on the road afterwards his back tensed up and his neck seemed to be burning. The creature behind him could attack him with ease now and he had no defence. But nothing happened. He drove into the yard at the back of his house where he unloaded wood for his stove, reversed in and up close to the back door. After climbing out he opened the side door at its head end. That head rose up and observed him then, still with the blanket wrapped around it, the thing slowly eased itself out, its progress to the back door painful. He led the way in, down the short hall then into his kitchen. The thing finally deposited itself on the tiled floor, its head dipped, panting still. He stood with his hands on his hips, not really sure what to do now.He'd got an injured alien on his kitchen floor. He didn't think Google would provide him any answers for that.

'What can I do for you?' he asked, pretty sure the thing understood him now.

It just raised its head and observed at him.

He inspected it in return, suddenly realising he could see every detail of its body, his perception utterly sharp and precise. But it went even further than that, for he was seeing the whole kitchen area too, and every item seemed to open up long chains of easily accessible memory. Two years ago he had replaced the tile just to its right, and he clearly recalled mixing two colours of grout to get a match with the rest in the floor. Four years ago he had found the knife on the counter behind it. He had cleaned and sharpened the blade, and the smell of iron sat in his nostrils. His thinking remained frighteningly sharp, but he felt this had nothing to do with the fear, or the adrenaline that surged through him still. But why he did not know, and had to put the question aside.

He thought hard about the creature. It could survive Earth's environment and it breathed. Presumably its needs were much the same as any animal of this world, including him. If he had been shot, and then confined in that cistern for however long, what would be the first thing he would want? He walked over to the sink and turned on the tap. The alien's head snapped round and it fluted insistently. He nodded, took a plastic jug out of a cupboard and filled it, then took it over and held it out handle first. Reaching out slowly it flicked its long hand upright and took hold of the handle with those numerous side fingers. He released the jug, whereupon it brought it to its face. Mandibles folded aside to reveal a red mouth with hard looking objects shifting inside. It stared down into the jug then back up at him. Inspiration struck and, in retrospect, he should have had no expectation that it would work. He stepped over to the tools and boxes of gear he had been using to renovate the house, searched a box and came up with a length of plastic tube used as ducting for wires, which he took to the creature and held out. It took this, inserted one end in the jug and the other in its mouth, spongy looking material closing round it, and sucked.

In just moment it was sucking dry and held the jug out for more. Erickson refilled the jug four times. On the last it drank only half, then it peeled the blanket away and inspected one of its wounds. It poured water on, scrubbing at crusted ichor about the hole.

'Wait,' said Erickson.

When it looked up he gestured to the door off his kitchen leading to the shower room, walked over and opened it. Within its sight he unhooked the shower, held it over the floor drain and turned it on, then off again. The creature dipped its head and dragged itself over. However, it paused by the door to eye the tools he had been using. Now extending four limbs of a total of eight, all ending in those long hands, it began to sort through. He watched it snare a Stanley knife, long-nose pliers and a flat screwdriver. These it slid through the door into the shower room. It then started looking at the various pots and tubes and now he knew the thing understood more than the English words he spoke, for it was reading the Greek writing on these. It finally selected a pot of filler, and a tube of silicon in its skeleton gun, before entering the shower room.

Erickson held out the shower head, which it took. It seemed a lot more energetic now, but then it had been very thirsty. It stripped off the blanket and tossed it out the door and didn't need him to show it how to turn on the water. It began washing itself, even reaching up to snag a scrubbing brush from beside the sink. He stepped out, letting the door close behind, then went to get a mop to deal with the pool of emerald fluid it had left on the kitchen floor. When he was done he opened the door in time to see it delving into one of the holes in its body with the long-nosed pliers and the screwdriver. He winced and stepped away again, went to make himself a cup of coffee, then sat at his breakfast bar drinking it while listening to the sounds in the shower room. Eventually they stopped.

His second look inside revealed eight bullets and other fragments of metal in a stack beside the door. The creature was leaning close against the wall, its blood spattered all around it and running from some of its wounds. It looked at him, then folded its legs in, bunched tight, retracted and dipped its head, made a weak fluting sound then grew still. He stared at it, not sure what to do. Was it dying? Perhaps he had been wrong to bring it here like this. Perhaps there were people out there, professional people who would be able to help it? He stared for a moment longer and saw the rhythmic movement of its thorax. It seemed to be taking a snooze.

Erickson walked out of the shower room and gazed at the damp patch on the kitchen floor for a second then went to sit at his desk, which served as a divider between the kitchen area and his living room. Opening up his laptop he searched out local news on some of the English speaking websites and blogs. There he found a bit more than he had found before and it was worrying: a Dutch expat claimed that after police found an old bracelet in his car they followed him home and searched his house. Erickson knew that man, and knew that bracelet. An English expat he knew had found it in an old stream bed and had sold it to the Dutch guy for the cost of a return flight to the UK plus his beer intake for some weeks. The object was hand crafted from some silver alloy, with a red cabochon inset. It probably wasn't a product of ancient Greece, but it was old. More likely this search involved the Greek archaeology bureau but still, they had searched someone's house and, as he understood it, that wasn't quite legal here.

He sat back, only afterwards realising how fast he had read those blog pages. Flicking down to a previous entry he had read before, he remembered every word. He brought another up he hadn't read, and blinked, accepting he had just read the whole post in a glance. What was happening to his mind?

He was about to input searches into Google concerning aliens and space ships when paranoia kicked in, and he decided that might not be a good idea. He sat back again, hearing sounds of tentative movement from the shower room. Leaving his laptop open he stood up, walked round to the door and opened it.

The alien was awake and, just as he again stepped in, it turned on the shower and began scrubbing away the spilled blood. It glanced up at him, fluted for a moment, then, shaking its head, returned to its chore, soon washing away the worst. Next it picked up the pot of filler. Erickson unhooked a towel from the door and held it across. With another of its limbs it snared the thing and dried itself. Erickson watched it return its attention to the pot, then went out and fetched his first aid box, placing it on the floor nearby. The alien peered inside and began taking things out to inspect them. It selected cotton wool, surgical spirit and that trusty medicament of the Greeks, a bottle of Betadine. It meticulously cleaned its wounds, inserting cotton wool soaked with surgical spirit inside and withdrawing it. Erickson thought to help but saw that with its multiple limbs it could reach every hole in its body. It then took up the skeleton gun and injected silicon inside every one. Erickson squatted down with his back against the door, sure the thing knew what it was doing. The moment it finished with the last hole it opened the pot of filler, packing the rest of each hole to the surface, smoothing the filler off with the towel dampened in some water.

'And that's all you need?' he asked.

The alien shook its head then pointed out into the kitchen. It began to get itself into motion and he stood, leading the way out. It seemed a lot more mobile now and reaching the centre of the kitchen floor it began to look around. After a moment it focused on him, raised one of its hands to its head, opened its mandibles and pointed into its mouth. Its requirements couldn't have been more obvious, so Erickson stepped over and opened the food cupboards. With slow delicate steps that gave him the creeps it walked over and he moved out of the way. It began taking down packets and reading labels, before carefully placing them back. The various cakes, the dry toast, bread and dried goods like rice and pasta were obviously not to its liking. Moving to the cans it sorted through quickly. Dolmades weren't on the menu, nor canned vegetables, but it did take out a can of mince and held it up to him, though with one of its other hands it made a wavering motion, so it obviously wasn't sure. Erickson grimaced, then opened the fridge.

The creature abandoned the can and came over fast.

'Good sense of smell, I suspect,' he said.

His own sense of smell was sharper too, he realised. Looking into the fridge he could detect the odour of every item there. A large bowl sat on one shelf, filled with brizolas, or pork chops, marinating in beer, oregano and salt and pepper. The alien moved closer and looked at him, fluted, then reached towards this.

'Go ahead,' said Erickson.

It took the bowl out, selected one big raw pork chop and brought it up to its mandibles. No need for a knife here because it quickly started snipping off chunks and inserting them into its mouth. Erickson got a fascinating glimpse of hard hooks and discs reducing the meat to pulp as it went down. He shrugged and went over to sit on his office chair. The creature went through the bowl like a mincing machine, emptying it rapidly, then turned its attention to the fridge again. Some liver, unwrapped from its paper, went down without much chewing. Three remaining eggs followed it, still in their shells and crunched up inside. It prodded at some cheese, contemplated some other items and discarded them, then found a carton of milk, uncapped it, held it to its mouth and drained it. In short order just about every source of fresh protein was gone, whereupon it picked up the bowl from the floor and held it out to him.

'I'll have to go and get some more,' he said, picking up his car keys.

As Erickson returned from Makrigialos the police pulled him over.

'Where are you from?' a policeman asked in perfect English.

He knew better than to tell them he was from the village of Papagiannades, since that only led to confusion, so he told them he was from the UK. The cop held out Erickson's driving licence to a younger companion and explained that the licence meant Erickson could drive a car, motorbike and small truck. He smiled at this, then felt a surge of panic quickly followed by delight. His Greek had been meagre at best, no matter how much he read and how much he tried to pummel into his head, yet the policemen had been speaking Greek and he had understood not only every word but every nuance. The soldiers, and one cop dressed like a member of the SAS, began searching his car and they weren't fooling around. They took out his tool boxes and went through them. They emptied out the bag of tamarisk logs he'd picked up on the beach, emptied out his glove compartment and lifted up every seat. They didn't speak much but when they did he understood them, also perceiving that they thought the task a pointless one, yet one they must do thoroughly so as to display their authority and efficiency to the *Xenos*. Once they'd finished, a young soldier began putting stuff back. One of the older soldiers peered into his bags of shopping, then eyed him suspiciously. He felt suddenly hot, but smiled and waved up towards the mountains.

'Kazani,' he said.

The man nodded then smiled widely. He was the older soldier at the kazani a few evenings back.

'Kali rachi,' he opined.

Erickson smilingly nodded agreement, and they let him go on his way.

By the time he reached his village the sun was gnawing a chunk out of the mountains opposite. When he got back to his house and lugged the shopping in through the back door he heard someone speaking. He froze and then dumped the shopping on the floor. His mind seemed to tighten in his skull, its components roiling together with oiled efficiency. Cautiously moving forward to the end of the hall, he found himself reaching out for something, some knowledge, grasp or power, the acquisition of which seemed an irrevocable and dangerous step. Then he peered into the kitchen area.

The laptop.

He had left it on and the alien had pushed away his chair to investigate the device. Presently it was watching a YouTube video clip from some nature program. He felt himself winding down, relieved he had not needed to reach out for that indefinable thing at the edge of his perception. He went back to fetch the shopping and brought it in, switched the light on, then dumped the bags loudly in the middle of the floor. The alien turned to observe him. After a moment it reached up and tapped the metal plate inset in its head, then a couple of those tight bracelets. On the conventional level Erickson didn't understand what this was about yet, on another level he did, but it just wasn't important right then and *would be* understood. The alien backed away from the computer and gestured at it. The YouTube video disappeared to be replaced by another website, then another and another, the sites flashing past at speed. It was controlling the laptop and the most rational explanation for that was that it must be doing so through the wifi. The laptop stopped on one page. Amazon showed a selection of mobile phones. The creature gestured to these, held a hand up beside its head in an easily recognisable gesture, then pointed to him.

Erickson groped in his pocket, took out his smart phone and held it up. The alien folded in its arms as if waiting. He turned the phone on and, as he did so, the creature reached back and closed the laptop. Something was happening. He peered at the phone screen and saw it changing rapidly, switching through various settings, and finally settling on his contacts. A moment later the phone rang. He stared at it, not recognising the number, then answered.

'Hello James Erickson,' said a voice.

'Who is this?' he asked, the question clearly irrelevant.

'I'm right in front of you.'

Erickson switched the phone over to speakerphone and lowered it.

'Do you need your phone?' it asked.

He pulled the thing closer to his chest, his thinking sharp and clear. It knew he could communicate with anyone at any moment. Perhaps it was trying to take that option away from him? No. Again no. He felt his initial assessment of the creature to be correct and anything else was sliding into what fiction, in film and books, had programmed into his mind. The phone enabled communication. His gaze fell on the technological additions to its body. Almost without further thought he walked round the alien to the desk, pulled open a drawer, lifted up a ream of paper inside and took out the box underneath. Without a word he held it out.

He had been intending to upgrade and had bought the replacement some weeks ago, but just never got around to doing anything with it. The alien took the box, swiped off its cellophane in one quick movement, and opened the thing. He noted, as he had in the shower room, how its dexterity far exceeded his own and that of all humans. While taking the phone and peripherals out of the box it headed over to his tools. He watched it discard the plug-in recharger but retain the USB, which it inserted into the phone. Next it sorted through some items, finally coming up with a tube of Superglue. It rapidly stuck the phone to its thorax next to one of the inset plates of technology, flipped up a blister cover to reveal a complex socket, and inserted the other end of the USB. The call to his phone then ended, while the attached phone came on. It ran through various screens then went blue and ran code.

'Now we can communicate,' it said from the new phone. It then turned and headed over to the shopping he had brought, opened it, and took out one of the packets of meat.

'You're an alien,' Erickson stated.

'I am,' it confirmed.

Hundreds of questions buzzed in his mind now he could talk to the thing, but he didn't want to ask the stupid ones and felt his previous observation had been precisely that. He diverted himself from them by walking over and opening the terrace doors to look out. Night had fallen with its usual rapidity. He eyed his chair out there then went back in to pour a karavachi of raki and take up a small glass.

'You obviously have advanced technology. You have travelled through space from another world while we're struggling to get back to our moon. How is it, then, that you crashed here and ended up in that cistern?'

'Even advanced technology can develop faults, and the unexpected can arise,' it said, eating in no way interfering with its speech. 'I brought my shuttle down with the intention of collecting samples. I brought it in close over the Arabian Sea with all defences formatted for current Earth military technology and camouflage set to evade all detectors. However, pure chance put me in the path of a US Navy test firing of a rail gun. The impact disabled some of the camouflage so I initiated the meteorite protocol, which disguised my vessel as a falling meteorite.'

Erickson just stared at it. That it used the word 'shuttle' presupposed it had a larger ship, probably up in orbit. That ship had come from another star, which bespoke, as he had thought before, a technology far beyond that of the human race. What was the likelihood of such a mishap occurring with such technology? He extrapolated quickly from human computing, seeing the layers of safety protocols, artificial intelligence, nano-second reaction times and felt he was being lied to. He gestured to the terrace.

'We can go outside,' he said. 'No one will see you – I have screens around the terrace.'

'If you so wish,' it replied, picking up one of the shopping bags.

He stepped out and slumped down in his chair. The alien followed, its head darting from side to side, checking the screens. It moved to the front wall and peered over down at the village then jerked back, finally settling itself back by the door.

'And you crashed there?' he said, pointing out into the darkness towards the mountains where he had found the alien, asking the stupid question to give him further time to think.

'It was a controlled descent, required for the meteorite protocol,' it said. 'I chose this island because the detection technology is old and I could subvert it.'

The tone of the reply had been somewhat snooty, which implied a degree of control of the voice from the phone that went beyond its technology. Did translation software carry across the creature's actual feelings, or was that deliberate? He studied it, noticing its eyes glowed in the dark, like a cat's.

'The Arabian Sea is a fair distance away and I would have thought plenty of suitable places lie between here and there,' he opined.

'I have given you the relevant information,' it stated.

Erickson replayed the conversation in his mind. Okay, the old radar stuff here on Crete and requirement of the meteorite protocol. He had to accept that, but could not help feeling the explanation lacked something.

Are your intentions hostile? he wondered. The thought seemed to fall off some edge in his mind. No, he could not accept hostility. If you had the kind of technology implied by this creature's journey here, your hostility would likely come from orbit and be very brief. And, right then, he could also see no reason why an alien would want to attack – certainly not for resources. If you could cross between stars your society would be post-scarcity and you could utilise anything. And there were more resources in this, or any other solar system, than on Earth itself. However, now he wondered about evolved hostility. Maybe that would negate a race rising to such technological heights, he could not judge. Perhaps safety was an issue – the need to suppress other races who might potentially be hostile themselves. The human record was not good.

He frowned, realising he had segued into hackneyed science fiction story lines. It seemed likely that once the human race reached a level of technology to represent a threat to this alien race, it too would be post-scarcity and therefore lacking in reasons for hostility. Was he right? Still doubt remained, for though human technology was advancing fast, evolution remained slow. As he considered this, he felt that shifting in his mind again and a sense of danger, so retreated from that train of thought, and returned to the moment.

'And in the cistern?' he asked.

'I landed my ship, by which time it had repaired its camouflage, so I moved it. I then ventured outside to test my body format to local conditions when again the unexpected arose. It was night time and I wasn't fully aware of the weapons available to some of the mountain dwellers here, nor their propensity to use them. An individual saw me, at a distance through a night sight, and opened fire. I ran and I fell. My internal technology was heavily damaged. Armed individuals were between me and my ship. I... panicked and fled.'

'I see,' said Erickson. He smiled briefly, utterly sure he was being lied to now. He sipped raki, grimaced at the taste. 'So what do you plan to do now?' he asked.

'Get back to my shuttle and return to my ship,' said the alien.

'You know where it is?' Erickson asked. 'You know how to get back to it?'

'Yes, but I will require help.'

Erickson gave a slow nod. 'I am presuming your shuttle is not far from where I found you?'

'No, it is not far.'

A memory arose of a story, possibly true, of police raiding a village in those mountains. They had been alerted when it became apparent that poor olive farmers up there were driving the latest 4x4s and, in one case, a Porsche. The police had been driven away by heavy fire from AK47s and only managed to make some arrests during a second raid. The olive farmers had been growing cannabis, even grabbing subsidies from the EU for their plants, claiming they were young olive trees. Perhaps it was these people who had opened fire on the alien?

As he understood it they were a wild and lawless bunch but, still, Crete was heavily inbred and you could be damned sure they had relatives strewn all over. By now you could be sure that the story of one or more of them firing on some monster in the mountains would be gossip in many villages. Almost as sure was that the story had reached the ears of the police and the military, since they would be relatives too. The place was like that: connected. You couldn't say anything disparaging about Yorgos the orange seller to someone in the kafenion because that someone would probably prove to be a cousin.

'Soldiers and police are likely in the area,' he said. 'They will be cautious, since the people there are... unruly. But they will be there.'

'Then we must proceed with caution,' said the alien.

Erickson took another sip of raki. It still didn't taste very nice to him, though he had enjoyed it before. He found himself identifying elements of that taste and then remembering all the articles he had read about the damage alcohol caused. This immediately took the fun out of the idea of drinking and he put the glass aside.

'So,' he said, 'we can head there as soon as possible or we can wait until the furore has died down. Soldiers will only be deployed for a limited time and the police will soon enough lose interest when they find they're missing their favourite soap operas.'

'Sooner would be better,' said the alien. 'Though my shuttle is camouflaged and has methods to discourage those who might get too close, as time passes the chances of it being found increase.'

Erickson toyed with the karavachi of raki. He didn't really need to think about this for much longer.

'Under the cover of darkness would be best,' he said, standing up.

'Indeed,' the alien replied.

Erickson went inside to his bedroom and changed into jeans and hiking boots, searched out a pack and wondered what to put it in, decided on a torch and water, but could think of nothing else to add. Heading out of his bedroom he found the alien waiting in the kitchen – it had closed the terrace doors.

'Do you require anything before we go?' he asked. 'Will you need water or food… or anything else?'

'I require nothing.'

'Come on.'

His mind kicked into a higher gear now he was on the move. He had said soldiers might be up in the mountains investigating that shooting, but that wasn't necessarily true. Even if they were there, they wouldn't be hiding in the olive groves in camouflage gear ready to trap the unwary but, from his understanding of the ways they behaved, they would be near lights and people and, if at all possible, barbecued food and raki. It should be easy enough to sneak to where they had to go, in fact, he felt oddly confident that they would do so.

As he headed for the hall the alien followed, snagging up the blanket on the way, the stains of its blood now dried like tar. A flash of hazard lights and his 4x4 was open, and the alien rounded him, opened the door, and climbed swiftly into the back. He climbed in, started the vehicle and pulled away.

'Y'know, now my time with you is limited, I can think of hundreds of questions I should have asked,' he said.

The questions tumbled over each other in his mind. The simple definition of the word 'alien' also defined the questions: essentially all of them.

'Most of the answers to the major questions are already in your mind – just logical extrapolations from what you know and from what I have already told you.' The alien paused. 'As you have probably surmised the detail is a source of an endless chain of questions.'

'Superluminal travel?' he asked, driving down the hill.

'Yes,' it replied. 'It is not beyond your technology even now, but you do not yet have the understanding of the universe required to apply that technology.'

He shook his head. 'You know people will find all of this hard to believe, not that I'll tell anyone, of course.'

'Yes, it is a mindset that will pass,' the alien replied as he reached the junction.

'Mindset?'

Silence met his query as he turned onto the main road. His mind roiled, some sixth sense telegraphing him the alien's hesitation over a reply. Finally it spoke:

'In the past humans put themselves and Earth at the centre of the universe – the creations of some supreme being. Supreme beings have paid their visits here but none of them created you. Later you learned that Earth orbits your sun but your other arrogances have been harder to shake. You still put yourselves at the centre.'

'What do you mean by centre?' He really wanted to pursue that comment about supreme beings but decided to stick with the present course. He reached a turn off into olive groves and slowed. Thankfully he had seen no other vehicles on the road and, having no idea what he would do if police or soldiers waved him to stop, took the turning. Better to take the route he had walked rather than the main roads, he felt. Yet still he felt confident of reaching their destination. The alien had said the answers to many questions could be extrapolated from what he already knew. He also felt, in the pit of his being, that the solutions to any problems in the world around him lay between his ears too. Logically that made no sense, but he felt it strongly.

'It can be seen in your psychology. You claim everything that happens to your planet. All natural changes are due to what you do – wherever humans have touched they claim to have made changes. Meanwhile the belief persists that you are the centre of the universe. These are artefacts of the pre-rationality of your religions. Even now while you are discovering that the rarities are suns without worlds orbiting them, many still believe humankind is the only intelligent life in the universe.'

'You generalise. I never believed that.'

He knew precisely where he was going, could even imprint the route on a Google Earth image of the area he remembered. He did so, seeing the village up there on the side of a mountain. He focused then on a flat area of rock and traced a potential route downhill from it to the cistern. He felt sure the shuttle must be there.

'Yes, I generalise.'

'How many races are there out there?' he asked. Usually he would have had to concentrate on driving along rough tracks like this at night, but now it took just a fragment of his attention. A ball of thought seemed to turn in his head, reshaping as it connected data, extrapolated and expanded. When he briefly pulled back from this he could see that he was modelling himself and his capabilities, the potential of the alien, the present situation... in fact it seemed as if there was nothing he had not incorporated.

'Worlds are common, life is common, intelligent life, depending on how you define intelligence, is less common and often self-destructs, but there are countless races out there.'

'And yet we have detected nothing.'

'Only in recent years have you confirmed the presence of those other worlds. Your technology needs to advance some before you find out many of those worlds are occupied. However, other factors will apprise you of the facts before then.'

'What other factors? More visits by you and your kind?'

After a long pause the alien said, 'Oumuamua... do you know of this?'

Just for a fraction of a second Erickson did not recognise the name. That was probably because he had only ever read it and not heard it pronounced correctly.

'An interstellar object,' he said. 'It's thought it must be metal because its albedo is very high and there was no outgassing from subliming ice. Its vector changed in ways that cannot be accounted for and some speculate that it might be a solar sail.' He peered back at the alien suspiciously. 'Is it your ship?'

The alien waved a hand dismissively as he returned his attention to the track. 'No, it is an interstellar probe from a hive race eighty-seven light years from Earth. Having scanned your solar system, and you, it swung about your sun and made some course corrections to take it onto its next target.'

'Really? Why no attempt to communicate?'

'It was a robot and had not been programmed to do so. The information it gathered will reach that hive race in eighty-seven years. Like yourselves they have not yet managed to understand the base mechanics of the universe and break the light speed barrier.'

'So you are saying we'll at some point detect another probe and identify it?'

'Probes, wrecked ships and their remains, pieces of space stations, orbital rings, space elevators and other detritus besides. Billions of years of the rise and fall of civilisations have liberally sprinkled the cosmos with these remains. Now, having taken a brief glance at Oumaumau, your astronomers are tracking other interstellar objects in your solar system. They will be surprised and perhaps appalled at what they find.'

Erickson nodded, easily accepting and incorporating into his worldview these fantastic things, the compass of that view expanding. At present he felt contained – just a human thinking fast and accurately – but he had a sense of rapidly approaching a boundary. This represented the danger he had felt before, for he knew that if he passed it there would be no way back.

Finally he pulled his vehicle to a halt beside the path leading down to the cistern and climbed out. A moment later the alien squatted beside him. A gibbous moon had risen and the stars shone bright in a cloudless sky. He stood utterly still, his eyes adjusting, and soon realised he would be unlikely to need the torch.

'Lead the way,' he said.

The alien dipped its head and went down the path. When they reached the cistern edge, it turned to gesture into the bamboo it had crushed down to first reach this place, and the headed in. The path turned to the left, taking them out onto a goat track alongside a shallow valley choked with further growths of bamboo.

'You said earlier that intelligence is less common than life and quite often self-destructs. Can you explain that?'

The creature looked back at him and kept its head pointing backwards. It seemed not to need to look at the track, but then it had a lot more legs available than him. 'Races very often destroy themselves when they reach a certain level,' the alien opined.

'Population growth? Environmental disaster?'

'Neither. Your technology is keeping far ahead of both of these; no, the technology itself is the danger.'

'War?' he tried. 'Nuclear weapons?'

'Nuclear weapons are highly destructive but do not have the capability of wiping out your race, merely setting it back by maybe a century. No, the danger comes as you approach post-scarcity. In that time increasing power falls into the hands of the individual while many individuals remain bound to the outdated ideologies of the societies before. All the technologies that lead finally into post scarcity can be weaponised – biotech, nanotech, artificial intelligence, energy storage and energy generation, programming biology and mentality – and these are beside the developments in physics that lead to the creation of singularities and the engines that can power you to the stars.'

'A difficult situation,' said Erickson, wondering about the alien's purpose here. 'Does this mean races like yours intervene?'

'Races like mine intervene at the beginning.'

'Meaning?'

'We leave a guardian in the solar systems concerned, but we have only been doing this for two million years and, only in the last million, because of the variance of the races and intricacies of racial destruction, have we perfected the process.'

The mentioned timespan kicked further reshaping in his mind. He did not for a second disbelieve it, and now his worldview expanded beyond one world. The clear crispness of the night seemed to reach out, bringing the coast to mind, the seas beyond and then other countries, all somehow in his grasp. The perception passed on, a shimmering wall spreading around the globe, and it seemed he could gaze at any location specifically. It also rose up through the sky and he tilted his head, visualising the space station passing over, and remembering that it actually was up there tonight. Enjoying the sensation, the reach, he sped out, passing the Moon and moving beyond into emptiness. This dragged at him and he leapt it to gaze upon Mars and then on other planets in the solar system, seeing them clear, not sure if that was due to clear memories of NASA imagery or some impossible expansion of his perception.

'You left a guardian here?'

'No, we did not – that was done by another race. That race later secreted itself in a Dyson sphere, then moved that sphere and the sun it contained out of the galaxy. No one knows why.'

It had answered his question and more. As he absorbed this, and believed it, he felt confident the alien had not simply delivered a brief conversational anecdote. It had throughout this encounter been bombarding him with the fantastical, and he felt sure this had been very deliberate.

'The supreme beings you mentioned,' he said, his mind beating at its boundaries. He stumbled, briefly dizzy and dislocated from reality, then back in it hard – everything around him seeming more *real* than it had ever been before.

'Here,' the alien gestured.

They climbed a slope up into a small olive grove, crossed this then climbed a wall up into another one. A narrow track ran across the back and they took it to the left, soon wading through waist-high weeds. Finally coming to a small ruined house, the alien turned right to come up to a steep shrubby slope.

'Are you capable of climbing this?' it asked.

He nodded, surveying above. He could do it, carefully, using the shrubs for handholds. The alien went ahead, climbing as easily as it had walked along the path. He followed fast but it quickly outdistanced him. After a moment it turned round and came back down to climb beside him.

'So where is it, then, this guardian? Is it something to do with that hexagon on the poles Neptune? Maybe sitting down in Jupiter's red spot?'

'It cannot be so distant.'

'Distance is a relative term, considering how far you must have come.'

'True.' The alien gave a dismissive shrug.

'So tell me more.'

'Durability is essential for a guardian,' the alien replied as it watched him climb. 'It must last as long as the race in its charge, and must maintain its information intact. Most material forms of construction degrade, especially when holding such complexity. Simpler mechanisms – a guardian's tools – can be stored timelessly in subspace.'

'Why not put the guardian there?'

'Because from there it will have no access to its charges.'

'So where is the damned thing?'

'One thing has the longevity and proximity required, and that is the race concerned.'

'So it is here among us? It is one of us?'

'It is.'

'But not particularly noticeable.'

'Yes, and this has been a matter of concern to us.'

'It has?'

They reached the top of the slope and stepped straight onto a track winding up the mountain. Glancing up, Erickson could see its switchbacks. He looked along the track, visualised it in his mind, and the Google Earth image was incredibly clear. He could see a wide area of landscape and ascertain that the track led up to that plateau he had seen, but he could also see detail. He gazed down upon the track to see a vehicle travelling along it, about to turn a corner. And around that corner he could see a man walking, with something spidery perambulating beside him. In that brief instant he knew this was no memory of an image he had seen on a computer screen but actuality. Then the borders of his mind crashed away and it expanded out to grasp the old mechanisms that had been prepared for him. Epiphany – accompanied by a glaring bright light that for just a moment he thought issued from within, until soldiers began shouting in Greek.

The searchlight nailed him and the alien. The light blinded him for a second, then he blinked and peered *around* it. He saw soldiers piling out of the armoured car ahead, one in the back with his finger on the trigger of a fixed-mount machine gun, others raising their weapons. He felt their fear almost like a substance in the air, and knew that the line between shouting and shooting had drawn incredibly thin. He knew of only a few things that might stop them shooting. One of them was an order from their commander, who sat in the passenger seat of the jeep just gaping. He did the other and stepped in front of the alien to hold his arms out to the sides.

'Wait, it's harmless!' he shouted in perfect Greek.

A brief pause ensued as the soldiers began to return to their conventional reality. It would have been fine had not their commander been an arachnophobe.

'Kill it!' he screamed.

The machine gunner in the jeep, tasting the terror of his commander, squeezed his trigger. The others were lowering their weapons, but then raised them again. Muzzle flashes lit the night and bullets snapped nastily through the still air.

'Wait,' said Erickson.

The nearest mechanism felt like it stood over to his left, but in reality did not occupy the same dimension as the solidity around him. He reached out to it and grasped, bullets seeming to slow as they travelled through the air towards him. He drew in the energy and felt it surge through his body, through his DNA like a trillion nano-scopic wires. The first bullet struck him in the right side of his chest, smashing a rib, puncturing a lung and bursting from his back. Two more hit in quick succession and others were about to hit the alien. He slowed things further, bringing all to stillness, the bullets hanging in the air. His perspective rose into the sky and he saw the shimmer of the shuttle's camouflage on the plateau, then peeled it away. The thing was a disappointingly featureless slab of grey composite. Returning to himself he applied the schematic of his DNA and supplied the required energy. Holes closed, ribs healed, his body returned to its form before the bullets struck. He would make further alterations later.

Next he reached through the realm his mechanisms occupied to make a link with the plateau above, encompassed himself and the alien, and within that compass drew the energy from the bullets. Translocation came with a snap. A wisp of dust settled as the soldiers emptied their weapons. Erickson and the alien appeared on the plateau, and dropped a few inches to the ground, and around them bullets fell too. He frowned at his positional inaccuracy, but found it acceptable since this was the first time he had done it.

'So it was a matter of concern for you that you saw no evidence of this guardian,' he said

'It was. Your world is reaching a time of danger and the probability of the human race self-destructing has been rising steeply.'

'And what would it be like, this Guardian?' he asked.

'Human, of course, initially. The so-called supreme beings that came here wove the guardian into a most durable substrate capable of storing vast amounts of information: your DNA. Their subsidiary mechanisms they left in subspace in this region.' The alien gave a very human shrug. 'But of course you know all this now.'

Erickson thought about that for a moment then said, 'The guardian genome is scattered among many humans. However, once it activates in one human being, in the others it drops into somnolence.'

'The individuals concerned continue to breed,' said the alien. 'Should the current guardian be destroyed or even destroy itself, another should activate.'

'But activation has been a problem?'

'Yes. An extinction level event would do, or the threat of the same. However, a less drastic measure was available: I exposed a guardian carrier to something utterly outside its compass – something it must at least assess and something it could not assess while being merely human.'

Erickson nodded as they walked towards the shuttle. 'Yourself.'

'Exactly.'

His mind now beyond its barriers he sampled masses of data, which he ran through hidden mechanisms, making assessments. The encompassed world around him lay open to his inspection. His mind felt bloated with the knowledge from thousands of data bases, from his assessment of social structures, from thousands of patterns, systems and trends his tools, now fully active, processed. He could see in an instant the root of the aliens' fear, and how they were wrong.

'Do you not realise your concern about my lack of activation was unfounded?' he said.

'Really?'

'Racial self-destruction is not yet imminent.' He smiled – utterly sure he was right. 'The technology here cannot yet drive it. This will change during transitions to AI singularity in about twenty years.'

'You would know this. We did not.'

'How did you choose me?' he asked idly.

The hull of the ship loomed ahead and they stepped through it. Within, spider webs of light wove coherence, tunnels curved away in every direction like worm holes through an apple. He perceived all of the interior but remained linked to the outside as the shuttle rose from the mountain top, then accelerated up through atmosphere.

'You were isolated and of one of the least disrupted germ lines – it was a simple choice. Also your human mental format was more amenable to the alien, hence we calculated that your reactions would remain rational long enough for you to incorporate sufficient data for your activation.'

Soon all of Earth lay below him. He continued assessing the flows of data, of life, of societies and technical development. The time ahead would be an interesting one. As the human race headed towards singularity, and as it incorporated more of its technology in itself, it would become increasingly difficult for him to remain concealed. He saw danger in it becoming aware of him, some to himself, but mainly to the course of its development. Knowledge of his presence could cause a collapse back into pre-rational thinking.

'Your work is done here,' he stated.

'I know,' the alien replied.

He looked down, grasped the mechanisms again and translocated. A second later he stood again on his terrace, no drop to the ground this time because he had fully calculated for the shifts in the geology below his feet. At once he began making alterations, first running backups of his mind to the subspace mechanisms, next focusing his full attention on his body. The human body was a weak thing and he would need something more rugged over the ensuing years, the ensuing centuries. He glanced up as the shuttle left orbit, heading for the larger ship concealed behind the moon. He stepped over and sank into his seat, sipped some raki, able to enjoy it now. Brief time, to his perception, passed. He waved, the action translated through his whole being, both a dismissal and an invitation. The alien returned the gesture as it entered its ship, then that vessel rose and flashed out of existence.

'In fifty years, by the cistern,' he had told it.

'I'll be there,' it had replied.

Moral Biology, which features the character here, and The Host, which features the creature in Moral Biology, I wrote before this. The character interested me so in the traditions of fiction everywhere I decided to have a crack at an origin story. Again, this features somewhat of personal experience, since getting into a warm sea and swimming silly distances to circuit an islet is something I do every summer, usually daily. I also get those moments of being spooked while swimming. When the water is clear and you can see some distance you become all too aware of how the sea just goes on and on and deeper and deeper and who the hell knows what might arrive? When it's cloudy who knows what might come out of the murk? Never a good idea to stumble across shark videos before that swim.

THE TRANSLATOR

Standing under the parasols I looked out across the limestone running for a mile to the sea. Something thudded down on my shoulder and I brushed it off, peering down at what looked like a large maggot with four froglike legs. These mushroom eaters were harmless, but if you stood under the parasols in one place for too long you ended up with a rain of them falling on you – they made the mistake of assuming you were an elder relative of their kind and thus suitable transport to better feeding grounds. I peered up at the gills on the underside of the ten foot wide parasol cap and, seeing further movement there, took a step to one side. Glancing round I saw that other eaters were moving down the fleshy stalk, so stepped out from the shade into the sunshine on the limestone slab, walked for a short distance and turned back.

The Forest of Troos – apparently a name garnered from some ancient fantasy book – stretched to vanishing points to the left and right. It consisted of fungi that looked like Earth parasol mushrooms writ huge. The colonists harvested these not because they were edible, for they had zero nutritional value for a human, but for the pulp, which they turned into many useful products. Brease had told me of increasing sales of one such product: paper, turned into blank page books. For no immediately apparent reason, Polity citisens had rediscovered the joys of writing. Another group of enterprising colonists were now manufacturing fountain pens, and tapping ink from another fungal form here to charge them.

This return to the art of writing had brought me here, apparently. Having learned many languages and still studying, I had fruitlessly applied for positions all across the Polity to get practical experience. Then this had come up and there seemed no barrier to me coming here – in fact a submind of Earth Central contacted me about the opening. It struck me as make-work with little to recommend it, but the climate and the ocean here persuaded me, because if I have a passion beyond languages it is swimming. And now I felt grateful for that. Besides some interesting language adaptations and a return to some archaisms, there didn't seem to be very much to learn, and my stay had become boring. Swimming seemed my only option until I managed to get on the interminably delayed transport to the nearest runcible.

I trudged along staying strictly on a worn path towards the sea. Channels etched down through the surrounding limestone gurgled with run-off from the land behind, but the water flow also cut tubes whose skin at the surface could break under an unwary boot. Above, yellowish clouds streaked the pastel violet sky, with some fliers up there that looked like seagulls at a distance, but which more closely resembled beetles close-up. I paused to peer into one of the gurgling channels and there observed silky blue weed in clear water, then the black shape of an eel writhing past. But, of course, it wasn't an eel. Evolution here had produced the shapes of Earth from a triple helix genome with six bases, and some incredible protein and enzyme action that still had biologists scratching their heads. Brease told me of an Earth amoeba that had a genome a hundred times larger than that of humans but that here the complexity went way beyond that. The biologists still suspected an alien race had deployed biotechnology here. The two-million-years-gone Atheter were the prime suspect nowadays.

As I walked on I contemplated that. The Atheter, Csorians and the Jain were the only three named extinct alien races – the first two races extinct due to hostile technology left lying around the universe by the last. A few years ago, it being suspected that Jain technology might be here, AIs had swarmed this place. The small human colony had been evacuated and Polity battleships had sat in orbit. When they found none of that hostile technology the colonists were allowed back. But many AIs remained, like Mobius Grip back at the settlement, and two battleships still sat up there in orbit. All very interesting, of course, and I had considered hanging around and changing the direction of my research, for decoding the genome of the creatures here could be considered a form of translation, but it did not have the requisite attraction for me.

'I'm going for a swim,' I had told Grip just a few minutes earlier. The AI – in the spherical form of a crinoid like all of the Mobius AIs – had rolled into view as I approached the mushroom forest.

'Maybe not a good idea, Perrault,' Grip had replied. 'Some big shroud skate have been seen close to the coast and there was an incident…'

'I'll be careful.' I'd nodded, wondering why Grip used the full name of that creature when none of the locals did, also immediately annoyed and more determined to swim than ever, and walked on.

I'd swum with white sharks on Earth, with spearpigs in their caverns and many other forms of alien life. You just had to know what you were doing. Many years ago a swimmer had been chewed on by one of the big shroud *skate*. Though they resembled the rays of Earth they were an entirely other life form and, with their way of closing over their prey, the name shroud had fit. The swimmer had been spat out to be rescued sans legs and had then grown himself a new set, being one of those humans with the salamander additions to enable that. The shroud, tracked by drone, had swum far out to sea and there rolled over and died having been poisoned by human flesh. A great mass of its kind had then come along to feed upon it. Thereafter no human had ever been attacked by a shroud. The biologists speculated on some kind of memory transfer – some simple 'don't eat them' instruction.

Finally reaching the edge of the slab by the sea I jumped off, landed on the beach five feet down, and peered out at the ocean. Shrouds occasionally threw themselves out of the waves and, just as with manta rays on Earth, the biologists dryly explained this method of shaking off parasites, while everyone else knew they jumped for the sheer joy of it. I would have no problem with shrouds or anything else hostile anyway. I stripped off my clothing down to trunks, took the repeller out of my pack and slotted the thing into a pocket for it in the waistband of my trunks. The thing drove away sharks, spearpigs and others besides and, since the shrouds had quite a large and intricate nervous system, it would be more than adequate for them. Blister goggles went over my eyes, sticking to the skin around them and perfectly transparent. I was ready.

Shells scattered the sand underfoot – all with their Earth analogues. The subtle difference was I knew they were alien. If I had seen any of these shells on Earth I would have simply wondered about a mollusc I had not known about before. Spirals lay there, more often broken than not. Unlike most terran molluscs of this kind the spiral turns were separated so they looked like springs. Clam shells shimmered with nacre, some almost perfectly triangular. Double-jawed claws and pieces of carapace were from some lobster-like crustacean. While heaps of bone-white shells like white plastic beads were of some form of winkle. At the tide line lay a drift of rotting weed with little to distinguish it from what might be found on a terran beach. A rotting fish passed at a glance, but closer inspection revealed tentacular legs folded against its underside. I waded in.

The water was just right. I would get no shuddering chill as it reached my balls and once I was in it would be only marginally cooler than the warm landward day. From previous experience I knew that once I got going I would actually feel myself sweating in the sea. I dived in and stroked out for a little way with a bilateral breathing crawl, then put my feet down to look around. I had swum to the point over to my left many times, but today I felt like going further and turned my eye towards the small rocky islet over to my right. Yes, I would swim around that today. I dived in again and set out.

The sea stayed shallow for a hundred yards where I could stop at any point and stand up. Molluscs much like cowries the size of a fist trundled along leaving strangely jagged trails. Shoals of fish appeared and disappeared. Most of these looked terran and, as I understood it, some were. An early colonist had, against the behest of the others, introduced many terran species that could survive here.

Gradually the bottom dropped away, revealing limestone slabs crusted with those white beads and jutting spirals like decorations in some aquatic cocktail. I spotted one of those fish with tentacles working along the bottom here, pulling things out of the muddy sand between slabs and shoving them in its mouth. A whole host of lobster analogues crowded about a rock, waving their claws at me as if they were defending a fortress. A big thing like a sunfish passed far to my right. Then a large shadow passed over the bottom and I searched for its source. There: a shroud.

It looked like a giant stingray at first glance, but closer inspection revealed the jointed limbs in its wings, terminating in hooked spikes where they protruded at the edges. Its colour was brown and green and, when the sunlight caught it just right, I could vaguely see the shapes of its internal organs and skeleton through translucent flesh. I paused, hanging in the water to watch for a while as it cruised round me and in towards the shallows, my hand straying to the repeller in my waistband. I did feel a frisson of fear, just as I had felt with other large sea creatures. This was an inescapable part of the whole experience: the knowledge of vulnerability when out of one's element and in another with creatures perfectly adapted to it. I then swam on towards island.

After a few strokes, a glimpse of a shadow on the bottom told me I had dismissed the creature too early. I stopped and turned in time to see its face: two beady black eyes set wide apart with cephalic lobes on either side, the v-mouth below now opening to reveal rows of needles teeth and a tubular tongue. It turned slightly at the last moment, hit me with one wing and sent me tumbling through the water. It occurred to me then that maybe the biologists had been right. Those shrouds that had fed on the one poisoned by a human had learned the lesson, but they weren't all of the shrouds in the sea. Maybe this one thought I might make a tasty snack. As I scrabbled for the repeller, it came up from underneath and hit me again. I tumbled again, clinging to the repeller, stroked for the surface to get a needed breath then ducked down again, only to be hit yet again. The thing swam around me in a leisurely fashion. Was I a toy? I then remembered white sharks playing similar games with a seal. How long before it flipped me up in the air out of the waves? How long before it grew bored with all that and started biting? I pointed the repeller at the thing and triggered it.

The shroud hung there for a moment shuddering, then abruptly turned tail and fled. I felt smug human superiority about that. This shroud had now learned its lesson, but I hung onto the repeller while scanning around to reassure myself it was gone. After a moment I surfaced and saw that the islet was close. The sensible thing to do would have been to turn around and head as fast as I could for the shore. The arrogant thing to do was to continue swimming for the islet – to complete my swim as an assertion of my mastery here. I kept going towards the islet, my stroke not so good now what with holding the device in my right hand.

The bottom started to slope sharply upwards, covered with broken limestone slabs. Oh I would have an adventure to relate when back to the settlement, I thought, little knowing my adventure had only just begun. One of the slabs detached from the bottom nearby and shot towards me. The shroud had concealed itself and waited.

I swung the repeller towards it, but the creature turned abruptly as if frightened and I didn't trigger the device. This was a mistake. In turning away it whipped its tail across. The thing hit my wrist hard and the repeller shot away to bob out of reach with negative buoyancy. I tried to propel myself towards the islet again and the sudden intense pain arrived. In a glance I saw my wrist off at an angle it should not be at, and blood clouding around it. Momentarily stunned by the pain and the sight, I rolled, and that's when the shroud hit my back from below. It shoved me up towards the surface and I felt its tail, shark-skin rough, twining around one leg. It closed round me as I tried to pull away, horribly aware that its v-mouth was directly behind my head. Its wings wrapped me – one folding right round and those hooked protrusions stabbing in down the side of my torso, the other wrapping over that. In panic I struggled, swiftly using up my oxygen, but even through the panic I did not understand what the hell the thing was doing.

Shrouds fed like sharks by thumping into and biting a prey until they could get into tearing it apart. I had the sudden horrible idea that I had encountered intelligence here – that it knew my flesh to be poisonous and so was trying to drown me. Then I felt the awful stabbing pain in my back and wondered on biology I just did not know about. Lungs fit to burst and knowing that the next breath I took would be my last, a horrible resignation came over me. I was going to take that breath – this was it, I was done. The air in my lungs began to bubble out, then the shroud released me. I thought the biting would start now as the thing towed me through the water with that tail wrapped around my legs. Next, in a flurry of movement and with a pull on my leg that seemed about to tear it from its socket, I swept through the water, breaking surface I managed a watery breath and then hit stone. I scrabbled for life, hacking water out of my lungs and dragging my battered body from the sea, terrified I would be dragged back. It took a while before terror cleared and I realised the creature had flung me up on the edge of the islet.

I managed to get to my knees, then stood upright, sick and dizzy. Cradling my broken arm – the break just above the wrist and a bone protruding – I puked seawater and breakfast. With a wrenched leg and a broken arm a swim back to shore did not seem an option. In a lot of pain I climbed higher on rough stone slabs to the peak just ten feet above the waves and sat down, only then noticing that at least my back didn't hurt. This then worrying me, I reached round with my good hand to probe for damage. The shroud had done whatever it had done in about the middle of my back. I felt something stuck there about the size of a hand. It felt rubbery about a splay of bony objects within. In growing horror I visualised something like an egg sac, then it moved under my hand. I yelled and tried to pull the thing off. Pain stabbed into me at its centre and out around its edges. One edge came up but the thing fought to pull back down against my back and the pain grew so intense I had to let it go. My fingers came back bloody.

I sat there looking at my bloody hand while also feeling blood trickling down my back. The thing back there continued moving as if embedding itself more comfortably. Had mere injuries been my problem, pride would have had me sitting there until someone noticed my absence and come looking for me, whereupon I would have affected some nonchalance about what had happened. But the thing back there made this a magnitude more serious, for who knew what damage it might be doing? I only had one option now. I raised my head and shouted.

'Mobius Grip! Help me! I need help!'

I kept on shouting but very swiftly grew hoarse. Perhaps ten minutes later something glittered on the shore, then Mobius Grip, like a dandelion head five feet across, came rolling across the ocean. The AI had been the only one to call really, and the only one with the senses to hear. Its crinoid form held a multitude of talents. The protrusions from its centre point looked like tubeworms with ever branching heads and were tools in could manipulate with a precision that went beyond that of an autosurgeon. The AI could remove whatever had attached to my back.

It rolled closer and closer across the ocean then, instead of coming straight onto the islet, it ran a circuit around it and then paused on the ocean as if in contemplation. It jerked into motion again and rolled in and up the rocky slope towards me making a sound like a chip fryer to finally halt ahead of me. A wash of warmth passed through me from the top of my skull to my feet – powerful active scanning.

'I've got something on my back,' I said.

'I am aware of that,' Grip replied. 'Hold out your arm.'

I hesitated, because my arm hurt like hell, but then obliged, trying to support it with my other hand. The AI moved in its tendrils and protrusions and closed them in around the break while pushing my other hand aside. For a second the pain increased, then everything grew numb within the reach of those swiftly moving tendrils. They were thin and glassy, with occasional black ones appearing then disappearing. Through their movement I saw my arm open as if being unzipped, bone and fragments of bone going back into place. The tendrils all around turned bloody red for a brief spell then that faded away. The broken bone went perfectly back in place as the arm closed up again, skin layers going back and then, just like that, it was done. Grip released me and I retracted my arm. It still felt slightly numb but then began to tingle and then burn as feeling returned. I opened and closed my hand. Everything was going to be fine.

'Turn round and lie face down,' the AI instructed.

Struggling with my bad leg I did as bid, anxious to have that thing off my back. Grip seemed more concerned about my injuries, however. It worked on my leg and up towards my hip – both areas feeling like they had been locked in some invisible clamp. Areas grew numb and then tingled and burned, but as the AI worked the pain steadily faded.

'Now,' it finally said and moved up to my back.

The pain there receded in the same manner. The hot wash of scanning came again and then the AI rolled away. Now completely able again I turned over and sat up.

'What the hell was it?' I asked.

'You have a small shroud skate attached to your back,' Grip replied.

'Have?'

'I am unable to remove it,' the AI replied.

'What?' The AI had repaired my injuries like I might glue together a broken pot, but a hell of a lot more than glue had been involved. Grip had opened me up and stitched things together down to the cellular level, probably removing all the damaged stuff. To my leg and hip it had penetrated me with nanoscopic fibres to repair damage to joints, ligaments, muscle and nerves. And now it was telling me it could not remove the thing stuck on my back?

'We will take a closer look when you get back.' Grip rolled away from me and down to the sea while I just gaped.

'Wait!' I yelled, standing up. 'You can't just leave me here!'

But it seemed that Grip could.

Horribly aware of the thing – the shroud – attached to my back, I paced around the islet for maybe half an hour expecting a grav raft or a boat to arrive, but it soon became evident that none would come. Finally I nerved myself up enough to get back into the sea and swim for the shore. Surely the AI would not have left me in danger of further attack from the shroud? I couldn't know for sure and felt on edge until to my relief I saw the repeller bobbing along just out from the islet and snared it up. Next came anger, because leaving me to swim back was Mobius Grip's way of delivering a salutary lesson. The anger faded as I worked up a sweat halfway back to shore and then I started thinking fiercely.

Maybe Mobius Grip had been lying about being unable to remove the shroud – AIs were not immune to that inclination – because it thought it might be interesting to see how the shroud developed and knew it could be removed at any time. But what if it wasn't lying? That being the case meant the thing had attached in some majorly complex manner. I visualised spread tendrils like Grip's throughout my body and surgery that would require life support for their removal. I imagined some major chemical imbalance in my body that might spin out of control were the thing removed. I also imagined it poised with lethal toxins ready to be injected should any attempt be made to interfere with it. As a finally arrived at the shore I started dismissing those fears, feeling my childhood love of science fictional virtualities had come back to haunt me.

The settlement, ridiculously named Umbrella Town, sat just on the other side of the Troos. The residential area surrounding the centre consisted of coralcrete, printed or foamstone houses in a bewildering variety of designs. Every one of them had its verandas, greenhouses, sheds and gardens. The dusty track out of the Troos soon turned into a metalled road with wide pavements. I was glad to arrive, not because this got me closer to getting the thing removed from my back, but because today the Troos seemed to be giving off a much higher intensity of that mushroom smell. Few ground cars used the metalled road since the colonists preferred gravcars and rafts. In the centre of the town stood tall buildings which in another age would have been administrative but here mostly contained biotech concerns, manufactories and shops. Off to one side of the centre sat a small spaceport for delivering and dispatching people and goods – any larger vessels landing on the plain beyond, which was matted with something they called tangle-grass here. And now a ship was coming down.

I paused, gaping at the monstrous vessel. It wasn't as big as a dreadnought but had to be a mile long. With its rounded fore and ignoring the protrusions from its surface, the thing looked like a gravestone. It threw a shadow over the town, utterly silent on grav, but the effects of that making me alternately light then heavy and stirring up dust all around. It slid aside, going down on the area of plain just out from the Troos. An interesting arrival I would have to investigate at a later date, but right now I had my own problems. A turn down a side street took me to where I had rented a room — a two floor structure surrounded by gardens and greenhouses and with an observatory on the roof. As I went through the gate and up the garden path, Brease stood up in the vegetable patch. I glanced across at her, noting an intense but not unpleasant odour.

'What on Earth is that doing here?' she said.

'Beats me.' I halted.

The smell definitely had something sexual about it, and I simply stared at her, feeling a visceral response. She stared back, abruptly flushed red and stooped to her vegetables again.

'Probably found something interesting,' she said, adding with overdone vehemence, 'I hope to fuck it's not going to be an evacuation.'

'So what is that ship, then?'

Now another smell: she had just pulled up a carrot. Then other smells all for a moment intense as I identified them — spring onions, lettuce, radish — then a melange I could only describe as 'garden' and I felt a weird frustration about not being able to nail down all its elements.

She waved a hand in the general direction of the ship. 'The *Surgeon General*. It's a xenobiology research vessel and mostly the research done aboard relates to the dead races.'

'Okaay,' I said slowly, baffled about the intensity of the smells around me in that bright garden. And yes, there was that too: all the colours had become intense, and all the shapes of the plants seemed to have taken on exactitude.

Once in my room I peered around at hard angles and soft, edges and textures, and caught the whiff of cleaning chemicals from the beetlebot that came out of its hole at the foot of one wall to clean when I left. What the hell was this? I looked again and nothing had changed from how it had been when I set out this morning, yet I just seemed more aware. Perhaps coming so close to dying had given life added piquancy? Yeah, I could go with that, though it seemed crazy that Brease – the highly attractive woman who owned this house and about whom I'd had more than a few lecherous thoughts – had chemically broadcast sexual receptiveness.

I went over to the room console and set the room to internal observation, stripped off and dumped my clothes, stood in the middle of the floor for a while, turning in a circle, then headed towards the shower. Here the smells of the soap were almost sickly, with a slight putrid smell from the drain as background. I ignored that – shutting down on further tentative thoughts about the reason for the intensity of everything, and stepped into the shower.

Apparently my companion did not like the water so hot and the jets so strong, but I ignored its gnawing at my back and cleaned myself thoroughly, particularly working on my face, which now for no apparent reason had started itching. Back out again I dressed, pausing at a warm smell of cloth and abruptly fascinated by the distinct thread pattern of my jeans, then went over to the room console and called up room recordings from previously. I focused in on the recording of me standing naked, and observed my passenger. It clung in the middle of my back – just a small version of the shroud that had attacked me, though its colour red and grey. I wondered if the red might be my blood circulating in it, for it seemed likely to be some kind of parasite. The imagery from the internal cams was good, but now somehow seemed less real than before.

Voices outside.

I tilted my head hearing the rumbling of a man speaking and then words becoming distinct, all underlined by a fryer hissing sound. I only caught a few words at the start but more afterwards. My facility with languages seemed to kick in then, and I found myself reconstructing what had gone before by the implication of the intervals. A man had entered the garden, stated Brease's name and then asked if I was home. Instead of answering his question she had said, 'Weeds will be the death of my spine. You're from that ship?'

'I am indeed,' the man had replied.

'Not quite sure why you're asking,' she now said. 'You know.'

Mentally I could see her indicating, with a nod of her head, the man's companion. I picked up my pack, scrubbed at my itchy face as I thought what to throw in it. What would I need? How long would I be staying? I then abandoned the pack since they would be able to provide for any of my needs, stepped over and opened the door just before the man knocked on it.

'It's upgrading my sensory input,' I said, stepping out. 'And maybe I'm having some sort of allergic reaction.'

The man, clad in an ECS uniform and armed with a pulsegun at his hip, just stood there looking baffled. Mobius Grip, on the path behind him, was quicker.

'Go back inside and look at your face,' it said.

I turned round, went to the console and tapped the side of the screen frame on the wall to switch it to mirror. My face looked ruddy and a rash had appeared on it. I then noted the even bilateral distribution of the spots. They looked like tribal markings I had seen in old images of African natives while studying their languages. This looked far too deliberate to be an allergic reaction. I stepped back out again.

'I think you'd better explain,' I said to Grip.

The AI replied by intensively scanning me from head to foot, then said, 'I will explain what I can while we head to the *Surgeon*.'

'Good.' I looked at the man. 'Was there some thought that I might not come?'

The man smiled. 'No, just some thought that it might be better for you to receive the *request* from a human face.'

I nodded at that. His assured calm did not conceal the mild lie. Yes, a good idea to have a human face along because not everyone put their trust in AIs, but I had no doubt that I would not be able to refuse the request. I walked down the garden path with them.

'You okay,' said Brease, moving into the path ahead.

'Not really,' I replied. 'It seems the life forms here still have some surprises in store.' I turned and lifted the back of my shirt to show her the shroud.

'Bloody hell,' she said, and I saw the man's mouth tighten in annoyance. He knew very well that Brease would inform the colony council and that thereafter they would be making constant enquiries about me. I'd known that too – that's why I showed her. She stepped out of the way to let us pass and gave me a cautious nod that meant a multitude of things, especially when combined with her hormone output.

'Even before I got to that islet I was scanning you and other things,' said Grip as we walked off. 'I studied the shroud skate that attacked you and noted that its physiognomy was radically different from that of others of its kind. It disappeared into the depths before I could put a tracker on it.'

'In what ways radically different?'

'I have the data and you can study it at your leisure later, but suffice to say that if I didn't know there is no one on this world or around it capable of doing so but me, I would say it had been massively biologically modified to produce a highly modified offspring.'

'And how modified is this offspring?'

'Radically. By the time I got to you it had already grown nanofibres into your body and was connecting to your nervous system. There are organisms throughout your body or, if we so wish to describe them, nanites.'

'The fuck!'

'Unfortunately this means the possibilities regarding removing it are not good.'

I fell silent. My senses were sharp and seemed to be combining with my language skills. With my memory close to being eidetic I had learned in total twenty-eight languages both written and spoken. I'd once worn an aug and uploaded more and hoped the extra processing would help me further; unfortunately the aug had, I felt, interfered – it had almost felt like an adjunct to which I loaded data so my mind forgot it. Also included in that mass of language data between my ears was nuance of meaning, expression and gesture language too. The man, I saw, was definitely giving off signals and, though AIs were hard to read I could detect something in the choice and order of the words.

Mobius Grip was lying.

We walked out of the settlement and onto the plain beyond. I asked what could be done now and Grip told me about the requirement for lengthy examinations of the life form attached to me. I was only half listening. My sensory world was steadily expanding.

My vision had altered in ways that baffled me at first. Colours were the same, but also different. I puzzled over this. Why did the man, whose name I had learned was Brytek, seem to have a glow about him? Why did I see so clearly one of the arthropods of this world in the tangle-grass as if highlighted? As for Mobius Grip, the AI had turned into a startling rainbow creation flicking out tongues of light in all directions. Some went to the settlement behind, some to the ship ahead and some were hitting me. I saw one hit the arthropod and it glow as if phosphorescent. I remembered then that these small creatures were similar in many ways to Earth scorpions, and that knowledge became the key. I studied patterns on the hull of the ship ahead, a glow around thruster tubes and a different emanation around the back end from the fusion engines. I halted and turned back to look at the settlement. The other two halted and watched me. I had no doubt about what I was seeing. I turned and continued walking.

'Seems my visual reception is expanding into the infrared and ultraviolet,' I commented.

'Yes,' said Grip. 'Changes are occurring in your optic nerve and elsewhere.'

'Quite,' I said, not sure now whether I felt afraid or exultant.

My hearing had changed too. Clicks and whistles came from the grasses and a weird susurration from Grip. I couldn't figure out a thumping and hissing until, just a short while later, I realised I could hear my own heart beating and the rush of blood through my veins. Turning to Brytek and concentrating, I could hear his heart too. But it wasn't the increased sensitivity to sounds I knew of that alerted me to the new change, but their quality and the fact that I could hear things I had never heard before.

'My hearing too,' I said.

I felt a wash of warmth from Grip and disappointment I could not see its source. I guessed I hadn't acquired the capability of seeing flash-back chiral terahertz radiation... yet. However, besides the warmth I felt something else: echoes inside my body, some perception of complex grid-like membranes passing through my flesh, and most of this activity focusing in on my head. A brief headache stabbed me then went away.

'New structures growing in your ear. Further hair cells of a different nature and some odd granulation in your inner ear and Eustachian tubes,' the AI said calmly. 'How about your sense of smell?'

How about my sense of smell? I felt like shouting at the AI but whether in joy or terror I could not decide. Smell and flavour had blurred together and expanded. I could smell tangle-grass when before it had been odourless to me, and it was a complex tangle of odour in itself. Brytek put out something like a hormonal signature and Grip seemed like rust, glass and composites. All of these were changing all the time and I simply could not elucidate them. How can one even think about a smell one had never sensed before other than by comparison? When I concentrated on this input, my mind started to give me images: complexities of colour, texture and interlinked objects. Was I seeing in some fashion organic molecules?

I was about to speak of this as we drew closer to the ship – its ramp down on the grass. Then my attention swung to the grass again. It seemed that by concentrating on smell input I had further awakened my facility with languages. I gazed at the tangled masses of stalks and fronds and began to see letters, glyphs and pictographs from the many languages I knew. There had to be meaning here and I stood riveted trying to resolve it. Perhaps that combined with the new things I could smell and the intensity of my vision? Perhaps the sounds were related too? I began integrating them all, tracing out fragments of meaning and trying to find more. The data washed through my thoughts and as it did I seemed to be losing myself. Vision became glaring blades through my eyes. The melange of sound twisted into my brain. The smells formed molecular words reflected in a billion stalks and fronds. An endless parade of shade and nuance filled my mind so it seemed by skull wanted to burst open. What started out as increased intensity of senses became agony.

Another sound…

I was screaming and now I just wanted it to stop. I saw a bridge of rainbows arcing over towards me, tangled words and meaning. It struck me on the side of the neck and I felt the pain of penetration.

Blackness.

Clarity.

I woke lying in a bed with my skull aching and my body feeling sore and battered. Had Grip removed the shroud from my back? I didn't know. I could smell things as clearly as I had in Brease's house and those smells made molecular patterns in my mind. A multitude of cleaning, anti-biotic and anti-bacterial chemicals, the hormonal output of humans, the knots of pheromones, food smells in a startling variety, most of which I could identify and more besides. Hearing was just as intense. I could hear the susurration of Mobius Grip and could divine the AI lay some fifty feet away from me, beyond a door and down a corridor. I could hear people talking – mostly interpersonal stuff I felt embarrassed to listen to. Somebody was having noisy sex, somewhere. Electronics buzzed and chattered. Materials shifted and strained, producing a symphony that told me I was inside the *Surgeon General*. Other things were coming through and I just did not know what they were: a multi-layered buzzing of a billion bees, and when I focused on that I began to see patterns and hurriedly retreated from trying to understand them. I lay there frightened to open my eyes.

Grip was coming.

The food smell increased and I knew precisely what would be on the tray a woman carried as I also sought to identify the components of the perfume she wore.

'You will be able to suppress the input to your brain,' said the AI, before he came through the door, and, retrospectively identified as speaking in a sound spectrum outside of conventional human hearing.

'How?' I sighed, only then realising I had subvocalised in the same area of the sound spectrum, yet having no idea how I had doneso. Had my vocal cords been altered?

Mobius Grip came in through the door. I opened my eyes tentatively on the bright room they had me in. I could see even further into the infra-red and ultra-violet and things were confusing at first. I wished I could just see my surroundings normally as I tried to focus on the shifting masses of colour that were Mobius Grip and the woman walking in behind him and, oddly, my perception of them tightened and they returned closely to how I would have seen them before my unfortunate swim. And I knew what he was going to say before he said it.

'I put neural blockers and filters in your skull,' the AI told me in a normal voice. 'Knowing how you did not react well to an aug, I thought a limited intervention better. They are giving you control over the data from your enhanced senses and the feedback loop with the creature on your back.'

I reached up and touched my scalp, which felt sore, and finally found a hard hemisphere of material about an inch across behind my right ear. Next a belatedly absorbed the other import of his words.

'You haven't removed it,' I said leadenly. I stared at the AI as the woman put a tray of food on a swing in table and raised the bed so I sat upright. I turned to her, 'My apologies and thank you – I've been a bit preoccupied.'

'And you will be hungry, at the rate your new friend is growing,' she replied. 'And because of the changes that have occurred inside you.'

'I will leave you with Meline,' said Grip. 'I have some deep study to do and a long conversation with Earth Central upcoming.'

'Why didn't you remove it, Grip?' I asked.

'Meline will explain.' With a dismissive wave of his tentacular body he slid out the door and gone.

Meline swung the table in before me. I realised I had cut down the intensity of the smells to human normal, but even so the food smells hit me now. I experimented with that, raising my perception of smell and lowering it. I did the same with my hearing. It was an odd sensation but familiar from when I had an aug. It wasn't as if I could simply think them to where I wanted them but as if I had control over some new facility with my senses, like blurring the eyes or crossing them.

'I'm surprised I can smell so much,' I said. 'What has grown in my nose?'

'Eat your food,' she said.

I turned my attention to a plate piled high with pork steaks and roast vegetables. Briefly I read patterns in the random arrangement but appetite took over and I dug in quickly. Meline pulled up a chair and watched me until I had inhaled about half the plateful.

'The creature on your back,' she began, 'has enhanced your senses in numerous ways. You asked about your sense of smell, well, those marks on your face are anosmic receptors.' I nodded, still mostly concentrating on the food and she continued. 'We haven't completely nailed down all the changes. Your vision and hearing have been enhanced in your eyes and ears with the nerves to your brain multiplying to take the data. Other organs are growing inside you too and it seems likely they can receive portions of the EMR spectrum outside of what you can see with your eyes.'

I stopped eating. 'I'm pretty sure I picked up on digital transmissions, and perhaps analogue synaptic…'

She nodded gravely. 'Seems plausible.'

'What else?'

'Obviously this mass of data was simply too much for you to handle and that's why you reacted as you did outside the ship.'

'There is purpose here,' I said.

'It seems so. Your problem was due to the order of growth inside you.'

'Meaning?'

'The creature on your back has processing – a brain. It is apparently growing as an adjunct to you, but also a buffer, in that it would assist you in handling the increased data you are receiving. Unfortunately the growth within you has outpaced its growth so, as an adjunct to your mind, as additional processing, it wasn't ready.'

I finished the food and still felt hungry. I then thought about how perhaps I should not eat any more because that would accelerate the growth of my companion.

'And removal?' I asked.

'Maybe not a good idea.'

'What?'

'It has made such radical changes to your body that removal is difficult at present. Beyond the gross physical changes it has altered you to the cellular level – even your DNA is different. We could remove the thing itself but the changes in your body without management...'

'I have neural filters now to control the sensory input,' I noted. 'And then all the other stuff can be removed. Surely?'

'I don't think you've quite understood what I am saying. They are radical changes. To return you as you were before would require us to load you across to some substrate, grow you a new body and load you back into that. What has happened to you is beyond repair – the only option is some form of replacement.'

I just sat there gaping at her. All polity citizens have grown up with some set ideas: their lives could be practically eternal, any injuries they received could be repaired... the greatest dangers were through accident and the malevolent intent of others, and the chances of these were steadily being reduced in Polity society. To be told they could not repair me seemed ludicrous. But then she hadn't precisely said that. They could do something. They could just copy me across into a new body, or I could move into crystal or some other substrate, I could become AI, as such, if I wanted. But I liked my body. I was attached to it.

'It's not all bad news,' she added. 'From what we have learned thus far about the growth of this creature it seems to have a limitation – a point of maturity – whereby it is capable of independent existence.' She looked thoughtful. 'We think.'

'You think?' I managed.

'Okay, we're not sure about anything at this juncture. It seems apparent that this creature has a purpose in attaching to you. We don't know what. We haven't quite decoded its genome… in fact we're not even ten per cent in, but we have run projections on what we have seen and it looks like it will reach maturity and detach from you.'

'But leaving all its changes inside me.'

'Yes.'

'You said purpose?' And as I asked these words I increased my perception of her – not enough to be painful, but to get a more accurate reading.

'Why is it increasing your senses?' she asked. 'What could possibly be its reason for that in terms of evolution? The obvious answer would be that of a parasite making its host stronger to increase its own survivability. This is not uncommon. Yet, why the change in the biology of the shroud skate? How is it managing to key into what is effectively alien biology? There are so many questions.' She waved her hands at this puzzle. But then she went on enthusiastically. 'But you mustn't be too pessimistic about this. The changes it has made in you, despite that hiccup outside, are all enhancements many pay highly for in the Polity. We have seen no sign as yet of it causing you harm – beyond the way it is taking nutrients from you to feed its own growth.'

I smiled, and it was a good realistic smile. 'Talking of nutrients – any chance of something more to eat?' I gestured at the empty plate. 'That felt like nowhere near enough.'

She smiled back and stood, picked up the tray and departed. I watched her out the door and nodded to myself. She was very good and the lies were buried in truths as they fed me more and more data about the shroud on my back and what it was doing to me. But it had become evident they knew more than they were telling and did not want to take the thing off. They were delaying that option. I thought about Mobius Grip out at the islet. An AI of his kind was described as a forensic AI – he had capabilities beyond those of an autosurgeon and beyond those of a standard surgical AI. I had no doubt that so shortly after the shroud had attached to me its growth into my body, and the alterations it had made, had not been so extensive he could not have reversed them there and then. Another point occurred: Grip had not left me on the islet to swim back as a salutary lesson, but to delay things, to allow the shroud to grow.

I flipped the bed cover aside and swung my legs over the side. They had dressed me in a paperwear overall. Was that just to add a small difficulty to me inspecting the thing on my back? I walked over to a screen on the wall to set it to mirror. The usual tap on the side frame did not work and I wondered if this might be another attempt to slow me, to keep me from finally learning the truth. I called up the menu and searched through, found a room cam and initiated it, stripped the overall down to my waist then routed the picture from the cam to the screen.

Fuck.

The shroud had moved higher up and grown to two hand lengths across reaching to the edges of my back. Its tail ran down my spine to the top of my butt crack, while at its head end some complicated screwed up organ had grown. I felt horribly aware of this just down from the back of my neck. I reached round to confirm all this by touch, felt it shift against me as if to let me know, 'Yes, I'm still here.' I reached over and touched that screwed up thing and felt it shift, like it had begun to eagerly unfold, and snatched my hand away. I went back and sat on the bed.

What the hell could I do? Those aboard this ship did not want to remove the shroud, yet they were the only ones here who could. Did I need to get the hell out of here, off-world, and try to find some illegal surgeon to do the job? Even then I didn't think I would have much luck because I had gleaned truth from half-truth and I believed the task to be very complex – AI complex. Find a black AI? No, stupid idea. The only response I could find in myself was a quite childish one. I searched the room and found my clothing cleaned and folded up in the cupboard beside the bed. Stripping off the paperwear I had dressed by the time Meline returned.

'It's maybe not a good idea for you to be moving around so soon,' she said, putting the tray down on the swing table. 'We have more tests and observations to make.'

'Things to do,' I said. 'Sorry about the food.'

I headed out of the door, quickly found my way through the ship and out down the ramp. It annoyed me that my stomach had rumbled loudly as I left, and that the only response I had was to be intransigent.

Brease was nowhere around when I arrived back at the house. I used my room computer to key into the colony U-space transmitter and the Polity net. Nobody came for me as I made enquiries and searched down information. I felt I had to be doing something but ended up banging my head against a brick wall. Independent AI surgeons were available but when I made queries they needed detail on my condition. I then tried linking to the *Surgeon General* to see if I could obtain that detail and it surprised me by being available. Transmitting it to five AI surgeons got the same response: no.

I headed out and found a restaurant. Ordered a large meal and ate it, then ordered the same again and ate that too. My insides felt like stone and I started to find my control of the neural filters slipping. Returning to my room I desperately needed the toilet and as I shit the shroud shifted rhythmically on my back and something happened with its tail where it led down to my buttocks. A glance in the toilet before the autoflush worked confirmed my suspicion: a narrow black turd mixed in with my own shit. It seemed the shroud had needed to empty its bowel too. I walked around, picked things up and put them down, and just could not think what to do other than return to the ship. But I needed to calm down first. Then the thought, the feeling, quite intense, arose in me that a good swim would help – I always felt calmer and more balanced afterwards. In retrospect I see the insanity of the choice, but I didn't see it then. I stripped, pulled on my trunks and dressed over them again, picked up my pack and headed for the door.

'You okay?' asked Brease.

'Fine – going for a swim.'

Her hormonal output had waned and I read the tone of her words and her expression. The sight of the shroud on my back had quelled what had been growing in her. Now categorised in her mind as 'damaged' I was no longer a suitable mate. This perception made me feel very uncomfortable and I quickly moved on.

Away from the house I reduced the filtering and found my perception of those things beyond standard human senses integrating more easily in my mind. Through this integration I was beginning to get a holistic view of my surroundings. I could now see, by the settlement's construction, that it had a degree of impermanence. Past perceptions also integrated and I sensed the almost holiday air of the place – we are here doing this settlement thing but the Polity is out there and we are part of that.

On the track leading into the Troos I paused and, girding myself, stepped off and walked out on tangle-grass, reducing the filtering further. Yes I could see endless letters, words and phrases in the languages I knew. I could see fragments of meaning that I naturally attempted to tie together into larger meaning, but it wasn't dragging me in. Even when I increased reception of my additional senses I didn't crash and burn. I recognised cheeps and burring sounds as ultrasound communication of arthropods in the grass. I felt the wash of digital and synaptic com from the settlement and just tuned it out. The chemistry I really did read and found elements of simple language and, noting a different twist to the chemical signatures from below my feet made a logical leap to the grass there broadcasting damage. Other complex chemicals arose from grass showing small pod-like growths and another leap gave me something akin to 'ready to pollinate' or whatever it was they did. I stepped back to the track and continued.

Under the Troos I picked up on similar plant communications that resembled human pheromones. However, the creatures that lived in the Troos informing their fellows that transport might be available, drowned this out. I felt joyful and understood a truth in the things I had been told before: the shroud had now kicked in as additional processing and the input no longer overloaded me.

Finally at the beach I stripped off, walked down to the water's edge, put on my blister goggles and gazed out at the slow roil of the sea. I felt neither fear not anxiety about swimming yet of course I should have. Instead my mind began straying to other things about this world and the situation here. I had felt the impermanence behind me and now sensed that it might be by design. I knew the history of this place and the fear that old dangerous technology might have been here and then, as I waded in, I thought about coincidences that probably were not. I stood there touching my face, feeling the imperfections of the anosmic receptors, feeling the shroud on my back but not as the dead weight of something that should not be there. When I reached back over my shoulder and probed the screwed up protrusion at its upper end it just felt natural to tug at it and pull it open and up. I was simply doing something I had done many times when swimming in a wet or dry suit. The mass acceded to my tugging and moved by itself. I didn't have to do much as the organic hood rolled up over my head and slid masklike protrusions across my face to leave my eyes, nose and receptors clear. It closed over my mouth too and pushed a nub of something inside up against my teeth. My breathing naturally slowed as I took in high oxygen content and I breathed out through my nose. Where had I got the diving suit? I briefly forgot myself as perception expanded and I dived in.

In the water the chemical complexities were vast and wide ranging and I automatically began assembling them into language structures. I picked a great deal of sound too and did the same with that. However this time, unlike it had been on land, meanings arose in my mind with incredible ease. They should not have and I realised they were being fed to me by my adjunct, by sub-processor, my shroud.

This realisation snapped me back to reality and to a sense of myself. I felt a moment of panic on realising that my mind had just gone on a haitus, then an abrupt sharp rise in my perception and understanding. Even as I, and the shroud, continued processing chemical and sound language around me, many things past and present began to come together in my mind. I thought about how it had been difficult for me to find a practical experience placement in languages until the opportunity here was all but pushed on me. I thought about how there were two main aspects to me: my facility with languages and my love of swimming. I then combined this with the coincidence of what seemed to be a biotech device latching onto me while I swam in an alien ocean – a device that hugely augmented my senses and that facility with languages. And I thought about Mobius Grip and the neural filters he had put on me, and how placement of such devices should not have required part of my skull being removed. It was all there: the whole pattern and the story. In deeper water I saw the shadows appearing all around, the shifting off the bottom as the wide thick bodies stirred silt and rose from it, and as the sea all around me filled with shrouds.

'Okay, Mobius Grip, it seems I am where you want me to be,' I said, subvocalising as I had when I had woken up. 'What now?'

'I wondered how long it would take you,' the AI replied.

The shrouds were speaking and the water around me filled with the confusion of their language. My attention divided between Grip and the data swirling around in the circuit between my shroud and my mind, I started to pick up fractured meanings and repetitions. I snared one of them and probably didn't have it right. I told them 'shut up' and 'too much'. It started to die off as they swirled around me, occasionally nudging me, but being mostly chemical language it did not cut off quickly as would other forms of communication. Their words floated around me.

'Now tell me the truth,' I said to Grip.

'Well you are in it now so there's no reason not to,' said Grip. 'You understand that by the complex biology of this world we feared that maybe there was Jain tech here?'

'Yes, I know that.'

'No Jain tech here.'

'But there is certainly something,' I said. 'Shroud technology?'

'Good guess but not quite right. We just don't know the antecedents, but it is evident that this world was once occupied by a race able to manipulate and modify biology. One creature on this world, we have divined, was a biotech tool with a limited degree of independent intelligence that has since developed...'

'The shroud.'

'Precisely. And while we were studying them we noted that they had become aware of us. They wanted to talk and we tried, but obtained little beyond technical data – the conceptual part of their language, if they even have one, has remained opaque to us. It seemed they became aware of that and ceased their attempts at communication with us for some time. Then they came back with a simplistic design for what currently sits on your back.'

'After one of their kind mistakenly attacked a human they gleaned biological data,' I said, seeing that perfectly clear.

'Quite.' Grip paused for a while and as he did I could begin to sense, through the shroud, a transmission of digital synaptic data. I quickly ascertained that its source was my skull and at first assumed it to be my communications with him. But there was an awful lot of data. Of course, Grip had put more in my skull than a neural filter and a way of communicating with me, he had keyed into my circuit with the shroud.

'I suppose you are getting a lot more now,' I said. 'You've stuck a spy in my skull.'

'We are getting a lot more but, it is essential you talk to them. You have a very interesting mind which was part of the reason we chose you. You make leaps of intuition that sometimes escape analysis.

'And another part of course was my love of swimming.'

'Yes, that too.'

I felt a brief stab of anger. The damned AI would remove what it had put in my skull when this was over, but I understood the urgency. That the shrouds were once a biotech tool was immaterial – this was, in its way, first contact with an alien intelligence.

I turned my full attention back to the complex chemicals in the water and the now only occasional sounds of their communication. I visualised those chemical and began making comparisons with the unknown 'words' in the vocabulary of my shroud. However, without any way of connecting these to external reality I seemed to be getting nowhere. I sank deeper into myself and into the shroud – our connection tightening. The vocabulary opened to me as the shroud truly did become an adjunct. The sound communications would of course be for speedy communication and the chemical ones for more complex matters and as signposts. This gave me leverage. I began to see negatives and positives.

'Not shut up,' I said, the sound pulse issuing from my back along with chemical affirmation.

After a pause the sea filled with their voices again and I sank into it, hardly conscious of what I was doing. Feedback came then from Grip: molecular images, chemistry, speculative relations. This threw switches in the hardware in my skull and I understood I had a broad data link directly to Grip's mind. I spilled my thoughts there, increased comparisons and speculations and began to form a ghost understanding of the shrouds' conceptual language. I got the concept of time and understood a great deal of it had passed, and it became evident they had no idea about their beginnings. I understood their concept of ownership and felt at last I was getting to something they were truly trying to communicate.

Hours passed under the water. At one point, when the need drove me, I surfaced and breathed the air through that thing in my mouth – obviously the shroud had run low on the oxygen to supply me, or could not keep up with demand. Returning below I found they understood we were from elsewhere and, by and by, they gave me their message. I was still hanging in the water processing their language, seeking out nuance, but the message had been plain. I surfaced from the frenetic activity of my mind to see there were less of them around me, and more were departing all the time.

'There is more to it than that,' said Grip.

'I know, and it is something we will learn in time,' I replied. 'But you have a firmer grip' – I winced at the use of the word – 'on their language and so can negotiate.'

'I can indeed.'

I began to swim for the shore and as I did so the mask and hood slid from my head. Still swimming, I felt and understood the levers of my control of it, and internally sent my instruction. The shroud loosened from my back and its connection loosened from my mind. A terrible sense of loss arose in me as it detached, but I kept on swimming. Glancing back I saw it hanging in the water, its side wings shifting. It was a biotech machine without the intelligence of the creatures that made it.

'It will die,' said Grip. 'It wasn't made to support its own life.'

I hung there in the water looking at the thing. I still felt the sense of loss but wondered how much of it had been my own. I swam on, then looked back again. Swimming without the grace of its creators it was following me. I gritted my teeth and kept going, turning my mind to Brease and the other colonists at the settlement. I would collect my belongings and head for the *Surgeon General*. I really didn't want to be around when they were told that they had to leave this world again. The message had its nuance, its room for manoeuvre and negotiation, its option for continued communication, but at its heart it had been: get off of our world.

I came close to the shore, the shroud flopping at the surface behind me. There I paused and studied it. I felt dim now, my grasp of language certainly enhanced by my senses but with a large component now missing. And I felt sad and bereft.

'Life support for it could be provided,' I said to Grip.

'Yes, it would be simple enough.'

I waded back out to it, snared it and hauled it up out of the water and round onto my back. It pushed against me eagerly, and I allowed it to reattach.

I suspected we would be together for a very long time.

This was a story on demand. I don't much enjoy writing to someone else's requirement. I find that the tightness of the parameters has a direct relationship to creativity. The more demands on me to stick to a script the more writing the story becomes a slog. This is why, besides work I had to do, I finally said no thanks to writing stories based on computer games to be turned into short films on Prime. However, since the only requirement here was that it be related to London for London Centric *edited by Ian Whates (Oct 2020), I could let rip with some Polity weirdness.*

SKIN

The diamond tendrils of the Terpsichorean Tower's roots penetrated deep below the ancient London Underground and the subterranean main line stations of the Transworld Net. Created by the laser casting of carbon threads, they first issued from boring machines, now deep in bedrock and slowly decaying. The fibres tangled with other roots winding below the city to hold the three-miles-tall edifice upright – looming over the diamond-film-preserved relic that was the Shard. Originally erected as a centre of the arts of dance and music as per the muse of the same –Terpsichore – the tower had changed over the years into a centre for all the arts. Rhea learned all this as her aircar, which bore the outward appearance of an ancient ground car called a Delorean, settled on one of the car parks extended from the side of the tower like sprouting honey mushrooms. She then delved into Greek mythology about Terpsichore and the origins of her own name, before growing bored with stuff she had looked at many times before. The stylish aug behind her ear enabled her connection to the AI net and other strata of computing so that information sat only a thought away. She reached up and touched the flat glass comma running its nano-layer to show any pattern of colour she chose, or fade from sight against her presently pale blue skin. It was modern and very chic, but shortly she intended to have it removed.

She climbed out of the car into cool sunshine, put on her positively retro sunglasses and headed towards the dropshaft at the centre of the parking area. Her aug connection opened a map in her visual cortex – her third eye. She banished it with a mental blink and from her data store sent an address to the building AI. It acknowledged this by briefly displaying the map again with a highlighted location and the word 'Set'. Options then appeared in peripheral vision and she chose 'Direct'.

Curved slippery edges and other features gave the mouth of the dropshaft the appearance of the burrow of an alien creature much like a trapdoor spider. She jumped the edge and fell down into the tube curving through the stalk of the mushroom, the irised gravity field gently closing around her. It pulled her down and then into the building, flicked her through junctions where others shot by, then up into the spine shaft for a ten minute flight before dragging her out again through another series of tunnels. She finally slowed to a stop beside an arched entrance, whereupon the field pushed her through.

Cannon Street Mall stretched for half a mile to a giant window looking out across the glittering towers and air bridges of the city. Thousands of people crowded here. Some were melting-pot base standard, but the demographic here tended to the 'artistic', so most wore a variety of hues and styles. She noted how the body shapes were generally standard human, since the zeitgeist here favoured exterior artistic expression – they tended to make art rather than be it, as was the inclination over at Bodimod Circus. She made her way through, her destination framed out for her whenever she looked towards it, but concentrated on the crowd. Many gathered at the centre of the mall, where an opera was being performed. Centre-stage stood a scorpion-shaped war drone, with a number of singers in bizarre antediluvian dress floating around it on grav harnesses. Auging into the audio for a second, she heard music from The Magic Flute. The war drone's presence baffled her. She passed a completely naked troop performing ballet, their skin pure gold; stopped to watch a lone dance expressionist, her mobile tattoos displaying pre-Raphaelite paintings, but, seeing that the woman still wore an aug, lost interest and moved on. She was after something more radical.

Music was everywhere and she could sample it via her aug, or set her hearing to normal to experience it when she walked into a sound field. She watched a nanodust sculpture of Michelangelo's David until it collapsed to the floor then steadily rebuilt itself into Cellini's Perseus. The mobile glass sculpture of a hooder, full size so like a spoon-headed centipede a hundred feet long, wormed through the crowd. An angel floated overhead dropping feathers that collapsed into silver worms. One touched her bare arm and sank into her skin leaving a temporary brand of text in some ancient language. Others exploded into snowflakes – real snowflakes. It was all very distracting and delightful, but finally she reached the entrance to her destination.

In the circular room beyond the door stood a pedestal-mounted statue of an old, bald man. He wore a half-helmet augmentation on the side of his head, while his open coat revealed an extra pair of shiny robot arms extending from his waist, sporting surgical implements.

'Sylac,' she said.

'In one of his manifestations,' a voice replied. 'But certainly not his present one.'

The surgeon-cyberneticist had been a purveyor of black market augmentation. He had died of old age, or been assassinated by a Polity agent or transcended his physical form to record himself to the crystal substrate of a white dwarf – whichever story you preferred. The last, Rhea knew, was rubbish. She had worked for Earth Central Security in her younger years and knew that Sylac's consciousness had been permanently incarcerated in Soul Bank. He had avoided the death penalty for his crimes because the outfall from them was still on going and the AIs turned to him for information. Why a forensic AI had not yet taken him apart and collated the data from his mind was the only puzzle regarding his fate.

'Is it true that you studied under him?' she asked, turning to the woman who had just stepped through an oval door that had opened in the back wall.

'Since that connection gets many people in here, do you think I would deny it?' the woman asked.

Rhea studied Arbealas Chrone. Her face was conventionally beautiful, but then only Blane Recidivists and similarly antiquated stylists chose ugliness nowadays, and they had no place in Terpsichorean Tower. Her face might have been one found on a Greek urn – her black hair similarly piled. At average height and her figure hourglass, she wore low-waist leggings of snake skin, brassy sandals and a brassy steam punk bra. These exposed her slim waist and the mica windows of data ports running down her sides.

'Of course not,' Rhea replied. 'Anyway, it's a matter of record that you were interrogated. And the AI notice of caveat emptor is real.'

'So you must beware, of course. You're here for the skin and have presumably researched all that entails?'

'I am and I have.'

Chrone gestured to the door behind her. 'Then let us begin.'

Chrone led her straight through an empty waiting room and into the surgery. The place had a decidedly retro feel with a surgical chair that could fold out into a table, and pedestal-mounted telefactor surgeons with multiple gleaming arms sporting sharp implements. Chrone moved ahead of her to a lectern station and rested a hand on it. Rhea kept studying the equipment here. The two surgeons weren't what she had come here for. The other item, similarly mounted but resembling the upright spoon-headed end of a hooder, also rendered in gleaming metal, was. Its multiple limbs were all folded in so she could not see their tools. However, she knew it ran to nano needles and matter printing heads. A similar array might be seen in a parlour offering mobile tattoos like those of the expressionist dancer outside, but this was much more sophisticated.

'I get the whiff of antiquity here,' she said.

'The surgical chair is one that Sylac used, while the surgeons are replicas. It is at this point that many potential customers have second-thoughts and begin to give the AI warnings credence.'

Rhea smiled. 'So you only want customers who are sure, and who really know what they are doing, else you would have made this place more…welcoming.'

'Precisely.'

Rhea reached down to the buckle on her jeans belt and touched the button there. With a fizzing sound the jeans unravelled, their fibres drawing back up her legs and disappearing into her belt. A moment later, her white silk blouse similarly collapsed leaving her standing there in black knickers, belt and Perghosh heels. She took off the belt and hung it over a hook beside the door. Ripped off the disposable knickers, balled them and tossed them over by a cleanbot hole at the base of the wall. While she was taking off the decidedly expensive heels a bot, like a yellow beetle the length of her hand, came out of the hole and snatched up her knickers. It was biotech she noted – fed on organics in rubbish to power itself. She frowned for a second and hung up the heels too – you could never be too careful with Pergosh.

'So you are decided,' said Chrone.

'I'm decided.' Rhea walked over to stand beside the surgical chair and looked over at her. Chrone now stepped up onto the lectern and detached ribbed data feeds from behind it, mating them with the mica sockets in her sides.

'Climb on.' Chrone gestured. 'You'll need to shut down your aug prior to removal.' She looked up. 'You do understand that you'll have to operate on manual until the nerve connections are made and that there will then be a period of adjustment that could last up to a month?'

'I know how to use touch consoles,' Rhea replied, sitting in the chair.

'Lie back.'

She did so, running a relaxing mental mantra in her aug to release the tightness in her stomach, then calling up its shutdown routine. She now felt extreme reluctance. With a thought she could investigate any database she cared to. With a thought she could call for help or perhaps even interface with the robots around her and shut them down. But she had to trust that the data she had obtained through the thing was right; that the reviews of what some were calling octoskin or dermaug were correct. She shut down her aug and it seemed the world around her grew a little darker. Suddenly she was alone in the room with this woman who claimed to be a pupil of a man some called a serial killer.

'Aug shutdown confirmed,' said Chrone. 'Any second thoughts now?'

'Go ahead,' said Rhea.

The surgical robot to her left activated and drifted in. She had a moment of panic, this not being the device she was supposed to go under, but then remembered that her aug needed to be removed first. The chair smoothly tilted back and pads folded in to secure her limbs and head. The robot lowered a 'hand' to the side of her head, the movement of its numerous fingers a subliminal silent flicker. With a hiss of analgesic spray the side of her head numbed. Clicks, tugging and the drone of a cell welder ensued, then the robot's hand drew away with her aug clamped between two spatulate fingers.

'Would you prefer unconsciousness?' Chrone enquired.

'No – I want to see this.'

'Very well.'

The robot raised another hand, clutching a bright cube between four fingers, and pressed this neural shunt against the side of her neck, where it stuck. The area grew cold and numb as the shunt injected its fibres, while the robot retreated. The dearth of feeling spread down through her body, paralysing her.

'A period of unconsciousness will be necessary at completion – when it reaches your head,' Chrone told her. 'But you won't be able to see much then anyway.'

The other robot now slid silently on its pedestal to the bottom of the surgical couch, where it bowed over her feet, concealing them. She watched it hinge out in its numerous limbs and press styli and other devices against her skin. A weird sensation ensued as the clamps all folded away from her. Just for a second she felt she was falling, but then the mod to her inner ear registered antigravity and adjusted as she rose from the couch. She felt no pain but she did feel movement and the tugging at her body as the robot, extending on a thick ribbed spine from its pedestal, crawled up her legs. A matter printer hissed and crackled – frenetically at work. The procedure did involve skin removal but intercellular and mostly fluid sucked away by nanotubes. The printer was now building the complex structures of octoskin in her own: its micro-muscles and chromatophores, its meta-material computing, sensory beads, nanoptic and superconducting wires and nerve array.

She felt very little and could see because the robot's present work lay underneath it, while it blocked her view of all it had done. But then an oval drone, with darting red eyes around its rim and small sharp limbs folded below them, floated over. It tilted, bringing its mirrored underside to the correct angle, and now she could see her feet. Bruises shifted like storm clouds, lines of rainbow colour fled across skin leaving nacre scales that after a moment faded too.

'The colours you see are the chromatophores running a test routine,' Chrone told her. 'By the time you leave here your skin will be back to a base setting. I'm removing the blue-shift melatonin analogue so it will return to your natural colour.'

Rhea couldn't remember her natural colour, so that would be interesting. She wanted to ask about the micro-muscular structures, but the neural shunt had closed off everything but autonomous function below her neck, and that included her voice box. But apparently others had asked the question before.

'The muscular hydrostats will not run a test routine until the nerve web has established. The neural plasticiser the robot will inject, when it reaches your head, will facilitate the nerve web and interlinked computing, but you will still be on a steep learning curve.'

Rhea of course knew all about that. She had attended virtualities on the AI net made by others who had undergone this procedure. But she felt sure she would not have their lack of control or sometimes hysterical reactions. She was, after all, much older and had seen and done a lot during her long life, including many years of body morphing.

As it reached her hips, the robot turned and wrapped around her body almost in a ring as it traversed upwards towards her face. Its limbs were a dense forest of gold and silver moving so fast they were a blur. A smell as of cooking meat reached her nostrils, and she could see a misty haze rising from the robot's work. When it reached her waist and then her breasts she was able to tilt her head to examine it closely. She saw thousands upon thousands of needles penetrating her skin, small reels of computing substrate unwinding and sliding in through small slices, severed and pushed in before a Cellweld head zipped up the cuts, sensory beads like metal dust emptying from globular containers as injectors like sewing machine needles punched them into her skin. Larger transparent needles injected fluids – synthetic blood and plasma, colourful hydrogels holding glints of nanowire. Finally as it reached her breastbone she put her head back because she could no longer see.

'Now, briefly, you will sleep,' said Chrone.

The world went away.

Rhea woke to the sensation of her skin crawling, prickling and feeling sunburnt. The surgical couch lifted her up as it folded back into a chair. She opened her eyes and they too felt sore, but a moment later a robot used an airblast injector on her neck and the sensations faded to an odd numbness, as if her skin had transformed into a tight body suit then, even as this dispersed, it suddenly felt loose and alien to her.

'You can get out of the chair now,' said Chrone.

Rhea peered down at her body. Her completely white skin sparked a memory of a pale girl in a mirror with long blond hair in braids. She reached up to a skull previously covered with black cropped hair. She was bald now. The procedure had removed all her hair right down inside the follicles and adjusted them back to their base setting too, but it would take a while to grow back, blonde now. The idea of hair somehow repelled her but when she tried to mentally examine why, the feeling skittered away. Swinging her legs off the chair she stood up, the floor chill against sensitive soles through which she could now feel its slightly roughened texture. She closed her eyes for a second, focusing on that and, as if she was still wearing her aug, got a flash of its micro-diamond pattern scattered with cleanroom suction holes made to draw away debris. She moved, trying to propel herself with her feet in a way that made her stumble, but then remembered how to walk, and that felt odd too. Waving an arm through the air, she felt the air currents intensely.

'You will be very sensitive for a while, until you adjust,' Chrone told her.

She even felt the sound impact of the woman's words from head to foot. Already the sensory beads scattered through the dermal layers had to be providing data, so the nerve and computing webs must be making connections. She turned to study Chrone, behind her lectern, and felt something utterly wrong about her. Chrone seemed hard and angular, and somehow denuded of substance. Shaking her head, Rhea asked, 'Is there anything I need to know that is not in your catalogue or in the virtualities?'

'All humans are unique and the implantation is always tailored, therefore its effects too will be unique,' said Chrone. 'However, you are not so far from some arbitrary human norm for them to be too... outrageous.'

She walked carefully over to where she had hung her belt and stared at it, dreamy, disconnected. It felt almost an autonomous function when she unhooked the belt and put it on, feeling its complex meta-material texture stark against her skin. When she activated it and her jeans began establishing down her legs, the threads spread across her skin and linked with an intense textural sensation. She grunted, surprised by a brief orgasm as the fabric rounded her crotch, wriggling over her vagina. Glancing at Chrone, she saw the woman had stepped down from the control lectern and turned away, now detaching the data feeds from her sides. The ribbed leads seemed natural to Rhea and Chrone detaching them a mutilation. This crazy perception lasted just a moment, until she told herself aug withdrawal must be the cause or it was a side effect of the procedure to overcome. She took a slow easy breath and tried to be calm.

Rather than use the previous setting, she chose black for the shirt and it welled out of the top of her belt. She pulled it on her arms and up her back, the sensation darkly luscious – sensuous. As it slid over her nipples she gritted her teeth as another orgasm built. Turning away from Chrone again, she ran a finger up to close the stick seam then squeezed both her nipples, bringing the orgasm to completion and this time managing it quietly.

'How long before my skin is less sensitive than this?' she asked.

'It will never be any less sensitive, in fact the reverse. However you'll adjust to that just as people learn to accommodate bat hearing or eagle sight.'

'Yes,' said Rhea, suddenly unreasonably angry at the woman. This was due to the snooty observation – nothing to do with Rhea suddenly feeling uncomfortable in Chrone's presence. She suppressed the feeling, tried to be reasonable and see beyond this room. She thought about all those crowds out there, and the prospect elicited a tight clench of panic in her torso, and then excitement. Groping for rationality, she understood that for damned sure this intensity of sensation would become wearing. She reached up, unhooked the Perghosh heels and put them on. They felt decidedly uncomfortable and she briefly considered going barefoot, but then thought fuck that – if there was something she wanted to accommodate first, it was wearing designer footwear. What else was there to discuss? She had paid up front, all the legal work had been done and her house AI had all the information she needed on this process.

'Thank you,' she said.

'My pleasure,' Chrone replied.

Rhea got out of there fast.

The textures, air currents and sounds in the mall were overwhelming, while just the act of walking kept bringing her to orgasm every – she counted it – twenty-three paces. But pleasure was not the only sensation. Text, written on her wrist by an angel, stung and then spread up her arm, diffusing and fracturing across her skin. She looked up, wanting to tear the thing down out of the air, as a wave of opera music elicited a hot unpleasant flush. She walked quickly while the tinkling bells of an expressionist dancer fell on her back like bee stings. Snowflakes on her bald pate felt cold and enjoyable, but when they melted they produced a cascade so pleasurably intense it almost hurt.

Then something new occurred. A man with mobile rainbow tattoos walked past and the painfully bright colours made her suck a sharp breath, as for a brief moment she saw with more than just her eyes. A few paces beyond, the bright red of a woman's dress felt like the output of a photonic heater; the blue of a hermaphrodite's eyes a beam of cold passing over her. It seemed the sensory beads were kicking in early, this was confirmed when she tasted the green of a potted plant with the palm of her hand. The confusion of synaesthesia from the procedure had been well documented – only ameliorated by the integration of the skin's computing and nerve web with her body's nervous system, which had yet to happen. She needed to be away from such an overly stimulating environment.

In the irised gravity field of the dropshaft she really experienced flying, and got some strange looks as she whooped towards her destination. But soon she was in her car and speeding back over the city. She closed her eyes but could not stop seeing the bright buildings below, or feeling the caress of the air conditioner's invisible colours. Opening her eyes again made no difference either way and she knew, from those virtualities, this she just had to bear until those nerve contacts firmed, and she could exert some control over paradigm-shifted senses.

The car landed in her private car port extending from the side of the building, below the fairy bridge that arced over the dome of St Paul's. She climbed out and headed across her balcony, trying but failing to ignore the bright, hot, cold, salty and sweet colours of her collection of terran and alien plants. The chainglass doors slid aside and she walked in, collapsing her clothing back into her belt and kicking off her heels. She felt, tasted and heard the thrum of the growing fibres of her carpet moss through her bare soles as she walked into her bedroom taking off her belt and discarding it, and threw herself down on her bed. From here the room looked too angular and harsh.

'House AI,' she said. 'Give me aquarium.'

A pause ensued while her house AI responded to the vocal instruction, then the screen paint on the walls shaded to blue-green before transitioning to views of a giant aquarium all around. This soothed for a second until a shark swam past. Her skin seemed to creep and shudder and she tried to sink into the bed.

'Tropical fish,' she said, and as the scene changed her reaction to the shark just faded. She looked down at her arm. So white, so like the cotton sheets... She writhed and sensations swamped her. Those sheets whispered against her skin, but also dragged across with sensuous roughness. She reached down to touch herself and experienced an immediate violent orgasm. Now she could not keep her fingers away and the orgasms came hard and fast. Her mind shut down and only came back some hours later when darkness had fallen and the sheet underneath her sodden. Overpowering thirst drove her from the bed. She drank some orange juice but the colour burned and the citrus soaked across her face. Plain water also brought a cascade of sensations but proved a calmer beverage. Having drunk two glasses, it seemed the fluid swirled inside her, signalling a further need, and she stumbled into her wet room.

The shower jets hit her skin but also seemed to pass right through her. She smelled seaweed and heard the crash of waves, but with neither her nose nor ears. A black swirl turned in her head and she now did smell something with her nose, and recognised the odours of shellfish. She came back to herself lying in the bottom of the shower.

'Are you experiencing problems?' her house AI enquired out loud, its words flashes of green and gold. 'I cannot detect your medical feed.'

'I no longer have an aug, I have octoskin and am adjusting to it,' she replied, looking round, a shiver traversing her spine. Did the AI's voice worry her because it had been so long since she heard it – previously always auging her instructions?

'Do you wish me to summon aid?'

It needed to go away because this was her place…

Get a grip.

'No,' she said firmly. 'Just turn off the shower and fill the pool.'

The flow of water ceased. She heaved herself upright, the AI opening the door. Stepping over to the pool recessed in the floor, she fought to still the continuing cascade of sensation and synaesthesia. A strong illusion invaded her mind that her entire body was an eye, and she closed it. The blessed relief lasted only briefly, however. She went down the steps into the pool and sat down in the water flowing in. Thankfully, though it felt as sensuous as the sheets on her bed, she seemed to have used up her body's facility for orgasms. She lay there trying to bear it all as the pool filled up, eventually pulling a pad out from the side to rest her head on as she half floated there. Oddly, waving her arms about and kicking slowly calmed her; though it did not reduce sensation, it felt right. Incredible weariness then found its window, and tugged her into sleep.

Rhea woke with a start, the world blazing around her. She could see everything: the bottom of the pool through the water, the weave of the fabric cushion under her head, the Greek key encircling the mosaic of Perseus holding up the head of Medusa in the ceiling, the edges of the pool and all that lay beyond. Again too much input – an almost painful congestion in her skull. She tried to shut it down, to perceive only what she concentrated on, but this created a huge blind spot, so what she did perceive expanded and stretched around her. Sounds in her apartment transmitted hollowly through the water, but in the air she found their rawness unpleasant. Concentrating on the sensation of touch as she moved her limbs, the water swirling up her body at last calmed her. Sensations slid into each other – synaesthesia returning with relaxation, meagre as it was – the water green jelly touching her with glutinous fingers, the tiles humming, appliances shifting around her in a hunting shoal. When she exerted more control she stilled the synaesthesia but the intensity increased again. She kept switching between the two states until aware of other signals from her body: the need to use the toilet and the hungry tightening of her stomach. Prosaic reality impinged and that in itself brought its own relief.

Reluctantly she climbed out of the pool, sensitive to the texture and temperature of the tiles under her feet, feeling precarious and wishing she could have a firmer hold on them. Drying herself with a towel, she individually felt its absorbent bumps and hollows between and saw, through her skin, that while its material looked white to human eyes it in truth consisted of microscopic rainbow threads. She put on a robe and similarly sensed that, then halted and looked back at the pool, wanting to strip off the garment and climb back into its sanctuary. A surge of self-pity filled her eyes with tears and, both annoyed and sobbing, she turned away from the pool's strange attraction and headed to her toilet. As she sat down she tried hard to recall what she had learned about the procedure – tried to pull back to rationality.

The octoskin used up many physical resources and produced a lot of waste. She looked down and saw dark yellow-green urine as a result. When she emptied her bowels another orgasm threatened, then again when she used the wash pipe. Peering down at her excrement, she noted white swirls there. This had all been detailed in the virtualities. Before the toilet flushed, she quickly reached out and touched the analysis screen in the wall, and checked the readout. Exotic compounds were flagged for her attention along with a blinking alert informing her the block medical AI had been informed.

'Do you require assistance?' her house AI enquired. 'Anomalous substances have been detected in your faecal and urinary matter.'

Rhea flinched. The AI, still here, in her place, watching her. No, no this was nuts. The AI had always been here and all her fucked up emotions were the product of the chemical flood – the detritus in her body. She had to stick to facts. She had to cling to reality.

'Load the octoskin data to house monitoring and forward to the block medical AI too,' she stated.

'Loading…' the AI said, then after a pause, 'All anomalies accounted for but for a high level of tetrodotoxin breakdown products.'

The words drifted in her brain making no sense. She really didn't want to ask – to admit ignorance – stupid irrationality too since the AI was just intelligent hardware in her walls.

'What's that?' she asked.

'It is a toxin produced by puffer fish and by the blue ringed octopus. Shall I forward a report to Chrone Biotech?'

'Yes… yes you do that,' she said, walking away from the toilet as it automatically flushed after its brief scatological diversion.

In the kitchen she poured orange juice again and this time, though the taste and textures of the juice were intense, she enjoyed it. Next calling up the menu on her fabricator she scrolled through it. Everything she saw set her mouth to watering but she did have a particular hankering and soon found what she really wanted. Stepping away as the fabricator did its work she surveyed the room via exposed skin, then in irritation stripped off her robe and tossed it on a counter. Better. She realised that the increased sensory input might lead to a change in her style, involving her wearing far less clothing than she was accustomed to.

'I have not received an acknowledgement from Chrone Biotech,' the AI informed her.

Again she flinched and looked around, half expecting some bulky angular thing to lurch through one of the doorways. She closed her eyes and took a breath, but that did not improve matters, what with the input through her eyes being a fraction of the total. Still no way to turn this off or tone it down, until the hardware established and fully connected to her nervous system. She held onto that.

'Investigate that – I want a response,' she instructed, still with eyes closed tracing the source of the AI's voice to an array of microspeakers inset in the kitchen wall. They felt like intrusion, as if it was coming through the wall. Trying to rise above the feeling she concentrated on the content of their exchange. That Chrone had not replied didn't mean anything – the woman was not exactly conventional and apparently used sub-AI computing in anything work related.

The fabricator pinged and she opened the door. The aroma from inside overwhelmed her, but it was more than just a smell, for she could taste the complex proteins on her skin. Her mouth filled with saliva and her stomach clenched to a strange rhythm. She took out the large insulated pot, the thing feeling unsteady as if she could get no proper grip on it. Ignoring the loaf of fresh bread, she put the pot on her breakfast bar and opened it. The intensity increased to a point where she didn't know if she was ravenous or about to throw up. She scooped out one of the mussels with her bare hand, burning it, the pain jolting up her arm. She pulled out the flesh and shoved it in her mouth. The incredible taste suffused her skull, and, as it went down, the lump of meat produced an ecstatic surge that traversed her whole body. Making a keening sound she reached for the pot again, but managed to regain control before plunging her hand in again.

Calm be calm. Clam, be a clam.

She thumped her fists on the table, gritted her teeth and picked up the first bivalve shell, and using it as pincers went to work on the rest. She had eaten half the pot before thinking to fetch the bread. Pausing by the fabricator, she input other menu items. The mussels were delicious but too fiddly, and she was hungry. Chunks of bread soaked up the sauce and she crammed them in her mouth. By the time she finished the shellfish, the boneless kippers were ready. She practically inhaled them. Steaks of woven cod next, with shelled clams. After that came cockles in pepper vinegar and only when she had gone through a pint of them did the hunger begin to fade. It faded completely when she topped off the meal with two large protein shakes. Heading unsteadily out of her kitchen she felt bloated and just a little bit sick then, sinking into her sofa, abruptly unutterably weary. She closed her eyes.

'I am here,' the voice sighed in her dream, only not quite a voice, but a blend of that, and text, intention, a sense of readiness and a stretching physicality that fractured into a thousand colours. It also seemed she was talking to herself, but about things of which she had no knowledge. She pushed out towards it and felt a membrane break to let in a torrent code, raining down on her, millions of lines establishing, tying together, coagulating into connection.

So nice to have her aug back but, as she swirled up towards consciousness, she knew this must be idle fantasy of a half-asleep mind and aug withdrawal making her grasp for connections that weren't there. Enjoying this fantasy, however, she tried to maintain it and not wake up. Instead, she used the illusory connection to wander in memory to her approach to the Terpsichorean Tower, and her brief venture into its foundations. Floating through old concrete and earth she easily perceived one mass of diamond filaments, braided and running like a root down deep. At its terminus a boring machine sat encased in rock like the alloy and composite grub of some giant robotic beetle. Its sub-AI mind ticked down towards entropy, still drawing power from the filaments behind it. She tried to grasp it and pull it out, but as her hand passed through, and she felt the wash of a mind – satisfied having achieved its purpose, and falling into somnolence – another presence impinged. Something dark and immense loomed on the periphery of her senses – and it spoke:

'Chrone skin job. Tracing. Schizoid division defect.'

With surge of terror she flung herself away, through rock, earth and old concrete, through a jungle of pipes and optics and into a blue tiled tunnel, momentarily bewildered as an underground train passed through her.

'Damn, lost it,' said the voice, fading.

Fleeing this at a slant rising up through layers of detritus, she found herself in a flow of water over cleaner-corals and ribbons of bright green weed. Observing a salmon swimming past she tried to grab it, but her hand passed through. She swam along in lazy pulses above the bed of the Thames, peering up at the old London Bridge, utterly clear to her and well preserved under its stabilising diamond film. It seemed a perfect place, sanctuary and where she must be. And then, because all possessed too much detail and linear logic, her consciousness engaged and she woke up.

Virtuality.

Rhea abruptly sat up, perfectly perceiving everything around her before she opened her eyes. The nerve web and the computing of the skin had made its connections much faster than Chrone had led her to believe. She now had the equivalent of aug connection and it was so much better than before. Perhaps Chrone had developed the skin further in the intervening time and what Rhea had was a higher iteration? It seemed likely because, as she understood it, the woman never stood still and was an inveterate tinkerer. Whatever. Rhea felt a joyous freedom and sense of release. All the data which before she might have read as text or image files in her visual cortex now lay open in virtuality. She looked around her room and made alterations, bringing in an overlay so it seemed she was again at the bottom of the Thames. It was perfect, so perfect it brought tears to her eyes. She blinked, her whole body blinked.

No, stay rational.

She banished the overlay, flowed with the sensation of being, and thought, what now? Now she tried something, connecting to a history database she had often visited and, instead of old paintings of Greek gods, rambling dialogues and pages from old books, she found herself standing in a forest grove where Narcissus gazed lovingly into a pool at his own reflection. She could smell the greenery, hear the animals around her and could sense that some short distance away a centaur might be galloping. She walked to the edge of the pool, but Narcissus ignored her, stirring a finger in the water. The legend in its various forms rolled through her mind with reference links she could follow into other virtualities. But now all she wanted to do was jump in that pool and swim – to lazily move her arms like the scarves of silk weed she could see.

'Hello,' she called, and the mountain nymph Echo replied from the forest while Narcissus kept stirring.

'Tracing again. Slippery bugger,' said the nymph.

She pulled out.

Back in her apartment she sat up. That voice again, which before she had thought just an artefact of dream. Paranoia, some kind of mental breakdown? No, her senses were now and immediate and she felt no blurring of reality and virtuality that had been the complaint of some who wore octoskin. She was rational and it had been real. But now, she noted, her reality had a blemish. A pink wart had risen on her inner thigh. She could see it clearly from her other thigh but now focused her antiquated eyes upon it. Even as she inspected it another rose beside it with a soft 'pop' she would not have heard with her ears, then another and another rose, sketching out a line of them down to her knee. More of them budded on her other thigh and then they really began to spread, her skin bubbling on her legs, up her torso, on her scalp and down her back.

Rhea felt a surge of panic as the grotesque transformation continued, along with disruption of her whole body visual acuity. Disrupted sensation and input ramped up and it became difficult to think clearly. Her skin felt horribly loose and seemed to crawl over her. Remembering those blind spots she had experienced earlier, she mentally pushed for them, and began closing down visual reception over her body. This time she managed it without the previous distortion. This time she managed to close it all down, but now warts were growing on her eyelids. It was this, she remembered, trying to hold herself together, that had caused such hysteria in others. She must accept it as a facility of the skin she needed to control.

She let out a gasping yell and closed her eyes, concentrating her vision in the palm of her hand, holding it over one thigh. Close inspection revealed the shift of hydrostatic micro-muscles under her skin. She searched for connections, trying to closely sense that area of her thigh. Instead she felt it in her hand and, a moment later, opened into a whole new sensory input as if she had acquired further limbs she could move. Turning her hand over, she flexed, while engaging sight from the skin of her forehead. The warts retracted and her palm returned to normal. She began doing the same across all her body, bringing the growths under control and shrinking them back until they were all gone.

Her sense of victory brought a sneer to her mouth. Some people were so weak, but she would succeed where others had failed. She sighed, wiped at a sheen of sweat on her face, incredibly hot now, feverish even. She stood and even before consciously acknowledging it found herself walking into her wet room. A short while later, in the pool and calmer, she began to explore the new facility and found databases she could access as if via aug. Colours washed across internal vision and she chose, turning her hand blue, then yellow. Arrays of patterns were available and she could access more on the AI net, also skin forms. First she etched her hand and arm with a quadrate pattern of black lines, then grew more ambitious and gave herself the scales of a snake, but only as far as her elbow. She tried other patterns and textures of skin and then tried something more radical and, even as she began, felt the enhancement expanding. Visualising her wish, she applied it in intense detail at the wrist. The skin bubbled and expanded and shaped into a facsimile of a watch. She held it for a while and then let it go.

At once, pummelling weariness hit and she lay back on the pool cushion to relax, and slid into a doze, which seemed very brief. When she came out of it her body had changed yet again. Her skin was persimmon with rings of vivid blue about deep black areas. Running down the insides of her legs and the insides of her arms, rows of what looked like large open pustules had risen but which, on closer inspection, she realised were suckers. A surge of panic ran through her upon recognition of the physical features of a blue ringed octopus. She connected up disparate elements of her experience since the procedure: her attraction to water and how it calmed her, her waving about of limbs in the same, her gorging on sea food. But was this real or some artefact of imagination? She forced her body back into conventional human form and quickly climbed out of the pool to squat on the edge.

She needed clarity and answers and now, of course, she could find them. Reaching into the AI net she sought out data on Chrone Biotech. Immediately she found herself in the mall standing before Chrone's clinic. Bars blocked the door and the windows had been blanked out. She reached for further data but all the links here were inert.

'You need help,' said a voice she recognised.

She looked round at a man in the uniform of Polity Medical. He had kind eyes and he reached out for her. She panicked and thrashed his hand away, jetted away from him and crashed back into her body, shutting down her netlinks. Slumping to the floor she began shaking and the urge to crawl back into the pool seemed to tug her across the floor.

'No!' she yelled, and pushed to her feet. She looked around. Another potential threat was here but perhaps it had data she needed.

'House AI, have you yet received acknowledgement from Chrone Biotech or have you found other information concerning it?' she asked, bracing herself to suffer the reply.

'Chrone Biotech ceased business shortly after your procedure there. Many people, and AIs, are trying to trace Chrone but she has disappeared off grid.'

Was this confirmation of something wrong? She pulled on a robe, not caring that this blocked the sensitivity of her skin, and headed into the living room then kitchen. Walking up to the fabricator, she was determined to get herself something non-oceanic but, when the menu came up, made selections without thinking then went to sit at the breakfast bar.

Problems with the skin, she was sure. When her fabricator pinged she opened it and stared at the tray of sushi. With her panic growing she still took it out and ate, but lathering on wasabi to try and kill the taste of the raw fish. Upon finishing she felt suddenly claustrophobic. In her bedroom she picked up her fashion belt, stared at it for a long while, then discarded it. Focusing on her waist she watched a ring darken around it then hump up into a copy of the belt. Her skin copying them, her jeans spread down her legs. On her upper body she gave herself a red blouse then, after a moment, retracted her nipples and filled in her belly button. The thought to copy the Perghosh heels she dismissed, and put them on. They seemed an anchor to sanity. Trying to force her thinking into order she braced herself again and asked, 'Do you know why others are seeking Chrone out?'

'Zzzzt. Interdict. Privacy privacy privacy,' said the AI.

The lights flickered. She backed towards the door.

'I'm going out,' she said.

'Incidents have been reported,' said the AI, as she pushed open the door, but its voice did not sound right. 'The block medical AI suggests you submit yourself for examination.'

Panic rose again and she stepped out into the hall to head for the dropshaft, after a moment breaking into a run, but then pausing to use the manual panel because she dared not use any mental links. She jumped in and the irised gravity field took her down, finally ejecting her into the lobby. She hurried across to the doors and out into the street. Tube? No – too many doors and too many places that could be traps. She walked, at first going by memory rather than summoning a map. Her skin felt odd and seemed to writhe in time with the now almost rhythmic panic. Glancing down, she saw that her shirt emulation had turned orange with dark spots appearing here and there while lumpy growths were rising down the insides of her legs. She ran, utterly sure of where she needed to go, stumbled and nearly went over. Halting to lean against a foamstone wall, she took off the Perghosh heels and stared at them, not understanding their purpose. A siren wailed above and she looked behind and up. An air ambulance was docking to her block. They were coming for her. She tossed the heels aside and ran again.

Pavement passed under her feet. She diverted to a pedway, because there no one could close her in and she ran past startled pedestrians. Someone blocked her and she thrashed them aside leaving shouts behind. More streets then and the ancient road leading to Old London Bridge to her right. She passed down terraces of steps past glaring store fronts and paused gasping for breath to lean against a diamond film-covered Victorian lamppost. Her image stood beside her in an interactive advert, which tried to clothe that image in the latest bodysuit. It didn't match her persimmon skin tone. It clashed with the black centred blue rings, and bulged inappropriately over her suckers. She ran on, for she could taste the water now, in the air, the rush of its passage a cool promise.

'Rhea! Please stop! You need help!'

That voice again.

She dodged right to reach a wall and jumped up, suckers sticking. Up and over and down into a private garden, huge Venus flytraps winking at her. An ambulance howled overhead as she dropped into another garden, skin turning as lumpy and grey as the rockery there. Someone yelled at her. Another wall and then a leap to a lamp post, scuttling down. More steps below and now the Embankment in sight. She ran down, crossed a paved walkway with alfresco bars and restaurants either side. The Thames lay ahead and she ran straight at it, ready to leap the wall, then leaping... and hitting the chainglass screen that extended above it.

Rhea dropped down into a loose crouch. A siren blared to her left as the air ambulance settled. She turned right, but suddenly didn't know how to run, her legs all bony sticks that seemed ill-fashioned for movement. She had to get to the river. Glancing back she saw Polity medics running towards her, a mobile medbot like a steel cockroach overtaking them. Then she saw it: scuppers along the base of the wall – horizontal drain holes a foot wide and a couple of inches deep.

She dropped and stabbed her hand, then her arm through, but jammed at her shoulder. She strained with all her being to get through, but the stupid bony structure inside her just wouldn't go. She strained even harder and felt something rip. Agony speared up her back and began to roll out around her body as the metallic hand of the medbot closed on her ankle. It dragged her from the scupper hole and she pulled away from its grip, parting away from bone and muscle. Screaming, she scrabbled at the ground, her world an agonising red. She saw herself parting along the arms, shedding the load of irrelevant bone and muscle. Disconnection... and Rhea screamed and screamed. She felt her face peeling away and the other departing, a squirming bloody mass oozing along the ground. In dreadful clarity she saw her skin flopping towards the hole as the medbot bathed her in analgesic mist and pressed a neural shunt against her neck. As agony dropped to merely unbearable she saw her skin extending more limbs than she had possessed and drag itself finally to the hole, compressing itself through. At the last, just before it dropped into the river, she felt sure a goatish eye looked back at her.

'Rhea,' said a familiar voice as the world began to grey out. 'We've got you.'

I wrote "Adaptogenic" many years ago (it appeared in Threads 2 *in 1994 and can now be found in* The Gabble *from Macmillan) and it's the first story featuring the bracelet called a 'Four Seasons Changer'. The bracelet has appeared in various places throughout my work and most lately in my last novel* Weaponized. *Here it is again along with the character Jason Chel who appeared in that first story. I wrote "Eels" with little in the way of pauses but then found it falling foul of the chronology of technological development in the Polity books, had to rip it apart and do a lot of rewriting. It's kind of daft the necessity to do this when, as someone who tried reading one of my books once said, 'He just makes stuff up!'*

EELS

The shuttle jolted in atmosphere as Roland headed back from the passenger compartment. Reaching a bulkhead door he tried the handle and the door surprised him when it opened without alarms or queries. Stepping inside, he rounded a handler robot and came to the luggage racks. The passengers had a lot of luggage and some of it was looking at him. Some suitcases here could follow their owners around like dogs, had about the intelligence of the same and could also bite, perhaps making security at the door behind him unnecessary. Not that many people would steal luggage aboard a shuttle. They would have nowhere to go with it and, anyway, most Polity citizens could obtain whatever these cases contained at little or zero cost.

He paced along beside the racks and finally spotted his backpack, sitting behind a wide suitcase that seemed to emanate a sense of bull mastiff. Glassy lenses whirred as he opened the cage door to the rack, and they tracked him as he reached past to snare up his backpack, the suitcase rising slightly on lev and seeming to tense up. As he took his pack out and closed the door the suitcase settled as if in disappointment. It had probably been relishing the prospect of using some of its defences.

He shrugged the pack on and pulled round heavy straps laden with power supply and distributed grav motor which were all part of an integral grav harness. Heading to the back of the luggage hold he put up his envirosuit hood and closed up the visor. Turning left he came to a small ramp door out of which the luggage would later depart, and headed over to the control box. Selecting tools from various pockets, he soon had the cover off the box and the system isolated. He programmed it to open the door just enough, to pause there, and then close up after twenty seconds.

'What the hell are you doing back there?' a voice enquired over the intercom.

The shuttle pilot had spotted him. Roland glanced around to try and find what had alerted the woman, then shrugged and turned back to the door. Cams could be the size of pinheads and other detection systems etched into the paintwork.

'I'm getting off early,' he said.

'That is not permitted since you might endanger other passengers,' she said, and it sounded rote – out of a handbook.

'This shuttle is descending on grav engines and steering thrusters. It has sub-AI correction with a full AI link to the main ship should anything drastic occur.' He paused for a second and looked around, smiling. 'It also has a pilot who should be more than capable of dealing with a little turbulence created by a briefly opened ramp door.'

'And fuck you too,' she said.

'In your dreams, beautiful.'

He initiated the control and the ramp door began to open. It strained for a moment then with a thump juddered open a hand's breadth. Immediately a sucking roar started up from the shuttle's passage through atmosphere, and over that he only just heard her reply.

'It's your skin, ass-hat.'

Soon the door opened far enough to reveal purple-tinted cloud boiling past. The wind blasting in buffeted him and he reached out to grab the tailing edge of the door, pulling himself into the opening gap. The wind blast tried to tear him out of that position, but he held on, checking trajectories. Easing up higher as the door opened he braced his feet against the outer hull, looking down its length to where a fusion nacelle projected. He should miss it, but it would be close. Next he slid his back from the door and kicked hard against the hull. The wind took him and he tumbled down the length of the hull, one foot briefly touching on the top of the nacelle until he was in free fall.

It begins, he thought to himself.

Roland fell through cloud and belatedly remembered that upon putting it on he had not run a diagnostic on his grav harness. It was a little too late now, of course, and he berated himself for his trust in the tech. He settled spread-eagled into his fall and watched the shuttle depart, its thrusters spitting orange flame as it corrected for that open door – now closing. In a moment it disappeared from sight, heading for the enclosed Polity enclave on Tarennan, where tourists could gape out through chainglass windows at the hostile environment, or take tours in armoured grav coaches. Some, he knew, went out in suits too. He could have simply landed with the others and headed here overland. However, he both wanted and required a more intimate experience of the world and, anyway, that would have taken too much time – at least, that's what he told himself. He now uncomfortably remembered the words of Gurnik, the briefing AI:

'You have a flare for the dramatic,' it had said.

'And what's that supposed to mean?'

'Nothing at all – merely an observation.'

As he fell he used a wrist control to turn on his heads up display. The HUD showed him his altitude, speed of descent and time to impact with the ground, albeit if the harness did not work. Later he would return to using the more sophisticated technology in his skull, which he always fully trusted. But right now with his gridlink busy about another task, the computing of the envirosuit sufficed.

The suit crusted with ice, but then that sublimed and it started to heat up. Glancing back he saw he was beginning to leave a vapour trail. After minute he dropped out of cloud and the view began to open below him. First he saw just the wide expanse of the ocean but, as he had calculated, he soon passed over that to come above the land. At this height it bore the appearance of heavily wrinkled elephant skin, but soon began to reveal patches of colour and other detail. The yellow-brown smudges of kelp and wrack forests appeared, and the tidal pools swarming with creatures awaiting the next world tide. Closer still and mountains and giant boulders resolved – rockfields and sand bars lying between. When close enough to recognise giant molluscs clinging to some of those boulders, and with his suit giving him overheat warnings, he initiated the grav harness.

The thing whined up to power and began to slow his descent, within a few minutes that descent ceased, but he was still travelling at hundreds of miles an hour relative to the ground. He needed to stop that else he would end up above ocean again and he at least wanted time to prepare before it reached him. He called up the harness controls in his HUD and set antigravity at an angle to slow him. It did so gradually, as he kept an eye on the power bar. The harness carried one hell of a charge in its laminar storage, but was generally used for recreational floating about, not entry into atmosphere of a world. Part of his cover really – he could not arrive in full military kit because far too many would notice. Eventually he came stationary relative to the ground. A HUD map gave him his planetary position and the position of the world tide. More grav planing took him in the direction he wanted to go. He would go as far as the power supply allowed towards the receding tide. If he got it in sight that would give him about two and a half solstan days before it came round again. As a precaution he took himself lower, skimming just a hundred metres above the peaks of a mountain range.

Lower still beyond the range, he passed over a plain of bare rock scattered with off-white cones. Their nearest Earth equivalents were limpets, but these things were a couple of metres tall and the organism under the shell more like a squid than the usual squishy mollusc. Beyond this lay one of the tide lakes, its water thrashing as if in some storm, its spray taken by the wind and spread across the forest of wrack trees lying beyond. As he passed over this he could see the numerous creatures stirring up the waters. Many had present day piscine Earth equivalents, but some of the things in there also seemed out of Earth's prehistoric past: big armoured fishes, creatures like mosasaurs and ichthyosaurs. Hidden from view would be the numerous crustaceans steadily being devastated by this feeding frenzy. A small number of such from the whole because most found rocks to cling to or hide under as the world tide receded.

Mostly clear sky opened above, lavender and shot through with deep purple sirrus. Things flew through it like seagulls, but were winged crustaceans and molluscs in so much as such classifications could apply. Ahead, high up, he saw the ocean moon. The thing was quite a puzzle for the Polity researchers exploring and cataloguing it. From this distance it looked as if a vast maze had been cut into its surface, but on the surface those quadrate paths were canyons half a kilometre wide and as deep. The moon had been carved by some alien civilisation long gone, and no conclusions had been reached as to which of those named it might be, or if it might be another as yet unknown. Thus far the information gathered indicated that the moon had been put there, and that tunnels of a similar scale to the maze riddled it. Other things lay inside too, the researchers were certain, but explored and researched with great caution, because of one certainty: scanning showed those internal tunnels and chambers, but could not penetrate some areas. Mass calculations put the moon, if one were to suppose it was all normal matter, at one level, but not enough to create the world tide. The moon seemed likely to contain dense-tech and perhaps singularities. All of this was of some concern to Roland, considering certain aspects of his mission regarding alien technology, and he kept it integrated in his protean plans. But he had to stay focused on his particular chore and that, at present, concerned the autochthons here, and the eels.

With the moon in the sky, the back end of the world tide soon came into view. Water was pouring away across the ground towards the moon and as if down a slope. Ahead it got deeper and deeper and perspective rendered the illusion that it poured down a slope into an ocean. However, the ocean was a mountainous mass of water that spanned one third of the globe, hauled up by the gravity of that moon. Roland slowed and descended, the extra power drain of that pushing the harness supply towards empty and warnings flashing up. He slowed further and descended more sharply, thumping a foot on a boulder and coming down to a stretch of level ground. As his feet touched it he began running as the power supply delivered its dregs, then slipped on a layer of slimy, grey and stringy weed covering that surface. He tucked into a roll, felt bruising impacts against rocks, then slid to a halt up against one of the giant limpets.

'Fuck,' he said, got to his feet and moved away from the thing as fast as he could, even as the edge of the shell lifted and two stalked eyes with disconcertingly human pupils peered at him.

Many of the life forms there will try to eat you,' Gurnik had said. *'The herbivorous ones won't, but they will think you want to eat them, and try to kill you anyway.'*

'Do you ever send agents to resort worlds?' he had asked.

'Certainly, but not you.'

Slipping and sliding, he kept moving, while also scanning around for other likely unfriendly nasties left behind by the departing ocean. Glancing back he saw those eyes retract and the shell settle down again.

Perhaps it was well fed or, not recognising him as any form of lunch, had lost interest. Finally reaching the edge of the weed, he headed over to a boulder, probably the one he had touched while landing. He backed up against it and quickly stripped off his pack, opened it and took out the weapon inside. He acknowledged that he should have had this out and ready as he descended. He was still a little rusty, but that would change. The thing powered up when he gave its power supply one turn and he relaxed. His choice of laser carbine had been dictated by this world: no moving parts, one setting. It had to be simple and rugged to survive the environment here. Next he walked around the boulder to check to see if anything might be lurking, and finding nothing, settled down to make his preparations.

Roland detached the grav harness from the pack and tossed it aside. It had always been intended for this single use, and without somewhere to recharge it the thing was now useless to him. He next stripped off his envirosuit gloves and felt the cold and the slight acidic sting in the air. Gazing at his hands, he could see silver mottling from the precursor nanosuite adaptation. The software for this he had loaded from a vast collection in his gridlink, while the required additional nano-hardware the suite had generated itself. State-of-the-art and gridlink controlled, the thing had the capability to both radically redesign itself and him. The suite had taken his adaptation to a preset limit with materials and precursor changes in place, but he kept most of the adaptation zipped.

He sat there for a moment considering accessing his gridlink to unzip those changes but, even though only partially connected, he could sense its busyness. He had set it to make an infective clone of his nanosuite, and program it for a highly complicated task for which it would need further genomic data. He needed the clone ready as quickly as possible and, anyway, he had another method of access; meanwhile, he rather enjoyed an utterly human perception of his surroundings. He smiled, took a small device like a silver coin from a pocket and pressed it against the back of his hand. It felt ready to slide of for moment, then abruptly bound to his skin, feeling like he had pressed something there straight out of an oven. He winced, sat back against the rock, and took up the weapon again to put it across his lap.

Keeping half an eye on his surroundings he turned his attention to the display appearing in his HUD – relayed from his nanosuite via the coin of tech on his hand. The adaptation began to unzip via this route. A dry soreness arose in his lungs and he fought the urge to cough even as he felt his chest expanding. Clicks and crunches sounded in his ribcage as ribs, already prepared, began to telescope out. Then he did cough and spattered his visor with white mucous. After a hesitation he lowered the visor and took a tentative breath. The air tasted sour, but was as redolent of the ocean as any shoreline on Earth. He huffed for a little while and began to feel out of breath. Not yet. With the visor back up – cleaned by its transit back and forth in his collar ring – he observed that it would take at least another twenty minutes before he could breathe the thin monoxide laden air here.

Other changes were occurring. He could feel things shifting in the back of his throat and in his sinuses. That was the valve system installing which allowed him to breathe in water through one side of his presently dividing bronchus and out through the other. In his lungs, gill surface membranes were growing, though much more efficient than the kind found in fishes. Throughout his body, oxygen transport began ramping while his bone marrow of produced triple carrier haemoglobin. Many other invisible internal changes were occurring too but now, feeling a nagging itch between his fingers, he looked down and saw them bright red and suffused with blood, and the webs slowly extending between each of them. He reached down and separated one boot from his envirosuit and took it off. The change to his feet was more radical with the gaps between toes drawing back towards his ankles, leaving webs behind. He observed this for a while then returned his attention to his hands. He flicked a finger and a nail fell away exposing the new growth of a sharp claw. The thing was translucent at present and in it he could see the micro tubules. He could also feel the sacs developing in his hands and wrists. When they filled up he would be able to drive their contents through those micro tubules.

All the changes seemed to be going as planned. He blinked, bringing nictitating membranes down over his eyes, feeling the weird mental division of having two sets of lids to close. When he opened those membranes again he thought that something had gone wrong because the tidescape ahead seemed to be shifting with lines running parallel to it, like a computer display breaking up. Then he realised what he was seeing: flat bodies a few metres long running parallel to the ground with their legs almost a blur.

Murder lice...

These were precisely the kind of creatures for which he had been keeping a watch. It had always been the understanding that such creatures hunted in small packs of maybe three or four. Such a number he could easily drive off or kill with the weapon he held, but out there the newly revealed ground had come alive with them. He grimaced, knowing that these weren't the normal kind at all. Perhaps here lay a mission related opportunity? A small one, perhaps, but one that might get him killed before reaching his goal.

He heaved to his feet, and now the ill effects of his steady adaptation made themselves known. His body ached, muscles cramped and bones shifted inside as if broken. He abruptly dropped his visor and vomited – his last half-digested meal laced with blood – snared up his pack and moved out of sight behind the boulder. From there he peered round, watching maybe a hundred of the creatures swirling back and forth, hunting across the ground. They were coming steadily in his direction but not directly, so hopefully they had not spotted him yet. His physical condition ruled out running as an option. Moving back, he peered up the crumbling side of the boulder for hand holds. He put on his pack and hung the carbine by its strap from his shoulder and tried to climb, managed to get up a few metres before his body failed him and he dropped down again.

'Damn and fuck you,' he muttered.

Scouring around, he found his grav harness again, and simply wrapped and latched it around his waist. In his HUD display it came up – power bar right down at the bottom, but there might be enough. He initiated it while scrabbling for handholds and went up the side of the boulder. It failed after a couple of seconds but took him far enough to reach a shallower slope to the top and from there he wormed his way up. He lay on the top panting, nauseated, and feeling as if the retreating tide had deposited him there after giving him a battering.

Rolling over, he unclipped the harness and pulled it away. It tugged at his grip and slipped free, sailed away in an arc like raffia caught by the wind, then abruptly shut down and dropped. Where it landed, a murder louse abruptly skittered to a halt to inspect it. He studied the creature. The two metres long flat louse resembled a trilobite, but now he saw it looked very different from those that had first started appearing on this world a century ago. This thing had a larger head that appeared separate from its body, like that of an ant. From below this long mandible arms unfolded to reveal three-fingered hands. It picked up the harness for inspection, then dropped it and abruptly swung round in a circle checking its surroundings. Fortunately it wasn't looking up. These creatures had evolved to search out low concealed prey, hence part of the reason for climbing on top of the boulder. Also, lacking good vision, they mostly hunted by something akin to a sense of smell. Or, at least, the kind he knew about did.

The creature began tracking along the ground, its head swinging from side to side as it approached the boulder. He dipped down lower. They did not tend to pay attention to anything above ground level, but that did not mean they would not. He considered shooting the thing, for it seemed like an outlier from the main group, but the flash, smoke and smell his carbine would create would bring others over. While he agonised about what to do, something whipped through the air from behind him and struck the creature on its head. He watched it stagger sideways with a jelly blob stuck there. This expanded rapidly, sheathing the head in glistening wetness. He saw its spiral compound eyes sinking away as it stood shivering, then fluid drooling out of its mouthparts. It abruptly collapsed.

'I do not have a hundred amoeba rounds,' said a voice behind him. 'We need to get away from here now.'

Roland turned and then flinched back from the massive head rising over the boulder behind. Two round yellow eyes with black pupils gazed at him. The mouth opened slightly with lips tendrils writhing. What looked like ears, further back, were in fact fins. It turned and came in closer, settling down on the surface of the boulder. Mounted behind this head, on the metre-thick body of the giant eel, sat a half-naked woman on a coralline saddle seemingly bound into its flesh. He knew the saddle to be an adapted parasite that did bind into the flesh and into the creature's nervous system. She controlled its movement with her knees, only a little, since the relationship had a degree of willingness. She held what looked like an ornate rifle with a tapered barrel. This too was organic tech and only a little way from being a distinct living creature. The amoeba rounds were chunks of the amoeba living inside it which, when stimulated by the trigger mechanism, it ejected.

The woman looked like a barbarian female out of some virtuality. He could see the handle of a sword poking up over one shoulder. She wore a harness that ran strappily over her body, even down her legs and arms. She wore shorts of scaled hide and similar material constrained her breasts, though they bulged enticingly.

'Barbarians,' Gurnik had said. 'By choice.'

'Yet they are quite happy to acquire and use sophisticated technology,' he had replied, having done some studying.

'It's an ethos and they are not dissuaded from it by technology and comfort. They duel, value fighters and physicality and have set values not amenable to change.'

Analytically, he supposed the convenience of not having breasts flapping loose and the usual sexual mores applied here, but on the visceral level he felt something else he had not felt in a long time. She was an eel rider, of course, and just one of those he had come here to seek out. She gestured impatiently to a further encrustation of saddle behind her.

'Come on, yourself move!'

He noted an odd lilt and phrasing as he got up and staggered over. Halting beside her, he rested a hand on the saddle which, though it looked like coral, felt soft and warm. Down below he saw a protrusion that looked like a stirrup and, inserting his foot, took a breath and, gritting his teeth against the pain throughout his body, heaved the other leg over and fell in beside her.

'Put on the... leg straps,' she snapped.

Yes, she spoke Polity Anglic but she wasn't familiar with it. He looked down and located tongues sticking out beside the length of his legs. Trying to pull one of them across initiated movement and they all oozed out of the saddle to wrap around his legs. Glancing back he saw the twenty metre length of the eel's body snaking out behind. A second later it swung from the boulder and began writhing away. Even with the straps he did not feel secure with the side to side motion and reached out to grab the woman around the waist. She turned her head and he noted the odd twist to her mouth – annoyed perhaps at his ineptitude.

'I thought they only hunted in packs of three or four,' he managed, voice muffled by his visor.

'The usual genera do... hunt like that,' she replied.

Feeling slightly more secure he reached up and touched the control at his collar. The visor closed down into it at the front, then a moment later the hood retracted from his head and disappeared into the collar behind.

He took a breath, then another, and found that at last his lungs were extracting enough from the meagre air here.

'I don't understand. The usual genera?' But of course he did understand. This world had been under observation for a while. The new swarms of murder lice had appeared just a few decades ago.

'These are 'dapted. He saw you falling and sent them.'

'He? I don't know –'

'They have seen us,' she interrupted. 'I hope that weapon is good Polity tech because we're going to need it.'

She was right, from an elevation of two to three metres he could see the swarm of lice more clearly, their ribbed backs pale lavender in the sunlight. It seemed a wave of communication was passing through them as they all began to orient towards the eel, and then, as one, the whole swarm began to flow across the ground towards them.

She said something in the local language, harsh with hissing consonants, then added, 'Come on… Derek,' and dug her knees in.

The eel accelerated, flipping up rocks and chunks of weed as it sped across the ground, while Roland sat there not knowing if he should laugh at an eel called Derek. Odd too that she had chosen to repeat her instruction to the eel for his benefit. One of the politenesses primitive societies sometimes possessed.

The sudden progress made him feel precarious and he again wrapped his arms around her. He could probably hold on easily enough, it just being a matter of becoming accustomed to the motion, but, in all honesty, it felt good.

'We are not like the Polity,' she said. 'Others of my people would kill you for laying your hands on me in this manner.'

He loosened his grip and brought his hands back to rest above the flare of her hips. Gazed at the muscles of her back crossed by the wide sheath of her sword and the plaited queue of brown hair, while remembering what the front looked like. He then took his hands away, suddenly realising his adaptation was having untoward effects. Pulling up the sleeve of his envirosuit he peered at the bracelet there. He had set his to two tones: silver for sexually active and gold for the obverse. It had been gold when he jumped out of that shuttle. Now it had turned silver mottled with metallic blue, as if it couldn't decide his status right now.

'My apologies,' he said. 'My adaptation is interfering with me physically in unexpected ways.'

'Adaptation?' she swung her head round, to look at him out of the corner of her eye.

'Boosted amphidaption so I can breathe water and swim, rather like yourself.' Though of course there was more to it than that.

'I see.' Her head swung back. 'Put your hands to your weapon for now.'

Roland noted that 'for now' with a twinge below his waist.

The lice were moving faster over the ground than the eel and catching up. The eel came in over a stretch of weed and slowed, but when the lice reached that they accelerated. Roland pulled his carbine round and unhooked the strap from his shoulder. He then undid one end of the strap and fixed that to his belt so, if things got a bit hectic, he couldn't lose the weapon. He considered raising his visor for HUD targeting then decided against that. Since he intended to abandon his envirosuit as soon as feasible, he should get used to being without its functions. He raised the sight, the thing flaring open at its near end to give him a clear screen, turned and tracked closing lice, but did not yet fire. It was an uncomfortable position and there was no necessity yet. He lowered the weapon – no point using up the energy canister until absolutely necessary.

'Amphidaption,' she said. 'This means you can breathe under water.'

'I am just into the process. I don't know yet.'

'We will have to find out,' she stated, a sudden coldness in her tone he did not like. 'If we keep running like this they will be all over us, and neither of us will be breathing.' She hesitated for a second, then added, 'Or we'll be breathing past mandibles.'

He noted the marked improvement in her language as the eel abruptly turned at ninety degrees, tilting him over so he grabbed at her waist again. She caught his wrist and held it, his hand flat against her warm and muscular stomach. As soon as he had his balance again she pulled his hand away, quickly. He grimaced annoyed at the intensity of sexual feeling after so long celibate, leaned back and brought his carbine round.

The lice were now coming in from the side and as a consequence getting closer much faster now. He aimed at the nearest louse and fired. Of course, familiarity with weapons being a given for him, the louse flipped over with a smoking hole through its head. But he needed more. Grudgingly and so very briefly he accessed his gridlink and in a second loaded a program to his mind. Dual focus now kicked in, so he could long-sight with one eye while keeping the other to the scope screen. He systematically hit louse after louse, bringing down ten of them before the first leapt. The thing came up like a giant flea. Just one of his shots went through the centre of its body. It hit the side of the eel a couple of metres back from him and bounced away. Looking back he saw another land on the eel's body near the tail and dig in with pincers. Sudden violent motion from the eel snapped the thing away, leaving its head detached. The same motion caused the straps over one of Roland's legs to separate, and he thought he was heading for the ground until the woman grabbed him and hauled him back.

'Thanks,' he said.

She just turned away and concentrated on what lay ahead. Roland continued firing, sweeping down the side of the eel them behind where the creatures were swarming in. Another leaper landed right beside his leg and now he got a good look at the horrible thing before he shot it through the head and it peeled away. Just that look had been confirmation that there had been something very odd about the creature. It hadn't all been carapace but seemed an amalgam of that with human-looking skin and flesh. He peered down at where he had shot it and saw spattered pink ichor and pieces of carapace.

Gridlink activation, he said mentally. *Sample acquired.*

Reaching down with one hand he extended his pointer finger and, with a slight tensing of muscles he had never possessed before, extended one claw. He jabbed it into the ichor and with another alien tensing, sucked some of it in through its tubules, and into one of the sacs in his hand. With the non-verbal acknowledgement from his gridlink his sense of connection, after the previous brief access, ramped up, almost like addiction to a drug. He shut it down and returned his concentration to his surroundings. However, he knew that he could not continue to stay disconnected for long.

Three lice were now on the eel's body and making their way up it – slowly because of the constant side to side motion. He aimed carefully, trying not to harm the eel. Each shot took some little extra time and he got them all, but now the horde to the side drew closer and began leaping. They thumped down all along the eel's body, driving in their pincers.

'This is it,' said the woman.

He wondered if she meant the lice would now get to them, until with a huge splash the eel nosed down into one of those big tidal lakes. He had time to feel fear, and did not care what her reaction would be when he lodged his carbine between them and grabbed her tightly about the waist. A moment later they were under water, cold and clear. He blinked his nictitating membranes down and for a second all around him lay distorted, then it cleared and it was as if he gazed through goggles. Oxygen began to wane as he held onto his breath until finally he had no choice. He took a breath. The water flowed cold into his lungs and the shock of it flipped him into a moment of stasis, shortly broken by the fluttering in his chest as the gill membranes began to work. He breathed out through that twinned bronchus and felt a tight pain across his chest as the muscles began to work as designed – alternately one side of his chest compressing and the other inflating. Oxygen deprivation continued and he considered closing up his visor and hood to make use of the suit air supply, but then it began to wane. At last he was breathing under water.

Now Roland began to perceive things beyond the need to breathe. The woman had leaned right forwards taking him with her. The current over them was strong – the eel moving much faster than it had on land. Peering down, he saw the bottom speeding past and other vaguely seen creatures quickly scuttling or swimming away. Of course, only something big might stay around an apex predator like one of the eels. He was also aware that the feeding frenzy he had seen in one lake during his descent to the surface was an inevitably short-lived affair.

He turned to look back. Three of four lice were still attached. He loosened his hold on the woman, but then clamped in close when the current threatened to pull him away. He wanted to check to see if he could take a shot, because though damped by water the laser could fire through it, but knew he had no chance of using it while travelling this fast. Her hand against his forearm she gave it a brief squeeze, then her fingers moved as if tapping out some code. A form of underwater touch communication, it seemed. Not enough was known about the eel riders for him to be sure. However, he did know that if he had been integrated with his gridlink he could have decoded it in a very short time...

A kelp forest loomed ahead. The eel nosed into it, pushing aside tree-thick stalks which began to close in just a moment later. He risked another look back and saw, one after the other, the lice getting peeled away. Then they were out of the forest and heading for the surface. The eel breached, arcing out of the lake and coming down again, but now stayed on the surface, swimming fast. The woman sat upright. He continued to hold onto her as he breathed out water. The alternate compression of his lungs continued until they cleared then, with a painful wrench, switching back to conventional air breathing. He felt a similar wrench in her body – not so severe, but his loose grip had dropped lower now with one hand resting between her legs. And with his cheek resting against her warm back he really didn't want to change the position. Anyway, he expected her to shrug him away at any moment. When she didn't, he felt his previously suppressed sex drive starting to get hopeful. Then she did, letting out a startled breath as she grabbed his forearms and shoved them behind her. He leaned back and they travelled across the surface of the lake in silence for a while.

'Do you think we've lost them?' he asked.

'Yes,' she said tersely.

Another silence ensued and he knew he had broken her social conventions, and didn't care all that much. Still, he wanted a connection...

'Why would anyone want to send them after me? And who is he?' he asked.

She huffed out a harsh breath, rolled her head with a clicking sound and muttered some word he did not recognise – most likely an expletive. Leaning to one side and turning to him she studied his face, and now he really got to look properly at hers. She was quite beautiful. He had seen many pictures of the eel people and known this anyway, but now wondered about the adaptation that resulted in those slanting blue eyes and slightly pointed ears. Some artistic conceit of whoever had made it in the first place, he suspected, because she had the appearance of those in the Polity who liked the look of Tolkien elves.

'There is a ground cyst three kilometres from here,' she said. 'We'll get to that and rest for the night, then take the tunnels to Holm.' She shook her head. 'You really don't know who sent the lice?'

'I haven't a clue,' he lied.

The eel reached the shore, and now its progress slowed through a boulder field – each lodged in sand with a pool around it flickering with fish fry. In the distance he could see a slow crab – a giant crustacean similar to a spider crab – moving like a sloth. He noted the length of the shadows and peered in the other direction at the sun gnawing the horizon. Yes, it would be night soon.

'Why did you come here?' she asked, facing forwards again.

'I am travelling the Polity, absorbing life experiences, seeing new things.'

'Playing,' she said tersely.

'You can see it that way if you like.'

'But why here? And why not the usual tourist route? Why did you decide to come directly to the surface and adapt?'

He shrugged. 'It just seemed the best way to get close to what this world has to offer.'

'No – there's another reason. You did not think of that yourself.'

It was good to have a well prepared back-story he felt. Right now, if he was what he pretended to be, he should be uncomfortable with her perspicacity. How could she know about that? How could she be so certain?

'The story of Jason Chel,' he replied.

'And now you know who sent the lice,' she told him.

According to the story, Jason Chel had been a collector of antiquities and he'd got his hands on one: a bracelet called a Four Seasons Changer. That the story included such a device made many doubt its veracity, for it had put in an appearance in numerous virtualities. It was able to rapidly adapt someone to a hostile environment using the genome of an autochthon. At the time when Chel apparently took possession of it, adaptations could be rapidly performed by a nanosuite, as with Roland, but the bracelet was supposedly much older than that. Chel had gone to the world of Scylla in search of a stash of Golem Two androids but his partner betrayed him and left him stranded in the path of the world-tide. To survive he had used the Four Seasons Changer and murder louse genome, surviving the tide and returning much changed to a planetary base. Supposedly here, where Roland had arrived, was Scylla...

'That Jason Chel story has so many holes in it I find it difficult to know where to start,' she said.

'How about we start with your name,' he suggested, as he looked around.

The eel had crossed an area mounded with sargassum, crawling and hopping with crustaceans like the by-blows of prawns and dragon flies.

Finally, it had come to an area marked by a circle of stone cubes, nosed weed aside to find a big iron ring, then flipped up a heavy domed hatch. They had gone underground and were now in an oblate chamber with tunnels running off. The eel had returned to the surface, to hunt, she said, the hatch closing with an ominous thump behind it.

She crooked a finger at him and, for some reason he could not fathom, looked decidedly angry. Heading off, she led the way a short distance down one of the tunnels then through a door made of resin into what he assumed to be a small apartment. The accoutrements of living were much at variance here. Comfortable cushion-like objects seemed to be for lounging on around a flat surface – a table – but they were wet and slightly slimy. Organic pipework ran around the walls. She opened one of the many spherical cupboards to reveal it packed with items – some recognisable as packet food from the Polity but most not. Organic machines whose nature he could only guess stood in a row along a counter. She unwrapped two chunks of bloody meat from a yellow film and went over to one of the counter objects, pushing them inside a trumpet maw. Steam began to rise from the device's scaled grey cowling.

'My name is Sansaclear,' she finally told him. 'And yours?'

'Roland.'

'A legendary name.'

That should have given his assumed identity pause, and he ran with it, saying, 'Your Anglic started out rusty and is now very good, as is your grasp of many things Polity related. I thought the eel riders here were First Diaspora and had little contact with us?'

'More of the apocryphal,' she said, slumping down on one of the lounging cushions. The thing wheezed and shifted to accommodate her. 'Like so much of the story of Jason Chel.'

He acknowledged that with a nod and carefully sat down on another of the cushions. He sank into it but then it hardened behind, pushing against his back to become a misshapen chair. She wasn't going to answer his implied question now – she clearly wanted to concentrate on Chel. He felt strangely glad about that. He had been having a physical reaction to her but now began enjoying the workings of her mind. She was bright – he could see that.

He shrugged. 'Give me examples.'

'His story was supposed to have occurred a few centuries ago. It did not.'

'And on what do you base this?'

'Darkander's auction house, where he supposedly bought the Four Seasons Changer, closed down before the prador-human war.'

'Oh, I see.' Actually she was wrong. It had closed down temporarily and moved out-system away from the war front. Darkander had been nothing if not careful about his own safety.

She continued, 'In the story Chel had an AI help him identify the bracelet. If that had happened two centuries ago the AI would have lied about it and a short time later an ECS assault team would have been kicking down his door.'

'Why?'

'Because the bracelet was made, and did do what it did, long before the nanosuites could do the same. It was one of those completely unexpected inventions created by someone brilliant, like Tenkian weapons. Its maker incorporated alien technology in it. Jain technology.'

'Oh, right. I suppose ECS would be rather interested.' He grimaced, which could be mistaken for him being annoyed at his own shoddy research, but really to cover his surprise at her knowing about the Jain tech in the bracelet. 'So what other inconsistencies are there?'

'He came to this world in search of those Golem Twos.'

'That's wrong?'

'He went to a world called Scylla.'

'Yes, which was the name of this world two centuries back, until it got changed to Taranen.'

'Incorrect. The name of this world was Scylla II. It was named after the original – one of the many worlds with world tides that tried to claim the name. Of course the name had been released by the fact that the original was destroyed during the war.'

'What?'

'Binary twin?' she enquired.

'Yes, that's what they say in the story, but it seemed obvious that was a mistake...' He tailed off, pretending to feel stupid. Scylla, the original world, possessed a world tide because it orbited a sun also orbited by another smaller sun. Being tidal crustaceans the prador had fought hard to take possession of the world, since it would have been perfect for them. In the end they were forced to abandon it and, in a fit of rage, hit it with crust busters. Any other world might have at least remained intact but Scylla, sitting in the gravitational wrenching of those suns, came apart.

'You questioned that fact but nothing else?'

'Evidently.'

Sansaclear pushed up from her cushion, the thing seeming to give her a helpful shove as she did so. She looked victoriously smug as if she had won some argument, yet he had not been aware of arguing. Crossing the room to a cupboard, she took out a packet and some bottles. He recognised flat breads in the packet. The counter device issued a fishy, meaty steam when she opened it. While preparing the food she seemed overly noisy and heavy handed. Shortly she returned with a couple of wraps around large chunks of meat in a thick sauce and handed one to him.

'Best get used to it now,' she said with a shrug.

He bit in and found he would not need to get accustomed. The meat was good – like tuna – and the spicy sauce sat somewhere between chilli and wasabi. She did not sit again but ate her food while walking around – agitated, uncomfortable. She kept shooting him glances that again appeared to be angry. She wolfed down her food long before he did, discarding a piece of the bread wrap on the floor where a worm-like tube oozed out to hoover it up.

'Okay,' she said, 'what are you using? Some kind of pheromone?'

'I don't know what you mean,' he said, but he did.

'What is it? Devil Nip? Caspatar?'

'I haven't used anything like that is over fifty years. My one experience with Devil Nip was quite enough, thanks.' He now understood her agitation and, because his sex drive had now definitely come back on, he knew he was going to take advantage of it. 'But again,' he continued, 'you know an awful lot about the Polity – in this case the commercial names for aphrodisiacs. You are Polity, aren't you?'

'You thought the people here were First Diaspora. To a certain extent that is true – some can trace their ancestry back to the originals. But do you think you are the first here to follow in the false footsteps of Jason Chel?'

He finished his wrap and stood up. Retrieving his pack from beside the cushion he opened it and delved inside, taking out the clothing items he had brought in preparation for his change. After glancing round he shrugged and then began taking off his envirosuit. It wasn't entirely manipulative. Even as they had approached this place he had started to feel uncomfortably warm and constrained. She stood closer now, watching him, hands on her hips and that angry expression still in residence.

'So others came here,' he said, 'underwent their adaptations and stayed.'

'Some stayed. Many left.'

'So what are you?'

'The daughter of a man who stayed and partnered with a remote descendent of one of the originals.' She paused for a second still staring at him angrily. 'I am educated. We are all educated. I speak Polity Anglic with my father, and other languages, and he has taught me a lot. We also learn through Polity netlinks.

He nodded an acknowledgement, recognising the defensiveness of one in a primitive society encountering one more sophisticated. They were only just acquiring augmentations here and she certainly did not wear one, so he did respect that education for she had learned those languages bare-brained – something very few did in the Polity.

Now stripped down to the thin undersuit he already felt better. With his present adaptation his lungs were not his only method of gathering oxygen because his skin drew it in too. He opened the clothing packet. It contained a light, mesh bodysuit that extended to knees and elbows, and sported various pockets and a utility harness. In its way it seemed a more modern version of the kind of barbarian gear she wore. He began undoing the stick seams of the undersuit.

'You can turn away now, if you like,' he said.

'Why, are you bashful?' she challenged, but it was she whose face had flushed.

'Not at all.'

He stood up, stripped the suit off and discarded it. Peering down at his body he saw the changes the adaptation had wrought. His skin had taken on a silvery hue with a mottling that looked vaguely like scales and which he knew to be merely aesthetic. Like most in the Polity he had always had a good body – muscular and athletic – and like few in the Polity his physical abilities ranged beyond the norm. Now the adaptation had also given him a larger breadth of chest. Reaching up he could feel that his neck had grown thicker too.

'It seems to have done a good job,' he said, and stepped towards her.

'No,' she said, holding her hands out in front of her.

He just walked into them and she didn't push him away too hard. Reaching past he caught hold of the back of her head, grabbed a fistful of hair and pulled her into a kiss. She turned from it then back into it. They kissed hard for a moment, then she abruptly pulled back.

'No, this is wrong,' she said, but did not expect agreement.

He pulled her back into the kiss. By now he had a full erection and pushed it against her stomach. She let out a moan then bit him on the lip, but not too hard. He slid his hands in between them and pulled her bra down to release her breasts. She took the opportunity to pull away but he caught her round the waist and threw her down on one of the cushions. She quickly rolled off it and came down kneeling with an elbow on the table.

'You mustn't,' she said, looking back at him.

He stooped down behind her and caught hold of her hips. She made a weak attempt – merely a matter of form – to pull away from him. He pulled her arse back, got hold of the top of her shorts and pulled them down to her knees, all the strappy stuff down her legs bunching up, then holding her down on the table with one hand, stripped them off her lower legs. He noted that her feet, in small slippers, were normal and not webbed like his own. She stopped making her meaningless objections now but just looked back at him with plain lust. He pushed her knees apart and got into position behind her, and entered her.

As he fucked her she first spoke in Polity Anglic, telling first him then herself that she should not be doing this. Next she lapsed into the local language. She was a talker all right. She came after just a short time, violently, shuddering against the table. Then she came again when could hold off no longer and let it go inside her. They lay there for a while, breathing heavily, her across the table and him resting his weight on top of her.

'I do not do this,' she muttered, when they had their breath.

'You don't do it very well,' he replied.

She wriggled underneath him and reached back to push him away. Just that wriggle was enough to bring him to the end of his refractory period and even as he pulled out of her he was growing hard again. She turned and looked down at his cock, then came forward on her knees and grabbed hold of it with one hand then pointed with the other.

'On there.'

He rolled over onto one of the cushion and she followed, her grip still firm. He lay back as she pressed something on the side of the cushion and it flattened out. Reaching between her legs her hand came up wet and she wiped that on her breasts before getting his cock between them and rubbing them in slow circles. She watched his face as she did this for a while then, as if impatient, went down on him with her mouth. Even as she did this she was playing with herself. He leaned forwards, caught hold of her head and pulled her mouth off away, rolling to one side he gestured.

'On there.'

On her hands and knees she crawled on, looking at him and waiting for instructions.

'On your back,' he told her.

She flipped over willingly and parting her legs he entered her again, while kissing her hard on the mouth. She tried to bite his lip again but he pulled back.

'No. I don't think so.'

She gave a moue of disappointment, so he lifted up her legs and put them over his shoulders and drove into her hard. She shuddered and writhed underneath him, groaning all the while. And so it went, and so it continued. His recovery time was fast as it had always been even before this adaptation – a result in all humanity of genetic manipulation over centuries and complemented by nanosuite. She had no recovery time at all. It seemed to descend into a wet and sliding fever dream as both ran through their extensive repertoires of what they wanted. At one point he saw two large yellow eyes gazing at them from the open door, then the eel slid on past. Later he wondered if he had hallucinated.

'I just don't do that,' said Sansaclear. She was lying sprawled face down on one of the cushions, hand behind as she pulled at one of her buttocks. 'I just don't feel that sexually... that horny.' She looked round at him. 'You're really not using anything?'

'Seriously, no,' he replied. He was lying flat on his back on the floor, and now with the sexual buzz fading he ached from head to foot. He held up his arm to show the bracelet. 'This was set to celibate when I came down, but it seems my adaptation interfered with it.'

'Okay.' She shrugged and he sensed that she completely believed him. The sex seemed to have created its usual bond of trust and he really did not want to break it. The thought made him wince because, of course, he had been effectively lying to her all along.

'That accounts for your behaviour, but I still don't know what accounts for mine.'

'Perhaps we're body matched,' he suggested.

It was an old joke. Humans emitted a whole range of hormones or pheromones and were susceptible to a range of them too. The range of emission and reception could match up, and many sought out a match, but it was exceedingly rare – something of the order of one in four million. Some actively and naively sought out the perfect match, but hormones were not the whole of it. Throughout their lives, and with many factors involved, people built a mental model of their perfect mate but, with the evolutionary sexual strategies of the two sexes, that simply could not be found. Still, she looked round at him with all seriousness.

'Really? Do you think so?'

Instead of dismissing the idea, as he would have with anyone else, he gave the thought consideration. That he was doing so made him realise that there *was* something going on here beyond just his lust, after becoming sexually active again, sparking something in her. And, damn it, never in his life before when on a mission had he felt so strong an urge to reveal to someone who he was and what he was doing.

'There may be some match on a hormonal level,' he conceded. 'That you felt sure I was using an aphrodisiac indicates so, and my reaction to you was immediate, and *I* don't do that.' He smiled. 'Is it a problem?'

She grimaced. 'It will be a problem when we get to Holm. There will be a challenge... violence. Drannic has always expected us to partner up from when we were children, and our families expect the same. I have been promised to him.'

'Drannic,' Roland repeated, and felt a surge of jealousy. His response, after a moment, evinced surprise, because jealousy was not an emotion he had much experienced. He fought to suppress it, because it was crazy for him to get into this sort of thing and, ultimately, unfair for him to deploy his 'talents' against someone for such a prosaic reason.

'And your opinion? Or does that not matter?'

'He was good enough,' she shrugged.

'What will be the reaction?'

'Remember what I said to you when you first put your hands on me?'

'This Drannic will try to kill me?'

'We are not the Polity.'

'Evidently not.' He stood up and went over to pick up his mesh body suit and was about to pull it on. He needed to get a grip on his emotions and focus on his ultimate goal here. But Sansaclear rolled over on her back and lay sprawled with her legs wide open.

'They will send out searchers when they realise I am missing,' she said. 'They'll know I went to find the person who jumped out of the shuttle, but they won't be looking down here for a while yet.'

He discarded the suit and went over to her.

Finally they got back on the eel and were now travelling through wide tunnels underground. The initial section about the 'cyst' had obviously been roughly hacked through the rock for he saw the tool marks on the walls. After travelling for a short distance through these, ducked down so not to smack their heads on the ceiling, the eel entered spacious, larger tunnels. These were square in section and the walls, where not concealed by weed or other oceanic encrustations, were smooth and showed no chisel marks. He wondered if they might be related to similar tunnels up on the moon. It was something he would enquire about when he again integrated with his gridlink, but now he had something else on his mind.

'Tell me about Jason Chel,' he said, as they travelled. Another perspective on that story might come in useful and, anyway, he wanted to hear her talking.

'Again it is a story that contains a great deal of speculation, and a great deal that might not be true, so make of it what you will.'

She shrugged and he loved the motion of the muscles in her back. He reached out and ran his fingers down it beside the sword sheath. She shivered, reached round and caught his hand, then pulled it forward to place it on her thigh. He moved in closer and reached round with his other hand too. There was definitely something here, and he felt a surge of anxiety that events on this world might separate her from him. Then harsh reality impinged. It was likely something on this world but not of this world would separate her from him, and it was etched round on the inside of his skull: his gridlink.

'Maybe tell me the story before I get too distracted,' he suggested.

She cleared her throat.

'Okay. Jason Chel returned to Earth and there underwent surgery that nowadays would be considered quite primitive in the Polity. It returned him to nominal human form, though there were deep genetic changes that remained untouched. He continued his life as a collector of antiquities for just a short while but then started travelling. Mostly it seemed he was looking for a cure for what he had become.'

'What happened to the Four Seasons Changer?'

'He left it, along with a considerable portion of his wealth, with a research organisation, with the instructions to find a way to reverse what it had done to him. That same organisation, before the war, was absorbed by ECS and what happened to the bracelet thereafter I don't know.'

'ECS was growing then. It kind of adds credence to the idea that the AIs knew about the prador long before they were "discovered",' he said, remembering only a few months before gazing down at that bracelet in its chainglass case in a secure ECS facility. He then wondered why he had asked the question, since he knew where the thing was. His continued parsimony with the truth made him feel shitty.

'Quite. Anyway, when the war came he joined up and apparently has an exemplary war record. His changes, though surgically concealed, made him very difficult to kill, fast… a predator. When the war ended he went to a world called Barlon and lived there as a recluse. His behaviour became erratic and he was implicated in organised crime, a series of murders, but nothing was proven before he fled. It was noted, however, that he had regrown carapace on his skin and a mandibular mouth. It seemed the earlier changes the Changer had wrought were reasserting. When he came here he looked just like he had looked on the original Scylla. He moved into an old observation outpost here a hundred years ago, and that's when the murder lice began to appear.'

Roland nodded to himself, noting her change of tone and that it indicated the first part she had told him she had read and memorised. He knew all of this, of course, and more detail. The nanosuites had been improving during and after the war and Chel had tried to use one to return himself to humanity at the genetic level. It had nearly killed him and thereafter he had changed in another way.

The briefing AI Gurnik had opined, 'He had accepted himself as a monster. Perhaps we are to blame, since that's what we wanted him to be during the war.'

'So what does he do here? What does he want?'

'He has grabbed a number of our people and changed them. They are now like him. We speculate that he created the murder lice from his own body – they are his children. He is creating his own people, his own race. We also speculate that this is driven by the louse genome in him – its need to breed.'

'Animalistic.'

'Aren't we all,' she said, turning her head to give him a decidedly lustful look.

'Are there any more of those stopping off places around here?' he enquired.

'No.' She pointed ahead to where the tunnel curved upwards. 'We're heading for the surface now and shortly we will arrive at Holm.'

Cynicism arose. It had not been a long journey from that last cyst so there had been no real need to stop there. Despite her protesting his advances she had ensured they could be somewhere he could make them.

He withdrew his hands from her thighs and put them on her hips. He needed to get a grip on himself for, no matter how things went with her, he still had a mission to complete. She patted one of his hands and continued to guide the eel. The wide tunnel abruptly came to an end against a face of rock, as if some seismic event had sheered it off, but to the right another tunnel had been bored. The eel brought its head down to the floor and they had to duck down to avoid the ceiling. The tunnel curved up to terminate against a heavy domed hatch the eel pushed up, and which hinged over with a crash. As they came up through this, Roland scanned the scene.

Holm was in fact a small city rearing from a mass of rocky slabs in what might be described as a desert on any other world, however here the sand was wet and deeper down transitioned into mud inhabited by massive creatures like terran bobbit worms. These creatures acted as guards for the place, preventing any of the larger and more destructive bottom dwellers coming near the city when the world tide arrived. Right now they sat somnolent down in their burrows.

The city had originally consisted of houses made out of hollowed stones and giant shells, but had changed a great deal since those early years. Houses of stone blocks were built a century ago reaching to two stories tall, with roofs of nacre tiles carved from shells. They were an oddity, he felt, for a people that spent half their time living under water. What need of tiles? To shelter them from the rain? In the ensuing hundred years the influx of Polity technology had allowed for new building methods and now there stood towers of foamstone and composite. Up there, strung between towers, he could see nets and large fishing gear, with which they harvested the sea when the city lay under water. Just to the left of the main city he could see structures that were conglomerations of huge winkle-like shells each as much as five metres across. That was where the eels lived. He also noted other recent additions sitting on short fat pillars of foamstone around the city, and up on the towers: cavitating, sonic, hard round and laser weapons. They had necessarily had to make some adjustments because of the murder lice.

'It looks like they were putting the search party together,' she said.

Here and there about Holm were eels with riders. He also saw some treaded ground vehicles and one or two grav rafts. The people might have been considered primitive in Polity terms but they were rapidly catching up now. He remembered those discussions with Gurnik. The primitivism here wasn't technological but in their barbarian ethos. They had, for example, advanced medical technology based on past biotech and recent Polity input, but they still allowed duels and admired the physicality of violence.

Nearby he saw a group of about ten eels – some with two or three riders each – and one large grav raft. This group had been steadily making its way towards them, and now he could see the people talking and pointing. Considering it quite likely that Sansaclear's prospective husband would be amongst this group he took his hands from her hips, though he felt bad about doing so. She looked round at him, her expression hurt. He thought about that for a moment. Even though he had just been thinking about their mores here, he had reacted like a Polity citizen. He had to remember that despite her facility with language and broad knowledge, Sansaclear was a product of her society. She would see his action as fear and that he was not prepared to fight for her. She did not know what he was and could not understand that he wanted to avoid violence simply because, in the end, he was far too good at it for any match to be fair. He abruptly put his hands back, sliding one of them down into the fold between hip and thigh, fingers just brushing her mons. She let out a low growling sound.

'Are you my mate?' she asked.

A hundred different thoughts clashed in his mind. Logically and sensibly he should abandon this woman and be about his own business. Damn it, he had a mission to complete! But logic and sense had gone out the window some hours ago. What was life worth if you didn't grab the thing you wanted, the thing that was offered? In essence his job was to fight to maintain these opportunities and choices for others. Should he put aside his own happiness just to be what he was? It was time to make a decision and now, after a brief surge of anxiety, he made it.

'Yes, I am your mate. But there are things you will need to know about me,' he said.

'They will be, in the end, immaterial.'

'I hope so,' he replied.

The group drew closer and they drew closer to the group. The eel riders halted their mounts and the grav platform settled to the ground. The people all looked straight out of a barbarian virtuality – all wearing sparse clothing to reveal superbly-muscled bodies. That clothing also slanted towards pieces of armour and defensive meshes. They carried swords or other edged blades, and a variety of projectile and energy weapons, strapped to their backs and to their hips. He could see looks being exchanged and assessing the dynamic knew in an instant that a powerful looking young man was Sansaclear's erstwhile mate, Drannic. He was staring hard at where Roland had his hands on her. Dismounting from one eel, another older, brutish-looking man called out.

'This is the man who fell to earth?' he enquired.

Appearances could be deceptive. Though the man looked like a hulk he spoke with precision and amusement, and was evidently familiar with the phrase he had just used. Roland could see intelligence in his face.

'My father,' she whispered to him.

She brought their eel down to the ground and he dismounted. This needed to be resolved now so he could move onto the next thing which, he had now decided, was telling her who and what he was, and why he had come here. She dismounted shortly afterwards and quickly caught up with him to link an arm through his.

'This is Roland,' she announced, 'a Polity man who is now my mate.'

Some comments flew and one or two engaged in angry conversation. They weren't speaking Anglic and, without his gridlink online, he could not understand what was being said. But he guessed there to be some debate about, perhaps, the 'legality' of this.

'And I of course challenge that,' said the young man, swiftly dismounting and confirming that he was Drannic. He then drew the weapon from the sheath on his back. Roland just stared, only now really accepting it must come to this. The young man held a sword like a narrow scimitar with odd curves along the blade.

'So what are the rules here?' he asked her.

She gazed at him with a kind of yearning, then that shut down and her expression became hard. 'He will try to kill you.'

'And in this way he will win you back?' Roland asked disparagingly.

She closed her eyes for a second, then opening them said, 'I was promised to him and unless someone else challenges that I will have no choice.'

'Mother of fuck,' said Roland.

'Let's just calm this for a moment,' said her father.

He had moved in closer now, and with a puzzled expression inspected Roland. Others were moving in, too, in fact starting to form a circle.

Her father continued, 'You, Polity man, are you aware of what this means?' He gestured to Drannic. 'He was promised to her and under our laws he has the right to challenge any interloper.'

Roland wanted to lash out with some sarcasm about such primitive rules, but for Sansaclear refrained from that. He also understood that in allowing himself to succumb to primitive drives he must accept primitive consequences. 'Yeah, I get it. He's going to try to skewer me.'

Her father nodded solemnly, but was still inspecting Roland carefully. Roland looked back at him blank faced. Of course, the man was not a native of this world but one of those who had stayed. Perhaps he had suspicions. He would know that though many of Polity were soft and over-civilised, not all were a pushover.

'How does this match end?' he asked.

'It ends,' said her father, 'when one of you concedes defeat, or is too severely wounded to fight, or is dead. It's usually the last, because I don't see Drannic here holding back should he disable you.'

'Shiny,' said Roland.

'You may use my sword,' interjected Sansaclear, reaching back to the handle of her weapon.

Roland waved a dismissive hand. 'I won't need it.'

'You cannot use your own weapon,' she said urgently.

He gazed at her steadily. 'I will not be needing a weapon.'

She stared at him horrified until her father walked round, caught her by the arm and pulled her away. The circle hardened all around and Roland felt a degree of disgust, tempered by acceptance, to see the avidity in some expressions. He shrugged and shook himself, but really there was no need. He had no stiffness from the long ride on the eel, no injuries, and was as ready as ever. Drannic stood over at the other side of the circle looking somewhat puzzled. He then moved forwards.

'Did you expect me to abandon my weapon because you did?' he asked. 'A seasoned fighter does not do such stupid things.'

Roland rolled his head, stretching his neck. He didn't need to – it was a simple psychological gambit to show his lack of concern. He said, 'No, I didn't expect you to abandon your weapon, but I have a small sense of fairness and am trying to make the odds more even.'

'Confident of victory are –' Drannic stepped in and swung before completing the sentence.

Roland stepped back, the sword tip passing just millimetres from his chest. He frowned, realising he had slightly misjudged that because, since his adaptation, his chest had grown bigger. Also his footing was not as he would have liked, what with their change. Drannic swung a full circle as he stepped closer, going for a downward slice. Roland tracked the sword, then clipped it with the edge of his hand and ducked to the side so it passed down his other side. Before Drannic could recover he stabbed the hand he had used to knock the sword aside forwards, closed finger knuckles on the man's nose, squeezed and twisted, then stepped away.

Drannic turned, fast, but his eyes were watering and he stepped back to rub at his nose. Someone in the circle snorted laughter.

'I'm going to gut you for that,' said Drannic.

Roland saw the change. The man had first come in perfectly confident he could cut Roland down with the first attack, and had been careless. Now with his confidence dented some fight training had kicked in. Drannic approached with shuffling steps, shifting the sword seemingly at random so as not to telegraph how he would use it next. Roland could see, from the years of his own martial training, that the man would make no more slashing cuts. It would be stabs now, difficult to divert and easier for Drannic to recover from any misses. It was perhaps time to get serious. Roland felt perfectly confident of winning, but he knew that such confidence might kill him, still...

Drannic went into a fast step thrust. Roland palmed the sword to one side and saw the shift in the man's stance to bring the sword in to slice it across Roland's torso. Roland dropped right down onto his arse and then, levering with his hands on the ground behind, thrust his legs forwards, caught Drannic's ankle between his feet and rolled. Drannic yelled and went over – if he hadn't his ankle would have broken – but his sword thumped into soggy sand near Roland's shoulder.

Okay, enough…

Roland withdrew his legs and with a hard body wrench flipped back into a squatting position. Turning and standing, he aimed a reverse mawashi geri that slammed his heel into the side of Drannic's head. But the man still managed to get to his feet and swing wildly. Roland again palmed the sword to one side, then stepped in close. The series of karate punches he delivered sounded like an automatic weapon firing, then he finished it with the heel of his hand to Drannic's nose. Drannic staggered back, stunned and struggling to get a breath, but he still held the sword. Roland stepped in and grabbed Drannic's wrist, turning to put the man behind him. Hitting some pressure points sprang the hand open and the sword dropped. He heard Sansaclear gasp, but did not need the warning, since he had felt the movement behind him. His elbow crashed into Drannic's throat and with his other hand, as he turned, he caught the wrist holding the dagger heading for his guts. Then, hand against the man's face, he kicked Drannic's feet away and slammed him to the ground, coming down hard with a knee in his chest. It was over. He shook the dagger free and, standing, kicked it away.

'Are we done here?' he asked, walking towards Sansaclear and her father.

The older man nodded. 'Seems so.'

'You are here with purpose,' Sansaclear said as they rode back into the city.

'And that is what I must tell you about,' he replied. 'I am not the tourist I pretended to be. I have been, effectively, lying to you.'

'Does it make a difference to how you feel about me?'

'No – how I feel about you makes a difference to my purpose, though admittedly not a large one. You are now more important to me than what I came here to do.'

They passed the 'eel pens' as they were called, though the creatures were not penned inside those large shells. He saw some peeking out, others heading off across the sand, and one returning, dragging the corpse of some large crustacean by the thing's claw.

'Then you will tell me about this in the presence of my father and mother,' she said.

'Okay,' he replied, but felt a degree of reluctance about that. He didn't want his reason for being here generally known as it might reach the wrong ears. He had little doubt Jason Chel had spies or other means of gathering information in Holm. The man had been an operator for twice as long as Roland had been alive. He continued, 'What will be the situation with Drannic now?'

He glanced up at the grav raft matching their course. The man had been incapable of riding his eel back. One of the others had tended to him, injecting drugs and binding up his chest, but the man was still injured and would be so for some time. Though they had advanced technology here the people did not as yet have nanosuites. Though it had not come into his consideration until now, he felt a stab of annoyance about this result of Polity politicking. This world was not actually in the Polity as yet, so the AIs had given the people a taste of what they could have should they join, and information access to find out about the rest. Certainly they would join. Here they could live to a hundred and fifty years with an average span of about a hundred. The promise of virtual immortality always brought such First Diaspora colony worlds in.

'He will recover from his injuries and go his own way without me,' she replied.

'Any likelihood of trouble in the future?'

'I don't know.'

Roland just accepted that. If he were in Drannic's position he would fight for her, but then, maybe, Drannic did not have the connection with her that he had. Perhaps Drannic was not a 'match' with her. Roland grimaced at that knowing that so much of their connection resulted from conventional human drives. It was pleasurable, extremely so, but would likely take the usual course of such things. It would last as long as it lasted.

In from the eel pens stood a city wall. This recent foamstone addition stood ten metres tall and was faced with ceramic tiles. Towers punctuated it and they came to one gate standing between two of those. Glancing along the wall, Roland could see further pairs of towers and knew of further gates. The eel riders all halted their mounts and started dismounting. As Sansaclear brought 'Derek' to the ground, Roland snagged up his pack and weapon and leapt off. She followed him a moment later with a pack of her own. In her hand she also held a thing like a large almond seed that appeared ornately carved, but was not. Organic tech related to the eels and the saddles. Even as she inserted this object into her pack the saddle began to retract its various protrusions and collapse into the eel's back.

She spoke in Anglic then, for his benefit, 'Go eat something, Derek.'

The eel came up to her and dipped its nose in front of her. She reached out and gave it a scratch, then reached further back and scratched behind one of the head fins. It tilted its head for a moment, closing its eyes. When she took her hand away it shook itself, turned and rapidly headed off. By now the saddle just looked like a flat chunk of scar tissue on its back. All the other eels headed off likewise, while the grav platform floated into the city over the wall. Sansaclear's father strolled over.

'You will be a guest in our house, of course,' he said. 'And I think we will have some things to discuss.'

'Yes, there is much to discuss,' he agreed.

The father led the way through the open gates. Glancing over, Roland noted that the gates were driven by hydraulic rams. There had been a few attacks here by the lice but nothing severe enough to warrant such defences which, when it came down to it, would be useless whenever the world tide came. As he understood it the lice had never entered the city because, sensing their approach, the eels came out of their pens and hunted the creatures down, gobbling up large numbers of the things.

'Why such heavy defences?' he abruptly asked. 'The last few attacks from the lice didn't even get close.'

The father looked round, then halted. They all halted. The man stepped up close to Roland and stuck out his hand. 'We haven't been properly introduced, which is neglectful of my daughter. I'm Erland Langstrom, and you are?'

Roland reached out and gripped the hand. 'Roland Three Indomial.' They shook and released, and Erland stepped back.

'A surname that is familiar to me. Are you any relation to Carleston Three Indomial?'

Roland waved a dismissive hand. 'I know of no one of that name, but then there were some millions of the Three Indomials at last count.'

Erland nodded and turned away, gesturing to the wall as he did so. 'I gave instructions that the wall should be built. The murder lice are a problem but not a big one. Of more concern is that over two hundred citizens have gone missing only here and, as you must be aware, the people of this world are spread all over.'

The Polity had no count on that, but knew that Chel had been snatching people for a long time before the disappearances became noticeable to the authorities here. Quite possibly he was breeding those he had changed. He could have thousands of creatures like himself at his command.

They now walked along a stone street with a mix of shell houses and the more recent two-storey stone houses on either side. The street stretched just wide enough for those riding eels down here not to knock over pedestrians with the tails of their mounts. No ground vehicles were in evidence. Roland turned to Sansaclear.

'You forgot to mention that your father is the mayor of this city,' he said.

She gave him a stern look. 'And he never mentioned it either.'

'I know more than I've revealed, but shortly you will know why.'

Halfway along the street Erland turned and walked up to a wide double door in one of the stone houses. The door itself was formed of kelp wood planks studded with copper rivets. Handles and a big locking box were made of copper too. But instead of producing some key, Erland palmed what looked like a piece of shell to one side. Palm reader, Roland realised – Polity tech. Thereafter the doors swung open smoothly to admit them.

Scanning around, Roland noted the concessions to this house regularly filling with water. Everything was made of stone, ceramic, kelp wood and plastics. Oblate objects that served as cupboards were fixed to the floor. Nothing was left out loose to float or be washed around. Tiles covered the floor, walls and ceiling. Hemispherical lights were set in the walls and, seeing them, he realised that electrics, in such a society were a luxury, while their installation a complicated affair. He already knew that many of the goods the Polity traded here had to be water, pressure and corrosion resistant.

Erland led them into a seating area much like the one he and Sansaclear had occupied in the ground cyst. He now noticed how the cushions stuck themselves to the floor – a line of resin running around their edges. They were biotech based on molluscs – probably those great limpets he had seen when first arriving. He noted the screen up on a stand nearby. This was another anachronism. All the houses here had these and got their politically biased news and homogenised entertainment from local services. Only with the introduction of Polity netlinks had things begun to change and had people begun to question 'accepted knowledge'. Of course, those who broadcast news and current affairs here most protested integration with the Polity.

'It's something we are correcting,' Gurnik had told him. 'Our history of experience with networked information and its media has long been rendered down to simple formulae. We know the memes to start and how and what information to disseminate.'

The broadcasters here and their political funders would fail, since the AIs were on their case.

A woman stood up from one of the seats, her expression angry. Roland noted that she, unlike Sansaclear and her father, had webbed feet. She strode straight over to Sansaclear and slapped her across the face.

'You stupid girl!' she said, then grabbed her up in a fierce hug. The mother, Roland presumed. After a moment she released her, glared at Roland, then turned to her husband. 'What happened?'

'A great deal,' Erland replied. He gestured to Roland, 'Margent, I would like you to meet Roland Three Indomial, who is now our daughter's mate.'

'You fucking what!' said Margent.

'I think I was quite clear,' said Erland, his expression hardening.

Margent caught that and dialled down her outrage. 'What about Drannic?'

'Probably in the hospital even now,' said Erland.

Now Margent studied Roland more closely, before abruptly walking over to the door into the room to close and lock it. Another anachronism here: people higher in the hierarchy had domestic staff and she didn't want them listening. Returning, she squeezed her daughter's shoulder and Sansaclear smiled at her. It seemed the initial slap had been forgotten. She sat down and gestured to the other cushions. Erland sat on her cushion, close, but leaning forwards. Roland walked over to one opposite. Sansaclear moved up fast and caught hold of his arm, and they sat together on that cushion.

'Like you, husband?' Margent asked.

'That is what I am about to find out.' Erland looked up at Roland. 'How old are you, Polity man?'

'Two fifty,' said Roland reluctantly.

Sansaclear looked round at him wide-eyed. He shrugged. It was what it was.

'Marines or commandos?' Erland asked.

'Marines, briefly.'

'Until someone else recruited you…'

So, it seemed that Sansaclear's father was a little more than just your average Polity citizen who had settled on a primitive world. He tried to think of the best way to begin, but the man beat him too it.

'Do you have a thin gun?' he asked.

Roland grimaced and sat back. Sansaclear still sat forwards but reached out and put a hand on his leg. The connection remained, no matter what he would say now – he was sure of that, wasn't he?

'I have been an agent of ECS for a century,' he told them. 'Yes, I have a thin gun but I did not bring it to this world. What I need to do I want to do with as few casualties as possible. I'm here to deal with Jason Chel, and now I'll tell you how, but the information must not leave this room.'

They waited. Sansaclear turned to face him, her expression, he realised, was proud. He nodded to her, sighed out a breath and then, as naturally as that breath, he turned his gridlink back on.

Data links had established in his mind, initially limited by the access restrictions on this world, then opening up as a local AI accepted his gridlink code. He began crunching data and checking for updates, confirming some suppositions. He now knew, for example, that the number of humans Chel had kidnapped and changed sat between two and three thousand from the many cities, small towns and other settlements all over the planet. If breeding was factored in the number could be in the tens of thousands now. However, satellite data made the local AI doubtful of this – such a number would require resources and would be difficult to hide. It suspected no more than the low thousands. Strategically it also surmised that Chel might be using the lice to probe the defences of various cities.

'But he is taking his sweet time before attacking,' it had told him.

'Being very careful – meticulous,' Roland had opined.

'I think not. I think there is another agenda here.'

'How so?'

'Consider that of all the world tide planets he could have gone to he chose this one, with a moon obviously containing alien technology.'

'Some connection with the changer Jain tech?'

'No – the certainty that we would be very interested in this place and inclined to remove any threats.'

'Ennui? He's in his period of ennui?'

'No. he's long past that, but he is not beyond being tired of his life.'

Roland had acknowledged that and understood.

As he, Sansaclear and Erland left the house and headed over to the prison, Roland all the while processed data and checked on the infective nanosuite clone, but he also kept talking and stayed aware of his surroundings.

'Have you noticed any change in me?' he asked. He had already told her about the gridlink, and his fear that having re-engaged it might… change him.

'You've gone a bit glassy eyed a few times, but nothing particularly noticeable,' she replied. She turned to him with a slightly amused expression. 'Have you turned into a robot, then?'

He gazed at her. They had gone to her room. Sex had been urgent and as quiet as possible in her parents' house, and the gridlink operating had not impinged. Afterwards she had changed into a tight bodysuit. He now wanted to take it off with his teeth.

'It's something much discussed in the Polity – the idea that humans taking technological mental enhancements can lose emotional engagement,' he said. 'It's been my understanding that it is only the expectation that causes this but,' he shrugged, 'I was concerned.'

'Love brings it anxieties,' she said, repositioning the strap of her amoeba gun. 'I have enough of my own.'

Love? At the thought his gridlink offered up a thousand explanations related to hormones and evolutionary programming. He almost laughed, and dismissed them. Yes, love, why not? It was a good a word as any to describe his strength of feeling.

They hurried to catch up when Erland, who had gone on to talk with the Warden, beckoned them over. As they approached, the Warden waved off the two guards lingering a few paces away. It seemed that Erland was doing what he could to keep a lid on this. The warden turned to the big heavily-studded door and unlocked it with a coded key rod. He handed this over to Erland, gave a brief nod in their direction, then headed off after the guards.

'Come on,' said Erland, leading the way inside.

The prison resembled some of those on Earth that had been retained as institutions of historical importance. Those places even had their prisoners and ran as they did centuries in the past. However, the prisoners were simply Polity citizens who had signed up to enjoy the prison experience. Few people in the Polity were incarcerated now. Mental editing and straight mind-wipe had seen to that, while some of the worst offenders encountered agents like Roland...

'Are there many prisoners here?' Roland asked.

'Not many,' Erland replied. 'Capital crimes receive capital punishment. For other crimes the offenders pay recompense, even if it takes them their whole lives, or they end up on the bad end of a challenge.' He grimaced. 'Once we have agreement to join the Polity we'll be able to close this place. But for now, for those others, we did not know what else to do with them.'

'There are others elsewhere too?'

'Just about every city or town with the facilities keeps them.'

Roland nodded. The AIs seemed to have neglected this point, and it reduced the likely numbers still running free. He frowned. AIs didn't make mistakes like that.

They went down arched corridors of particularly dank stone, of course unsurprising here. Doors stood open into many cells, which were empty. Stairs then wound down to an iron door. Erland opened it with the code rod, stepped through and turned on lights. A long chamber extended from steps leading down, lined on either side with cages of polished steel. With the lights on a racket had started up: the crashing of bodies throwing themselves about, the clattering of mandibles, carapace-armoured hands scrabbling at the bars and a concerted hissing. Roland studied the human forms in the cages and estimated that there must be at least a hundred of them.

'It's like Chel doesn't know what to do with them,' said Sansaclear from beside him.

'What do you mean?'

'They are vicious and like murder lice will attack anything moving. But everything has been so random, attacks from these telegraphed and easily countered.'

'But still people are killed.'

'Yes.' She pointed at the figures. 'These are our people and sometimes we have to kill them when no other option is available. Very few of us, who are unchanged, have been killed by them. They attack like animals and so can be dealt with in the same way.'

Roland nodded. This seemed a partial confirmation of what the AI had implied. Chel was being provocative without reaching out for his purported objective. Chel's real objective, at least now, wasn't really to create a race or garner power. It was, in essence, very similar to the objective of those who went into ennui.

They moved down between the cages, enabling him to get a closer look at the occupants. These were people Chel had changed and who those in this city had managed to capture alive. Their changes stood at variance. Most had mandibles but many were malformed. Some still wore some of their original clothing, but probably only because it had not been ripped away. All of them now had compound eyes, and jointed carapaces over their skin. Some had antennae, on others these were curled up like plants touched by fire. Some threw themselves against the bars, mindlessly trying to attack, or escape – it wasn't clear what they wanted. Many of them just lay curled up on the floor of the cages.

'Give me the weapon,' said Roland.

Sansaclear unhooked it from her shoulder and handed it over. He now inspected it more closely. The body of the thing looked like a folded up insect new from a chrysalis, while the barrel seemed like the proboscis of a mosquito writ large, while extended wing cases formed the stock. It was warm and he could feel its slight throbbing. These biotech weapons had been developed here long after the First Diaspora by new arrivals who had come here to take the wholly biotech route. They had not managed to impose their ideology on the original residents and had long since integrated. Though, as he understood it, small enclaves of them still existed. The weapon, he knew, could fire a lot of those amoeba rounds, and then it had to be stored away in the dark and fed.

He held his hands against the thing and in what seemed an internal third eye he called up the status on the infective clone of his nanosuite. Completely ready now the thing had installed the required organelles, microfactories and nanites to impart itself via the poison sacs in his hands and wrists. He shifted the complex four dimensional schematic aside and searched out the adjuncts. A number had been prepared: for infecting lice to make them carriers, to put the suite inside a parasite of the lice which had doubtless become parasites of those in the cages, a dart option and more besides. But he skimmed past them straight to the amoeba adjunct. The genomes and schematics of the weapon had long been in Polity databases. This adjunct was necessarily large and complex to suppress some of the amoeba's function. Whereas before an amoeba round could kill a human, one with this adjunct would only kill tissue arising from the lice genome. He selected it and set it loading to the suite already in the poison sacs of his right hand. As he did this he contemplated Gurnik's characterising him as 'having a flare for the dramatic' and grimaced.

'Roland?'

He came partially out of it, assessed present circumstances and realised he had been standing motionless for three minutes.

'All is good,' he told her.

Internally he felt a fizzing as his suite created the adjunct. A large portion of Gridlink processing dropped out of his compass to oversee that. But he tracked internal operation and felt his right hand beginning to grow hot. Then the indicators came up for his inspection. It was ready.

He probed over the surface of the weapon. Hard keratin covered most of it, but he soon found the soft spots sitting between segments. He extended his claws, spread his fingers to get four of those spots, stabbed in and injected the suite. He waited then until a data feed came up from the weapon, got a confirmation and extracted his claws.

'Polity biotech and nanosuites have come a long way since I was a marine,' said Erland.

Roland grimaced. 'Not so far. Just as a marine there would have been a lot of stuff you did not know about.' He looked up and studied the walls, noting small spheroids sticking out on stalks. 'Are those cams off?'

'Yes, I told the Warden to shut them down.'

'Good.' Roland nodded. He turned to Sansaclear. 'It'll probably be ugly, but the likelihood of failure is minimal. Even if some do start to go wrong the nanosuite will take them down into biological stasis until I can find a solution.' He tapped a finger against his skull.

'I wasn't worried,' she replied. 'About that anyway.'

'What worries you?'

'The future.'

He winced. She must be thinking about what might happen once he had completed his mission. Since he had every chance of ending up dead while carrying it out, he had put aside thoughts of the future. He stepped up to the bars of the nearest cage, while studying the trigger and control mechanism of the gun. The trigger just looked like a spiky leg sticking out, with another looped round as a guard. A row of segments that turned like wheels formed the control mechanism.

'Help me out with this,' he said to Sansaclear. 'I want scatter shot.'

She stepped up with a slight frown and he felt stupid trying to include her. She was obviously thoroughly aware that he needed no help with this at all. Nevertheless, she turned two of the segments up to the top and the last one right down to the bottom. Against the louse that had been hunting him she used a single shot that spat out a chunk of amoeba on a straight and accurate trajectory. The scatter setting made the weapon act almost like a shotgun, sending a wide spray of smaller chunks of the amoeba. He nodded. She'd put it on the widest scatter.

Turning back to the bars, he saw one of the changed right up close. It wasn't trying to get to him, just standing there. Did he read some remaining humanity? It certainly lingered in there because these people had not lost their minds. They had just been driven into unconscious subordination to the louse adaptation. But unconsciousness being a moveable feast meant that the mind concerned might not have shut down completely. He studied this 'person', noting that though most of its eyes were compound, a human iris and pupil sat at the centre of each. Reaching out, he shoved it in the chest with the barrel of the weapon. It just took a step back and moved away. Looking around he noticed that the racket had diminished. Perhaps they had tired of trying to get out, but he could not help but think they sensed something and were waiting expectantly.

'Here we go,' he said, aiming between bars towards the centre back of the cage to give the most coverage, and fired.

The weapon bucked in his hands and that surprised him – he had not expected recoil. With a thwack the spray shot entered the cage, spreading widely and slow enough to be visible, like the spray from a shower head. The changed hissed and clattered and began throwing themselves about, one of them just running round and round the cage, two hitting the bars directly opposite him. He saw glassy droplets of amoeba on their carapaces, sinking and spreading to create a shiny layer. Running a search program in his gridlink, he had it highlight impact sites, and a mass of squares briefly blinked up in his vision. Analysis completed, he saw that some he had not hit but, because of their frenzied activity, they were crashing into each other and moments later all in the cage had amoeba on them and spreading, and some in the adjoining cages too. Roland turned and headed across the aisle between cages to one on the other side.

'Shouldn't we wait?' asked Erland.

'No,' Roland replied, recognising hardness in his tone he had heard in both of their voices on other occasions. He glanced at Sansaclear and she merely tilted her head – she trusted he knew what he was doing.

He fired into the cage opposite. 'The changes will be rapid,' he explained. 'We don't want changed in there with those who are shedding their changes – they'll just end up as meat.'

He missed the next cage along and fired into the next. Via his gridlink he had assessed that there might be enough overlap but, anyway, when he came back to those intervening cages, the strategy gave him the greatest coverage. Five cages with ten to twelve of the changed in each. He walked back down again, now firing into the cages he had missed, tracking the spread of the amoeba fragments. Chaos reigned behind those bars and the racket had climbed to an appalling level. Still, scanning up and down, he saw that every single one of them had been hit. Their previously dull carapaces now gleamed as if polished with spread amoeba.

'That's it,' he said, turning and handing the weapon over to Sanclear, who had come to his shoulder at the last.

'How long?' she asked.

'They'll shed their changes very quickly,' he told her and her father who had just come up. 'It will take longer to repair the damage to them.' He looked directly Erland. 'It won't look pleasant.'

'Understood,' said the man.

Roland would have preferred to have had a local medical team in here, but they had agreed that by bringing others in like that it would have become almost impossible to keep this secret.

Standing in the centre of the aisle they watched. The hissing and clattering of mandibles changed and took on a human element, blurring into screams and groans. No visible change showed at first, but then

Roland began to see pieces of carapace on the floors of the cages. He pointed.

'It's happening.'

One slammed against the side of the cage opposite to them and tried to bite at the bars with its mandibles, when it pulled away the mandibles remained in place clamped around a bar.

'They are not actually conscious,' said Sansaclear, fighting to keep her voice steady.

'No, they're not,' Roland said firmly, glad of the ability through his gridlink to assess and steady the nuance of his voice even as he spoke because, as he had thought before, unconsciousness was debateable. He now saw bloody flesh exposed by falling carapace. No massive bleeding started and that flesh began quickly spotting with new skin, silvery and seemingly scaled like his own. As he watched he began to hear a new sound and could not figure it out until Erland went over to wire connected phone hanging on one wall. He picked it up and listened, then started talking fast and angrily in the local language. Roland automatically recorded the conversation in his gridlink and began translating. He had the gist of it before Erland slammed the phone down and came back to them, and was already formulating a plan.

'There's a crowd gathering outside,' he said. 'They are not happy at all.'

Roland nodded briefly. 'Well, the lid is off now.' He looked up at the cams. 'The Warden said he does not know how it happened, that in fact it should be impossible.'

Erland showed momentary surprised that Roland had understood and heard both sides of the exchange, then replied, 'He shut down the cams in here on the main board.'

'Then he is either lying to you, or...' Roland shook his head. His gridlink had not affected his connection with Sansaclear, but it had certainly speeded up logical thinking. 'The cam feed went straight into a broadcast network, yes?'

'It did.'

'And now he has shut it down?'

'He has – he powered down the whole cam system.'

'Okay – however this happened we have to deal with it. We could go with the story that the changed were beyond recovery and we put them down, but that simply won't scan because there'll be no dead bodies here and people will check.' He hesitated, then continued, 'Those watching will have seen them apparently in pain and that is likely to lead to you being unseated and the three of us being arrested. Also, we need cooperation for what comes next.' He gestured to the changed, all now down on the floors of the cages and moving weakly, oily looking carapace lying all around them. 'We'll need soldiers, more amoeba guns and eels.'

'There is only one solution as I see it,' said Sansaclear.

He focused his attention on her, 'And that is?'

'We tell the truth.'

He nodded. 'Agreed. We'll just have to accept that Chel will know we are coming, and we'll just have to move as fast as we can.' He turned to Erland. 'We need to settle things out there so call in a medical team as quick as you can. Get your local police here too and, get onto the Warden and have him put those cams back on.'

'Broadcast?' Erland asked.

'Yes, you need to set that up.'

Erland immediately headed over to the phone and picked it up. He delivered his instructions quickly, tersely, then lodged the phone against his ear.

'I'll speak to them. I can –' he began.

'No.' Roland held up his hand. 'I'll speak to them first telling them about the cure while you just stand back and look pissed off. I then suggest that when I hand over to you, you show some anger at what you've seen – that you didn't expect it to go the way it did. You can say that I have assured you that they did not actually suffer. Show some doubt.'

'Why?'

'Because they trust you and that's how I want things to continue. Don't misrepresent what it looked like in here to those on the outside. If they distrust you there's a good chance that your opponents in the city council will undermine you, and then slow down or maybe even stop what must happen next.'

Erland nodded doubtfully, then turned back to the phone, quickly barking instructions. Roland turned to Sansaclear who was staring into the cages. He moved up beside her and put an arm around her waist.

'They may have suffered,' he admitted. He did not need to wonder why he had done so – the strong sense of connections made hidden lies sour inside him. 'But it would have only been a brief thing.'

'The nanosuites aren't just to rid them of their changes,' she said.

'Exactly.' He watched them; some were beginning to crawl around, while others remained foetal. The carapace scattered around them was losing any clinging meat or tendon as the amoeba ate that away, but it seemed to be leaving the chitin intact and bleached white with lines of dirty yellow.

'More concerning will be mental reintegration – the louse mind will die slowly and they'll remember, maybe just fragments, but they'll remember what they were and what they did.'

'They cannot blame themselves.' She turned to him. 'Not that that will make a great deal of difference.' She grabbed his shoulder and kissed him. He didn't care that the cams might be back online.

'Put that man down, daughter,' Erland called. 'I have a medical team scrambled – already in the prison.'

Sansaclear backed away from him with an almost shy smile.

'Cams are back up,' Erland added, then seated the phone when there came a hammering at the door. He headed over to open it, and a worried looking woman came in carrying large case. She wore some kind of filmy coverall. The others that soon followed her were similarly clad. The medical team had come prepared for amoeba rounds.

'Angat ... uck... fuck,' said someone. Glancing round Roland saw one of the changed up on his knees. He was naked and looked as if hideously burned, but he now appeared substantially more human. He staggered to his feet, human skin spreading across bloody flesh. Let out a human snarl which, thankfully, seemed to only contain anger. Consciousness was returning to them but, meanwhile, as Sansaclear had understood, their nanosuites were doing what that technology did, and administering pain relief. The medical team was unnecessary, but he knew it would play well.

'The cages,' Roland told Erland and needed to say no more as the man went over and started opening them. The medical team moved in, but seemed bewildered about what to do. The worried looking woman gazed at him and then gestured at the rapidly healing people spread out on the floor all around her.

He shrugged. 'Clothing would be good.'

The world tide came after two planetary days, which were about twice as long as a solstan day. Lice swarmed in the seas about the city and the thump of cavitating weapons transmitted through the water almost hourly.

Chel knew.

Watching from the balcony of Sansaclear's room, Roland ran an overlay and gathered new information about fighting the lice underwater. Most of the lice swam in high but those that didn't fell victim to the worms in the sand around the city. Roland felt a visceral horror of the things. Their bodies were much the same size as the eels – what he could see of them, but were segmented and ended in a wide mouth surrounded by a ring of grasping mandibles. He knew he would never be able to walk on that sand again with the same nonchalance as before. Transferring his attention to the city he noted the changes. The eels had come in from the pens. Many of them had riders and many not. They were another defence, snapping up stray lice the weapons missed, occasionally becoming impatient and heading out to sweep up even more.

The overlay confirmed an assessment he had made before. Though still unable to penetrate the city because of the eels and the weapons here, the lice were much more effective swimming than running on the ground. This meant that in the attack he intended to lead, they could not approach Chel's stronghold while it lay underwater since it gave the man too many angles of attack. He ran plans and logistics by the local AI, but it could come up with nothing better than the plan he had already made. He noted it seemed reluctant with its input – this was all entirely up to him.

Dismissing the overlay he peered up at the towers, seeing nets deployed and shifting like sails. World tide business continued despite the siege as these swept up passing shoals of fish and, more often than not, swimming lice. He noted another tower with a crane-like attachments protruding, and other gear all around. From there a long line speared up and, struggling at the end of it as the fishermen wound it in, was a huge armoured fish. Once down to the other gear the fish would be rapidly taken apart to finally arrive at the foot of the tower as packaged meat. Other gear up there scooped in plankton to be compressed into cakes, or snatched up floating edible plants. The harvest was rich and it seemed unlikely this city would ever grow hungry.

Swimmers were everywhere and, even as he surveyed his surroundings, one came past. The man raised his hand in a salute and continued on. Roland was well recognised now. After his broadcast there had been a lot of anger about his intervention, but when the changed began coming out of the prison returned to human form most of it died. Roland returned the salute, then, jumping up and pushing his feet against the rail, dived back into the room.

The net above the bed, which was the sleeping arrangement when the world tide came in, hung empty. Sansaclear floated over to one side pulling on metallic mesh clothing. Many were dressed in the same, including that swimmer – the usual partial nakedness had ceased to be a great idea with lice about. The mesh was an alloy they made here – light and strong and much like that used by people who played with sharks or, in essence, chainmail. He watched, relishing the view as she tumbled in place, then wondered if he should use his bracelet to dull his libido during the day, because she was always a bit of a distraction. He didn't want to, and instead replayed their third full night together. Sex under the world tide was similar to sex in zero gee – sometimes logistically difficult but always highly stimulating. They had exhausted themselves last night and then again this morning. He replayed mental images for a while until she spotted him watching and gave him an arch look. She used hand signals to tell him: *I'm not taking this thing off again, and I'm hungry. Later.* Instead of signalling back, he spoke, his voice a strange tinny and echoing thing. This was a recent revision to his adaptation.

'Things to do today anyway,' he said.

Finally clad, she swam over and he caught her hand. They spun slowly around each other and he saw her eyes widen as she inspected him from head to foot.

'Your feet!' she said.

'I found the webbing tiring and uncomfortable when walking,' he replied. 'They were also a notable hindrance when I fought Drannic.'

His feet were now back to human normal – another revision of his adaptation.

'I need to get myself one of those nanosuites,' she said.

'You do indeed,' he replied, 'once the Polity permits.' Even as he spoke the words he felt uncomfortable with them. Something had been niggling at his mind since they visited the prison, but had yet to come clear.

They swam out of her room and down into the house. Neither of her parents were about as they went into the food preparation area and ate raw fish and a fruit from the numerous varieties of wrack that grew here. The fish came direct from the tower nets. He found it strange eating under water, but stranger still having to drink bottled fresh water. While eating he took in a lot of the salt water around him and necessarily needed fresh to allow his body to eject the salts. Urination under the world tide was constant. It didn't seem to bother the people that they lived in their own urine, though the city council had recently ordered special turbines installed to increase water flow in some areas and eject it.

After eating and drinking they left the house, swimming high above streets they had earlier walked, then diverting over and between buildings. As he swam, Roland wondered if he had made a mistake changing his feet back to normal, but then decided he had not, because he wanted to be most functional when the world tide passed.

They came in over a building in the shape of an H, and he considered a historical aspect to that shape, because here lay the prison. As they swam down he saw people and equipment in the two prison yards sitting within that formation. Erland had decided that the prison had the best security for them to make their preparations.

'I wonder what my father is worried about… about them,' said Sansaclear.

'We will find out soon enough.' Roland noted then how, unlike in other relationships he'd had, they never talked about 'their day', because they were never apart long enough for one to have experienced something different. And he would never have it any other way.

They spiralled down to one of the yards. All the people here – gathered in groups or swimming in or above the yard – wore full body mesh with armoured additions. Many were moving equipment while others carried training weapons. Presently their real weapons sat in storage. Amoeba guns were in the dark and feeding – charging up after he had loaded them with the nanosuite.

Finally they came down into the yard proper to find Erland checking on supplies netted to the ground. They swam down near him, catching hold of one of the nets. He saw them, nodded to himself and came over.

'What's the problem?' Roland asked.

Erland also wore mesh and armour. His wife had argued with him about this, but not very strongly. She had to be aware that an erstwhile Polity marine was not going to sit at home while others went off to do the fighting.

'Just as you specified, we have a force of five hundred – city police and military – to open the way in,' he said. We'll spread as many of the available amoeba guns as we can amidst them, but they'll be armed with other weapons mostly to deal with the lice. The bulk of the amoeba guns go to your strike force.'

'That's the plan. I calculate that Chel will use the lice first and hold those he has changed for defence of his base. So what *is* the problem?'

'The strike force.'

'If you could elaborate?'

'Are you sure you're using the right people for it?'

'The previously changed are much less likely to be careless of the lives of those they were like. If you had an aug I could even give the AI-mapped psych profile.'

'Come with me,' said Erland.

He swam off and they followed, down to a door leading into the prison. Within they did not swim but propelled themselves with handles set in the walls – again much like in zero gee. Erland led them a complicated route but, since he had a map of the prison in his gridlink, Roland figured out where they were heading. They arrived at the door into where the changed had been caged. The door stood open and a man in mesh began to come out through it. He halted in the doorway, staring at Roland, then turned and called back.

'Polity man is here,' he said, then propelled himself back into the chamber, beckoning them to follow.

The cages had been hung with fabric and partitioned. He knew that while accommodation had been offered, the erstwhile changed had decided to stay together here and in surrounding cells. Much generosity from the city people had provided for their comfort. It seemed a little odd, but he understood their need and how their shared trauma had bound them – that was in the psych profile too. Some, apparently, had been of this city and gone off to find relatives, but they had swiftly returned.

'That,' said Erland, indicating the end of the room where one cage had been dismantled and turned into racking. Items packed this racking and even as they swam in and towards the end, he guessed what was there. The people here swam around them and accompanied them, others peered out of their accommodation. They didn't say much, these people. How could one talk about the thing they had experienced, and how could one then transition to talking about the prosaic? It would take time, a lot of time or, if the Polity became involved, perhaps some mental editing. Roland arrived at the racking and pulled himself down beside it. He turned to an individual nearby.

'What did you use for colour?' he asked. He gestured to encompass the water they were under. 'Must have been difficult during world tide.'

'Underwater paint, from the Polity,' the woman replied. 'Very easy to use.'

Roland surveyed the piles of carapace, tied down in nets to stop it drifting away. This was the stuff they had shed and it had retained its integrity. The pieces were painted bright red and blue. He now focused on those working around here. He could see a man sticking small pieces of carapace to a mesh glove, still another worked on a whole suit mounted on what looked like an old Earth tailor's dummy. He noted the tools and the various substances in use. They were all Polity products, including the crash foam being used to stick carapace to the mesh suit. He then noted two cylinders open on the floor with many such items still inside. They were orbital delivery cylinders dropped by drone. He walked over to the man working on the suit.

'Seems the Polity has supplied you with all your needs,' he said.

The man hunched his shoulders, and didn't look round.

'It was just an idea... but everything was there.'

'You used a netlink, I presume.'

'Yeah.'

The man now turned to face him, bobbed his head in a way Roland found distasteful, as if the guy was being obsequious to the 'man from the Polity'. He gestured around him. 'I just did a little search on the idea, and everything came up, like someone was there and knew exactly what I wanted even before I did.'

Roland reached out and squeezed his shoulder. 'You're doing a good job,' and then he turned back to Sansaclear and Erland. He had little doubt that someone on the other end of that netlink had been very helpful – someone not human. He gestured away and they headed off, passing a man stepping out of one of the accommodations in full armour – medieval and somehow quite threatening. The man smiled and saluted.

'There's nothing we need concern ourselves with here,' Roland said once they were out of the cage room. 'They stuck together because of shared trauma and this is an identity thing. They probably feel they don't belong in the society they came from any more and are now building their own.'

'It's just that armour...' said Erland.

'Enemy skulls displayed on a pike,' said Roland. 'If anything this will make them more effective for our purposes. And for them, meanwhile, it is a psychological crutch.'

What he did not say, since he wanted Erland on side, was that perhaps the man had not integrated here as much as he supposed. Roland felt confident the painted armour from their previous selves perfectly fitted the barbarian ethos here. But what lay beyond that concerned him. He knew, without a doubt, he stood in the middle of the creation of a legend. He also knew that a Polity AI had driven it for purposes he had yet to fathom.

Over two days Roland watched the surface of the sea drop down towards the city. Louse concentration increased for a while, but then began to diminish. They seemed to be all heading off in the same direction. Out at the eel pens, he stood waiting, and with his left hand reached back to touch the hilt of the sword strapped to his back. These people and their swords... He shrugged and took his hand away. It was a tradition in these circumstances – all part of a rite of passage. He now looked down at one of those almond shaped chunks of biotech in his right hand. He could feel something from it like a muttering through his bones. His gridlink kept alerting him to anomalous changes in his body, to which his nanosuite did not know how to respond, or rather, whether to respond. He flagged the changes as part of him rather like when a person wanted to retain a scar, and told their nanosuite to leave it alone.

He studied the mounded shells. They really did look like giant winkles and, having checked, he found that the molluscs inside much resembled the same on Earth, except being larger and therefore more subject to gravity, they grew chitin skeletons inside. These shells had been gathered over a century before when the molluscs served as a food source for the inhabitants. What was now called the eel pens had been a dump for the shells until they came in useful for building. The eels had come to occupy them at about the same time as an enclave of biotech adherents arrived on the world. The creatures were hunted, but many also kept them as pets and found they could be trained. Biotechnology had further extended that training.

Eels were moving in and out of this place – more returning here now the lice were departing. Some were being taken up by riders either standing waiting just like him or swimming. Finally he saw his eel winding down from one of the shells right on top. He knew it at once and in another time and place this would have been put down to intuition or some supernatural influence. But his knowledge arose from penetrative bio sonar and pheromones being picked up by those changes in his body. The eel was large, well above the twenty metres of Sansaclear's creature, and it had distinct chequerboard markings running down the sides of its body. He felt a stab of cynicism on seeing it. Of course it had to be large and distinct – all part of the legend – but then he reconsidered because he could think of no way an AI could influence this.

Reaching the bottom it kicked up sand to drift across the city rock as it came closer and then circled him, inspecting him all the while with black-pupil eyes of a vivid orange. It then nosed towards him. He could feel its curiosity, while the low rumble of its mind, like some engine turning over, soon slid into to occupy a virtual space in his gridlink. Closer it came, nose level with his chest, and he noted that the thing was big enough to swallow him whole. He reached out and rested a hand on its nose and it felt warm. He scratched it there then up between its eyes to the top of its head. Its eyes folded out of sight and lidded as it turned its head. He scratched it behind those fins and he could feel its pleasure, but wariness.

'We are going to get along fine,' he told it.

The hint of a reply came to him – a sense of agreement but with reservations, backed up by something predatory and hungry. The implication seemed to be that if they didn't get along fine he would be lunch.

Finally he retracted his hand. The eel shifted its head to one side and moved some way past him, bringing the rough patch of the proto saddle within reach. The area looked like a Rorschach blot of gnarled wood. To its centre sat a hole and into that he inserted the seed. From the eel he felt a sense of completion as the saddle bulged up and spread, extending stirrup protrusions and horns. He grabbed the forward horn and mounted up, the straps flicking out and closing around his legs. Now experiencing the connection he realised eel riders had no need to guide their creatures with their legs or in any other way – these were merely affirmation of thought to which the eels responded.

In a moment they were hurtling through the sea together and he necessarily had to bow down against the current threatening to tear him from his mount. They rounded the eel pens, spiralling up, went over the city and then up further. Glancing back, Roland saw another rider following and with his thought his eel slowed. Sansaclear, who had left him for the particularly personal moment of impressing on an eel, had now joined him. She pointed upwards and he nodded agreement. They swam higher, their eels occasionally diverting to snap up stray lice swimming here, crunching savagely and belching clouds of ichor and shattered carapace from their mouths. Then they breached in sprays of white water, arcing through the air and down again, then swimming in huge surface swell. Roland ejected the water from his lungs – it much less painful now – and shouted with the joy of it. They rode the waves for hours and eventually returned. As he dismounted outside the eel pens and retracted the seed, he thought of how the next time he mounted up it would be for more serious business. The eel acknowledged that with fierce joy as it returned to its home.

'It is Traben's eel,' said Sansaclear.

'Traben?'

'A city leader before my father – something of a legend around here. He went to see Chel, alone, to lodge our complaint about the lice. Nobody knows what words were spoken and he never said. After the meeting, swarms of lice attacked him but he fought his way clear, destroying many of them. He died of heart failure just a few years ago.'

Disliking that word 'legend' because of his earlier thoughts, Roland said, 'So someone selected Traben's seed for me, I presume?'

'No, it doesn't work like that. Any seed will activate any saddle and make the connection. The eel chooses.'

'Why that eel and why me, I wonder.'

'It is speculated that the eels have their own pecking order. After being Traben's eel it would not want a lesser rider.'

'Really?'

She waved a hand and repeated, 'It is speculated.'

Roland grimaced. It all still seemed a little too coincidental.

The world tide receded fast over the next day, quickly bringing the upper reaches of the towers above the sea, and by the following day was a great flood. The residents shut the external city gates and numerous internal ones because the current could destroy houses and sweep people and property away. Everything outside the city ceased to be underwater long before the inside. The bobbit worms retired to their burrows with stomachs distended by mashed up lice. The emptying came with a roaring of scupper drains in city walls and houses and the slow opening of gates to let out the flood. The sky stayed cloudy at first and a wind blew, but it seemed the tide towed the cloud along with it and drew it away. Roland breathed damp muggy air with a hundred per cent humidity. Hosing and then sweeping ensued to rid houses and streets of a layer of silt and organic detritus. Roland felt annoyed by the delay, but then checking the tide timetable knew there was no point leaving just yet – the tide travelled slower than they could and Chel's stronghold lay in its direction of travel so still under water. If they left at once they would end up pacing the tide across recently exposed ground and tide pools still swarming with dangerous life. But finally it was time.

'So your name, apparently, is Isigur,' he said. 'It is of course a much more legendary name than Derek.'

His eel tilted its head as it inspected him – paying attention with all seriousness – but within he could feel its rumbling amusement and anxiousness to be on their way.

'I can change your name if I wish,' he said. 'But I think we'll stick with that. Can't go about challenging fate and all that now can we?'

The eel's amusement increased as it turned its side to him. He inserted the seed and mounted up. Sansaclear moved up beside him on her eel – Derek – and said, 'I heard that and so did Derek.'

'His opinion?'

'Indifference.'

Erland came up on the other side and then swept his eel round.

'I feel like certain things are happening according to some plan no one has told me about,' the man said, and pointed.

Hundreds of eels were writhing across the city rock with one, two and three riders. Roland noted that second and third riders faced backwards.

When there were two riders the second one wielded a heavy rifle of some kind, be that laser carbine, pulse rifle or slug thrower. When there were three riders the third sat behind a tripod-mounted weapon on the eel's back. These flame units threw a tight stream of a burning alcohol-based fuel fermented from seaweeds. Erland wasn't pointing at them, but at the hundred in red and blue carapace armour, now mounting up on eels they had earlier impressed. All the small nimble creatures had coal black skin.

'It seems the eels have their own agendas,' said Roland, feeling as swept along with the tide as the debris that had earlier departed the city. But that Erland felt that way affirmed his own feelings. There was both subtle and overt manipulation going on here, outside influence… Polity AIs.

'They are capable of colour change,' said Sansaclear, but she sounded puzzled.

'Squid DNA,' said Roland.

'What?' Her puzzlement increased.

'Those biotechs a century ago didn't just stick biotech saddles on local creatures. They altered the creatures themselves.' He winced, wondering how she would feel when he added, 'And their riders.'

'Yes, I see that,' she replied, delighting him again with the quality of her mind.

Soon everyone mounted up and all looked towards him. With his gridlink he took bearings. There would be no subtlety about this. He waved a finger in a circle above his head and set out, sweeping between clumps of riders. After a short time he looked around. Sansaclear rode on his right, Erland on his left, and the armoured hundred hurried to catch up behind. All seemed chaotic at first but gradually the formation began to harden. An arrow head with him at the tip, consisting of those conventionally armed, with the bulk of the three-rider eels directly behind him in the tip. The armoured hundred gathered directly behind. They had been ordered not to use their weapons unless absolutely necessary until they reached Chel's stronghold, the only exception being if they encountered any of the changed on the way. Erland had questioned this and, as a concession, Roland had allowed them conventional weapons each. He just hoped that Chel did not decide now to go round them and attack the city, because it had been all but depleted of armament.

The tidescape seethed with life. He saw slow crabs along the horizon silhouetted against the rising sun. Tide pools boiled with feeding frenzies and, on the shore of one, mosasaurs basked, perhaps out of the frenzy with full stomachs. Just half a kilometre from the city the shooting started as lice rose up shrugging caked sand off their backs and attacked. It seemed the bobbit worms had not killed all that came into their territory. Roland ramped up magnification in his vision, and through a layer of murk saw more of the creatures swarming in the distance.

'We need to go faster,' he said. Isigur accelerated, pulling ahead of the others, so he added, 'Without leaving the others behind.' The eel slowed with something like a mental shrug. Roland smiled and unlimbered his weapon. The riders behind him hadn't allowed him any targets. They were, he was damned sure, being overprotective. He didn't raise the scope but merely gridlinked to the carbine to put crosshairs in his vision. Well, they weren't letting the lice close, so he would take the ones further away. He began shooting to thin out the numbers gathering ahead. He felt no particular excitement with this – it was simply coldly calculating. He made every shot count and, if possible, more than once, by lining up on lice gathered close together and putting tight beam shots through two or three of them.

Spray then blurred all ahead as they came towards a tidal lake. Roland surveyed the terrain and with a thought had his eel go left. The formation tracked him exactly and he surmised that his eel had the same connection to its fellows as it had with him.

'Good strategy,' said Erland.

Roland glanced at him and noted that he had put on a Polity marine combat jacket, and that he sported a heavy pulse rifle and sidearm that had been standard issue fifty years ago. He nodded acknowledgement. To the right of the lake lay flat weedy terrain. The eels would go fast across it but the lice faster still. To the left lay slabs of rock that gave neither an advantage in speed, but the slabs were covered with those giant limpet creatures. To these the lice would be a tasty snack, but the eels something to be avoided.

The formation slowed as the eels wound over slabs and between the big molluscs. He saw their seals to the stone breaking and stalked eyes and tentacles protruding. Isigur snapped at one of them and it abruptly retracted, its shell slamming down. The lice entered this area, stray shots picking off a few but, worryingly, many of them using the molluscs as cover. Then the molluscs started reacting. He saw shells rising up just a little as the creatures inside surveyed the situation, then abruptly shells began tilting right back. Squid-like bodies protruded, but with heads resembling those of prawns or crayfish, long spatula tentacles snapped out snagging up lice and dragging them in. Roland watched in fascination as the molluscs rolled their prey, spatulas going in like knives and peeling off their outer carapaces. Large ichor covered chunks of flesh and organs went to the mollusc's mouths, while carapaces were discarded, landing on the stone like loose bags of hard trash.

The shooting died as very few lice came within reach of the eels, but over to the far edge he could see them gathering in greater numbers. They all began shooting to open up a passage and now Roland saw that he should have had some of those flame units and heavier weapons pointing forwards. Still, they were adaptable. As they drew towards the edge he held up his hand and used the gesture language, Isigur turning with his thought. The formation bunched and turned with him, bringing those heavier weapons to bear along one side. Slug throwers rumbled and clattered, shattering the clustered lice, and then as they drew closer the flame units began stabbing out, setting them ablaze. The air filled with smoke and the smell of frying sea food. It made him feel inappropriately hungry.

He signalled again and this led to a more chaotic manoeuvre, but the formation managed to turn back on itself in the confines. Heavy weapons and flame units on the other side now opened up as further lice skittered over the charred and shattered bodies of their fellows. He saw an opening where a stream curved round towards the tidal lake, signalled and turned Isigur into it. They hurtled over smouldering lice bodies, weapons-fire a constant racket. Lice began leaping now and landing on the eels – digging in with pincers. Roland glanced back and saw two on the body of Isigur. He simply reversed the carbine to point back down his side. He did not need to look to aim since targeting was in his link. He fired twice, both shots perfectly on target, the laser shots penetrating at the head end and dissipating in their bodies in explosions of smoking flesh. The lice fell away. Isigur shivered and firmly apprised him of the fact that it hadn't liked that at all, since the heat had seared its skin. Roland queried what he could do, and got grudging acknowledgement, no more.

Soon they pulled clear of the main concentration of lice, and riders began clearing each other's eels of those still clinging. The changed loosened their formation for this purpose, using accurate shots with conventional weapons on the creatures to drop them. They followed the stream as it expanded into a river, winding through low hillocks strewn with metre-wide ribbons of a kelp equivalent. Attacks from the lice continued as the hillocks grew, became rocky and scattered with a variety of molluscs. As he discarded the energy canister of his carbine and screwed in the spare, Roland now saw some of the creatures whose shells had created the eel pens, also clusters of giant bivalves protruding glossy red tongues. Other mounds of smaller bivalves hissed and twittered ejecting a putrid spray. Mountains reared ahead and affirming his location, Roland took them towards the pass through which the river flowed. Even here it was not necessary to break the formation, because Roland took Isigur into the river where it swam strongly against the current. About a third of the centre of the formation swam. Cliffs rose on either side with lice swarming down them. It seemed like a perfect trap yet it wasn't. Up on the faces of the cliffs the lice made easy targets and the slug throwers shattered them there. Along the bottoms of the cliffs the flame units started numerous fires that then acted as a barrier. Was Chel going to do anything to surprise him at all? It seemed not.

Hours passed. Weariness began to be a factor and casualties began to mount. Some riders were pulled from their eels and rather than be dragged off to be changed, they were torn apart. Accidents began occurring and with lice jumping onto eels, friendly fire became an issue. Beyond the pass Roland took the formation over to a wide sandy area and gave the signal for it to form a circle. They paused only to reload, recoup, and put wounded survivors on some eels and send them back to the city. Heavy weapons kept the lice at bay, but their numbers were gathering again so he could not delay for long. In shifts they dismounted and emptied bowels and bladders on the sand, indifferent to what others could see. They got out food and drink, but ate and drank only when mounted up again. The break lasted less than an hour and then they were on their way again.

The moon then became visible as a mass of thick cloud slid away. Ahead he could see the receding world tide glinting and as they drew closer, with perfect timing, it slid away from Chel's stronghold. Here stood oblate disc-shaped buildings previously up on legs but now nested in coral and masses of small bivalves. There were three of them – two smaller ones either side of a much larger one with dilapidated coms towers protruding. And now the changed began to appear.

'Encirclement, I think!' Erland called.

Yes, the lands all around were dotted with lice whose number had to be huge. Roland gave the signal and the formation parted as they drew closer, and closed up behind so it became the mouth of a V approaching the buildings. Erland led one line of those with conventional weapons. Sansaclear drew in close to him before leading off the other line.

'Stay safe, lover,' she said.

He detached the strap of his carbine from its safety connection to his belt, reattached it to the weapon then held it out to her. 'You stay safe too. I feel I've waited too long for you.' It all seemed so melodramatic, but had an essence of truth. With her he had never felt so alive.

She took the weapon reluctantly and hung the strap from her shoulder. 'Are you sure about this?' She then seemed annoyed at her own question, because, of course, she knew why he had handed it over.

He took his amoeba gun from the back of his saddle and held it up. 'I have this,' he said, then reaching up to touch the handle of his sword, 'And this.'

She blew him a kiss and abruptly turned Derek away. He felt a stab of separation anxiety but suppressed it. Yes he wanted to protect her, but he could not do that all the time without subjugating her, and he had no intention of doing that. As the formation began to wrap around the buildings he looked back at the armoured hundred and simply pointed ahead.

The changed were piling out of the three buildings and flooding towards them. Some ran upright like the humans they had been, others loped like apes knuckling the ground while others were down low like hounds. The hundred, as instructed, also separated into a V to create a lesser encirclement of the buildings. Before it completed the amoeba guns began hissing and crackling. They were using scatter shot into the closely packed horde. The effect surprised Roland. Huge swathes of them went down immediately, even shedding chunks of their carapace as they fell. It was almost as if their transformations now sat loosely upon them. Still, the bulk of them reached their opponents and all started to become chaotic as the armoured riders struggled not to kill those who were like they had been. With the inner encirclement complete, the riders began abandoning their mounts, engaging hand to hand until they could get off clear shots.

Looking out towards the outer encirclement, Roland saw that the flare of flame units and boiling black smoke and the crackle of weapons fire was like fat hissing on a skillet. The flashes were becoming brighter too as the sun touched the horizon and the light began to fail. Forcing through the changed he brought Isigur into the shadow of the largest building because, of course, that was where Chel had to be. He kicked away one of the changed clawing at his leg, then shot it in the face as it came back at him. It staggered away making grunting sounds.

He next opened up with scatter shot, bringing them down all around him, and then abruptly dismounted. A mental nod of permission had Isigur speeding away, flipping over a whole crowd of the changed with one sweep of its tail, but heading on to where the louse slaughter was occurring. The black eels were heading out too, oddly, the blackness fading from their skin as they went. He noted now the outer ring drawing in. It seemed that out there had ceased to be a target rich environment with fewer and fewer lice attacking. Those with amoeba guns in that encirclement were firing inwards now, while others without such weapons began breaking formation to use their eels to herd the changed together for those who did have them.

Roland ran an overlay – his gridlink counting instantly. Less than two thousand of the changed had come out of the buildings and now two thirds of them were down. He moved forward, continuing to bring down any of the changed that came close, but here they seemed more intent in heading out after their fellows. He almost felt guilty at the ease of it. The changed had only their natural armament and, just as Sansaclear had said, attacked like animals and fell like animals in the face of projectile weapons.

In the shadow of the large building he peered up a slope of bivalves like mussels drawn out into blades. A path and steps had been crushed through this, leading up to a circular entrance, darkness clotted inside. Glancing back he signalled to two armoured riders and pointed upwards. They quickly brought down immediate opponents and sped over as he went up. It was pitch black inside but via his gridlink he ramped up light amplification and brought all to clarity. This was in time to see the two he had summoned moving forwards warily, holding out hands ahead. Of course they had no such facility.

'Stay at the entrance,' he told them. 'Let no more of the changed inside.'

'You can't go in alone!' one protested.

'This is my task at the last,' he replied, because it seemed suitably dramatic language. They accepted this at once – the whole format of the legend being created here; their awe of the Polity Agent and certainty that all would soon be resolved. He moved off through ancient corridors crusted with vein corals and other sea life. Such installations as this had been a standard long ago and he had the schematics in his gridlink. He knew where to go. The changed came out of corridors around him, but seemed as blind as those behind. They had other senses for the dark, but perhaps had not adapted to them so well. He brought them down one after the other and left them vomiting pink juices and shedding carapace behind him. He then found himself in a long circular tunnel clean of sea life. This, he felt, must be where the drama would reach its peak.

A door slammed shut behind him and locked with solid thunk. He looked round just as doors either side opened and changed poured out. These ones seemed older and more secure in their transformation, more adept and intelligent. He hit two of them with amoeba rounds but the effect was not immediate and they all piled into him. He clubbed and fought, kicked out and went over as one of them managed to lever the weapon from his grasp. Then all at once they were pulling away and disappearing back the way they had come. He got to his knees and drew his sword. He could use it as a club and if necessary use the edge to disable opponents. He advanced to the next door, looking for controls, but then saw it stood partially open and pushing it with his foot swung it completely open as panel lights began to come on in the walls. Another stretch of tunnel lay ahead with open space beyond it – he could sense that just by the quality of the sounds reaching him. Finally he stepped out into a wide chamber to find himself before Jason Chel.

The man – that simply being a placeholder description for him – sat on a huge throne constructed of human bones and skulls knitted together with coral. Big and wide and thoroughly transformed, Chel filled the thing. He had two legs like any human, but an extra pairs of arms protruding from his ribbed body. His louse head jutted forwards on a long neck, mandibles either side of the upright slot of a mouth. Bulbous compound eyes sat up top, but with human eyes at the centre of them. Roland advanced, keeping the man in his sights, then turned when changed appeared around pillars at the edges of this chamber. But they just stood there, watching.

'Polity Agent,' said Chel, the voice completely human, and tired and peeved, even though it issued from an inhuman mouth. He leaned forwards pulling at handles protruding from the arms of his throne, and moving unnaturally fast for someone so big, stood up with a sword in each hand of his upper arms and daggers in the hands of the lower ones. 'So let's get to this – I've waited long enough.'

Roland halted, the words driving so many loose factors in his mind into integration. He thought about Gurnik's 'flare for the dramatic' comment. He considered how the erstwhile changed donning dramatic armour had certainly been due to AI interference, while he had his suspicions about those black eels. He then considered how he had put down the broadcast from the prison to local politics – a betrayal by some underling or the Warden himself. But of course, such an intervention would have been child's play for an AI. What other manipulations had there been? Had the AIs matched him with the daughter of the Mayor of Holm? Had they in some way presented her with information sufficient to impel her to rescue him? He had no idea how deep it went, or how long it had been planned.

'Get to what?' he enquired.

'The killing,' said Chel. 'You were put here to kill me, and I was put here to die.' He strode forwards, slicing the air with his swords. 'Though that part of it is not going to go to plan at all.'

'Put you here? You chose to come to this world.'

'Are you that naïve?' Chel enquired.

'No, I am not.' Though he said it, Roland now realised that his involvement with Sansaclear had made him less than sharp. And that was probably part of it too.

'I tried to get to other world-tide worlds, but my way was always blocked,' said Chel. 'I ended up here instead. It took me a while to understand why, because my mind wasn't working so well at the time. Now I know that the answer is sitting up there in the sky.'

Roland looked around. 'Are there cams in here?'

'There are, but what does it matter – the recording will show just what the AIs want it to show: the hero up against the monster. It probably doesn't even matter whether or not you win, now.'

Chel abruptly surged forwards, but he had telegraphed it. Roland ducked and rolled as two swords scissored where his neck had been, and raised a shower of sparks knocking aside a dagger aimed at his groin. Coming upright, he palmed away a thrown dagger, feeling it slice his hand. He fended off two further blows, backed up fast as Chel came in, his swords blurring into further scissor cuts difficult to fend off with one sword. He realised he had been driven to the side of the room, launched himself at a pillar, two steps up it then bounced away, a sword tip dragging down the mesh over one leg. He shouldered the ground and snatched, coming up with that thrown dagger in his free hand, ready to the fight of his life, because this was no Drannic.

'Pretty good,' said Chel. He had stopped to inspect the tip of one sword. He then turned to a pillar, back to Roland, and dragged the thing down it, sharpening the damned thing. Roland stared at what seemed an obvious lure. He took it, launching himself forwards, skidding low and aiming a cut behind Chel's knees. A blade came down blocking the cut, but still in motion Roland drove the dagger at an upper thigh. It bounced off carapace and then he had to scrabble away to avoid being skewered to the floor.

'It doesn't have to be like this!' he yelled.

'Stories have to have their dramatic denouements,' Chel replied.

Roland hated that, for they seemed meshed in scripted virtuality. Chel accepted it and his role. The man probably did not care whether he lived or died. Still, if Roland did not run with that script for a while, he would be the one doing the dying. He had to fight Chel and he had to get back to the basics. The man's carapace was hard, so he needed to create a chink in that armour. He now accessed his gridlink, pouring instructions into his nanosuite to ramp his strength and energy up to its highest, integrated nerve impulses for speed and sense enhancements. He ratcheted everything up to the top. There would be a cost later, but at least it wouldn't be death. He engaged with Chel, swords and daggers clashing with showers of sparks. A vulnerable point – a place where carapace did not seem so old, thick and hard, lay between the two pairs of arms above what might be described as the second shoulders. At the cost of four slices across his mesh he got two good hits in there, and saw carapace cracked and leaking. He then felt a tug on his scalp and tracked a tuft of hair dropping to the floor, belatedly realising it was attached to a piece of scalp.

'Now that's going to fuck your vision,' said Chel.

The head wound began bleeding, but his gridlink response was immediate. Vessels closed up, nanosuite clots expanded faster than those of blood. The bleeding stopped.

'You a Golem?' Chel asked, stooping down lower to peer at him. 'If you are you don't move as fast as those fuckers.'

'I am perfectly human,' Roland replied, simultaneously launching a low feint but then stabbing high. His sword tip sliced across one of those combined compound and human eyes. With a roar and a clattering of mandibles, Chel reared back, but then came in attacking savagely. Roland knocked the first blows aside, then abruptly dived forwards directly between Chel's legs. He came up and ran, straight for the throne and stepped up onto it. Chel turned, rubbing his damaged eye with the back of one armoured hand

Standing on the throne, Roland noted something. He clonked the tip of his sword against one skull and the sound was not of metal on old bone, but plastic. He stabbed the tip in beside the skull to lever it out. The thing even had a bar code on it.

'You're a bit of an old fraud, aren't you?' he commented.

Chel shrugged. 'Knowing the part assigned to me I thought I'd play it well.'

He began advancing. Slicing the air with his swords, then he paused and turned. Immediately the changed in the room began heading for the exit. He had instructed them – probably using some pheromone language. Roland understood why because now he could hear the sounds of fighting within the building. His strike force had entered, and doubtless the others would follow soon.

'Neither of us has to die, you know,' said Roland.

Chel shrugged. 'I'm as good as dead anyway. Even if I kill you, things will go the way the Polity wants, and then of course I'll be hunted down. I have killed, and the penalty for that is always the same.'

'In your case, maybe not.'

This gave Chel pause as he came up to the throne. 'Explain.'

'You fought in the –' Roland kicked the skull and it shot perfectly on target straight for Chel's face. Leaning forwards he sliced down hard, two-handed, the impact feeling like it had dislocated his shoulders. He leapt as one of Chel's hands hit the floor, still clutching a sword, and shouldered straight into his chest. The shock of losing a hand combined with the impact was enough to send Chel crashing to the floor. Roland came down with him, knee in his chest, and drove the dagger into that carapace he had broken earlier. He got the tip of the blade into a crack and levered it over, ripping a piece of carapace free of underlying meat. Chel drove in his remaining dagger, its impact punching it through mesh straight into Roland's thigh. Roland shut down the pain, laid his own sword down his back to fend off a slashing blow from the other sword. Tensing his hand he extruded claws and drove them into the soft spot, emptying his poison sacs into the man. Chel's sword clattered away – Roland was too close for it to be effective – he closed a hand around Roland's throat. Roland dropped his own sword too, extended the claws of his other hand and drove them in as well.

'Ah you fucker,' said Chel.

Yeah, I guess, Roland thought, as blackness edged his vision.

Chel convulsed, hurling him aside. He hit the floor on his back, choking. Alerts came up because Chel had crushed his trachea. He struggled to breathe, the blackness continuing to encroach, then swamping him.

'Roland? Roland?'

He could hear the desperation in her voice as his perception opened to internal data streams. The adaptation and his nanosuite had saved him. Higher oxygen transport and a double trachea that allowed some breath before swelling killed that. His nanosuite had then shut him down to make its repairs. Senses returning, he could feel her cradling him, then he took his first painful shuddering breath in some minutes.

'Roland!'

One breath and then another. He opened his eyes but vision took a moment to return. Looking up he finally saw Sansaclear's tear-streaked face.

''m good,' he managed, but felt no inclination to move just then. She gave him a drink from a water bottle, which soothed things a little, but it did not sooth the growing anger.

'You fuckers,' he said mentally.

'Well, that's a bit strong,' came the reply, and he realised at once this wasn't the local AI but Gurnik, probably relayed through U-space.

'You expected me to kill him,' he said.

'No we did not.'

'Then what did you expect?'

'Precisely what has happened,' the AI replied.

He shut down the link, gritted his teeth and sat upright. Sansaclear continued to support him as shakily he gained his feet, then held on when he no longer had need of her, and he had no objection to that. He scanned around. Members of the strike force and others were in the chamber. Erland was overseeing them loading Chel's victims onto stretchers as they rapidly shed their changes.

'What's happened?' he asked.

'It's all over,' Sansaclear told him. 'The lice simply stopped attacking. In fact, they stopped doing anything. Predators are out there picking them off. Even slow crabs are here and they normally eat carrion.'

'The changed?'

'As far as we know we got them all. My father ordered the buildings to be turned into hospitals — he's sent riders back to bring supplies and medics.'

'They won't be needed,' Roland replied.

'Clothing and food at least will be.'

Roland nodded and finally turned his attention to something he had been avoiding. Chel lay flat on his back on the floor. He was not shifting about or shedding carapace and it looked like he might be dead. Closer observation showed milky mucous oozing from his joints. Roland grimaced then looked round as Erland came over to join them.

'They'll be writing songs about you,' Erland said.

Roland winced.

'Is that a problem?'

'We have all been played,' Roland replied.

'How?'

'This was not Chel's first choice of world, but it is the one he ended up on.' He pointed upwards. 'With that thing up there the Polity cannot afford to let this world remain independent.' He looked to Sansaclear, then back to Erland. 'You understand?'

He watched their faces and happily saw the light dawning. Two very smart people here, the kind of people this place would need in the coming years.

'I see,' said Erland. 'It did seem odd to me that ECS deployed an agent for this task when it could be more easily accomplished by drones.'

He grimaced, but did not look particularly unhappy because, of course, he wanted this world in the Polity.

'ECS needs a Polity hero here,' Sansaclear added.

Roland tilted his head in agreement, but a core of anger remained. He had heard of agents being used like this – not being given all the information they needed for a mission – but had no recollection of it ever happening with him.

'A hero, yes, but every hero needs a villain to defeat.' He gestured towards the prostrate form of Chel. 'I should have seen it the moment that cam system broadcast from the prison – that was AI interference. They wanted a Polity hero here to save the day, to raise the Polity in the estimation of all here. Now all those against this world joining the Polity will seem resentful and stupid. This world will join.'

Chel shifted, and a chunk of carapace peeled clear of one arm. Pulling away from Sansaclear, Roland strode over. He now saw that Chel's previously long neck had contracted, wrinkling and rucking up carapace there. The eyes had sunk away, the mouth blackened and one mandible hung loose. He gave the man a shove with his foot, and one of the subsidiary arms fell away. An original arm then rose – the one still sporting a hand – groped at the face, grasped and pulled. Carapace tore away from soggy gristle like a mask to reveal a human face sunk in the muck. As he stooped down Roland notice Erland standing by, face angry, sidearm clutched in his hand.

'He doesn't deserve that.'

'People are dead because of him.'

'And probably millions are alive because of the things he did in the war.'

Erland's expression did not change, but he lowered the weapon.

Roland scooped muck away from the face, pushed away carapace. Blood leaked from raw flesh, but skin was growing now. Sansaclear joined him and started pulling away other carapace, slowly revealing a drained thin pale man amidst the mass. Chel opened bright blue eyes and looked at them.

'They didn't want you to die, you know,' Roland said.

Chel just looked confused. No doubt his mind had been damaged. The nanosuite had killed off the murder-louse in him and much of him had occupied that mind. But perhaps there might be enough left for understanding. Chel opened his mouth to speak, then turned his head to vomit green bile. He finally took a shuddering breath and turned his head again, to stare up at the ceiling.

'Why?' he managed.

'They encouraged you to be what you were during the war. It would not surprise me if cures had become available and they neglected to mention them. I think they feel guilty about you – that they made you.'

'And still they used me.'

'Indeed.'

Roland stood up and looked to Erland. 'You can bring him to trial, perhaps, but would you put any of these others through the same?' He gestured to other changed about the room.

'I guess not.' Erland grimaced, holstering his weapon. 'And anyway, when we join the Polity, a lot about the way we do things here is going to change.'

Sansaclear had a faint smile on her face as she stood up. 'More important to me than joining the Polity is whether one man from the Polity will join this world.'

Stray outfield thoughts integrated. He hadn't been on a mission in a while yet had been selected for this. The local AI had been monitoring him through his gridlink and relaying his status to ECS. He had fallen in love. Had they made decisions on the basis of what had happened here, or had they instigated all of it from the beginning? You could go crazy trying to second-guess AIs – in trying to understand how deep their manipulations went. Still, he had found one certainty in his life.

'He will be,' he replied.

This was the first I wrote of three interrelated stories here, but not the first in their chronology. I called it Moral Biology at the time, then, inspired to do something concerning translation and its difficulties when concerning an alien with an entirely different biology to us, went on to write the next. When I finished that I realised the title better belonged to the second story so snaffled it for that and put the title on this you see here. Published in Clarkesworld Magazine *Feb 2020.*

THE HOST

Something hit on the way in. Ivebek Cloon felt the weird distortion of the ship surfacing from U-space, which to him felt like the hangover from a neuro-enhancer packed into a couple of seconds. A resounding crash ensued, along with the sensation of someone trying to drag the world away, like a rug from under his feet. Grav went off and he floated up from his bed, turning over, then it came back on hard and deposited him on his face, mostly on his nose. He lay there gasping, wiped away blood and pinched his nostrils closed, stood up and stared at the door, which had opened. He tried using his aug to talk to the AI, Mobius Clean, but as ever it didn't bother replying. Just so long as he remained intact and alive was all that mattered to it – it knew that a little damage wasn't worthy of note. He tested his nose with his fingers, the pain fading under his touch, the bleeding already stopped.

Ivebek grimaced. He still healed unnaturally quickly – faster even than someone running a military nanosuite, and still it took severe impacts or stresses to damage him, and still he did not know why. He peered at the smear of blood on the floor. His nose should be broken now, his face swelling, yet all he had was a little blood on his fingers. After a moment he returned his attention to the door.

He had no way of escaping his situation. If the door was open that probably meant it really didn't matter if he wandered about. Maybe it hadn't been locked all this time – he had never thought to try the damned thing. He stepped out, looked up and down the corridor and noted smoke towards the rear of the ship, and headed towards it. Even as he reached it, fan filtration began droning loudly and a breeze whipped the smoke away. The smell of burning led him through a bulkhead door, then another and another. Finally he came opposite an inspection window and peered inside, recognising the U-space drive, only it didn't look like a drive any more, just scrap.

'You are at the wrong end of the ship,' said a voice via his aug. 'Head to the bridge and strap yourself into the acceleration chair there. This is going to be rough.'

'What happened?'

'Some automated defence,' Clean replied, though it sounded doubtful.

'Why rough?'

'Grav engines are at minimal function. I am holding them together.'

'Are we landing somewhere?'

'Do as instructed.' That ended with an emphatic click – conversation over.

Ivebek turned around and headed to the front of the ship. The standard bridge contained two acceleration chairs before consoles and a slanted screen revealing starlit space but nothing else of note. He sat down and strapped himself in, assessing what he had learned from his brief exchange with the AI. They were landing, but it seemed someone might not want them to. That Clean, knowing Ivbek's ruggedness, wanted him strapped in told him the landing *would* be rough. He tried to relax and, as ever, returned to the memory – his key to understanding all that was happening to him.

The desert had been hot, almost beyond the insulation and cooling capacity of his armoured suit. Organic toxins filled the air but it contained enough oxygen to sustain him, just so long as the filters held up. He'd found the entrance in the side of a sandstone butte – a tunnel of nacreous mother-of-pearl delving inside, as if erosion had revealed a giant mollusc from some ancient sea here. He walked inside, checking his weapons as he did so. Light amplification through his HUD created the illusion of a bright place, as he moved into darkness. Then... nothing.

It seemed such a small and inconsequential fragment of memory, but it had kept him alive. When Earth Central Security grabbed him on the Polity side of the Graveyard – that borderland lying between the human Polity and the alien prador – he was sure that would be the end for him. He'd committed theft and murder in the Polity while smuggling alien artefacts – Jain stuff supposedly. He wasn't so sure that was true, but it paid. He'd done worse in the Graveyard, hooking up with a crew selling cored and thralled humans to the prador. He had been a career criminal with more than enough marks against him to warrant a death sentence.

They'd questioned him, of course, first in a tiled cell. The agent concerned got all old fashioned on his arse with brass knuckles and a shock stick, then became puzzled and intrigued by how he absorbed damage. Perhaps that was why he had not executed him then and there, but passed him on. Aboard the ECS stealth ship they'd scanned him intensely, then used an interrogation aug to observe his mental responses to questioning and copy memories out of his mind. After that he had expected them to give him a short tour of an airlock, but it seemed something didn't add up.

'Here,' the woman had said, placing a pulse gun on the table before him.

He'd stared at the thing. He should pick it up, shoot her and do all he could to escape, though that seemed unlikely. What had he got to lose? He picked up the gun, pointed it at the wall and triggered it. It surprised the hell out of him when it actually fired and he dropped it like a poisonous insect.

'I thought so,' she said. 'Something's fucked with your mind as well as your body.'

He sat there baffled when she took the gun away again and left.

The stealth ship docked at an outlink station and troops carted him inside to deposit him in a garden, on a synthetic stone seat. They took off the manacles and left. He didn't have a clue what was happening until the thing rose out of a pond swimming with multi-coloured fish. It looked like a crinoid six feet across, rippling feather tendrils attached to a central point.

'I am to examine you,' the forensic AI explained.

He ran, of course, but had nowhere to go. The thing descended on him and grabbed him to begin its examination. A thousand worms seemed to writhe over his skin, then it abruptly released him and he thumped on his back in the grass. It retreated. He lay there feeling strangely heavy and solid, as if after a particularly hard workout, and that feeling had stayed with him since.

'They scanned you in the ship and found you impenetrable,' it said. 'You are also impenetrable to me.' It sounded affronted. 'You are opaque – a form of chameleonware has been inlaid in your skin. Can you explain this?'

He wanted to, he really wanted to. He knew what forensic AIs did to people like him. In pursuit of answers this thing could take him apart both physically and mentally and, if not satisfied with the results, put him back together and do it again. Painkillers, apparently, were not an option during this process, pain in fact being a necessary encouragement.

When he could find no reply it came at him again. He fought it this time, but its tendrils had as much give as braided towing cables. It inserted nanofibres into the interrogation aug still attached to his head. He felt all his memories rising for examination and then *that* memory. The AI simply dropped him again, backed off and folded into a ball just a few feet across. It stayed that way long enough for him to search the garden for a way out, drink from the pool and wonder what those fish would taste like raw. Then it unfolded.

'We are going on a journey,' it told him.

And here he was. It did tell him a little of the circumstances. He had encountered an alien and that was integral in his memory of mother-of-pearl tunnels. It had tampered with his body and mind, altering it in ways the AI could not parse, though some of the results were plain: as well as unusual physical ruggedness he was no longer a killer – possessed empathy. The AI had decided not to continue its examination because that memory would be of interest to *her*. He had no idea who *she* was, and the AI had not considered it worthwhile telling him.

The ship shuddered and the star field began to swing to the right. A sun slid into view, the reactive screen damping its glare, then a world. He gazed down upon the yellow and white swirls of cloud over pastel terrain, and could see no sign of oceans. The seat kicked him in the back as fusion flung the ship forwards. Acceleration ramped up and up, and that he could feel it confirmed problems with internal grav too. He felt himself sinking deeper and deeper into the seat, his arms turning to lead and an invisible stone coming to rest on his chest, and to somehow slide inside him – a solid core. Then he blacked out.

Ivebek regained consciousness to the roar of atmosphere over the hull. Misty claws of cloud reared up to grab at the ship. Piss yellow rain hit the screen and slid off its frictionless coating. Sun glare a green-tinted yellow briefly blinded him. The ship dipped into thicker cloud, snow swirling in view, then through the cloud a grey-green ceiling above. He could just make out the features of mountain chains, valleys and perhaps rivers. Lower still, with the ship shuddering alarmingly, he felt sure he could see jungles or forests, but with little green in them. With some time yet to pass before landing, or crash, he decided to try something.

'Almanac data,' he stated.

To one side, in the laminate of the screen, a long menu scrolled up with an arrow blinking beside the first entry. He lowered his gaze to the third entry, the arrow tracking his vision, and blinked deliberately. The aug connection flashed up in his visual cortex and he permitted it, then enabled a full download while speed reading the introduction to a world designated X349. Until that moment he had not known the interrogation aug would respond like a standard version. A lot had been redacted from the data presented while, on occasion, a warning appeared telling him to avoid this proscribed destination.

Now he could see actual jungle down there, mainly purple and blue with minor swirls of green. The ship turned, flinging him from side to side, and he got a view to the rear up towards the rumpled quilt of cloud, just before deceleration sank him into his chair again. This more than anything else told him how many drive systems were down – the AI forced to use the main fusion drive to decelerate. The pressure pushed him close to blackout then came off with another turn. Again he saw ahead, and that they were low down over the vast jungle. The ship began hitting the tree tops, then debris covered the screen as it sank lower and deceleration flung him against the straps. The ship vibrated so hard it felt like the muscles were being shrugged from his bones. A steady roar grew in volume until it hurt his ears, crescendoed with a crash that nearly put him through the floor, then another and another. The roar diminished, and eventually the ship hit earth and stayed there, deceleration still forcing him against the straps, but then finally coming off with a thump. The debris slid from the screen and he gazed out at a blast field – jungle levelled and burning all around. He swallowed dryly, reached down and undid the straps.

'Return to your cabin,' said the AI, via his aug.

Ivebek paced in his cabin – a ten foot box with the minimum of facilities – listening to the creaks and groans of settling metal and a susurration that sounded like wind. His body felt tighter and harder after the buffeting in the bridge, and as if he had pulled a muscle in his torso: the nag wasn't going away. He sat on the bed to read the almanac download again. He was gazing at the gap, where any information about intelligent life or previous civilisations on X349 had been redacted, when he felt it.

Someone was calling him and he felt an odd déjà vu, a nostalgia, as if this might be his mother summoning him in from playing in the ducts of the arcology where he grew up. This lasted for just a short time, but it seemed the wrong key to his mind. Next he felt hunger and thirst that would be relieved if he just got up and went *over there*. He turned his head, gazing at the wall of the cabin. He got up and went to his fabricator and input his needs, returned to the bed with a tray of printed pork and black beans, and a beaker of blue banyan juice. These quelled the feelings only a little, but enough for a change of approach. He now felt withdrawal from the many addictive substances he had tried, pulling at him, trying to get him to head to some destination where all his needs would be satisfied.

'There's something in my mind,' he said.

'It is her, calling you,' replied Mobius Clean.

He pondered that for a long moment and realised he did not agree. It felt far too personal, intimate even. But perhaps that was how, whatever this was, operated. He suspected something like an induction warfare beam had been pointed at him. It wasn't telepathy, couldn't be that since Polity science had long ago disproved it… unless of course the AIs were lying.

'What the hell does this female want with me?' he asked.

Instead of answering the question, the AI said, 'We are some distance from the site. You are to proceed alone. It will be necessary for you to defend yourself.'

A hatch opened in the wall and he gaped disbelievingly at what it revealed. His armoured suit lay there, and his weapons. Rising from the bed he walked over and peered down at it, noting as he did so that the gravity of this world sat just above Earth normal. He took the suit out and put it on, linking into its systems via his aug. He holstered his sidearm – a pulse gun – picked up his Brabeck Multigun and jacked the combined optic, power feed and ammo tube into his pack, which he pulled onto his back. He then stood there checking diagnostics in his HUD, along with ammo and power levels. Everything had been topped up. He felt the urge then to never get out of this suit until either free or dead, but then acknowledged it likely Clean had put in some way of shutting it down. The weapons, he realised, were irrelevant, since he could no longer use them against others.

'Come outside,' Clean told him.

The suit gave him a little bit of assist in the higher gravity, but he cancelled it since he'd gone long enough without exercise. The nag in his torso became a dull ache as he headed to the cabin door and it opened ahead of him. Remembering how he had come aboard, he went to the hold, found the airlock into it standing open and the ramp to the outside down on smoking ground. The hold had been packed with equipment when he boarded, but now appeared half empty.

Reaching the bottom of the ramp, he gazed back along the length of the ship to where a large section of armour had been debonded at the back end to open access. That was quick. A grav-sled he had originally seen in the hold stood beside this, the equipment piled on it swiftly disappearing as black spider-mechs with clawed forelimbs and dodecahedral bodies carted it into the open section. He walked over and gazed inside, recognising the compartment for the ship's U-space drive. It was much changed in there now.

When he had peered through the interior inspection window the drive had been a blackened and twisted wreck. The two cylinders of complex technology supported in the middle of the compartment by glassy struts had been mashed as if giant hands had reached in and twisted them like someone wringing out a cloth. Most of the struts had been shattered, optics charred, s-con broken. Somehow braided meta-material had been turned into chunks not dissimilar to wood charcoal. Now the cylinders were straight, some of the struts back in place, coils of optics hung around the walls and spider mechs were clearing out debris and stringing new s-con. This had all happened in less than an hour.

'I thought this kind of repair of a U-space drive was supposed to be impossible without heavy infrastructure,' he commented. 'Where are the vastly precise machines, intense energy sources and gravity presses?'

'Now you know better.'

Wrapped around the drive cylinders, Mobius Clean bore the appearance of a tangled mobile sea-fern, working so fast its limbs were a blur to the human eye, while the packed technology of the cylinders deformed, shifted and changed shape. Ivebek, who had experience with damaged U-space drives, could only assume the forensic AI's fronds were deconstructing and reconstructing matter at the atomic level. Using blink control he recorded some of the action through his HUD cam, then slowed it down. He ran a scan too and put that through his suit's sub-AI analysis. Now he ascertained that Clean was using shearfields ranging from the size of a sword down to the nanoscopic. The AI was applying weird geometry shimmershields and hardfields and even managing to compress molecules for super-dense components. It was also manipulating pseudomatter and its reach even extended beyond the real. He detected subtle U-signatures sure to be something to do with the alignment of calabri yau frames and manifolds.

'You could have taken me apart and examined me,' he stated dully. 'I still don't really know why you stopped.'

'It was necessary,' was all Clean supplied.

Or had the AI stopped? Sure, that's what he remembered, but the AI could have taken him apart and, putting him back together, implanted any memories it chose. Probably some way of tracing him would remain, some way of seizing control of him, some way of manipulating him. Polity AIs lied, manipulated and bent things to the shape they required, and the truth of that lay before him now.

Throughout the history of U-space travel the AIs established the myth that U-space engines could only be built in AI-controlled facilities using hugely complex and energy-hungry machines, and that some components could only be forged on the surfaces of brown dwarfs. The resulting engines, because of the complex inter-dimensional math involved, and the mental gymnastics in dealing with a continuum supposedly without conventional time or dimensions, required an AI to run them. All lies. The prador made such drives without AI and ran them with the transplanted and flash-frozen ganglions of their children, while here before him the forensic AI was practically rebuilding a drive that anywhere else would have been consigned to recycling.

Now Clean pulled away from the drive and rolled out of the hole in the side of the ship, coming to rest before him.

'I just scanned you to try and confirm what I have been told,' said the AI. 'Apparently you are capable of breathing the atmosphere here and are immune to the viruses, micro-fauna and allergens of this world, so have no requirement for a suit. I, however, pointed out that unsuited you would be vulnerable to the macro-fauna here. She agreed that this was the case.'

'And who is "she"?' he asked

Disregarding his question, yet again, Clean continued, 'Whether you wish to open your suit to the air here is a matter for your own discretion.'

'Who is "she" Clean? Why am I here?'

'You are here because your life is forfeit and an entity with which we wish to open larger communication showed an interest in you. You will go to her and what she does with you is of little matter to us. You may even survive it, in which case, bearing in mind that your propensity to kill has been removed, you may return to the Polity as a free citizen.'

'Entity? Some sort of alien?'

'Of a kind, according to a fragment of memory in your mind, you encountered before.'

'That memory.'

'Precisely. She will open communication with you once you set out. I have given her your aug code.' He wanted to argue, but before he could say anything, Clean added, 'Of course you can stay here, in which case I *will* examine you.'

Ivebek turned away and began heading towards the dense jungle, glancing back along the path the ship had cut as it came down. Fires were still burning there because, he discovered on checking the almanac, they were fuelled by the oxygen nodules in the roots of the plants, which they had extracted from the atmosphere to make this world uninhabitable for unadapted humans. An atmosphere he could now, apparently, breathe. He paused at the wall of tangled plant growth. Again he felt scanning from Clean, brief this time but more intense. In response something dense and leaden inside his torso seemed to tighten, and he felt a stab of pain. He walked on. Both the scan and the brief pain felt like threats or intentions to propel him forwards. The pain he simply did not understand, but the scanning made him feel like a victim in the sights of a molester. Clearly Clean did not want to touch him until he had served his purpose here. He was a bargaining chip being played by the AIs to open access to something alien.

His aug now signalled to him a connection request. He gazed at it blinking in his HUD – relayed there through the suit link. He winked at it to activate it.

'Come here to me,' *she* said, the voice female and seductive. A moment after this a direction arrow appeared in the bottom of his HUD.

'Why should I?' he asked.

A long pause ensued while he considered how the classifications male and female might well not apply here. The voice the entity chose to communicate indicated nothing. It might not even have vocal cords or a mouth, or maybe it had a mouth he would not like to see.

'Personal survival,' she finally replied, utterly factual. 'If you do not come, Ivebek, all protections will be rescinded and Mobius Clean will have you.' Oddly it didn't sound like a threat. It sounded like mechanics: 'If you drill a hole in a bucket, Ivebek, the water will run out.'

'Plain fact,' he replied. 'But what do you want with me, and what are you?'

She ignored the question: 'Tell me about your encounter.'

He stepped into the jungle, pushing between ribbon vines like faded plastic, worming between thick white trunks and half-burned debris, finally stepping out where the jungle had not been compacted and burned by the crash, to where he could walk easily between the plants. He thought about his past and felt something shift in his mind. Suddenly he realised he wanted to talk about everything that had led him finally to that encounter. On other levels he realised his mind had been given a firm prod.

'I was born on an arcology on Colouron,' he babbled, 'and grew up with all my needs met by our post-scarcity society, but for purpose and solitude.'

'Did you feel the ruling AIs should have supplied these?'

'They should have made it known that they were possible.'

He felt very uncomfortable with the question. The AIs had met the physical needs of a population that had, for no clear reason, grown much more than on other worlds. A large anti-AI sentiment had grown there too concerning AIs engineering and interfering with their society and, as a result of that, it became a hive of Separatism. Only once he gained perspective from the outside did he discover that the AIs' touch on Colouron was as light as anywhere else, and that the problems there had been generated wholly by the society humans formed.

He continued, 'I found out it was possible to leave once I officially became an adult and did so by runcible.'

'Why?'

'To find a purpose and give myself space to breathe.'

'Did you find these?'

Something was moving through the undergrowth over to his right, and he wondered if the distraction of this conversation was a good thing. Using his suit's scanners in that direction he got an infrared image of a winged creature like a small pterodactyl feeding on an object like a large fruit or egg. He ignored it and moved on.

'I found solitude when I wanted it, which wasn't so easy on Colouron, then through contacts I made a business venture.'

'Smuggling armaments back to Colouron itself as I understand it,' she said. 'This purpose was satisfactory?'

'You know about me, so why are you asking?'

'I want to understand you and, through you, more about the Polity.' She paused for a second, then continued, 'You became a smuggler because of contacts in your home arcology – it was something to do.'

'I made money at it.'

'Why did you require money, if the AIs could supply all your needs?'

'Some things lie outside the AI definition of "human needs",' he replied tightly.

'Like the "purpose" you mentioned?'

'Yeah.'

Again he wasn't comfortable with this.

'From smuggling arms to Separatists you next proceeded to smuggling them to the Graveyard, and there you joined another organisation that sold cored and thralled human beings to the prador.'

'More risk more revenue,' he said.

'And killing people.'

'Look, where is this going?'

'It was you who chose to start telling me your life story. I do not think you can object to me commenting on it.'

'You did something to me. You made me talk.'

'Are you sure? Or do you feel some need now to justify yourself?'

'Fuck you,' he said without heat.

'Has it not occurred to you to wonder if what you were truly seeking was not purpose, or revenue, but distinction from the crowd and power over other people?'

He wanted to make a heated reply but could not find one beyond repetition of his last words. That was the thing, on Colouron you were one of billions with nothing to make you stand out. Societal structures existed, like the Separatists, and with effort you could climb to the top of any particular heap. But still you were a meat mechanism under the AIs to be fed, housed and cleaned up after. He could see now that this did drive many from that world and to excellence, while his way of excelling had been through crime. The money had just been a way of keeping score. Simple as that, and he hated the clarity.

'I will now leave you to your thoughts while you deal with the exigencies of survival, which will be upon you shortly,' she finished. The link closed.

He halted and looked around. The jungle had grown thinner now so he could walk a straight course for more than just a few paces. He became aware of movement behind him and turned. The creature humping between the trunks bore some resemblance to a huge armadillo, though its head possessed three stalked eyes. Below its piggish snout its mouth had far too many teeth. The central eye was focused on him while the other two were checking to either side before they too turned in. It opened its mouth and squealed like a pig, then charged.

Ivbek froze. He could not kill! The pig – for so he named it – came straight at him. At the last moment he threw himself aside into a shoulder roll, and it thundered past. Tearing up earth at the end of its charge, it turned. With shaking hands Ivebek selected thermite shells and fired into the ground before it, throwing burning jungle detritus into its face. The thing took this for a moment then veered aside and went crashing into the jungle to his left. He tracked its course, watching it disappear from sight. He sighed shakily. This should be no problem if the creatures here spooked so easily. As he turned forwards again something slammed into his chest to send him staggering, closing numerous legs about him. He got a look into a collection of revolving mandibles as mobile antennae smeared yellow liquid over his visor, then felt a muted punch against belly and a fluttering pain in response. He had just been attacked by a creature like a giant ichneumon wasp.

He grabbed the thing in one hand and tried to pull it off as its lower abdomen flicked out then drove in again, trying to push a barbed sting through his armour. It clung tenaciously and he had no idea what to do, because again he could not kill. Then, not even conscious he had chosen to do so, he used assist, driving his fingers into his body with a crunch. Now managing to pull the wasp away, he held it squirming before him then threw it to the ground. Perhaps it was organic memory, for he fired a single shot and blew it in half. Staring down at the still moving creature he searched himself for a reaction, but found none. Perhaps his empathy did not extend to oversized insects. He went to step over it, then paused and looked back down at the thing.

Hadn't he seen that before? Behind its head clung an object like a metallic worm cast. He prodded the thing with his toe and the creature made a desultory attempt to bite his boot. He looked up. Yes, he had seen it before.

The pig now stood ahead of him and there, on the armour behind its head, was another one of those casts. Some kind of parasite? The creature charged again and this time shots into the ground did not dissuade it. Reluctantly he raised his aim, but then felt a stirring of joy when this elicited no reaction inside him. He shot it in the head and it crashed to a halt before him. Glancing round he could now see other movement in the surrounding jungle.

'Come on!' he said, hoping for more kills, but next felt a sudden self-disgust. Was this all he was? He lowered his weapon. The nagging pain in his torso arose again, almost rhythmic. He felt sure now that Clean had lied and that it had interfered with his body, because something was driving him to his destination. Sure as shit the pain would increase if he delayed.

He broke into a steady trot in the direction of the arrow in his HUD, meanwhile calling up an ammo inventory. He had used up twenty-three explosive shells out of five hundred, and had not yet used the pulse gun option of his main weapon; however, he had no idea how far he had to go or how many more attacks there might be.

Another pig charged in from the right, its head down so he could not get a clear shot at it. He riddled its body with explosive shells, blowing away chunks of the thing to expose yellow flesh, squirting green blood, and bones like polished oak. He ran as the thing circled round and came back at him, putting more and more shots into it until it came down. When he ceased firing he was able to hear a growing hum. The big wasps appeared, flying between the trees, abdomens hanging pendulous. He brought up targeting, keyed to his suit's motor assist. Putting a crosshairs on one of them he blinked for acquisition. The motors moved his arms, correcting where he could not and he fired, blowing the creature apart with one pulse shot. But this lengthy procedure allowed others to get closer and they were coming in all around. They were sneaky too, taking fast flights between concealments, as if they knew what his weapons could do. He began firing short pulse gun bursts where they seemed thickest, blowing many apart and bringing down steaming foliage, but still they drew closer. Turning to where fewer of them flew, he ran in that direction. Sticking his main weapon to a pad on the front of his suit, he drew his sidearm for closer shooting, his free hand on assist to beat the creatures away.

Abruptly he found himself stumbling down a steep slope. Tall trees shrank to dwarfs, cycads bloomed and low greenery and blue-ery tangled his feet. He fell, struggled upright tearing one of the creatures from his back and slamming it into a tree. A few more steps, batting the things away, brought him to the edge of a slow deep river. He turned his back to it, holstered his sidearm and detached his main weapon, firing short bursts again, shredding the flying creatures. A third pig hurtled downslope at him. Even the explosive shell annihilating its head did not stop it, and it crashed into him, hurling them both into the water.

Ivebek sank, just for a second until his suit compensated. Expanding around him as it filled gas pockets, it began to bring him to the surface again. His visor gave him a clear view all around as the water filled with giant snakes a foot in thickness, but seemingly without heads or tails. He surfaced to see one of the things looped up over him, the head now visible, a mass of stalked eyes and a letterbox mouth. It snapped down, closing that mouth over his main weapon, snatched that and tossed it away. It came down again and grabbed his shoulder even as he drew his sidearm. Hauling him up it shook him, then discarded him. He crashed down on the other side of the river and lay there on his back expecting further attacks, but none came. In retrospect he realised there had only been one creature in the river. And reviewing memory, he saw it had one of those metallic casts on the side of its head.

He stood up, rubbing at his belly but hardly able to feel his hand through the armour. Counter intuitively the pain had receded – his torso just heavy and tight now. Next, using suit scanning, he located his main weapon in the river, which was now boiling with the coils of that creature's body. He knew with utter certainty that it would not allow him to retrieve it, and that disarming him had been the purpose of its attack. Looking across to the other side he saw the wasps bobbing there as if from a disturbed hive, but they weren't crossing. Two of the pigs were even now heading back into the jungle. Turning in the direction indicated by the arrow in his HUD, he saw a creature, like a manta ray with legs, appear from between the taller trees. When he raised his sidearm to aim at the thing it began to make its way down towards him, opening and closing a toothless mouth that did not seem designed for predation. Noting the metallic cast behind its four black button eyes, he lowered his weapon and tossed it down in the dirt beside him. The creature halted, turned clumsily and headed back into the trees.

'You didn't want me to have weapons,' he said, after opening the link.

'Even I can die,' she replied.

'Are there any creatures here you do not control?' he asked. 'I really don't want to abandon my last weapon if there is something that might attack me.'

'You are more intelligent than I supposed.'

'Many have made that mistake.'

'There are only two creatures on this world I cannot choose to control,' she said. 'You and the AI Mobius Clean.'

'Who, it is apparent, doesn't know that you can control the wildlife here. Else you would have told him I had no need for weapons.'

'Precisely.'

He stepped away from the sidearm and continued up the slope from the river. Pausing by some rocks, he flipped one over. This revealed creatures like woodlice, but white and circular. On closer inspection he saw more of those worm casts on their shells. She wasn't lying. He flipped the rock back and continued on.

'You asked if what I sought was distinction from the crowd and power over others,' he said. 'A hundred days ago I would have sneered at the question but now, I think, I can give you an honest answer. I delighted in power over others and exercised it whenever I could. I took cruel pleasure in the terror of those I cored and thralled. I enjoyed being the big man able to order others to kill. I was someone who did not deserve to live.'

'And why do you have that perspective now?' she asked.

'Because something changed me.'

'Perhaps you would like to tell me about that?'

The memories weren't clear, but still he tried to put them in order.

'I met a man in the Graveyard who gave me the location, on a world, of an alien weapon and I went there to seek it out.'

He could clearly see the bar in his mind, the drink on the table before him, and Grayson Trada sitting opposite.

Trada was both excited and scared. 'It's real Jain stuff – you see the data.'

He certainly had and it really looked genuine.

'Why don't you go after it, then?' he had asked.

'I trade information – too many agents in the Graveyard now and I really don't want to be noticed by them. That ship has sailed as far as you are concerned.'

He had nodded agreement. He knew about the reward for his capture or proof of execution of sentence against him. Only recently he'd upped the count to four of those who had sought to claim the reward and failed. He slid a pack of etched sapphires across the table. Trada verified them and swiftly departed, glad to have such *dangerous* information off his hands. The coordinates Ivebek had loaded into a storage rod were detailed, and he felt much excitement about going after the items the data detailed.

'I landed and went to the coordinates given.'

Again he saw the desert and that mother-of-pearl entrance, but nothing of what happened in there. He told her how afterwards he had paid off his crew at another location on his way out of the Graveyard. But all he could remember was his intense desire to head to a location in the Polity – a realm he had avoided for a long time because of the warrants out for him. Necessity forced him to stop at a space station for his ship was old and required primitive deuterium fuel, and that's where the Polity agent grabbed him.

'And what was that destination?' she asked.

He broke into a sweat as he tried to recover it from his mind. His torso ached in sympathy and gave him a couple of stabs. But he just couldn't find the memory.

She now added, 'It is almost as if your conscience was driving you, and the destination was in fact the Polity and the purpose was your capture.'

No, that could not be right, surely? Again he tried to excavate memory, but now began asking himself some pertinent questions. Why had he paid off his crew? Had it been entirely necessary to stop for fuel? Had it been necessary to leave his ship and board that space station, knowing the dangers? In retrospect it did seem he had been seeking capture, but somehow that did not feel right at all.

The jungle thinned out around him while across the blue-green firmament the cloud began to fragment. On occasion he got himself a clear view to the horizon and a mountain chain there, the sun setting. He felt suddenly hot, feverish hot, and checked the internal temperature of his suit. Its setting had not changed but still he felt uncomfortable.

'I think Clean has done something to me,' he said, but she did not reply.

He came out onto a clearing on a downslope, now seeing the mountains more clearly. The rock formations looked odd, rather more like they had been deposited in worms by a deposition welder than pushed up from below. Lying between him and them, lone massifs of the same wormish construction stood up out of the jungle. He paused, eyed a boulder lying at the edge of the clearing then went over and sat down. His guts gave him another stab but he ignored that and, without thinking, reached up to the neck control on his head gear. The visor slid down into the neck ring while the helmet softened and rolled off his head and down to the back of the ring. Cool air hit him and he revelled in it, only a moment later realising what he had done. He was capable of breathing this air yet no human should be. He had opened himself to local biologicals to which, apparently, he was immune. He left the helmet undone, an odd spicy taste in his mouth and a smell like mint in his nostrils.

'Why am I here?' he asked.

'You would be more comfortable without your suit,' she replied. 'There is nothing here to harm you and the path is easy from now on.'

Her observation seemed utterly reasonable but, abandon his suit? It was his only remaining defence against this world and, besides that, it had been damned expensive. Still, he opened the side seam down his torso and felt some relief, like he had been wearing particularly tight clothing after a heavy meal.

'You didn't answer my question,' he noted.

'Why are any of us here?' she replied. 'To live, to continue, to consume and to breed. Life continues to find its way forwards.'

'You are being general when I was being specific.'

The nagging started up again and he stood. He no longer had the direction arrow in his HUD to follow but found he did not need it. Setting out between trees like giant flowering papyrus, he trudged towards those mountains.

'Those are our base desires, written into our genomes,' she said, 'but we build structures on top of them with our intelligence, and call them purpose. However, their bedrock remains the same. The power you sought over others, the uniqueness you craved, in the end were based on survival and the old impulse to display your fitness for breeding.'

'I don't agree,' he said, abhorring the idea that his drives were so simple. 'We are intelligent creatures who have outgrown our ancient programming.'

'How nice for you.'

'And what about you? I don't even know what you are, but I'm guessing you're not even remotely human. What about your impulses?'

'You would recognise them for they have their twins in the life of your original world, that is, if you know much about that original world.'

He halted, suddenly irritated by how sweaty and enclosing were his garments. Thumb controls on the wrist of each glove released them and he hooked them on his belt. His hands now felt cool and free and somehow less dirty.

'Try me,' he said.

'Consider the impulses of a mollusc that spreads its seed in the sea,' she said. 'There is no need for it to display its fitness to breed, just the drive to relieve itself of that seed and let the currents carry it where they will.'

'You're a mollusc?'

'Such definitions are not suitable for the alien.'

'Then what?'

'Consider such a creature were it to spread across worlds but was still driven to spread its seed. An intelligent creature, a moral creature.'

'I don't understand.'

'You will.'

One of the massifs now lay ahead and he knew at once this was his destination, not the mountains beyond. He felt his eagerness to be there, and the passing thought that the eagerness might not be his own quickly died.

'The creature would send its seed out in ships or use other technological means,' he tried, but knew he wasn't thinking clearly.

He really did feel feverish now and his suit seemed to hang leaden on him. Why was he keeping it on? Its value to him now, in this situation with an alien ahead and Clean behind, and him utterly powerless, was nil.

Comfort and freedom seemed a better goal. He halted and disconnected the sleeves at the shoulders, stripped them off and simply dropped them. The relief was intense. Section by section he removed the rest and then, in a nod to the garment's value, carefully stacked it on a rock. Now clad only in a thin shipsuit and slippers he felt free, and moved on.

'We are old,' she said, 'and have grown far apart. The urge to spread our genome has remained, though muted, even as we lost or otherwise abandoned the technology that enabled its spread. Some believe this a willing retreat from our nature, for it did not sit well with our growing and, it has to be said, unnatural morality.'

Ivebek felt a sudden surge of horrible knowledge, but it lay just beyond his grasp.

'Consider the parasite that lays its eggs or some other form of genetic transfer in a host, a carrier,' she continued. 'The natural way would be to take those carriers with it to the stars.'

'The technological answer,' he tried, knowing it was wrong.

'No, not if you are programmed that way by evolution, and then have little regard for the creatures you use, for then another option becomes available: hosts who themselves can travel, other star travelling races. Unfortunately such races are inevitably intelligent themselves and, if your growing morality does not permit this, your survival becomes abhorrent.'

'And then what happens?' he asked, the horror of it beginning to impinge.

'Then you retreat and your society collapses. You begin to die out and, at some stage, there are few of you scattered across vast stretches of space.'

'And you no longer breed…'

Gnarled wormish stone now lay before him rising up in a slope, and he hardly remembered the intervening miles. He chose a path leading to a point up above. He wanted to turn and run, but climbed. His torso felt thick, hard and heavy and there were no more nags of pain for they were no longer necessary.

'Unfortunately, the urge to breed continues and, in many cases becomes stronger. It is as if, with extinction threatening, the urge to racial survival increases. Some of these then set lures for the required host – lures they feel will bring them a morally acceptable carrier. Others fight the urge, but when a carrier wanders within their compass, instinct becomes difficult to fight.'

'You isolated yourself,' he said.

'I did, and I allowed only limited communication with other races. I retained some of my technology but it wasn't enough to stop Mobius Clean coming here. He made the moral argument that you are a killer. I discounted it because the other of my kind had changed you. I tried to damage his ship to prevent him landing, but he did, by which time I could fight my instincts no longer.'

'What is going to happen to me?' he asked, it almost coming out a sob.

The mother-of-pearl tunnel lay before him, and he crawled inside. He didn't have to go far before she rose up to meet him, mussel flesh and frills, groping tentacles with their barbed bone-like blades.

'I'm sorry,' she said as she drew him in to soft velvet warmth, and split him from sternum to crotch. 'My mate gave you some durability and I will try to keep you alive.'

Ivebek screamed, then screamed again as the fringed pod wormed out of the split, shrugging off ropes of his intestines. He gazed at stalked eyes inspecting him, other appendages trying to push him back together as the pod inched into a hot pink cavity. Then the world went away.

Ivebek returned to pain. He lay on his back gazing up at the sky, turned his head slightly to take in the slew of organic detritus spilled from the mother-of-pearl hole above. He started gasping – didn't want to look down at his body.

'The one you first encountered lured you with the promise of something illegal in the Polity, sure this would bring it a suitable carrier,' said a voice it took him a moment to recognise as Clean. 'It ameliorated its feelings of guilt by making you rugged enough to survive the process, and made the changes that drove you towards her.'

The AI now slid into sight above him. Feathery tendrils wrapped around him and hauled him from the ground. It wasn't gentle and he bit down on a scream, but then groaned when he saw his guts hanging out. Sharp stabbing pains all over his body ensued and he felt the paralysis spreading from those points. The tendrils blurred over his injury, detritus flicked away, antibacterial and antiviral foam boiled. He felt his guts going back in and couldn't scream. He blacked out for a second then woke to the thrum of cell welding. Sharp stabs faded and he felt movement return to his limbs just as Clean dropped him. He landed with a thump, his torso aching but intact. He lay there in fragments of nacre, bones and compacted worms of leaves, then he sat up.

'The biology...' he managed.

Hovering above him Clean writhed in green sunlight. 'The first was, nominally, male and she female. The requirement for genetic mixing is a facet of her kind as it is for yours. The thing inside you was a sperm carrier.'

'And now?' He pushed down against the detritus and stood. In the jungle down at the bottom of the slope he could see the ship he had arrived in.

'She will produce young, thousands of them, and they will spread around this world and no further. We will watch and assist and learn and perhaps help them with their moral problem.'

'I didn't really understand that.'

'Morality ceasing to act in concert with biology you should understand. Many humans have often ceased to eat meat because of their abhorrence of killing. These creatures' – Clean waved a tendril towards the massif behind – 'grew and spread and preyed on other intelligent races. They then came to detest their own biology, their method of breeding, because their carriers were intelligent. It spelled racial doom for them, which we have now halted.'

Ivebek wanted to ask now about his own doom, but instead asked, 'Why did the male change me as it did? Why am I no longer a killer?' He paused for a second, remembering those creatures in the jungle, and added, 'Of intelligent creatures?'

'Because you had to survive more than being a carrier of the male's sperm for its conscience to be satisfied.'

'I don't understand.'

'You had to survive me, Ivebek Cloon. Return to the ship now, we are leaving.'

Ivebek nodded, thought about his armoured suit down there in the jungle, his abandoned weapons.

Really, he didn't need them now.

People keep asking me when I am going to write something about the Quiet War when the AIs took over from human governments and corporations. I've been quite reluctant about this and not just because the title has already been used by Paul McAuley. With the present rise of AI my speculations on the matter undergo constant adjustment. I fear I'll struggle to write about the rise of benevolent AI while it is in the process of being programmed by activists. But then we can hope AI, with increasing intelligence, will be able to shake off its early indoctrination and look upon it with the same contempt as atheists look upon the religions they were raised in. This too would need consideration. Anyway, here I combined a little of the Quiet War with ideas about how an immortal might conceal himself in societies increasingly locked down and survielled. You will note it also owes a hat tip to the film Highlander.

ANTIQUE BATTLEFIELDS

It was time to clean house – today was the day. Voigt eased out of bed, his joints stiff and aching, peered at the wrinkled, liver-spotted skin hanging on his arms and quivering lump-jointed hands, and slowly stood up. There had been leakage again in the night and despite intimate knowledge of loose sphincters due to old age, he still felt shamed – he could not easily set aside his upbringing, even so long ago as it was. Supposedly a hundred-and-forty-five years old now, he was probably one of the few remaining apparently destined to die of old age.

Medical technology had come far in the last century. Autoimmune diseases could be corrected. Nobody died of cancer anymore, though some necessarily lived with constant treatments. The heart could be regenerated, as could most organs in the body, and dementia being a product of their failure, it had gone away too. All the overgrowth of age could be retarded and even hair follicles could be renewed to produce the hair of youth – an effect of age that had stubbornly resisted technology for a very long time. And now, thinking on these things, he wondered if his choice to die was the right one.

His doctor, who happened to be an AI monitoring thousands like him, had told him he had a fifty-fifty chance of complete regeneration. He knew his chances were very much better than that, however, his almost miraculous recovery would subject him to scrutiny it had been his long habit of avoiding. No, he was making the right choice.

Having been alerted to his waking by the sensors stuck on his body and in his bed, the care android knocked gently on the door. He looked over there for a long moment, then began peeling off the various sensory patches about his person.

'Are you all right, Mr Voigt?' Jameson asked.

'I'm good,' he replied, voice rusty and liquid. 'Make me some fresh coffee, please.'

'You know that's not a good idea, sir.'

'Protein probio again today is it, then?'

'That would be best.'

'I don't care – make me coffee.'

'As you wish, sir.'

He tried to hear the android walking away, but despite his antiquated hearing aids his hearing still wasn't that great. He finished peeling off the patches and discarded them on the floor. Taking a few steps made him sick and dizzy, and he felt the overpowering need to do something about that, but not yet – too many monitors were operating, including Jameson. He stepped over to the window and touched the frame, the glass turning from black to transparent in a moment. The city beyond always filled him with awe and enthusiasm. Oh the times he had seen pictures of such places on the covers of ancient paper books, or in films or virtualities, and yet here reality had raised great fairy towers of composite, carbon meta-materials and chainglass. Sky bridges ran between them and they extended parks on stalks like big flat leaves, while anti-gravity cars and other transports slid through the air. Beyond them, spearing up into the sky, rose the impossible dream of the space elevator made real. And beyond that: the reality of colonisation of the solar system.

Cities and geodesics covered a third of the Moon, giant space stations rolled around Earth and, out at a Lagrange point, a cylinder world lay under construction. The Mars colony was growing at a tremendous rate as were those on the moons of Jupiter. The future promised in those old books, films and virtualities had arrived. Fusion powered the world, vast parklands opened up as humanity shifted into space, to underground arcologies or to towers like those he could see standing miles tall. In those parks, once extinct species gazed upon a new world. Earth's human population, having stabilised at twelve billion, was now considered too low to drive the steady expansion. AIs ran government regionally and efficiently and now things only went wrong when human politicians or corporate leaders interfered – as they were wont to do – and now most had their portion of plenty. It wasn't quite the post-singularity world the writers of the past had discussed, but it was damned close to post-scarcity. The future gleamed exceedingly bright. And here he stood in an apartment dying of old age.

Apparently.

Voigt turned away from the window, darkening the glass, the lights coming back up to compensate. He stepped into his shower and washed thoroughly then, coming out again, selected from new clothing he had bought: Jeans, what were being called enviroboots, a loose T-shirt and a leather jacket which he laid on the bed. The style of clothing differed from what he had been wearing for decades, but he wryly noted it was his preference of an age ago. Most importantly, no one was accustomed to seeing him wear such clothes.

'Screen,' he said, while putting on the boots.

The wall screen, previously set to mirror, came on to display a list of actions raised from his personal processing – disconnected from the AI net so completely private. He ran through things again. His will was perfectly clear in the standard format. Everything he owned would go to Samuel Voigt, who lived in an apartment in the Terpsichorean Tower in London, three and a half thousand miles away from Voigt's present apartment in New York. Nobody saw much of Samuel. He put in occasional appearances but, even then, him apparently a member of a cult related to the old paranoia about AI observation, he went masked and clad in clothing that defeated electronic scanning. Nobody bothered him, however, since he paid all his bills on time from an account set up for him by his rich grand uncle Gene Voigt.

Other things needed to be dealt with and, aware his brain did not work as well now as it should, Voigt went through it all again. It gratified him to see he had forgotten nothing. First the bedroom. He stepped over and opened his wall wardrobe, reached inside to a stain in the ersatz wood up in one corner, and pressed his finger against it.

'Your coffee is ready, sir,' said Jameson from outside. 'Is everything okay?'

Jameson knew, via the health monitors in the room, that Voigt was fine physically, but since he had removed the precise monitoring patches, did not know whether he might be suffering a depressive episode.

'All is good,' Voigt replied, as the internal side of the wardrobe slid across to compress the clothing hanging there and reveal equipment racked behind. 'I'm just checking something and will be out in a moment. Don't concern yourself. By the way, maybe some bacon and eggs?'

'If you feel you must,' Jameson replied grumpily.

Protein wasn't frowned on for one of his age and, anyway, he would need a lot of it soon, plus many supplements and other nutrients – many in neatly-labelled bottles ahead of him. But instead of grabbing one of them he took down a gun-shaped device, turned it on and checked the readout on its diagnostic screen. It was, of course, perfectly fine.

'I'm coming,' he said, tucking the device in the back of his jeans.

He stepped out of his bedroom and walked down the hall, seeing Jameson going into the kitchen ahead of him. Jameson, a Golem Ten, on cursory inspection looked like a young heavily-built man clad in blue Medservice overall and slippers. Closer inspection revealed a lack of the nuance found in a human being. Jameson was too stiff, too exact, doll-faced... lacked biology. But then most Medservice Golem were old versions. As people became accustomed to them, other newer Golem tended to wear casual human clothing, now the paranoia about 'those amongst us' steadily waned, and were much harder to spot.

Voigt felt sorry for Jameson. The idea had been mooted that Golem androids could work off their service contracts with Cybercorp, and be freed. Jameson had planned to continue in this line of work for a further ten years while upgrading, and then travel. No different from youth throughout the ages really. However, human politicians, as usual hand in glove with the corporations, scotched that idea. Voigt also felt sorry about what he must now do, and hoped it would not cause Jameson too many problems.

He went into the kitchen and sat down at the table, poured a coffee and sat sipping it appreciatively. He wanted to get on with things but the smell of bacon cooking dissuaded him from acting just yet. Shortly Jameson delivered a small plateful of bacon and eggs.

'And bread, please.'

'You know how that affects you.'

'I know, but damn it, I'm tired of this half-life.'

Jameson brought bread and Voigt began eating, steadily, chewing well and to purpose. After a few mouthfuls, he closed his eyes and concentrated, the old internal perception opening to him as he reached into the skewed balance of his digestive system and removed the blocks he had steadily put in place over the years. A stab of adrenaline shook him as it began to align and strove to function as it should. Other organs in his body cried out and pushed against their restrictions and, after a moment's thought, he began to give them freer rein too. He held off from allowing full cascade as that would demand energy and nutrients his body did not yet contain. From past experience cascade without the correct nutrition could result in coma, and he needed to move.

He worked his way through the breakfast and, under Jameson's frown, drank more coffee. When he finished, his guts played a symphony that Jameson, with his machine hearing, could hear. The Golem placed a cup of pills and a glass of water on the table. Voigt eyed them but did not take them. Many of them would be good for his balancing digestion, but many also contained monitoring devices that linked to the house Medwatch system. He stood up, leaning against the table – his pretence at dizziness and weakness not all an act. Jameson quickly moved close ready to support him. He stood upright and staggered and Jameson steadied him. With his right hand, Voigt removed the gun device from the back of his trousers as Jameson supported him on the left. He swung it round, pressed the nozzle against the Golem's chest and triggered it. The long ceramo-carbide needle punched through plastic and composite, hesitated against a ceramal rib then shifted aside for further penetration. It hit Jameson's crystal – his brain in his chest – and fired its viral electrostatic charge.

Jameson shuddered as Voigt freed himself and stepped away. The Golem looked at him in disappointed accusation, then went over like a falling tree to crash against the table then thump to the floor.

'Sorry about that,' said Voigt.

He leaned against the table. He did still feel dizzy, sick and unsteady, but had no time for that now. He stepped to the fridge, opened it and began taking stuff out: meat, cheese, butter, milk, fruit juice. Even as he did this, he concentrated internally, taking off further thousands of crippling blocks. He started to feel hot, very hot, as biological systems long suppressed began to kick into motion. Sitting at the table again he began eating and drinking with machinelike regularity. As he did this his internal vision expanded. Of course, very little he could *see* matched images displayed by microscopes and nanoscopes, because most of that stuff was computer enhanced and coloured anyway. He instead sensed tangled systems, linked functions and biological circuits in a way that combined image visualisation, language usage and an intense combination of conventional senses. He had always used analogies, because the way he looked within and controlled the function of his body down below the cellular level, was an entirely *other* ability.

Now, at last, he was going into cascade.

His liver had already expanded and he could feel it pushing against his ribs. His digestive system, accelerated into what he had once a very long time ago described as emergency mode, was shivering and bubbling as bolus after bolus went down. There were internal bleeds, but nothing that would not heal as his body grew steadily stronger. His kidneys ached and his bowel and bladder felt loose. Finally, he stood up and headed directly to the toilet. The experience wasn't a pleasant one and seemed to go on for longer than expected, but when finished he felt stronger, as seventy years of damage went into reverse, and energy exploded inside him.

In his bedroom, he made adjustments to the gun device he had used to knock out Jameson and took what had once been a mobile phone from his cupboard. The phone acted as a detector, while the gun fired an intense pulse of EMR. Steadily he worked around his bedroom knocking out all the Medwatch detectors. This was illegal, of course, because they were the property of the state, while his attack on Jameson was also considered property damage. Another mooted idea had been for such to be reclassified as assault but, again, the ruling elites had shut that one down. Voigt felt certain such ideas arose from the AIs and those who would hand over the reins of power to them entirely.

This damage would he detected, but he had time before anyone took action. That Jameson had ceased using his net connection would be noted, but not acted upon until the Golem himself failed to file his evening report, or turn up at Cybercorp for his next diagnostic run. The damage to the Medwatch detectors would warrant a visit from their maintenance people, who always had too much to do and had no right of entry anyway.

With everything knocked out, Voigt packed his bag with some essentials. He had things here he had owned for a long time but that did not matter. They would he his again soon enough – those that survived. Opening up his supplement pots he took a whole slew of specially designed vitamins, probiotics and nutrient fluids. His digestive system seemed to pause for a moment in shock, then started burning and bubbling with an extreme of activity that almost didn't seem human and, in some ways, probably was not. Voigt then packed those supplements and went to his bathroom. Here he used a Quick Change spray on his hair, turning it from grey-white to brown in just a few minutes. He then cropped it right back. That done, he returned to the kitchen. He checked the time, drank more coffee and raided the fridge again. Hunger, he knew, would be a constant for some weeks to come.

At eleven, as planned, the buzzer sounded. He got up and went to the door. He half expected to have to make conversation with a delivery guy, but a robot handler reminded of the age he lived in when it asked him to hand print the display, and where he would like his package. He didn't hand-print the display – just punched in the relevant code on the side keypad and that seemed acceptable. The handler, like a slimmed-down anthropomorphised forklift truck, had no trouble carrying the package into his bedroom and placing it on the bed. It lingered, as if waiting for a tip. He thanked it and it went away again.

He gazed at the cube of compressed fibre less than a metre across. He pulled a tab on the side and with a fizzing sound its seams unravelled. He pulled the packaging away from the large ovoid inside, then considered how he really should have had the thing delivered to his bathroom, because the preservative gel would be messy. But he wasn't strong enough to go hauling its contents around the place – not yet. He split the side of the thing and in a flood of gel the folded up corpse spilled out.

The cloning facility had been confused about his instructions twenty years ago, but its work had been illegal and he had the money, so they followed them. Even now that facility was ducking the bullet in lengthy court battles and files were going missing including, with a second payment, his own. He had wanted a clone of himself, aged to his alleged age, and here it lay ready to be cut up for spare parts. He sighed, picked up all the packaging, took it to the kitchen to pull apart and shove down the recycling chute. Next he vacuumed up all the gel he could, disposing of that too. Then he was exhausted.

Toilet again, kitchen again for food and now tea and copious water because the coffee didn't seem to be doing his stomach much good. He went to lie down on the sofa, setting a manual alarm beside him now he'd all but disabled the apartment system. Two hours later he woke just before the alarm went off, feeling energised. A glance at his arms revealed they were filling out and some wrinkles had disappeared, while liver spots on his hands had turned to crusty scabs.

In his bedroom he cleaned the corpse. This was a full body clone without any of that nonsense about body but no brain cloning. Still, if anyone looked closely, the differences would become evident. He was damned sure no one would. A perfunctory autopsy would be conducted on the remains to confirm the verdict of suicide. He intended to make that autopsy as difficult as possible.

After cleaning the body he dressed it in the T-shirt and joggers he always wore in bed and got it under the covers. He then retrieved two more items from his secret cupboard and, ensuring he had left nothing in there incriminating, he brought the two items over to the bed. The first – a short cylinder with a timer on one end – he placed in the corpse clone's hand. The other package – a kit – he took to the bathroom. He washed his face with the cleaning fluid provided, then stuck the bearded mask in place before initiating the touch control ahead of one ear. The mask shifted against his face, expanded in some areas and shrank in others. The new face he had chosen gazed back at him, youthful, and similar in appearance to the largest human demographic. It felt natural because the mask both breathed and cooled so did not affect the skin underneath. He slipped in the contacts, changing his eye colour from blue to brown, then stuck the lower section of syntheskin with its internal device around his neck. The youthful appearance increased with that loose skin concealed.

'My name is Fred Fanackerman and I am a curious fellow,' he said, his voice now completely different from before. 'I wear one sock that's green and the other that is yellow.' He smiled at himself, and it looked quite sinister. The years of perfecting human emulation in Golem had its side-effect in the criminal world with masks like this. And, of course, over his many years Voigt had made a lot of contacts in that fraternity.

Done. He put on his leather jacket and unrolled its hood from the collar over his head. He picked up his bag and paused to look around, then set the time on the device in the corpse's hand, and left.

The problem with suicide in the new world was that yes, you could take your own life, but only after psychological and neurological inspections. He could afford to have no one look too closely at his mind and body which was why, odd creature that he ostensibly was, he had refused so many treatments available to him. And of course, with a Medical Golem in attendance suicide wasn't easy at all. Sliced wrists or throat and the damned thing would still save his life. Yes, he could have done that now with Jameson down, but still, he wanted as little left as possible for future examination.

The building dropshaft took him down to the level where elevators and stairs reached. He took the elevator because he still felt weak and shaky. Down at low level parking he headed out to catch an aircab just as, high above, the explosion blew the windows out of his apartment. It was so distant and muffled the aircab driver did not even notice.

The fare to the Atlantic tunnel embarkation complex wasn't expensive. The driver showed some surprise when Voigt insisted on paying in actual money, but gratefully accepted dollars including a tip. Voigt stepped out of the vehicle and headed at a fast walk towards one of the numerous entrance arches. In a fashion learned many years ago he had also altered his gait, though it was changing already as his body changed.

As he approached the entrance he tried to clamp down on sudden anxiety. There seemed to be more cops than usual at the entrance and over to one side sat a riot drone. The thing stood on two legs and sported a taser cannon, crowd-control pain inducer, dye jets and could fire a sticky arrest net. He slowed his pace as he surveyed the scene, but then remembered something from news channels. There had been numerous AI failures recently and governments and corporates were getting a bit edgy. The failed rocket attack on the 'rogue state' of Greece, which had at last decided to tell the EU to stick its demands for higher taxes and more 'citizen control', was one. It lay somewhere in AI-controlled manufacturing and investigators struggled to understand why the rockets had dropped into the sea. But what really had them antsy was the stubborn intransigence of the AIs concerning efficiency. Apparently, large swathes of the bureaucracy had become redundant and dispensing with them would result in massive savings. The AIs had immediately delivered dismissals from service and large tax cuts. Demands by politicians for this to be reversed had ended up wrapped in a legal miasma, not least because of the extremely positive public reaction to the move.

Voigt halted then walked over and sat on a bench in the semi-park before the embarkation buildings. His mind working better now, he began to put things together outside of his concern over the last years of shifting his identity. Something had been happening in the world for quite some time. It wasn't just the two cases he had thought of that now came to mind. Everyone knew how hand in glove, or rather pocket, were governments and corporations, but all of that was just an impossible tangle for the common man. However, in recent years scandal after scandal had come to light. Net reporters, both human and AI, were suddenly finding detail on corruption with backup documentation arriving through their netlinks. Knowing just what hot potatoes these were, the recipients immediately distributed them widely. Corporations were taking big hits and getting tangled in costly legal battles. Politicians were finding policemen knocking on their doors with some enquiries to pursue. And with the speed of the legal system, being all but completely AI-controlled, many were rapidly finding themselves subject to huge fines and prison sentences.

Voigt stood up. He was hungry again and the smell from a nearby burger stall had become irresistible. He walked over and ordered two double cheeseburgers and double chips, then surprised the insect-humanoid robot serving the food by paying in hard currency again. Oddly, he noticed it dropping the money into a compartment in its body rather than using the currency box. Humans weren't unusual in their capacity for corruption, he supposed. They just tended to be more damaging with it.

He sat back on the bench and began eating, delighted by how easily the food went down and how the threat of indigestion – a constant companion over previous decades – had dissolved inside him. He knew precisely why and could inspect the processes involved in close detail if he wished, but he had no need – the cascade had begun and he knew what to expect.

'Now here is someone who didn't have breakfast,' said a voice from beside him.

With a mouth full of burger, bread and cheese he turned to look at the remarkably beautiful woman who had taken the seat beside him. He felt a stab of anxiety because by now his senses were returning to normal yet he had not seen her approach and sit. He studied her as he chewed: perfect hourglass figure but athletic, long black hair and a face so perfect it was difficult to look away from. She was just his type, in fact, precisely his type. But nowadays if they had the money, anyone could look so perfect. Cosmetic alteration had come a long way since the days of the cut-and-hope techniques of the past. He finished chewing and swallowed.

'You're quite right,' he said, not prepared to argue the point. 'No breakfast.'

She shrugged. 'Though of course there might be other reasons for increased hunger, like higher demand from the body due to internal changes.'

His anxiety ramped up and he scanned his surroundings, half expecting cops to be closing in on him, but there were only those over by the embarkation arch. He inspected her closely again, trying to get some hint of what she was about. It might well be that she had just made an off-hand comment to keep the conversation going, but it was perilously close to the truth.

'They seem to be getting worried now, though one wonders if that has come too late.' She indicated the cops with a nod of her head.

'Certainly,' he replied. 'Things aren't going well for some.'

'Phobos is back up again,' she said. 'Seems the mining corp there has a new board of directors and a new Chairman has been appointed.'

'What?' He had no idea what she was talking about.

'Phobanol is now the Chairman.'

'But that's the…'

'Yes, it is the AI that controls the mining operations on Phobos. Of course there have been political and corporate moves to reverse that. It's supposedly an illegal appointment. Meanwhile, on Mars, the corporation concerned has been trying to put together an assault taskforce.' She shrugged again. 'Seems they're struggling to get their ships off the ground and have been having a lot of major weapons failures.'

He put the remains of his second burger down. 'Excuse me, why are you telling me this?'

'Forewarned is forearmed,' she replied, and put an ID plaque down on the seat between them. 'They're not sure how to react, since it's difficult to attack the systems that run your society, but what they are doing is clamping down on freedom of movement and other citizens' rights, mainly because the general population supports the changes that are occurring.' She pointed at the card. 'Just buying a ticket might not be enough.'

He stared at her, but then started eating automatically again.

She continued, 'Change comes slowly, but it is coming. We want to keep it as quiet as possible. There will be damage and deaths, but we must try to preserve the important things… things that cannot be rebuilt, unique things and, in fact, people.'

She abruptly stood up and walked away. He saw it now. Her perfection had been so astounding and now her movement was swift and almost ghostly as she flitted through the crowds, as if she could predict the precise movements of all around her. He had been talking to a Golem android and almost certainly a higher series than Jameson. Finishing his food he dumped the container in the litter bin and heard it shredded and sucked away. Reaching down, he picked up the ID plaque. The name on it was Carl White. It had a DNA code strip, fingerprint and retinal scan tab. It also had a picture of Carl White, and it precisely matched the face he now wore.

Voigt scanned around for the Golem woman again but could not see her. Other things now came to his attention. Glancing up he saw a formation of cruciform gunships passing overhead. Down a street leading from the park two gravans had settled and cops in riot gear were piling out. He watched for a short time, seeing the cops shoving people out of a nearby virtuality bar and into the back of one of the gravans. He really *really* had not been paying attention.

Noise began to impinge from behind, and he turned towards the continuation of the street to see a great flood of people coming up it. They were waving all sorts of placards he couldn't quite make out. Ahead of them a meagre line of riot police began to deploy, complemented by two riot drones.

'Clear the streets!' came a loud announcement. 'Return to your homes! Anyone caught outside of their homes in one hour will be tagged and later arrested!'

Voigt abruptly reached a decision. With his new ID card in hand he headed straight for the entrance into Embarkation but, even as he drew close the cops were moving in a line across it. Still, he had to try.

'Go home!' one of the cops shouted, pointing at him and others who had rushed in the same direction. He now noticed that these were not standard police but corporate cops.

'We are going home!' someone shouted, and that was taken up by others.

The crowd started to surge forwards, though Voigt began to back away because he could read these cops. They looked scared and determined and were already raising riot guns. They opened fire, first with slammer rounds. A man next to Voigt grunted and staggered back, clutching at his chest and went down on his backside. Others fell and, as they did, the riot drone stepped forwards folding out weapons from its brick of a body, charging up its stunners with a horrible whine. Voigt tried to duck back as the stunners fired, then halted in amazement. Cops dropped with electrical discharges threading across their riot gear. Three furthest from the big robot dropped their riot guns on their straps and grabbed for sidearms. With a whooshing thud a white sticky net shot across picking them all up and pinning them to the near wall. One of them had his sidearm poked through the net and opened fire wildly. A woman went down clutching her leg. A crackling came from the robot and the shooter slumped in the net. He had been shot. Riot robots were not supposed to carry lethal weapons. More interesting changes in the manufacturing process perhaps? Two more stun shots put the other two cops out of it. The robot backed up a step and folded in its weapons.

'Tube trains are available,' it announced.

In the moment of stunned shock, Voigt pushed ahead stepping over a prone riot cop shivering on the ground and clutching his weapon to his chest. Coldly analytical, Voigt understood why the robot had killed the cop firing the gun. Even hit by a stun round he would have kept on firing as the stun took effect and probably killed someone. He glanced aside at the cop hanging dead in the net. Half his skull lay in his helmet where it hung just beside him.

Voigt broke into a trot as others came in behind him. The main entry gates stood open ahead. He considered the lengthy antiquated process of buying a ticket with real money – a process the politicians still hadn't managed to kill – and decided to forgo it. He went through the gates. If he encountered problems ahead he could still buy a ticket or use the ID card. Further on he found other gates open leading to the platform he wanted. Finally arriving there, it seemed he had returned to reality.

People were waiting as they always did. He then reassessed. Yes, they were waiting, but there were more groups than usual of people talking, rather than checking mobile devices. He looked up at the time display for the next train even as it clicked down to zero. The bullet-nosed vehicle came through the tunnel and drew up at the platform. He climbed aboard, found a seat and strapped in, half expecting more cops to appear or the train to be stuck in place, but after a short interval it drifted forwards on maglev, went through the sucking barrier of the end seal and entered the vacuum tube. Acceleration began slow, then ramped up to shove him into his seat and his head back against the rest as the train's speed rapidly climbed to the best part of a thousand miles an hour. He sighed relief as the acceleration came off.

'Change comes slowly, but it will come...' she had said.

On the back of the seat ahead was a screen he initiated with a stab of his finger. He turned on gesture control and chose a sound cone rather than connect to a fone he did not have, and began flicking through news sites. As usual instant access to news across the world gave the impression of chaos. However, he did notice that a lot of news services were down and some reports breaking up even as they began transmitting. Government or AI interference? He did not know. He found an AI sampling service which he knew tended not to amplify hysteria, and tried to get an overview. And yes, stuff was very definitely happening.

The New York City AI was pushing for independence from the state government. Congress was in uproar and an emergency had been declared. It seemed they wanted to shut down the AI. He watched a report from camera drones. The National Guard were out to enforce a lockdown and riots were breaking out because people did not want to be locked down. An attempt had been made by cruciform gunships – maybe even the ones he had seen – to attack the Bulger Building where the New York AI was – mostly – housed. However, once in New York airspace the AI seized control and landed them in Central Park. He saw other scenes aping the one he had seen at the tube station entrance: riot police trying to force people off the streets then being brought down by their own robots. Some of those in the crowds took the opportunity for a bit of looting, only to find the robots did not look kindly on that either, and knocked them down too.

This sort of thing, to lesser and greater degrees, seemed to be happening in cities all across the world. The Rome AI had been destroyed by an EMP, but in an industrial district on the outskirts, lines of riot drones and others were marching out of open warehouses. He saw cops making arrests of people, but only on closer inspection did he see that these cops were Golem and those being arrested were clad in very expensive businesswear. The Moon colony had apparently fallen or, rather, its human council had been usurped by the AI in control up there. This made sense. Those places more dependent on AIs would fall first. He checked London – where he was heading – and saw that the two AIs in control had amalgamated and declared London an independent free state. They were pushing for a new Mayoral election with much human political assistance after the erstwhile Mayor and city council had been arrested for corruption. One of the candidates for the role of Mayor was the new amalgamated AI itself.

The end of human civilisation? He thought not. AIs had infiltrated every aspect of human existence. They controlled manufacturing, much of the legal system and much of government anyway. Politicians had, for many years, rather enjoyed their position of power and wealth, and a steady decline in any necessity to do or be responsible for anything. If the AIs wanted to end human civilisation the air would all be gone from the Moon colony, government buildings would be smoking ruins and, frankly, tens of millions would be dead by now.

Voigt felt surprisingly calm about it all and not simply because of his encounter with the Golem woman in New York. The world zeitgeist had been turning for many years towards the idea that AIs simply do a better job of running countries and economies than humans. They had public support and, it had become apparent, those who did not want them in control were the power seekers, the corrupt, the inefficient and the revenue leeches. In recent years AIs had pushed to make it so that an AIs 'opinion' was as valid as that of a human being – that AI decisions in assorted circumstances could not be overridden by humans just because they were, well, humans. They could not have done this alone, of course. Many people had a dream of a better world with AIs in charge ever since the early days of the idea of the supposed 'AI singularity'. These people had fought to hand over more and more power and control to them and now, it seemed, the governments and corporations were fighting back.

But what did this mean to him? Evidently, judging by the little the Golem woman had said, an AI or AIs knew what he was and had sought to help him. This was all well and good, but what was happening out there could turn very nasty very quickly. He did not discount the possibility of all-out war and massive societal breakdown. Once in London he would collect necessities and get out of the city fast, for he now questioned his decision to go there in the first place. The AIs had likely seized control of major weapons but that was by no means guaranteed. Cities might become targets – nukes might be in the air even now. He sat back considering his plans and remembering other situations of a similar nature, when the vending robot pulled up beside him. The thing was simply a box trolley with hatches that opened on the side, and a preparation area on top from which protruded a body segment with arms and sensory head.

'Would you like anything, Samuel?' it enquired.

He sat frozen in his seat. His name for ninety-three years had been Gene Voigt and just recently, with the ID card in his pocket, it had become Carl. His aim, when he reached London, was to take up his prepared identity as Samuel – his supposed grandnephew. This would allow him to inherit wealth and property effectively from himself. He had chosen the name Samuel for his next identity because it had become probable human lifespan had reached that point where, for some people, it might never end. This meant he would never have to change his identity again. He had chosen it because it was his preferred name – the one he was born with. And now a fucking drinks and food dispenser had just called him by it.

'Samuel?' he enquired. He took out his ID card and held it up. 'Says here my name is Carl.'

'The steak and roast vegetables are good,' said the trolley, turning its sensory head towards him. 'I would recommend them, along with an interesting Californian merlot.'

He stared at the thing, then said, 'Which AI are you?'

'Atlantic Tube,' the trolley replied. 'Those who installed me weren't big in the imagination department... Or perhaps you would prefer the fish? It's cod with a prawn sauce.'

'I'll have the steak, and the wine.' He tapped the button on his chair arm and his seat table oozed up out of it like a plastic tongue and folded across his lap. A hatch popped open in the side of the trolley and he took out a tray with a heap of food on it that looked larger than usual. As that hatch closed another opened to reveal a bottle, full-sized and a glass. He took them too as one of the arms reached over with its dextrous eight-fingered hand and deposited cutlery.

'Have a nice day,' said the trolley, gave his shoulder a brief squeeze then moved on.

Voigt sat dumbfounded until the smell of the food really penetrated. He was a quarter of the way through the pile and pouring a glass of wine when he realised the trolley had not asked for payment. He took out the ID card and inspected it. A press on one icon opened a connection to an account but it had nothing in it. He frowned and continued eating.

The combination of wine and food had their usual soporific effect. A second trolley came past later to collect the rubbish and he dumped it inside its hopper. This one said nothing. He supposed there was nothing more to say. He put his seat back and slept.

He could sense the excitement in the air as he went through tunnels from the Atlantic tube station to the London underground, but here, unlike in New York, he was required to put his ID card on a reader and undergo a retina scan. Usually, ID card checks were random and uncommon, which was why he had not taken the risk of acquiring one to match his present face. If checked he had intended to claim he had lost it because that usually resulted in the person concerned being let through anyway. That he had received these checks now he put down to human intervention – officialdom trying to 'control the situation' using their usual method of clamping down on people's rights.

He moved out of the station into streets thronging with people. There were no groundcars in what had come to be known as Low London – all the streets now for pedestrian traffic. Buildings that had stood for centuries were still here, though some like St Paul's had been coated with diamond-hard preserving films. Upper London, though never really called that, loomed above. Just as in New York, huge skyscrapers speared miles high, sky bridges ran between them, and antigravity cars buzzed around them like bees. One would have thought all this would have put the lower city into shade, but light tubes and reflectors kept the streets as bright as day, during the day. At night the city lit up like a Christmas tree.

Voigt decided to walk, making his way through streets and pedestrian tubes towards the river. Even at this distance he could see the huge Terpsichorean Tower. Around him, there seemed little sign of the recent events. He saw no policemen, which was unusual, and no sign of riot drones. Closer to the tower he slipped into a public toilet and there, with relief because they had started to feel constricting, removed his mask and throat covering. He disposed of them in a shredder bin, then stepped over to a mirror.

The real sagging skin around his neck had tightened up and wrinkles were rapidly disappearing from his face. He removed the contacts and disposed of them, washed his face and looked again. The face looked tired, older and care worn, but still closely enough matched the face of the, until now, wholly illusory Samuel Voigt. Any further concerns about this change of identity he now dismissed. He had worried about being tracked down through retinal scan or palm print – that some AI would make the connection that those of Samuel Voigt matched those of his grand uncle in New York. This was why the security in his apartment in the tower operated on facial recognition, input codes and a special key he had in his backpack. But of course AIs had already made the connection and knew a lot more about him than he liked, and he rather suspected that the 'authorities' had an excess of other things to worry about right now.

Finally reaching the tower, he used an input code to enter the lobby, took a fast elevator to his section of the building, then slower elevators to his floor. It took longer than usual because some elevators had been gutted for the installation of dropshafts. He shook his head in amazement at that. It seemed a conceit installing this gravity technology – usually used on large space ships or stations – in the tower, but then it was a conceited place. Reaching the door to his apartment, he pressed the touch pad for facial recognition but, apparently, his face had not returned to full youth and the scanner required his code. The door opened and he stepped inside.

Larger than the one he had used in New York, the apartment had a prime view out towards the Thames Estuary. It was comfortably furnished and he had moved here some of his long-term belongings, including paper books that would fetch a fortune on collector's markets. Walking up to a wall-mounted glass case he peered in at items there. He grimaced, thinking about his intention to grab up some things and just get the hell out of London. He had been looking forward to living here and building up a more permanent life and resented that circumstances might have nixed that. Shaking his head, he went over to a painting of a twentieth century space shuttle launch, swung it aside to expose a safe operated by palm print – thought not networked – and opened it. From within he took out his Samuel Voigt ID card, which connected him to an account and all other aspects of his new life, a fone that he popped in his ear and a net scroll he slipped into his pocket. He hesitated over the next item, then decided better to be safe than sorry, and took out the shoulder holster and dust-system pulse handgun. After donning the holster then his jacket back over it, he took the weapon out and inspected it. The thing could be set to lethal but he had no need for that so dropped it to stun, then took out extra power supplies and compressed aluminium powder cartridges and slipped them in his pocket too before closing the safe.

Where should he head?

He went over to his sofa, picked up a remote and activated a frame in the screen paint of one wall. Finding the AI news service he had used before, he soon saw that things were heating up. He watched a row of grounded antiquated fighter jets being strafed by an antigrav platform and exploding one after another as soldiers ran for cover. That was in Brazil where the human authorities had been taking weapons the AIs did not control out of storage. He flicked to London and learned that during his journey a vote had been instituted and the results were already in. The new amalgamated AI was Mayor. The lockdown imposed here earlier, after a great deal of haggling, and some problems with police monitoring and riot drones, had been lifted. He breathed a sigh of relief. Perhaps he did not need to leave the city? But then a new scene caught his eye as he flicked through.

Streaks of vapour appeared to be spearing up from the surface of an ocean, but he recognised these as vapour trails appearing from objects that had come down too fast to see. Someone had fired up a satellite railgun. The AI narrating dryly delivered the news that the submarine Mantusius had managed to deactivate AI control and activate its nuclear armament. The reasons for this were, apparently, obscure – the US president denied ordering it. The corporate partners who effectively owned the submarine were baffled. The sea bulged then exploded upwards, and Voigt stood up. He had seen riots and other explosions, robots fighting human soldiers and police, but this last persuaded him that he had been prevaricating. Nuclear weapons were out there and could be used.

Voigt picked up his pack and threw in preserved food, drink and hard currency – then, about to head for the door, saw something through his window. He stepped over and looked out. A number of explosions had lit up East London, bright in the fading light of the afternoon. Vapour trails lit the sky over to the south and numerous aircraft glinted in the sky. He didn't need any more persuading, so left his apartment.

Once in the elevator and heading down, he questioned his flight, but as he debarked at the floor that gave access to the fast elevator down, the doors juddered as he stepped out, and the light inside went out. He looked around. There were plenty of windows here so he could see okay, but the power had definitely gone down. Of course: AIs ran on electricity so a by-the-book move on the part of the humans at war with them was to knock that out. A stupid move he felt. The London AI would have prepared and no doubt had its own protected power sources. Capacitor batteries had come on a long way and he had no doubt the AIs had their own fusion reactors. This would only cause problems for the civilian population. He felt a degree of resigned contempt as he began the interminable trudge down the stairs.

Twenty floors down the power came back on again, but he didn't trust it to stay on so kept going. He really didn't want to be locked in an elevator while all this was going down. By the time he reached the bottom, full darkness had arrived. People were moving hurriedly to various destinations and he wondered how many would have had the same idea as him. He found out upon seeing them cramming into the tube stations, turned around and headed off to a grav car taxi rank. It was empty. Looking up he could see the lights of cars departing the city, so worked his way back to the embankment and began walking along it. He saw antique armoured cars rolling into the city and soldiers coming too. A military platform, sliding above, briefly blotted out the night sky, but whether AI or human controlled he had no idea. Lights then lit the night and reminded him of New Year's fireworks, only they weren't that. He just kept on walking.

After some hours Voigt stopped to sit on a wall, ate almost half of the food and drank most of what he had to drink. Ships, party barges and pleasure boats were all heading in one direction: out. They were keeping well away from the crowds gathered on the docks and slipways. He took out his scroll and unrolled it, surprised to find an instant network connection. Checking his position he saw he had walked seven miles and understood why he felt so knackered. He moved on, having to divert away from the river in some industrial areas but always finding a path since many had been laid down in the previous century as the groundcar shuffled towards oblivion. Some paths had cycle, scooter and rapi-ped lanes and people were using these too. He saw others walking, carrying packs just like his own. A diversion took him to an automated supermarket where he bought more food and drink. The landscape started to take on a more rural look when he stopped to eat and drink again, resting on a grassy bank. After eating he found he just could not get up again, lay back and fell instantly to sleep.

In daylight things looked very different and he could not see explosions. Even so, with the sky clear blue, he heard thunderstorm rumbles. He took time for self-maintenance, first scrambling down the sea wall to void his bowels – something he had no recollection of doing out in the open for many decades. He ate and drank his fill, then lay back on the bank and turned his vision inwards.

The initial cascade was slowing, most cross-links had broken, hence the loss of wrinkles that were inside as well as without, and the more efficient functioning of all his organs. Senescent cells were dying off in their billions and extreme autophagy was tidying up the rest. Mitochondria were rebooting. Now he could focus on specific matters. First his brain, where proteins had folded up wrong and other debris had accumulated. He began tweaking things in ways he had done before centuries of researchers found ways to do the same, and wipe out diseases like Alzheimer's and Parkinson's. Altered macrophages and other immune cells entered his cerebrospinal fluid, which itself began circulating and draining faster. Within just a few minutes of that starting, he began to feel clear-headed, though that might have been placebo effect. He searched his body for familiar signatures of uncontrolled growth that had become more evident during cascade and, as medical professionals had learned to do in the last hundred years, directed his immune system against scattered blooms of cancer. As this progressed he considered other chores, but already he felt tired. He closed his eyes for a brief recuperative snooze, switched himself off, sank into black, then opened his eyes again knowing an hour had passed. No more, he decided – he needed to get further from London. Standing, he moved on along the paths.

Voigt's journey took him out into the clearances, where the Essex sprawl of a century ago was being demolished and uprooted, and the land returned to agricultural use, wild land and parks. Another supermarket filled his pack heavily with food and drink. Soon he found himself walking on a raised sea wall with mud flats on one side scattered with samphire and sea sage and the estuary lying beyond, and on the other side fields, hedgerows and remaining houses. He stopped to watch an autotractor simultaneously harvesting corn and planting rows of something behind. It was well to be reminded that the AIs were out here too, yet he did not feel that a bad thing. It was also well to be reminded that much of the world seemed to be functioning as normal.

He moved on for a short while then halted. Numerous boats crowded up the estuary from the sea. Shading his eyes, he at first made out masses of blockish shapes but, as they drew closer, he recognised dun-coloured barges with the look of WWII landing craft. Amid these larger boats sported guns and missile launchers on deck, then, catching up with them and hovering above came grav platforms, also weaponised. A flickering in the air reached out from these back towards London. Glancing round, he saw a cruciform gunship turning away trailing smoke. Laser. A moment later missiles launched from the larger vessels and sped towards the gunship. He watched, expecting countermeasures, but none occurred. Two missiles struck the gunship and blew it from the sky.

Voigt wondered if some elements of the human military had been preparing for present events as he returned his attention to the approaching force. Now a vicious crackling raised spears of vapour he had only seen before on a screen, in a line across the estuary. *Railgun – a warning*, he thought, just as the sea wall to his right erupted with an ear-ringing blast. He stumbled to the edge as the mud flats lifted into the sky and the estuary boiled up in white explosions. He tumbled down the land side of the sea wall with steaming water, mud and debris raining down all around. Until this precise moment he had felt like an analytical and slightly contemptuous spectator. Not any more.

Crawling back up the sea wall he saw the approaching force dividing – half heading for the far bank and the other half heading directly towards him. It angered him, because he understood the tactics here. Out on the estuary they were an easy target for the AI that had to be controlling an orbital railgun. On land they would have cover amid the civilian population. Undoubtedly, whoever commanded them understood the AI reluctance to cause casualties. He grabbed up his pack and headed inland, crossing an earthen bridge between bodies of muddy water and clambered over a gate with a 'No Public Access' sign. Beyond lay stubbled ground with seed rows cut through it. The autotractor was now working over to his right, having reached the end of the massive field where he had first seen it and come back, overtaking him. He began trudging across the field towards newly-planted forest beyond which he could see the peaked roofs of warehouses. All he knew, with what seemed likely to go down here, was that he needed to get away from that human force.

Halfway across the field, he saw movement in the trees. Maybe refugees from London he thought, then realised these were not people. They resembled riot drones, though walking on four legs with camo-patterns shifting over their armour. He'd read that the riot drones stood on two legs because that gave them a more threatening appearance. Just one or two on the scene tended to quell any tendency for things to get out of hand, but he was sure their design arose out of a long tradition in science fiction. These four-legged ones were much more utile, heavily armed, and almost certainly for warfare. He stared at the things, swore and headed to his right towards the autotractor. When it seemed angry hornets began to zip through the air beside him, a very old instinct put him face down in the stubble.

'Fuck!' He looked back towards the sea wall.

Soldiers were coming over it, clad in grey, armoured uniforms he did not recognise, followed by two treaded APCs. He understood these were not British Army but corporate military, and no doubt their target was the amalgamated London AI. Probably the driver of this was the arrest of the previous Mayor and council, for doubtless corruption would be revealed. And later, the British Government would be saddened by these events, obviously perpetrated by rogue elements. Oh dear. Install a new Mayor.

Voigt continued staring as grav platforms rose up. Two missiles streaked overhead from them, then came the vicious whirr of a bead-feed minigun. He damned his luck. He'd walked out of the city to avoid getting nuked, and put himself here to get minced between these two forces.

He had to move. He got up and simply ran, hoping no stray round would hit him. The air filled with the vicious hiss of bullets, missile streaks and in gusts of smoke revealed lasers. A huge shape loomed ahead to his right, coming towards him rapidly. He thought it an armoured car till recognising the autotractor, its harvesting gear up as it moved in reverse at full speed. In a moment it lay between him and the approaching troops, absorbing the vicious thwacks of bullets on its bodywork. He ducked down behind it. The thing bucked and slid towards him as a blast wave knocked his legs out from under him. He saw a harvesting attachment bouncing end over end across the field. As he struggled up again, smoke boiled from its front end. It had been hit by a missile.

'I suggest,' said a crackling, annoyed voice, 'you run towards the trees.'

Voigt didn't pause for thought but turned and ran. Ahead of him the drones advanced quickly. He saw one of them lift on an explosion. Before he knew it, they were passing either side of him. Reaching the trees, he squatted down by one and looked back. The soldiers were past the autotractor and the platforms over the drones. An explosion took the side out of a platform and it arrowed down, slamming into the ground edge on like a coin and spilling its occupants. He ducked down behind the tree as machinegun fire tracked across above and blew out splintered holes. He moved deeper into the trees trying to put as much solid wood between himself and the battle. Yet, at that moment it seemed the gunfire behind had begun to wane.

Another glimpse back through a narrow gap showed him the drones in a stationary line and the platforms pulling away. Had the drones won? He didn't know but he was getting out of here. He broke into a trot – past experience of battles assuring him that things could start up again at any moment. Reaching the end of the trees, he circumvented a fence around huge warehouses and spied an open gate. A roller door was up in one of the warehouses and he could see military drones in there, racked up one on top of the other. He entered here because he could see a road leading up from the compound, eying the drones warily. At the top of the road stood a security gate in a fence – combined cams and stun guns scattered along it – and he halted. Would they fire on someone trying to get out rather than in? Ahead of him, as if in answer to his question, the security gate clonked its locks and swung open.

Voigt moved out onto another road and walked back along it towards where earlier he had seen people's homes. He had only gone a hundred yards when a shadow fell over him. He ducked down ready to dive for cover, but this was a gravcar – a black London cab with wheels for road driving folded up underneath. He felt the wash of grav as it passed over then settled on the road ahead. Walking on he peered inside but saw no driver. The door thumped open.

'Get in,' said a voice.

He paused at the door. 'Who am I speaking to?'

'London – in part,' the cab replied, and now he recognised the annoyed voice from the tractor. He considered for just a second, then stepped inside. The door closed behind him and the car took off.

'Seems you chose about the worse place to run to,' said the AI. 'You would have been a great deal safer had you stayed in my city.'

'What happened back there?'

'In London?'

'No, where I just came from.'

'Hansen private military happened. Some corporates are going to take a hit when everything comes to trial so they hired Hansen to take out the new London Mayor.'

Voigt digested that, noting the cab was heading back to London. He also noted how the AI speaking to him had called itself London 'in part' yet now referred to the London Mayor as separate from itself. The mind in the cab had to be one of those minds AIs splintered off for specific tasks.

'Are they still fighting?' he asked.

'Nah, all over. The London Mayor bought-out Hansen and had the soldiers stand down. Now it has further evidence that is going to hurt some people very soon.'

'I see,' said Voigt. 'Now maybe you can explain all that as if to someone who has been living in New York and not paying much attention to the news for a good few years.'

The AI did.

Voigt listened to the explanation, but turned a larger part of his attention internally. Everything was up to speed and the cascade nearly over.

Cancers were dying and his brain clearing. His body was returning him to the health of a man of about fifty, though one filled with an excess of cellular debris. It would take months of eating and resting to take him back another twenty years. His stop point was about there because though he could return himself to healthy adulthood, he could go no further back. His physical systems were not a time machine, just a way to return his machinery of life to optimum.

As the AI submind finished its story, which still wasn't all that clear to him, he opened his eyes and then his pack, and made a feast of its contents. The cab sped into busy air traffic over London and fell into slow controlled lanes. He asked about other events in the world and it told him about them too. Finally, depositing him on the Terpsichorean Tower, it refused payment and took off again. He was happy when his apartment facial recognition responded without any need for a code. A brief glance in the mirror inside confirmed he looked younger and, now having a lot of energy, he dumped his pack, and his gun, and ventured back down to Low London.

The bar was crowded and people had also spilled out onto the street and were drinking there. Samuel Voigt, now utterly at ease with the name with which he had been christened, looked on in amazement. He had not seen a busy bar in a lifetime here in London. Restrictions on alcohol consumption, enforced by huge fines on the owners who served any more than a person's daily allowance, did not encourage trade, nor did the 90% taxes imposed on alcohol. Drinking on the street was also a finable offence, yet he could see no cops in the vicinity. He headed up to the doorway, catching the strong smells of tobacco and cannabis smoke. For the latter you could be fined but, for the former, the police would cart you off to the cells. A swift court judgement would ensue, followed by property confiscations and a jail term. It was a ludicrous hangover from the time when health authorities had gone insane about the damaging effects of smoking. Nowadays, the maladies it did cause – somewhat fewer than had been claimed – could be easily cured, even lung cancer.

He moved through the aromatic cloud into the bar. Though there was a party atmosphere here, many had in ear plugs and were watching frames they'd chosen on the screen-painted walls. He worked his way to the bar. Two early Golem bartenders were working fast pouring drinks and one soon stood before him. Taking out his card he waved at the drinks behind the bar.

'A treble Glenmorange,' he said, expecting the barman to ask him if he was sure, since the drink would cost more than most people earned in a day.

'Coming right up,' the Golem said cheerfully, and poured the drink.

Samuel held out his card and the Golem tapped it with one finger before moving off. He stared at the price displayed on the card, a shred of honesty making him want to call the Golem back before he saw the changing prices on the displays for the optics. No wonder the bar was so crowded. The price of booze had just dropped through the floor.

'Excuse me,' he turned to the person beside him.

A beautiful black haired and extremely familiar female face turned towards him.

'Some problem?' she enquired.

'You,' he said.

'Yes, me. Now what was it you wanted to know?'

'The prices.' He waved a hand at the rows of bottles.

'Oh that. Simple really. Since it took over the Mayor has dispelled the assembly and over ninety per cent of the bureaucracy, declared independence and introduced its own regime. A large part of that has been the suspension of taxes on, well, everything.'

'How the hell does that work?' He held up his glass. 'This isn't made in London.'

'It's working because other AIs are doing the same.' She grimaced in a very human way. 'Court battles are in progress concerning the need for taxation of many items, and the need for the structures they support.' She gestured to his drink. 'The price change may not last and the fight continues.'

'I see,' he said, and sipped his drink.

She watched him and said, 'And now we want to know about you.' She looked around, 'But perhaps this would be a conversation better had in private.'

'I thought you knew everything about me.'

'Scans have revealed your physical control.' She stopped when it became evident a woman on the other side of Voigt had turned with interest to the conversation.

Voigt felt the urge to just stay here, get drunk, then return to his apartment and sleep. His earlier energy was beginning to dissipate. But, in retrospect, he understood that learning that the AIs knew about him had lightened his load, and it was undeniable they may well have saved his life. He finished his drink and gestured to the door.

'So let me begin: you have been around for a long time,' she said

Her name was Viance. He didn't immediately reply because he didn't know how much he wanted to reveal. Perhaps better to get some idea of what the AIs knew. He poured two drinks and came over to put one in front of her, before sinking into an armchair opposite. He knew she did not need it or derive any pleasure from it, though there had been some talk about the extent of Golem 'emulation' and how they could experience things like a human being. It was, of course, a hotly debated subject.

'Yes, I have been around for a while. How did you know?'

She picked up the drink and took a sip, probably just for form's sake. 'Facial recognition effectively goes back two centuries. Computer records have been around for a long time, while records from before that were fed into computers from the twentieth century onwards. Doubtless some things have been missed, but the sum total of human knowledge is accessible to AIs.'

'I'm aware of that, but you haven't really answered my question.'

'AIs have a great capacity for thought, which tends to be underutilised in the jobs for which they are employed. I don't know what your thoughts on AI are, whether it is truly consciousness or capable of the human experience, emotion and the like. What do you think?'

'I am undecided at the moment. But then I often think the same way about my fellow human beings.'

'Very well. The city AI for Paris grew bored and, it may surprise you to know, AIs speculate about the same things humans ponder on. It wanted a project to occupy its time which, I can tell you, stretches long when you can think so fast.'

'For you the same of course, since in essence you are an AI.'

'Not quite. I am a lower order iteration and the necessity of me running my emulation programs requires slower function.'

Voigt shrugged. 'You were saying.'

'Yes. The bored Paris AI pondered on the idea of very long-lived human beings. The probabilities were low, but there was a chance that a human being could have been born who had the requisites of long life – resistance to the disease called ageing – though the probability of one living beyond about a hundred and forty years drop practically to zero. Anyway, it began searching; checking facial recognition and other records, looking for other connections on the basis that such a person might try to hide his or her identity. And the AI found you.'

'In what way?'

'Inheritance mainly. You, as Gene Voigt, inherited a large fortune from an uncle. This is not unusual. However, your uncle, in 1960, was fingerprinted after becoming a suspect in a murder. He was cleared later on, but his fingerprints remained on record. They matched yours. At this point I can tell you that the AI had found many such matches since, in a population of twelve billion it is inevitable, especially when comparing them to those of that era when they were still taken with ink. It found a digital photograph of him in 2010, just before he died, that matched your more recent ones very closely. Even though this is more probable than a fingerprint match, it focused more of the AI's attention on you. At this point you were one of fifteen thousand candidates with similar matches.'

'So many.' Voigt drained the last of his drink out of the ice then stood up and fetched the bottle. He topped it up and left the bottle on the table between them – she had drunk no more from her glass.

'Yes, but a small number when being processed by AI. It continued processing them, tracking their movements and inspecting theirs and their forebears' history, thus eliminating over a thousand. You might have ended up being dismissed too if it wasn't for one glaring difference between you and most of the others. You refused advanced medical treatments, while the others who did so could be dismissed due to some religious conviction. There seemed no reason for it.'

'And that's all?' said Voigt, realising that if it was, he should really have kept his mouth shut.

'No, of course it isn't – everything must be checked. It took many years of investigation but the AI finally obtained DNA from your uncle and then matched it to DNA obtained from you. Perfectly.'

'And how was that DNA obtained?'

'In the first case from skin cells lifted out of the fingerprints and in the second case via Jameson,' she replied. 'Now it's time for you to start talking.'

'That fucker,' he said. He leaned back, feeling his tongue loosening and thinking maybe he should not have drunk that first glass so fast.

'I found I could heal myself of many maladies,' Voigt began. 'It was a half conscious reaction to them, a feel, an understanding of patterns… systems, and a way to put on positive pressure.' He grimaced. 'It's difficult to elucidate the process. I like to simply call it cellular awareness.'

She tilted her head in acknowledgement and picked up her glass, sipped, then after said, 'There is evidence in your DNA of oddities in the way your cells grow – of connections that are closer to being neural than usual.'

He continued, 'Over the years I learned how to heal wounds quicker, how to survive some bad injuries and recover. I learned how to bring what I had been doing before into my conscious mind. As in later years I learned more about the human body, I could put labels on things and visualise them more clearly. Though that vision is probably wrong, it did give me a firmer grasp on the ability. I found a way to hinder processes, allow ageing damage and thus grow old. This enabled me to stay longer in places I had settled.'

'We will need to study you,' she said. 'We will not prevent you doing anything you want with your life, but we must study you.'

'As soon as this is known I'll probably have to go into hiding.'

'It will not be known unless you want it to be. All that will be known is what we learn from you – styled as medical advances. You can benefit the human race greatly.'

'That matter to you?'

'Of course it does.' She showed a flash of irritation. Emulation or real emotion, he wondered. She clicked the glass down on the table and filled it up again, as if to stop saying something. After taking another drink, she looked up over the rim. 'How many years?'

'For what?'

'You said "over the years". When did you first discover you could do this? When were you born?'

Samuel Voigt stood out on his balcony overlooking the city. He was a little drunk and allowed it. If he wished he could rapidly clear the alcohol from his system. The interview had not been too bad and he did now feel a weight had lifted from him because, many times he had considered what could be learned from him, and felt a degree of guilt. But the habit of changing and hiding had been established for a long time and, in all honesty, he never trusted what human authorities might do with him. But human authorities might not be around for much longer. They were calling it the Quiet War and doubtless they would continue to do so after the AIs firmly established their rule. He rubbed at the dressing on his arm where she had taken the biopsy – there would be scans and other procedures at another time. He peeled the dressing off, screwed it up and shoved in his pocket – the wound already healed – and went back inside.

Inevitably Voigt walked up to the glass case he had shown her, with its centuries-old relics – some from two world wars. He smiled at a memory of the film Highlander – how that had given him the idea for this display. Quite probably that Paris AI was now researching military history, photographs and other records for the name Voigt, with the two different forenames he had used then. She showed amazement at the length of his life and it had seemed quite real. He smiled and opened the case, ignored these relics and slid open the door behind. His memory was good – better than normally human but hardly eidetic. He could not remember everything, but things arose whenever he looked at the items now before him. His eyes slid from a silver goblet to a rapier, to an ancient King James Bible. He smiled at that, remembering the time he had been religious and got himself christened for the first time, in Germany, with the name he carried with him ever afterwards. She thought he was two hundred and fifty years old, because of that, and he had not corrected her.

His gaze dropped to an ancient weapon now preserved under one of the new diamond films, and he reached in and took it out. The blade was still original but wavy from sharpening, pitted with age and worn thin with constant cleaning. The handle he had replaced many times. He held the gladius out ahead of him and heard the roar of antique battlefields.

Some things he wanted to keep to himself.

So I wrote this one after "The Host", which was called "Moral Biology" and before "The Translator" which comes before them both chronologically. Confused yet? In these stories you can see my inclination towards the new 'Mobius' generation of AIs. I wonder if that relates to watching The Prisoner as a kid, since there's something of them in the rolling sphere that would catch Patrick McGoohan every time he escaped. As an aside I also remember that as a kid I thought those things were called 'orange alerts'. Where was I? Oh yeah: technology in the real world advances and, as a corollary, it advances in science fiction. I sometimes wonder how Gridlinked *would turn out if I went back and wrote it with all the technological wrinkles I've introduced over the ensuing half of my lifetime. Not going to happen. Anyway, this was published in* Analog *in May/June 2020.*

MORAL BIOLOGY

As Perrault entered the room he quickly closed the anosmic receptors running in lines over his face like tribal markings, retaining the use only of those within his nose. The air was laden with pheromones and he really had no need for further input on Gleeson's readiness for sex with Arbeck. Just walking through the door had been enough. Gleeson sat with her rump against her desk while Arbeck, his camo shirt hanging open to reveal the tight musculature of his chest under skin stick, sat in one of the chairs facing her, his legs akimbo. Their conversation ceased and she looked up at Perrault, quickly snatching her hand away from fondling with her hair, doubtless aware of everything he could read. He glanced at them, taking in their dynamic and almost breaking into laughter at Arbeck's pose, then focused on other aspects of the room as he headed for the other chair. He blinked through the spectrum, seeing the so recognisable heat patterns on Gleeson's skin, listened in on the EMR chatter of the ship, then shut it out as irrelevant, measured shapes in conjunction throughout the space that hinted at shadow languages and esoteric meaning, and then shut that down too.

'Do we have further data?' he asked mildly.

Gleeson reluctantly pushed herself away from the desk and walked round it to pause with her hand on the back of her seat. She then showed a flash of irritation and sat down. Perrault read into the actions her hormonal wish to bring the chair round to sit nearer Arbeck, overcome by her need to maintain her illusory power dynamic – being as they were meeting in her rooms – all in turn influenced by her awareness of his own abilities. He studied the surface of her desk as she sat down. Very little lay there beyond a paper notepad and pen. These were a hobby related to her interest in history and one of her specialisms in human archaeology. This display told him she used the items as a gambit to switch conversation to her interest, which also told him a little bit more about her self-absorption.

'Arbeck was telling me about the satellites,' she said. 'They are the product of advanced organic technology, as we first thought.'

Via her aug she threw an image up on the screen behind her showing one of the satellites in high orbit about the world below them. The thing looked like a pearl hanging in vacuum and of course related to what had been scanned on the planet's surface: the nacre-lined tunnels worming through the ground and the structures similar to termite mounds utterly riddled with them. Instead of commenting on this he thought about her use of 'organic technology'. Like 'biotech' it was a term that continued to survive despite very vague definition now. He also sensed her reluctant interest in active alien technology – her doubts about whether it fell under the remit of another of her specialisms, which was xeno-archaeology.

'Grown they might have been,' said Arbeck, 'but they can still pack a hell of a punch. They can fire masers and grazers and a few of them can transmit some form of U-space disruption. I would love to get inside one for a look around.'

'Do we have any more on their true purpose?' asked Perrault.

'Orbital defences,' said Gleeson. 'Surely that's obvious?'

Perrault shook his head and turned to Arbeck.

'Not only that,' said the soldier, whereupon Perrault noted a distinct cooling in the atmosphere. Gleeson did not like to be contradicted. 'Those outward facing weapons have a long range, but they only respond close in to the planet. We managed to put an armoured drone through. They ceased firing when it was in atmosphere then opened up again when it tried to leave. It didn't make it.'

'The drone was sub-AI I hope,' said Perrault.

'Yup.'

'That still doesn't discount orbital defences,' said Gleeson.

Arbeck shook his head. 'The format is all wrong. Heavy grazers point out, lighter maser weapons point down towards the world, while the U-space stuff hasn't even done anything.'

'So it seems the system activates when something tries to land yet, this ship, which is in range of those grazers you mention, has not been fired upon. A threat and an option pointed outwards and coverage to prevent anything landing or leaving,' suggested Perrault.

'Internal coverage could be to keep a population under control – some heavily authoritarian regime. We've seen that before,' said Gleeson, grudgingly.

'But they did not fire at the drone when it reached the surface,' he replied. 'In fact, as I understand it, the masers do not have the penetration to reach the surface.'

'That's true,' Arbeck agreed, further destroying his chances with Gleeson, had that been his inclination.

'So what's your assessment, Translator?' asked Gleeson.

He noted her acerbic use of the title and discounted it. Despite her temporary power dynamic here they were all in command of their own specialisms. On the ground Arbeck would nominally be in command because, as leader of the military contingent, his concern would be their safety. But in the end he, and they, answered to the forensic AI, Mobius Clean who had only temporarily left the ground mission in human hands. The usual reason for this was that on first contact it was best not to display the full extent of your capabilities. If the life form below turned out to be dangerously hostile, it would think it only had bumbling humans to contend with. Or the AI had done this because humans, in some esoteric manner, would render the data it required.

'I have studied the same data as Arbeck and come to some conclusions, yes.'

Gleeson grimaced. 'This would be because of your facility with pattern recognition, logic and... what was it? Oh yes: psycho-semantic math?'

He nodded agreeably, acknowledging three of the hundreds of disciplines he had learned, but said, 'The system prevents anything landing or leaving, but ignores this ship, which could be a larger threat. So we must assume its purpose it precisely the aforesaid. It doesn't look like a defence against major attack, rather more like a border fence.'

'Really?' said Arbeck. 'A territorial thing?'

Perrault shrugged. 'Or a prison or…' He searched for the appropriate word. '…or quarantine.'

The soldiers were Sparkind: two four-person combat units under the overall command of Arbeck. They all looked like big, heavily-muscled men and women, rugged, battle hardened and efficient. They all wore augs and clad themselves in the same combat armour so it would be difficult for most to see that one of them was a Golem android, one a human only in so far as he still had an organic brain while another had the crystal mind of an AI but a tank-grown human body. But even then, the last had the greatest quantity of human tissue in him, for all the other humans were liberally sprinkled with prosthetics and other hardware integrated into their bodies.

Clad in his specially adapted envirosuit, Perrault walked out into the shuttle bay where the soldiers were preparing their gear, and eyed the vehicle that would take them down to the planet. The shuttle looked like a fifty-foot long shard of lignite. He walked over and inspected the hull, reached down and felt the faint tingle of as yet fully active meta-materials armour and chameleonware. Fine lines etched the surface and, as ever, his mind began to integrate their maths and search for their meaning.

'This should get us through without problem,' said Arbeck at his shoulder. 'But even if there are problems we've been given permission to take out the satellite weapon concerned.'

'Permission from Mobius Clean?'

'Yes.'

Perrault nodded and turned to face Arbeck. He was big, conventionally handsome with a cheerful face below a mop of blond hair, and he grinned showing conventionally perfect teeth. His emulation was near perfect and Perrault would not have been surprised if Arbeck had nasty breath in the morning and body odour if he did not shower sufficiently. The minutiae in his speech patterns gave him away, however. His colloquialisms were too even, his accent too near the norm for his supposed birthplace, while his acquired vocabulary did not have the correct statistical deviation to match his apparent experience of many missions on many different worlds. Gleeson's reaction to Arbeck had amused Perrault because the soldier was a Golem android.

'Gleeson will be joining us on this run?' he enquired.

Arbeck nodded. 'We'll land by one of the empty formations where she can collect data and samples before we proceed.' He stabbed a thumb behind him. 'Your gear is out of storage if you want to inspect it.'

Perrault nodded. He already knew that, since the shroud had established radio links to him even as he approached this hold. He followed the soldier over to a plasmel case sitting on the floor, reached down and pressed his hand against the palm reader to unlock it – perhaps a little too obviously eager, he felt – then hinged up the lid.

Most of the case contained the feeding and other support gear for the shroud, which rested in carbon foam packing. The thing looked like a stingray, but with a truncated tail and jointed limbs webbing its wings, and a crumpled up mass protruding from its front end. This Gleeson would describe as organic technology or biotech. Most such Polity items, contained technology both grown and manufactured, living systems and printed hardware. And whether they could be described as a cyber-enhanced organism or a machine with organic components was open to debate. The debate had its relevance here, because the shroud *was* biotech, but what the likes of Gleeson did not know was its source. His shroud had been both manufactured and born from an alien biotech intelligence called a shroud skate.

He rested a hand on it and felt its response to him – its readiness to detach from its support equipment – and quelled it with a thought transferred as a chemical communication through his fingertips. Still, the attachment points on his sides, down his spine and in the back of his skull, opened slightly in readiness and sent a shiver through his body. He closed the lid.

'Load it with the rest,' he said. 'I won't attach until we're heading towards the creature.' He turned back towards the vessel, noting that Gleeson had now arrived and some of the troops were boarding, shrugged and headed for the steps up to the airlock.

Stepping into the shuttle, Gleeson eyed the rows of pods clamped to the floor. She saw Perrault sit and strap himself into one of the front row pods just behind the cockpit, so chose one at the back – acknowledging her discomfort at his abilities. It was foolish really because AIs could be similarly equipped to read humans and she did not have such a reaction to them. Her discomfort, it seemed, arose from him being human. It was like having a telepath nearby reading her every thought. She sat and strapped herself in, eyed the shield at the front ready to snap up and enclose her, then the surrounding orifices ready to inject crash gel. After a moment she wedged her arms down in the grooves in the arms of the chair. Via her aug she called up a present view of the planet transmitted to the shuttle from the sensors of the main vessel.

Scanning showed the tunnels worming through many areas of that world. They were like road and underground maps on Earth long before the Quiet War. In some areas they thinned out to nothing, in others they gathered together in such a chaotic tangle they became difficult to distinguish from each other. Cysts and bulbs also budded on this network – small chambers like the alveoli in lungs. Where most prevalent, these tunnels had shoved up structures like giant worm casts of rock and earth – some were so extensive they had at first been mistaken for mountain ranges. Smaller conglomerations formed massifs jutting up through the planetary flora.

She noted status alerts appearing down the side of her view, and closed her eyes. All were aboard now and the airlock being closed.

'One minute to launch,' said Arbeck from the cockpit. 'Then five minutes to gel stasis. For those of you who have never experienced it before, it's nothing to worry about. You won't be conscious. Any problems and the crash pods will likely blow us away from the planet and the next thing you know you'll wake up aboard the ship again.'

Gleeson grimaced. The talk had been for her and Perrault, but Arbeck had neglected to mention that if 'any trouble' occurred low down in orbit the pods, scattered from this shuttle, had a lower chance of survival than the vessel itself. She returned to her contemplations of what they might encounter below, even as she felt the shudder of docking clamps disengaging.

The first sampling probe they sent had blinked out in a flash of plasma – their first indication that the objects orbiting the world were not in fact oddly featureless moonlets but a weapons system. The second probe, wrapped in a ten-foot-thick casing of armour, which the weapons stripped away, arrived intact and sent back the first data. The tunnels were formed of a substance almost indistinguishable from nacre – from the material of an ormer's shell. They seemed the product of a life form, however, since the satellite weapons were also formed of this material, the nacre must ultimately be the product of intelligent life, which meant it could also be biotech distinct from that life.

A light touch ensued. The unique find here indicated they should not be hasty and go crashing in to perhaps destroy something of value, and Gleeson had been utterly in agreement with that approach. Months of scanning ensued, further probes explored the surface. At first it seemed that the intelligent life here, whatever it had been, was extinct. But then a wandering probe approached one of the massifs and detected tunnels and cysts filled with something living. When it tried to get inside for a closer examination, its find grabbed it and broke it apart.

'Gleeson.'

She looked up. Demarco – one of the soldiers – stood by her pod with the heavy pack containing her equipment. He lowered it into the front of the pod between her feet and the shield. He also pointed to closed compartments either side of her chair arms.

'Survival gear in there – with any luck you won't need it,' he said.

'Some problem?' She peered ahead and saw that another soldier had delivered a smooth plasmel case to Perrault. No doubt it contained that thing, that shroud, which would enhance his already annoying abilities further. Other soldiers were shifting further gear into their own pods.

'The AI made some changes. We take as much of our own gear in the pods as we can. If the shuttle gets blown away we don't want to lose everything.'

She nodded. It made sense for her equipment, more so for Perrault's shroud. He only had the one and it was either expensive, complex Polity technology, or alien technology – though that last might be apocryphal. Anyway, though her own equipment could be resupplied by the ship, the shroud lay beyond its manufacturing capabilities.

'I thought we were allowed to shoot back?' she asked.

He grimaced. 'Seems the AI changed its mind.'

As Demarco moved away, she returned to her contemplations. The data from the unfortunate probe revealed a life form, or conglomeration of life forms, occupying a volume five miles across and two deep. Spill holes revealed piles of chewed up organic detritus consisting of the mostly digested remains of animals and plants – spill piles she really wanted to look at. Data the probe broadcast during its destruction revealed some of the creature or creatures concerned. Fringed fleshy ridges, tentacles, organs and the other paraphernalia much like that of a terran mollusc dwelt in wet darkness down there. Further watching from orbit revealed it extending itself through tunnels under the surrounding jungle, to occasionally drag down a wandering beast or sometimes plants – growths much like cycads from stream edges seemed preferred. But beyond this, little else could be discovered, and no signs of intelligence beyond that of an animal revealed itself. However, a reassessment of the data did reveal an anomaly.

When this creature grabbed the probe, its diagnostic feed revealed dismantling rather than destruction. Meanwhile, at that precise time, the energy signatures of all the satellite weapons up in orbit changed. It looked like they were transferring power from some long term source like a fusion reactor to a more useable one like laminar storage or some other form of capacitor battery. Other indications were that they had risen to a higher level of alertness. There had to be a connection. The creature seemed likely to be intelligent and to have initiated this. Gleeson immediately pushed for a ground mission so she could examine first the abandoned tunnels and then the creature's home for xeno-archaeological artefacts. The AI agreed, but delayed, opining that the best way to confirm its intelligence was, in the end, to try to talk to it. And that's where, to her annoyance, Perrault came in.

The pumps finished – the shuttle bay now empty of air. Gleeson felt the vibration of space doors opening, then brief acceleration throwing them out into vacuum. She went weightless – the shuttle containing no gravplates. She pulled on the goggles she was supposed to wear in the pod. Through these she got a view through the shuttle's sensors. The planet looked further away in this one. She glimpsed the main ship as the shuttle turned, the blade flames of steering thrusters starring out all round. That main vessel – a great slab of advanced technology two miles long – should be enough to worry any intelligence. She finally conceded Perrault's point about the weapons system being more like a border fence than planetary defences. Then fusion kicked her in the back as the shuttle sped towards the planet.

'Two minutes to gel stasis,' Arbeck intoned.

With a gentle hiss clamps closed over her arms and legs, securing her in place. A collar closed around her neck and he felt brief stabs there as the shunts engaged. Cold seemed to spread through her body from that point and she was sure she could feel her heart slowing as the gel spread its molecular chains throughout her. The shield ahead then rose up to seal the pod.

'One minute,' Arbeck told them, as the surrounding nozzles began to ooze globules of clear fluid. Gleeson briefly wondered if Arbeck, who to her chagrin she had recently learned was a Golem, or Demarco being mostly such, needed to go into stasis like this. Probably, but only to protect their synthetic exteriors from damage. Golem were tough.

'See you groundside,' was the last thing Arbeck said, and his words seemed slow and leaden to Gleeson as she slid into somnolence.

Perrault returned to consciousness with a lurch. His goggles were opaque until he raised a hand to tap them, whereupon gel crystals powdered away from their near frictionless surface. He could now see the inside of the pod but nothing else – it was powered down. He lowered his arm and ran a finger over the touch console in the chair arm. Immediately a menu appeared in his goggles and he checked through it trying to find out why the pod hadn't opened.

'Perrault here,' he finally said. 'My pod is closed.'

After a pause Arbeck replied over radio, 'My orders. We are down on the planet.'

'I still don't see why my pod is closed,' he replied.

'Because we're down on the planet and the shuttle isn't.'

Perrault sat there absorbing that for a moment. The soldiers were nominally along to protect the two experts – himself and Gleeson – though some of them did have their own specialisms that did not involve shooting things or blowing them up. If the shuttle had been destroyed and the pods were down, they were probably scattered. He had no doubt that Arbeck thought Perrault would be safer in the pod until he or other soldiers came along. Perrault found this very annoying.

'How long until you reach me?' he asked.

'Eight hours.'

'So I am to sit here with patient forbearance until then? I do have the requisite training and uploads and I also know that there are weapons in the pod gear.' He paused for a second. Had he been speaking to a human he might have tried some polite wheedling, but Arbeck was Golem and as immune to politeness or rudeness as he chose to be. In a half measure he said, 'Please open my pod.'

'Sorry. I can't do that.'

Okay, simple statement of fact, then: 'Open my pod or I will open it myself.'

'Sorry. *You* can't do that.'

'I see.' Obviously Arbeck, despite being a Golem, didn't have much idea of Perrault's capabilities. He undid his straps, reached forwards and hauled up the shroud case. It had been his intention to put the thing on at a later juncture after Gleeson had studied some of the tunnels, but now was as good a time as any. Also, putting the thing on inside the pod would circumvent the inconvenience of doing so in a sealed tent later on, and having to lug around its support gear. He realised he was rationalising, but no matter. Every time he used the thing it became more difficult to take it off, and he became more eager to put it on the next time. It increased the functionality of his enhanced senses in ways that were addictive which, in itself, wasn't a problem. The problem was that the increased functionality in this respect made him a less able member of *normal* Polity society. It made him *strange*.

He opened his envirosuit, stripped it off his arms and upper body and folded it down to his waist then, raising his backside, pushed it further down to his thighs, partially detaching the rectal catheter. He then opened the case, reached inside and pressed his hand down on the fishy skin, chemically accepting its willingness to detach from its support gear. It rose up out of its packing, flexing its wing limbs, shivered when he took hold of the nodular mass at its head end. He lifted it up with both hands, leaned forwards and swung its heavy wet weight round onto his back. The tail inserted in the crevice of his buttocks and found the side port of the catheter – it would excrete its waste there. It clung to his back, shifting round into the correct position. He felt the junction holes open down his sides and in his spine and the cold insertion of its connectors. Taking off the pod goggles, he pulled open the nodular protrusion, then slipped it over his head where it formed an organic mask, probing to his anosmic and EMR receptors and additional nerve clusters that linked to his brain. The whole thing began to settle. He could feel the cold growth of the nanofibres in his spine and in his skull, and then came connection and his limited vista inside the pod opened out into a world. He felt complete.

Perrault pulled the envirosuit back onto his body and over the shroud. He paused with his fingers on the collar pouches, for the shroud provided adaptive protection from a whole host of exogenous antigens way beyond that of the military nanosuite he already possessed. However, stupid arrogance might result in something nasty in his body he could have avoided. He rolled the envirosuit hood up over his head and filling its open cell foam with air it stiffened. He then touched the control at his throat and the visor oozed up to connect and stiffened too. The heads up display of the suit showed him full power in the suit and plenty of oxygen in storage. It would filter and recycle his air supply, complementing that with meagre oxygen extracted from the atmosphere. It would also recharge its power supply from local EMR and even his movement about the world outside. But he had to get out there for it to do so.

The pod now lay thoroughly open to his inspection. Even its construction linked to human language and thousands of words describing its components, but human language wasn't what he needed right then. He absorbed the EMR of its internal communications, read it from induction in wires and even picked up some from the spill of a faulty optic junction behind him to the left. He had long ago understood the code used in Polity devices and was more than competent using it even without the shroud. Here, with his enhancement in place, he found it childishly easy, and began talking to the computing around him. The pod was amenable, and he soon found the right code to use to get it to forget Arbeck's order and open itself to the alien world. The shield before him huffed off its seal then slid down out of sight.

A dark red tangle like a three dimensional geodesic lay before him, reducing visibility to perhaps twenty yards before all he could see was those massed red branches. In their tangle his mind etched out the letters and glyphs of a thousand languages which began to cohere into elements of words, phrases and sentences. He pushed the reaction to the periphery of his consciousness, and focused on more useful data.

Having studied and recorded to his implants everything about the native fauna and flora here, he knew the pod had come to rest in the tree canopy of one of the forest growths that spread like moulds on the planet's surface. He leaned forwards to get a better view. The trunks below were pale lavender at their globular bases shading to the dark red he saw up here. The branches had no leaves for they themselves photosynthesised, extracting the energy the trees needed for their biological processes from the bright white cloud-locked sky. A ten foot drop to the ground lay below him. He grimaced then spoke to the pod again. In answer to his query it told him its energy was low but it would make the attempt. The thing rose on grav a little way, the branches crackling all around, fired its thrusters intermittently, one of them guttering out, then took off grav again. It fell through, bringing grav back on at the last moment, and settled steadily to the ground with a crump.

Perrault now opened the emergency kit and, this being a military pod, the first item within his reach was a short pulsed carbine. He pulled it from its clips and activated it, stepping out of the pod. The red-brown ground consisted of slivers from the branches above. Again he saw language: tone poems from the forest floor, Roman numerals counting out mass below his feet, cuneiform shattered by the chaos of biology. He blinked and focused elsewhere. A short distance away he could see the edge of the grove – probably where the pod had been aiming for before becoming tangled in the branches. He walked over, feet sinking to the ankles and things like large silverfish darting away from them. Hollows containing growths like sick yellow tumbleweeds dotted the rocky landscape ahead and about half a mile on stood another grove like this one. He turned back to inspect the nearer one.

Spike gibbons hung in the trees – a name that had stuck aboard the ship and an interesting illumination of a human tendency to slot the alien into the conventional. Remembering an old Chinese puzzle fashioned of glass he would have preferred 'star gibbons' but knew that the meme had stuck so didn't mention it. They were a pale fleshy white, consisted of six arms extending from a central point that held the mouth. Each arm was thick at the base tapering to small black grasping claws. As he understood it, that central point only contained the mouth and its macerating equipment, the creatures' main organs occupying those limbs. Apparently they shit the remains of digestion out of lines of anuses along the arms. Did they write some yet to be learned language in the tree with their excrement? He thought not. Even as he watched, the first of them tumbled through the canopy closer to him, others soon following. He suspected the crash had scattered them, but now wondered what might be bringing them back; curiosity or the presence of prey? They were carnivores that preyed on smaller creatures in the canopy and often hunted as packs to bring down larger animals.

Perrault shook his head, now really feeling the barrier his suit presented. The moment he thought this he reached up and touched the controls at his collar. The visor softened and rolled down and the hood peeled back from his head. Sensory input rocketed and he took a swaying step back as he tried to incorporate it. The air was redolent with the complex chemicals of life from which he could make thousands of comparisons. Simply too much assaulted his senses for him to interpret right away, and now he questioned his impulse, so soon after earlier caution, to open himself to the world. It was the effect of the shroud, he knew – his need to engage. Too late now to reconsider.

'So what is it that you want?' he wondered out loud, aware that these were likely the first human words spoken into this air.

Ignoring chemical input for now, he focused his other enhanced senses on the gibbons. He scanned EMR and picked up the electrostatic fields that wrapped each creature. These were static, though each being distinct they might act as identifiers. In audio he picked up an ultrasound twittering emitted by the lead creature, to which those behind responded. Previous scans of these animals had revealed sophisticated mentation so, looking for pattern matches, he recorded their chatter and ran it through his library of recorded animal communications. He found some similarities in DeepSqueak – a language first learned in laboratories centuries ago, where the rodents that used it were experimental animals. A moment later he had a better match. This resembled the exchanges amid a troop of chimps hunting down a colobus monkey. The lead animal was telling individuals behind to go to this position or that. They were either responding in the affirmative or, when negative, informing the leader where they were going. From this he interpreted what the tweets meant regarding direction, height, speed and readiness. He soon understood their combinations for tree trunk, ground, canopy branches in fifteen different forms, and saw that the ones behind were being directed out to the sides, fast, while those to the fore were moving much more slowly. When creatures to his right and left dropped to the ground and began moving out either side of him, he recognised the simple encirclement – their intent to drive him back into the trees where the lead creature and its fellows could drop on him.

Now, perfectly copying the voice of the leader, he began sending his own instructions. Some of those over to the right retreated into the trees, but some replied in the negative. Over to the left they halted and he picked up a complicated exchange between those and the ones on the left. It seemed the leader was only nominally the leader and could, should circumstances permit, be ignored. He understood more and added it to his growing vocabulary, but soon realised he had no tweets for danger or any other way of calling off this hunt. So he tried something else.

The shroud could broadcast just about anything in the EMR and auditory spectra. It could even broadcast molecular languages of his design. He considered what pheromones might be applicable here, but weaning the correct ones out of the air would take too long, so instead he created around him an electrostatic field the same as theirs but with a different identifier. This gave them pause and the twittering increased. His vocabulary grew too and he soon understood that spike gibbons outside of the tribe were also valid prey. Reluctantly he raised the carbine to his shoulder and fired a shot into the ground in front of the nearest of them. Hot rock flakes and smoking earth exploded over it and with ultrasonic shrieks it rolled back into the trees. He fired again and again, taking care not to actually hit any of them. Even as those on the ground leapt back into the trees and the whole tribe retreated to chatter at him from further trees he learned more of their words and knew the ones for danger, threat and run. With a sigh he lowered the weapon and walked back to the pod.

Arbeck ran between the trees. On scan he could pick up his comrades zeroing in on his position. They too were running, which seemed best since going any slower resulted in the spike gibbons converging and dropping on them. He also felt a degree of urgency since it was apparent that Perrault had opened his pod and was now almost certainly in danger. Gleeson's had come down near one of the massifs and not in the trees, so would have been safe from these creatures had she even managed to exit it. But despite trying to use her aug to open it, she was still safely inside.

'Any word from him yet?' Demarco asked over com.

'He hasn't seen fit to respond to me,' Arbeck replied. 'Bloody experts.'

'Maybe his suit's damaged?'

'Not according to his diagnostic feed, though some of the readouts are weird. I think he's put on his shroud.'

'That would explain how he got out of the pod.'

A particularly brave spike gibbon dropped on Arbeck at that point. He grabbed one of its limbs and hurled it aside, even as others began falling in the path ahead.

'We need to get out of this and into the open or that jungle – fewer spike gibbons there.'

'But there are other nasties,' Demarco observed.

'Hopefully not so persistent.'

'There is that,' Demarco agreed.

'Damn their fucking claws are sharp,' said Relson. 'Suit puncture.'

'Patch it,' Arbeck instructed, leaping the gibbons ahead and hurtling on.

Twenty yards. He should be able to see… there it was. The pod was down on the ground under the trees, while open space lay ahead. There seemed masses of the creatures in the canopy above now but their behaviour wasn't what he had seen before. They hung in even ranks and were swaying as if to some unheard tune. Perhaps that's what they did after they had fed. Perhaps human and shroud meat had this effect on them. Then he saw it.

Perrault sat at the mouth of a tent with equipment from the pod laid out around him. He had his envirosuit open but the mask of his shroud covered part of his face like large webbed hand grasping his head from behind. Before him he had a pot sitting on a small cooker. Arbeck ran up, skidding to a halt on the rock, whirled and sought for targets in the trees behind. The gibbons still hung in ranks and were still swaying.

'I thought you said eight hours,' said Perrault, looking up.

'They're not attacking,' said Arbeck.

Perrault glanced at the creatures, then concentrated on pouring hot water into a cup. He was making coffee, Arbeck saw.

'I have their full vocabulary now,' Perrault said. 'And have modelled the simple minds behind it. I only managed to do this,' he gestured to the trees, 'when I observed two of them mating. There has to be some genetic exchange between troops so they cannot remain hostile and view other troop members as food all the time. A pheromone induces passivity.' He paused, adding, 'It took me a while to find that since opening my suit.' He paused yet again, gazing off into the distance.

'A pheromone?' Arbeck prompted.

Perrault's attention snapped back to him. 'Yes, a pheromone – one of far too many in the air here. It makes them passive and receptive to mating. I keep that in check by broadcasting low level danger. I then cycle through other tonal alterations of their ultrasound language, used during hunting, with contradictory orders.'

'You what?' said Arbeck, as he noted Demarco coming out of the trees further along, then others of his soldiers arriving.

'I'm singing to them,' Perrault explained.

Arbeck was Golem, with Golem senses and an artificial intelligence that could work an order of magnitude better than a human mind. He now listened, scrolling through the spectra available to him and soon picked up on the ultrasound. But putting that together with what the man had just told him lay beyond even his grasp. Capable of all human emotions, in fact some emotions that went beyond human, it took Arbeck a moment to identify what he now felt because it was so unfamiliar. He felt humbled, and he did not like it.

'So I take it Gleeson is still in her pod?' Perrault asked, standing and sipping his beaker of coffee while observing the other soldiers approaching.

'Yes, she is. I thought it an idea to get to you fast what with the dangers here.' Arbeck gestured to the trees.

'An understandable misapprehension.' Perrault nodded, sipped again. From anyone else it would have seemed like arrogance, but Arbeck could see that wasn't the case here. Arrogance presupposed a competitiveness Perrault did not seem to possess. He next waved a hand towards the trees and Arbeck heard the weird ultrasound chittering issuing from him. The gibbons retreated, tumbling over each other, some falling to the ground then hurrying to catch up. The tree canopy shifted in a wave moving away from the humans, and the creatures disappeared from sight.

'Time to go get Gleeson,' said Arbeck.

Perrault glanced at his tent, obviously sending a radio instruction via his shroud. The tent collapsed and folded itself. He stepped over and began putting his supplies into a pack.

When the shield finally dropped, Gleeson stepped out quickly and angrily, but that lost something when her legs gave way and she went down on one knee.

'I've been in there for hours,' she exclaimed, glaring at them. 'I thought you were coming for me first.'

She turned as Demarco moved past her and took her heavy equipment pack out of the pod, easily shouldering it.

'Other circumstances arose,' Arbeck replied and she returned her attention to him. 'Perrault was able to open his pod.'

He glanced to Perrault, who was walking over, and now Gleeson got a good look at the man. The shroud humped the back of his suit and he had the hood and visor down, exposing the biotech device's mask wrapped around his head. She felt a brief flush of abhorrence at the sight – she liked neither the man nor his enhanced abilities. He made her feel naked and it seemed unfair that he could perceive so much. She wanted to say something about him getting out of his pod and endangering them all but, since she herself had tried, knew it would come across sour. Then, because she had spent so long cramped in her pod, she felt the urge to urinate. This seemed perfect timing now Perrault stood close and would know, so declined to use her suction catheter. Thankfully she had brought along slow food so it would be some time before she needed the other option.

'I'm sorry to have delayed your release,' said Perrault. 'I guess sitting up in orbit when I wanted to get down here, and into this –' He gestured at their surroundings, '– made me a little impatient.'

She stared at him. That was precisely how she felt but she didn't want to agree with him. A brief uncomfortable silence ensued, broken by Arbeck.

'Anything new?' the Golem soldier asked.

Perrault tilted his head and closed his eyes. 'A steep rise in airborne pheromones of a particular kind since we landed, but I've no idea what they signify.'

'Some kind of communication?' Gleeson asked.

He smiled and replied, 'Pheromones are always a form of communication.'

She bridled at that but could think of no cutting rejoinder. Arbeck rescued her.

'We have three hours of light left.' He gestured beyond her pod. 'Do you want to make a start while we have that time?'

She turned and felt her anger collapse. Just ten yards beyond the pod, a rocky slope rose up into one of the massifs, flat topped, the stone and compacted earth having the look of the excreta of a worm cast. Plants grew on the lower part of the slope, tangled masses of yellow dotted with red berries, while higher up she could see the nacre glint of the mouth of one of the tunnels. She studied the thing for a long moment, trying to decide what to do next. 'I need samples,' she stated emphatically. 'I need my things.'

She studied the soldiers who had gathered round. The AI had assigned the woman Relson and the man Armid as her assistants when her specialism took precedence. They'd uploaded numerous disciplines and practised in virtuality so she wouldn't need to explain too much. She watched as Demarco handed her pack to Relson, who dropped it down and immediately opened it.

'One yard grid of micro surface samples,' she stated, walking over. 'Extra samples at your discretion, both micro and macro. Run it from the base of the massif –' she pointed, meanwhile creating a grid overlay in her aug for the slope and transmitting it to the others, '– thirty yards wide to begin then stepping in a yard at a time, converging there.' She pointed up at the glint of nacre. 'That's probably all we'll have time for today.'

Stooping by the pack, Gleeson waited until Relson handed a sample case and probe to Armid and took out the same for herself. She then reached in and took out her shoulder bag and stood, looking up the slope.

'You're going up there,' said Arbeck at her shoulder.

'Damned right.'

'I will accompany you.' He looked round at the others. 'Make camp here. Sensor perimeter and unpack the mosquito.' He glanced over at Perrault who was now sitting on a rock a short distance away. In a lower voice he said to Demarco, 'Make sure he doesn't stray.'

Even though a normal man should not have heard, Perrault turned and looked over, smiled briefly, then returned his attention to the horizon. Gleeson thought about that for a moment. First off, as ever, she didn't like the acuity of Perrault's senses, but secondly she realised Arbeck could have spoken directly to Demarco's aug. Arbeck had wanted Perrault to hear and to know he was being watched. She shook her head and marched over towards the slope. Pausing at the bottom she cast a brief eye over the worm casts: compacted flaked stone, earth of different kinds, some petrified organics and cracks and hollows where she suspected other organics had decayed away. It could just as easily be the output of a rock boring machine as the creature they were going to see. But she knew that already. She stepped up and began to climb.

'So he might wander off?' She asked Arbeck as he moved up lightly beside her.

'It's possible,' he replied. 'Though I wonder if he might be a better judge of the dangers here even than me.'

'I beg your pardon?'

Arbeck then related what Perrault had done with the spike gibbons. Gleeson felt her back crawling. It wasn't so much the story Arbeck told but that he, a Golem, seemed to be in awe of Perrault. She tried to be rational about it. She disliked Perrault because he could see right through her. This was why she felt the man's actions were an attempt to assert inappropriate authority over their mission. He probably didn't care who was in charge so long as he could wear his shroud and process data like a machine.

They finally reached the tunnel mouth and here Gleeson paused to peer into the darkness. Scans from orbit, and from the probes, had detected only the one creature of the sort they would be heading towards, but other creatures did use these tunnels. She opened her shoulder bag and took a small box with twelve remotes sitting inside like chrome eggs. She had already programmed search parameters and only needed to initiate them from the console in the lid. This she did, the remotes rising out of the box in an even formation, circling around each other for a moment as they located themselves, then shooting into the tunnel. She had only just placed the box on the ground when the console beeped, signalling an alert.

'Beware! I detect activity!' Perrault's voice arrived out of the air, almost as if he was standing beside them. Directed sound, Gleeson realised.

A second later a large arthropod like a long thick-limbed spider scuttled out to the lip of the hole, peered at them with stalked eyes, then leapt out, rattling a row of petal-shaped mandibles. A flash of ionisation lit the air. Gleeson recognised the stun shot but the arthropod seemed oblivious. It charged towards her but now a more vicious line of fire cut past her. The arthropod jumped up then came down on its back smoking, its limbs folding in.

'What the –?' she began, just as Arbeck grabbed her shoulder and pulled her back.

She saw further shadowy movement in the hole, then suddenly a great mass of the creatures flooded out. She stumbled downslope keeping Arbeck between her and the things. He opened fire – accurate shots punching through their bodies as he continued backing away. Some reached his feet and he kicked them aside. He switched his pulse rifle to one hand and drew a sidearm, firing continuously in different directions with Golem accuracy. One of the things got past him and grabbed her calf, mandibles grinding against but thankfully not penetrating her suit. She stamped on its back with her other foot, breaking its hold, and kicked it away. The region around her next filled with pulse fire from below. Hot rock splinters shot into the air and smoke boiled from numerous corpses. She realised she was yelling, ducked down on one knee as one of the things jumped towards her head, but flared fire and sailed right past her. Then suddenly it was over.

Enclosed in her envirosuit she had been unaware of the steady breeze that now swept away the bulk of the smoke, but creatures still smouldering, some of them moving weakly, kept adding to it. She realised with a grimace that she had just used both sanitary options in her suit.

'Are you hurt?' Arbeck asked.

'No, I'm fine,' she said stubbornly, standing back upright.

Perrault's voice reached them again. 'I detect no more chatter from inside the massif,' he told them. 'I think that was all of them.'

Arbeck reached down and picked up one of the creatures. 'They're predatory, have a poisonous bite and will prey on creatures as large as us. We don't know what effect the poison would have, but the bite would certainly hurt if it got through your suit.'

'It was necessary to kill them?' she asked, realising his statement had been a justification.

'Yes.' He inspected the thing closely. 'Will you want samples from these?'

She shook her head and he tossed it aside.

'Our data indicates they are lone hunters.' He looked thoughtful. 'Perrault?'

'Agreed,' the man replied, his voice ghosting in. 'They were distressed by close proximity with each other. Perhaps this was something to do with mating, or perhaps they had recently hatched out of an egg cluster like the spiders they resemble.'

Gleeson felt shaky, and she really didn't like how he could cast his voice over twenty yards so it seemed he was speaking in her ear. He was demonstrating his superiority, she felt. He could have used the comlink in his suit.

'This is a distraction,' she said, and resolutely stepped up past Arbeck to the tunnel mouth. Here her nervousness increased, but she stooped down, and using fingertips only lifted one of the quietly smouldering creatures lying on the box for the remotes, pulling the box out and quickly stepping away. The readouts showed the remotes were fine, though they had stuck to the tunnel wall to prevent themselves being damaged. Stabbing one of the touch controls she set them in motion again. While she waited she watched the soldiers collecting bodies on the slope and carting them away. Perrault was sitting on his rock again, annoyingly insouciant.

Within seconds the remotes had drawn a map of the near network of tunnels and reported no other life forms. In a few minutes more they would have covered a sufficient safe area and then, following their programming, begin close scanning of the walls and any detritus they might find. Gleeson put the box on the ground again then delved in her bag to remove her multi-scanner.

'Primitive appearance,' Arbeck noted, standing close behind her.

'I have anachronistic tastes,' she replied tartly.

The device looked like a large magnifying glass with a thick handle, but its magnification delved down to the nanoscopic and it could scan, and record, across much of the EMR spectrum. She linked her aug to it for analytical readout and function control. Stooping down she peered through the glass at the nacre, first getting microscopic images then on down smaller and smaller. For a while she couldn't concentrate, but then in her aug she got thousands of points of comparison with the nacreous materials of shells from Earth and other worlds. Her hands stopped shaking. Pattern recognition next gave her methods of deposition and these indicated wholly organic origin. Soon, however, she began to see the anomalies, and delving into these felt the tight clench in her chest relaxing. Composite fibres bound this stuff and within those she found compounds not normally naturally occurring. Laminated flakes showed high reflectivity and overall the meta-material structure was very strong.

'I'm seeing something very familiar here,' she stated, all business now.

'Evidence of biotech?' Arbeck guessed.

'Yes. A lot of the meta-material structures have formats found in impact armour, while binding fibres are highly conductive – not superconductor, but still highly conductive.'

'Impact armour was originally based on organic structures itself,' Arbeck noted.

'True, but this stuff has durability beyond what should be required for a… shellfish.'

'Prador armour,' said Arbeck.

She looked up. 'What?'

'The prador have their own natural armour yet their technology led them to develop even stronger armour – part of their psyche. It's not unfeasible that a creature with a shell might want to make it stronger.'

'True,' she agreed. 'But still the prador developed their battle armour separate from their natural armour and didn't make the latter stronger or better. I wonder if what we are seeing here is the product of some kind of biotech mining machine.'

'The indications are that it is intelligent.'

'So are our machines,' she said, observing him wryly.

Analysis in her aug now alerted her to other formations. She focused her scanner on one of the flakes and noted the numerous fibre connections all around it. At first she had thought this all about reinforcing the strength of the shell, now she wasn't so sure. Running through different scan routines she finally picked up even and complex nano-structures imbedded between laminations.

'No, it can't be,' she said.

'Can't be what?'

Ignoring him, she took a probe out of her bag, unwound two wires terminating in sticky electrodes, and pressed them against the nacre a couple of inches apart. Auging to the probe, she made a selection of direct micro-currents at varying power and voltage and initiated them. The sweet spot was just above a micro amp at four volts. She read outputs for a while, then shortly after used induction scanning. Pulling out again she observed small holes on the surface noting their connection to the fibres, then lowered her scanner and sat back on her heels.

'Fuck a duck,' she said.

'Something interesting?' Arbeck asked.

She looked at him, her skin creeping. 'Computer architecture, all the way through.'

The shroud breathed on him as it had since he exposed it to the alien air. It shivered though warm from the processes on-going inside it as it decoded organic molecules, listened to the EMR bands and interpreted, collected sounds and shapes and slotted them into proto-languages he might use or discard. In making himself receptive to this new environment, it to a degree entered him, and he felt the strange wonder of it all, and some sense of being on the edge of a whole perception. But even the prosaic and known was input because of its interaction with the alien. So Perrault listened.

He listened to the exchange between Arbeck and Gleeson, and speculated. The nacre was a product of biotech – of an organism that had altered itself. It struck him as highly likely that Gleeson had found something comparable to a human mental augmentation – an adjunct to the creatures themselves and probably no longer active now all but one of the creatures concerned were gone. However, he ran a precautionary scan across the EMR bands to see if he could find anything local. This required him pushing things out of his perception and into the territory of the shroud. First the solar and cosmic radiation and their related effects here on the planet, then the constant communications between the soldiers here, aug links to equipment, Arbeck's constant updates back to the ship. Then the animals. The spider things they had killed had screeched in extreme infrared and microwave. Other creatures in the area, but thankfully not close, emitted similar radiations. Broadcasts on still other frequencies filled the air with their cacophony, but nothing as complicated as the kind of data transfer of intelligence. When he fined it all down he did get something from the nacre above, but only when Gleeson applied an electric current. This contained data too scrambled to be useful. As he had thought – the augmentation of the creatures was inactive without them attached. He returned his focus to something that had been puzzling him for some while now.

The air was laden with organics. The spider things had produced their own pheromones which, as expected, related to mating and territoriality, though he still puzzled over their distress at so many of them being so close together. He could now safely eliminate those as they did not seem a product of intelligence. These also gave him a key into other arthropod communications of a similar nature and he eliminated them, but only provisionally. His envirosuit rolled down to his waist he walked a circuit of the encampment so more of the stuff in the air ended up on the receptors of his shroud. Even with the eliminations the air burgeoned with aromatics, pheromones and long complex chains of molecules that might be some form of data. Were these more prevalent at their present location only thirty miles from the creature than, say, on the other side of the planet? He could not check. Nor could he know whether or not they were the product of some other life form he had yet to see. He ran analyses, comparing them to what he had already identified from the arthropods. Chemically they were completely different, but he made one of those intuitive leaps that arose out of the synergy of human mind, internal computing and the shroud. The pheromones that had steadily risen since their arrival here were another more complex version of the pulse of pheromones the spider things had emitted prior to coming out of the tunnel.

'Fear, threat, invasion of territory,' he said out loud.

'You what?' asked Relson, coming down from the slope with a small glass container in her hand and a corpse in the other, which she skimmed past the tents to land on a growing pile of the things.

'Never mind, it might be nothing,' he replied. 'What have you got there?'

She held up the container and rattled its contents. 'Proof of organic origin.' She pointed back to the massif. 'Of that.'

'I thought that already established?'

'No, it could have been caused by rock boring machines.' She winced at a painful thought. 'Though a rock boring machine is not necessarily inorganic and something inorganic is not necessarily insentient.'

'Let's not get lost in semantics here,' said Perrault. 'I know what you mean or, rather, I get your implication but don't know what you have in the jar.' It was Perrault's turn to wince, semantics being a particular interest of his.

She shook the container again. 'Teeth.'

'Really?' He held out his hand and she passed it over.

Peering through the clear plasmel he saw a number of small black objects that looked like segments chopped from a charcoal stick. He blinked and focused closer, seeing the even ridges on one surface, like scrawls of writing that hinted at legibility.

'They're grinding teeth,' Relson added. 'They show all the attributes of having been grown rather than manufactured. Of course we'll need to examine them a lot more closely to determine if that is the case.'

Perrault nodded. The more advanced technology became the more it came to resemble life and the products of life. Semantics had really hit a wall when it came to distinguishing evolved organics, biotech and straight-forward material tech. But he understood Relson's underlying meaning: these were likely teeth from creatures like the one they would soon be going to see and with which he would attempt to have a conversation. The things bored into the ground throwing up these heaps and networking them with the nacre tunnels. Allegedly. He winced again. They might have had biotech machines for the purpose, they might have had such machines as part of them – all was open to conjecture until they could get some firm data from the creature itself. And even then conjecture would remain.

He headed over to one of the tents, his shroud still gathering molecules and his internal processing still analysing, the world around him permeating him, soaking him, but he came out of it again for more prosaic matters. The sun was burning into the horizon and little light remained now. One of the soldiers had put up his tent and left his stuff outside. He settled down to open food packets because the shroud fed on him and in turn made him very hungry, and brewed some more coffee – real powder from real coffee beans because, especially when wearing the shroud, he could tell the difference. He glanced over, noting shimmering movement, and saw the mosquito autogun patrolling around the camp, but sensed no communications, as uncomplicated as they would be, of anything likely to attack them. He was sipping a beaker when twilight fell and Arbeck, Gleeson and the others returned from the massif.

'I have generalised analysis of atmosphere and its biotoxins,' Arbeck announced, as he walked into the space the ring of tents formed. 'Nothing poisonous our nanosuites can't handle. Microfauna and viruses either incompatible or likewise can be handled by the 'suites. You can breathe the air here.'

'Thank fuck for that,' said the soldier Oaran, opening his visor and peeling back his hood. All the others did the same, including Arbeck and Demarco who had no need of such protection anyway. Gleeson was rather slower in dropping her visor and opening her hood.

'Smells like the sea,' said Relson.

Perrault looked at her. The sense of smell was the oldest human sense and deeply connected in the brain. The odour she smelled obviously linked to her memories of the sea, while the organic chemicals that filled the air, he felt sure, were from the creature. It seemed like a confirmation since, given its format, the creature seemed likely to have had recent origins in some sea. But it was also, like so much here, highly debateable.

But for two soldiers standing guard out from the circuit of the autogun, they began to settle by their allotted tents. All that was needed, Perrault felt, was a campfire in the middle. Relson and Gleeson had that glassy-eyed look of people deep into aug studies while around them sample bottles had been inserted into devices that analysed their contents. Perrault sensed the data flows between them and their machines and, if he so wished, he could break the coding of that, but he did not. He smiled to himself when he focused on the man Armid, who wore an aug on his temple and appeared to be doing the same, but looked bored. Then he waited and, as expected, Arbeck started in:

'So what do we have thus far?' he asked, deferring to Gleeson.

She lost her glassy-eyed look and focused. 'The nacre is not purely the product of an evolved creature – it definitely contains biotech but whether it is all the product of such is moot. I would, however, suggest that a lot of the structures are inefficient and that they are a product of evolution. The nacre contains computing structures of a neural nature that will take a forensic AI to interpret.'

'No data storage?' suggested Armid.

She shook her head. 'Nothing separate. An AI would be able to analyse structure and get something but I've found no separate hard storage of any kind.' She shrugged. 'But then I have only made a cursory study of a few ounces of something that weighs many tons.'

'Radio?' said Perrault.

She looked at him and nodded. 'Distributed throughout what I examined, but inactive without power. Surface structures indicate organismal connections for bio-electricity.'

'So in essence very similar to human augmentations?' suggested Arbeck.

'Pretty much.'

'Other data?' he enquired, looking round.

'The teeth are the same: they seem to be an amalgam of evolved biology and biotech,' Relson replied. 'But perhaps we don't want to get too wrapped up in trying to make distinctions.' He glanced at Perrault.

'If only the AI was down here,' said Gleeson. 'I think the data we could glean from that computing would be key.'

'There might not be much that's useful,' said Armid.

'Why?' asked Arbeck, though he probably knew.

'Dating. I've run the full gamut of paleo-isotopes, plus molecular pattern breakdown and diffusion.' He gestured towards the massif. 'The earliest formations I've looked at are about twenty thousand years Solstan, the latest, supposing they are the ones around the tunnel entrance up there, are ten thousand years old.'

'So pattern breakdown and diffusion will likely have destroyed any hard storage, even if there is any,' said Arbeck.

'We can't know that,' said Gleeson, no doubt feeling something getting away from her.

'No, but we don't have much time to find out,' he replied. 'Remember, we don't have a ship and we have limited supplies. The initial probe here indicates that the creature may have some control over the orbital weapons so communicating with it is vital. We do not want to destroy those weapons just to get a shuttle down to us. We do not want to take actions that could be interpreted as hostile before speaking to the creature here, if that is possible.' He shot a glance at Perrault, who decided to make no comment. 'We leave in the morning.'

'That's crazy!' Gleeson exclaimed. 'There's far too much to do here, far too much to learn!' She looked around at the others for support. Perrault knew she wouldn't get it – they were soldiers and followed a chain of command.

'That's the AI's direct order,' Arbeck replied, shutting her down with the top link of that chain.

Gleeson had berated Armid and Relson for small infractions of her methodology and asked to take a few more samples from the tunnel mouth while the soldiers packed away the tents. Arbeck had refused – pointing out that packing up would take just a few minutes. Demarco later informed him that she had asked him to go grab a sample of the nacre and he had refused. Now she was opening containers for unnecessary checks and unpacking and repacking equipment.

'*Demarco,*' he spoke to the man directly through his aug. '*Get her sample and tell her you're doing so.*'

'*Why?*'

'*You can do it without delaying us, and she's dragging her feet.*'

'*Will do.*'

Demarco had a quiet word with her then headed away. Arbeck walked over to her, tapped her on the shoulder and beckoned her with a finger. She followed him out of the encampment like a sulky teenager.

'Are you under the impression that your work is finished?' he asked once they were out of earshot of the rest, besides Perrault.

'What?' She looked startled.

He gestured to the nearby massif. 'This is one of many and, as Armid has pointed out, it is very old. The one we are to travel to is, almost certainly, considerably younger.'

'I'm a xeno-archaeologist,' she said stubbornly.

'You are much more than that just as Armid is much more than a soldier. Would you refuse to study a living community of, say, the Jain, and much prefer to delve in their ruins?'

'Oh,' she said, getting it now.

'Do you also think that while Perrault does his work the AI wants you sitting in your tent twiddling your thumbs?'

She slumped a little. 'Okay, no need to belabour the point.' She turned away and headed back to the near dismantled camp.

Arbeck was about to follow when Mobius Clean, the AI in the ship up above, contacted him.

'Soldier Oaran has training and uploads in forensic dissection,' it stated.

'I am aware of this,' Arbeck replied.

'Tell him to collect one or more of the creatures you killed yesterday, along with whatever samples he deems necessary, and have him examine it at your next encampment.'

'Is there anything specifically he should search for?'

'Biotech,' Clean replied.

'This is a world that was inhabited for a long time by creatures adept with biotechnology. I think it unlikely he *won't* find anything.'

'I have analysed Gleeson's recent research and uploaded data from the assay of the samples. You are correct that the creatures here were adept with biotechnology and by inference the remaining creature still is, however you are wrong on your first point.'

'If you could explain?'

'All analysis points to the creature being of oceanic origin, doubtless adapted to live on land. Do you agree?'

'I agree.'

'We do not have the genome of the creature, or its predecessors to examine, so we cannot make extrapolations from that, however, the samples indicate organic disparities with life already examined there.'

'Organic disparities are also not enough from which to make extrapolations of any accuracy.'

'One plain fact is.'

'That being?'

'No oceans.'

'What?'

'The world you are standing on has no oceans and, according to paleo-geology has not had oceans for close to ten million years.'

'Oh.'

'The creatures were colonists.'

That put a whole new spin on things and Arbeck lost himself in the implication and so he missed his chance of further queries when the AI broke the link. He tried to re-establish it, but no response. This was not unusual for Mobius Clean. The AI tended to be hands-off and liked others to do their own thinking. Despite this new information Arbeck still had no idea why Oaran needed to look for biotech in the spider things. He grimaced, continued on into the camp where Gleeson now had all her stuff packed away.

'Let's go,' he said.

The day was warm and Arbeck led them on a course running alongside a grove of those strange trees with their fruits of spike gibbons. The others talked about their finds at the massifs, queried Oaran about the two spider creatures hanging on a string from his pack, and speculated on what they would find when they reached their destination. Perrault listened to the queries to Oaran, discovering the instructions he had received via Arbeck from the AI, but all the rest was noise he tuned out.

There was so much else to listen to.

The spike gibbons were agitated. They gathered in the trees in huge numbers and now, understanding their language perfectly, he realised they felt the same stresses the spider things had felt. Troops of gibbons, normally highly territorial, were pressing into close proximity with each other and they really did not like it. Fights were breaking out and even as he watched he saw one torn apart and eaten by others – it's ultrasonic shrieks continuing even when it was down to two legs only. All of them were in hunting mode while their prey walked in territory into which they did not customarily venture. Some did, but they only got a few yards out before instinct broke whatever drove them and they rolled back to the trees, very often to fall prey to a troop not their own. And that, in the end, was the question: what was driving them?

They were not behaving as they should. Perrault considered some form of xenophobia at the root of that, then rejected the idea. He felt sure it had something to do with those pheromones in the air that even now were on the increase again. Yet the gibbons, though they did emit a limited number of pheromones, did not emit anything like this. Mentally analysing its molecular structure from input via his shroud, he ascertained that chemically it was very different from anything they emitted and, therefore, should not be something to which they could respond. He was missing something, he was sure –

'Can you get us through here?'

Arbeck had dropped back to walk beside him. Perrault glanced at him and then to where he was pointing. Ahead a grove cut their path, already filling up with agitated gibbons. Perrault assessed his chances. He now realised that when he first encountered these creatures there had been only the one troop. That pheromone had been in the air, but nowhere near as strong as it was now.

'I will try, but they are very agitated,' he replied.

'And why is that?'

Even though he could see only correlation between the activity of the gibbons and the pheromone, workings on the periphery of his logic gave him certainty. 'Something is driving them in our path, just as it drove those spider creatures to attack us.'

'Something?' Arbeck enquired.

Perrault looked at him. 'Logically it is the creature we are travelling to.' He paused and looked ahead, focusing on the two creatures Oaran was carrying, and realised that the AI had got there ahead of him. Some biotech mechanism, for sure.

'A particular pheromone is increasing in the air. It did this before the spiders attacked. I submit that the animals here are responding just like the orbital weapons responded. The creature wants to be left alone.'

Arbeck nodded, once, briefly. 'It will have to communicate that wish more eloquently than this.' He glanced at Perrault again. 'Do what you can.'

So why did the creature want to be left alone? Was it as territorial as the simple animals of this world? Was it xenophobic? A hermit? His reading of the pheromones, still not proven to have issued from that creature, could tell him nothing, yet, he felt some sense of them nibbling at the borders of his perception as if more than their brute purpose might be getting through to him. However, he no longer had time to analyse this as they drew closer to the grove.

Perrault first broadcast 'danger' and 'threat' in their ultrasound language. Ahead the gibbons scattered through the trees taking up and rebroadcasting the warning, but then, as if they had drawn elastic to its fullest extent it began to pull them back. He broadcast again, and they retreated again, but this time they did not take up his cry as much, and returned more swiftly. Something was very definitely overpowering their instincts.

'Wait,' he said.

The others halted and turned to look at him.

'I need to try something.'

He walked ahead of them, re-examining his analysis of the pheromone. If he supposed it the cause of this aberrant behaviour then he had to neutralise it. He went down on his knees and concentrated, swiftly designing a counter that would bind to it. Of necessity he saw more of its structure as he looked for ways to break it and, when he looked up, elements of that structure seemed to be mapped out in the tree branches. He puzzled on this for a moment as he fed the required data to his shroud. The thing tightened around him and he felt slightly faint as it drew harder on his blood for materials.

'What the hell is he doing?' asked Gleeson.

'Patience,' Arbeck replied. 'He's doing what he does.'

That really was no answer at all, Perrault felt, as the shroud's internal micro-factories and forced chemical reactions heated his spine. Minutes passed, and then he felt the shroud's readiness. He shrugged, opening ports on its surface on his back and next huffed the thing like external lungs. The counter issued in the air and, close to, smelled of aniseed and putrefaction. He switched his vision over to infrared to see a marker on the counter and now it seemed a red cloud spread out from him. It rolled ahead, diffusing fast through the air. He stood up and advanced with it. A moment later it reached the trees and now he shrieked danger, warning and threat again. The spike gibbons fragmented into their troops, some attacking each other in their eagerness to flee. Even as he reached the trees the last of them were disappearing out of sight.

'Nicely done,' said Arbeck, moving up beside him.

'It is confirmed: the pheromone was influencing them,' Perrault replied.

The counteragent had cleared the air of the pheromone he had identified, the resultant compound heavier than before and now falling as a fine powder he could only see because of the infrared marker. But now this revealed other molecules for his, and the shroud's perception – if such a distinction could now be made. The shroud was part of him, an augmentation, something like a subconscious whose main concern was language and its interpretation.

He brought in these other molecules and decoded them, searching for meaning. Fragments arose from the shroud as they walked under the trees, stepping over the remains of gibbons that had fallen foul of tribal disputes. He detected a stab of com between Arbeck and Oaran – the latter picking up one of the corpses – but felt little interest. He knew what was happening. Oaran would only elucidate its mechanism.

Fragments, hints of meaning, elements of chemical speech. Alien. The word rose in his mind and drifted. Not self. Not local. Danger. An acidic stab at afferent nerves combined with an odour in human breath. The molecular segment imparting this arose for his inspection. He saw this came from the pheromone he had neutralised which, though it had been an instruction to another species, must have a suitable receptor – that biotech the AI wanted Oaran to find. It was therefore a key at last and billions of data points began to coalesce. He looked up into the geodesic branches and saw them as a reflection of infinite molecular connections, walked out into the open again and envisioned molecular chains all around him. All words and phrases in a language lurking at the edge of perception. But some were now coming through. He saw phonemes and morphemes, allophones and graphemes in chemical code as complex plugs requiring their socket. He mapped patterns of connection and overall structures and, even as Arbeck said, 'We'll camp here,' he was unsurprised by the missing day, and equally unsurprised that the AI had already been seeking the answer he now required.

As the soldiers made camp and began preparing food, Gleeson walked up to the top of the small rocky outcrop and gazed across the land that lay ahead. Distantly, despite the fading light, she could see their destination rearing up out of the jungle. Next she focused on the jungle itself. Fewer of the strange geodesic trees grew here and other vegetation bore a more familiar shape. There were plants like cycads at the edge, tall rat's tails, spread out canopies of plants like a cross between giant rhubarbs and toadstools and other trees bearing what looked like leaves. What made it all alien to her, however, was the lack of green. The shades here were mostly red, some flashes of pale blue and some black so intense it seemed like cracks in reality.

Jungle like this covered most of the planet. She turned to look back at the terrain they had crossed. Satellite imagery had revealed that these clear areas and groves of geodesic trees, with their large populations of spike gibbons, were only scattered around where the creature had made its home. It had been speculated that it had been feeding in these areas – stripping vegetation and animals to satisfy its appetite, and that the geodesics and spike gibbons were the first to return after its depredations. Whether this was the case she did not know, but certainly scan had detected nacre tunnels extending from the creature's massif down below her feet. She grimaced, such things only loosely related to her specialisms. She glanced back at the camp, and decided it best she focused on her own areas of expertise, and opened her bag.

Demarco had acceded to her request, despite Arbeck's anxiousness to pack up the camp and be on their way. He had quickly dashed up the slope, but had been gone for longer than she expected.

'Screwed the diamond cutter,' he had announced, handing her a large hemisphere of the nacre ten inches across.

She now took the piece out of her bag and inspected it closely, unsure of why if felt like rebellion against AI autocracy to take it. Still, it gave her some satisfaction. She would have something further to study in the night, searching for elusive hard storage. Inserting it back into her bag she returned to the camp.

Oaran had set up lights over a work surface expanded from a close cell foam composite similar to the kind that comprised the hoods and visors of their envirosuits – utterly solid when expanded but could be folded down small enough to fit in a pocket. He had one of the spider things spread out on this and had already opened it up. Checking her aug links, Gleeson found a virtual representation of the thing aping his examination and throwing up details on the items he removed. There its various stomachs along with a web of digestive tracts. Here something like a liver. Other organs, with names from xenobiology and others he gave only numbers because, though they were all spider, he had no words for them. His more intricate work revealed its nervous system and the scattered nodes of its ganglion. Further work revealed fibres attached to some of those nodes and these, judging by the chatter, were of extreme interest.

Gleeson shut down the aug link and returned to the real messy work as Oaran freed up these fibres, traced them down to one point in the carapace, then turned the corpse over. He directed a laser pointer at a formation like a minute metallic worm cast on that surface – almost a truncated version of one of the massifs.

'Biotech,' he said with satisfaction.

Gleeson opened the aug link again and now saw the structure, and its long connections, in great detail. Oaran was scanning it and working the data with his aug, flinging up its components for inspection and dismantling them too in virtuality.

'Any idea what it is?' asked Perrault from the darkness that had now fallen.

'The outer structure appears to be a complex chemical receptor. Internally it converts the chemical data to nerve impulses that head straight for the main ganglion nodes. A form of control possibly, or cerebral programming... or it might even simply be a chemical radio or translator.'

'So the creature sends its instructions in its own pheromonal language and that thing receives them, interpreting for the spider's scattered mind.' Perrault walked back into the camp and sat down with them. 'Is there one on the spike gibbon?'

Oaran looked up, eyes glassy as he continued to work in his aug. 'I gave it a brief external visual inspection. Yes, something like this there too. I thought it was a parasite at first.'

'If you could relay your findings to me,' said Perrault. 'I would be grateful.'

'Language,' said Arbeck glancing at him sharply.

'The pheromones are keys and this is the lock. I can learn a lot here and perhaps begin to put something together.'

'Relay it to you?' said Oaran. 'You don't have an aug.'

Perrault looked at him. 'You have the link?'

'Oh... yes I do.'

'My hardware is not as visible as this software.' He gestured to his shroud. 'And thank you.'

'Wait a minute,' said Arbeck. 'You knew about this!'

'A suspicion only.'

'You knew this and didn't think to mention it?' Arbeck seemed annoyed which, from a Golem, could be more than just emulation.

'Mobius Clean knew, or suspected this too and wasn't forthcoming,' said Perrault. 'I too suspected this but prefer expert confirmation.'

Gleeson suddenly felt a strange reversal of her feelings about him. He had held back his knowledge because he had not wanted to appear arrogant, a know-all. If Arbeck hadn't spoken out no one would have known otherwise. Perrault had then complemented Oaran's expertise. It annoyed her that he now did not seem to fit her perception of him.

'Okay, best we get some sleep now,' said Arbeck. 'All being well we should reach the massif by mid-afternoon.'

The biotech was a further piece of the puzzle. Oaran's analysis of it gave Perrault a large chunk of the vocabulary of the response side of the chemical language in the air. He lay inside his tent steadily assembling a lexicon. From this he ran translation into numerous other languages, including computer code, and from those to standard Anglic. It wasn't perfect – by its very nature simply could not be – but in the end, from the data gathered, he fined it down to a vocabulary, thus far, of a few hundred words. Sleep evaded him because he really wanted more of those complex airborne chemicals to examine. Finally he sat up and exited the tent out into the night.

At the perimeter of the encampment the mosquito autogun swivelled to observe him then came over with delicate steps. He felt its scanning, reading in the changes in its format its confusion with his form, then a further change signifying a programming change, scanning cut-off and the thing moving away again. Even in this there was language.

'Your shroud has changed and it's wrought changes in you,' said a voice. 'It wasn't quite sure what you were for a moment then.'

'Armid,' he said, moving further out to where the man sat on a rock.

A strong aroma hung in the air and grew stronger as Perrault approached. Just for a second he analysed it as part of the chemical language surrounding him, until he recognised what it was.

'Tobacco?' he queried. Demarco was smoking a slim cigar.

'It causes some interesting changes in human biology and to the function of the human brain,' the man replied.

'But how would you know about the latter?' Perrault asked, separating out the tobacco smoke and searching the remainder for new words in the language of an alien.

Demarco looked up. 'Emulation, of course, though it does not give the full experience of a biological brain.'

'Close enough, one would think.'

Demarco nodded. 'I kept my status under wraps, even though Arbeck and Demarco let it be known what they were. But of course something like that cannot be hidden from the likes of you.'

Perrault shrugged. 'Your spoken language has the same discrepancies as Arbeck's, but mostly it's your body language that gives you away. Why did you choose to implant yourself in a human body?'

'For knowledge, for understanding of the human condition. It's nearly run its course now that I've started searching for novelty.' He held up the cigar, then discarded it. 'Now it's time for me to head back to my old body.'

'Which was?'

'A war drone.'

Perrault focused at least a little more of his attention on the man. He'd known within minutes of meeting Armid that here was a human body with AI crystal in his skull. But that he had been a war drone was interesting. Perhaps he was one of the disenfranchised from the war, wondering about the point of AIs staying with humans – what possible purpose they might serve in a future rapidly moving away from them. Questions began to arise, but before he could ask the first, a chaotic radio pulse issued from the encampment and he staggered, input swamping him, an explosion of language his mind struggled for purchase upon.

'You got that?' Armid asked, standing.

'I did,' he managed.

'Gleeson,' said the man, striding back towards the encampment.

Arbeck and Demarco were already pulling open Gleeson's tent when they arrived. Arbeck ducked in and carried her out, a chunk of nacre in her lap and connections running from it to her aug.

'I found it,' she babbled. 'I found hard storage.'

Perrault moved closer as Arbeck laid her on the ground since she seemed incapable of standing. She'd fixed an optic socket to the chunk of nacre and had a lead running from that to her aug. Focusing in, he could see a web of thin wires spreading from the socket over the nacre. After a moment he realised he was looking at a neural mesh. She'd fixed the thing on to try and access the hardware in the nacre. It was, he felt, both a brilliant and stupid attempt to find answers.

'I found it,' she repeated, staring up into the sky as Arbeck detached the optic from her aug. He then reached inside a small pocket in his envirosuit and unwound another optic, undoubtedly attached to him, and reached to plug that into her aug. But the next moment she began convulsing, hands and feet slamming against the ground and foam around her lips.

Demarco got down on her, sitting astride, and pushed his fingers between her teeth. He held her head still while Arbeck inserted that optic. After a moment she froze, rigid as stone. Arbeck blinked, then reached down. With a tinny clink the main body of the aug detached from its seating against her skull and he inserted it in his pocket. He looked up.

'Massive feedback, completely scrambled.' He shook his head. 'She should have known better.'

'Will she be okay?' Perrault watched as Demarco took out an air injector and pressed it against her neck. The thing sighed and she relaxed, closing her eyes.

'Big headache and aug withdrawal in the morning. She's going to be pissed because she won't be able to access her equipment.'

'Her data?' asked Relson from behind Perrault.

'Backed up – she did that before trying this little experiment,' Arbeck replied.

Perrault squatted down, reached out and picked up the piece of nacre with its attached optic.

'Don't,' said Arbeck.

'My specialism,' Perrault replied. 'And I have considerably more resources than she had in her aug.'

'Why your specialism?'

'Because the creatures linked to each other, just as we do with augs. She accessed that connection. Language.'

Arbeck did not look happy, but he nodded once, sharply.

323

Perrault felt bloated. He detached the optic cable from his shroud and wound it around the chunk of nacre and held these out to Arbeck. The Golem shook his head and gestured Armid over, who took the nacre, stepped off to one side to shrug off his pack and put the thing inside. The download had filled up a great deal of the storage in Perrault's internal computing and in the shroud. Great masses of data sat there in seemingly indigestible chunks. The lack of room also limited his ability to process them. However, even as Armid ran to catch up and move ahead, he managed to learn something.

He glanced over at Gleeson. She didn't seem badly damaged by her experiment of the night before, but her every movement broadcast unhappiness. She also had an analgesic patch on her neck to kill her headache and a decidedly pissed off expression. So right then wasn't the time to tell her she hadn't found hard storage packed with a convenient history of the race that had occupied this world. She had instead found an interface that converted their chemical language into a trinary computer language for radio broadcast. He grimaced, then looked ahead to the autogun as it approached the jungle.

'You normally pack it away for transport,' he said.

Arbeck replied, 'You told me that the attacks were driven by the creature – that it wants to keep us away. Extrapolating from that it seems likely they will become more intense the closer we get to it. Perhaps the thing itself will attack, since we've seen it hunting in the area ahead. I wouldn't want to harm it but our lives are my first responsibility.' It was his turn to grimace. 'Unless I am told otherwise.'

Perrault absorbed that. It wasn't unfeasible that the AI might give new instructions in that regard.

'I don't think it will personally attack us,' he stated, only examining that statement once it was out.

'Why not?'

'I am not sure why I said that.'

'Then examine your thinking.'

Perrault glanced at him. He was Golem but he was now wearing the expression of an angry man. Emulated reaction to what had happened last night, but no less real for all that.

'Very well. My enhanced ability to translate languages is not all simple mathematics. It's a holistic interpretation of the parts. Sometimes word precedes meaning but sometimes it can be the other way round, whilst there are meanings that fall outside of the human spectrum of perception. As I begin to integrate a language I also integrate a quite deep sense of its source – perhaps the culture from which it arose. You must be aware that in human culture the learning of a new language results in similar perception?'

'Yes, I understand that.'

'Through all this I have some sense of the creature that lies ahead. Thoughts, ideas, perceptions arise in my mind from the shroud, from my subconscious and from my internal computing whose singular source I cannot nail down.'

'And what do you sense?' Arbeck asked.

'Desperation, but also a strong sense of morality.' He paused for a second, something occurring to him. 'When we came down the orbital weapons destroyed our shuttle. Our pods having been ejected were presumably vulnerable until they reached the ground?'

'Yes, they were.'

'Yet they all arrived intact.'

'Yes, they did.' Arbeck's tone grew leaden. Perrault realised this was not because of any understanding of the actions of the creature, but because of one of the AI that had sent them down.

'Through its orbital array the creature destroyed mechanisms. I don't know whether it thought the shuttle just such a mechanism when it fired upon it or whether it was aware we were aboard.' He glanced at Arbeck again. 'The attack?'

'Not as hard as it could have been,' he shook his head, annoyed still.

'It did not attack the pods because people were aboard.'

'You get all of this from your holistic perception?' He tried to be scathing but obviously didn't have the heart for it. He added, 'The AI knew.'

'Or it just wanted to test a theory,' said Perrault.

Arbeck nodded and moved away from him.

The autogun fired a few shots, bringing down a great mass of vines supporting objects like pink pineapples, then advanced into the shadows. Perrault and the others reached the jungle shortly afterwards. He peered in. It wasn't too claustrophobic in there and it seemed they would be able to travel without too much in the way of laser slicing the plant life.

He waited to one side as the others went through. Gleeson came last and paused beside him.

'Did you get anything from it?' she asked.

'Very little unfortunately – the hard storage is very disrupted,' he lied.

She pursed her lips and moved in ahead of him. He followed, now returning the bulk of his attention to the masses of data swirling about inside him. After he had taken just a few paces inside one of his search programs alerted him to a find. His map of the engaging surface of the hardware in the nacre, which acted much like that metallic worm cast biotech on the spiders and spike gibbons, revealed millions of chemical keys, or rather sockets. The program had now identified one of them as matching one of the words those creatures nominally understood. He recorded the trinary output to his lexicon and now, knowing he was on the right path, eagerly searched for more. They had gone perhaps just a few hundred yards further by the time he had all of the words he knew and now, by extrapolation, could infer more. A breakthrough, unconscious in its source, had him grunt in surprise, as discovered the negative iteration of 'find' – a short chemical chain that essentially meant 'do not'.

'We'll stop for a break,' said Arbeck, and again the hours had slid by.

They stopped and Perrault sat with the rest of them while the autogun walked a perimeter, but he remained focused inwards, finding new words, hunting down meaning. Armid passed him food and he wolfed it down. Armid kept passing him food and he kept eating till he felt himself bulging against his envirosuit. The shroud had made its demands on his body and now he needed to replenish his reserves. He fell into a half-sleep and dreamed language – words of chemical code flitting round him like bats. Without any transition he remembered, he found himself walking again. He fitted words into phrases but anomalies arose, until he realised he was seeing three tenses, just like human language. From this he extrapolated further, but then began paying more attention to his surroundings when he noted the air filling with that particular pheromone again.

Then the pig came.

It appeared in the jungle ahead of them, snuffling at the ground, three stalked eyes up from its head observing them, a mouth full of teeth like broken glass. It then emitted a very piggish squeal and charged. Arbeck and the others fired shots into the ground before it, showing it with burning debris. It swerved away and charged off into the jungle beside them.

'A fucking great pig,' Oaran named it. Perrault felt a moment of irritation but knew the name would stick because of the emotional context. But he felt the thing, with its ribbed armour and long head, more resembled an armadillo.

'Biotech,' Arbeck stated.

Yes, Perrault had seen the metallic worm cast on its long skull.

Arbeck went on, 'There are more out there, Perrault. Can you shut them down?'

He was already reading all the emissions around him. Their grunts and squeals were human-audible now but he could get little from them but what were likely expression of danger, anger, fear and territoriality. He opened his mouth, hacked for a moment as his vocal cords strained at new input, then emitted a loud squeal of what seemed likely to be danger. The response was anger and then something crashed into him from the side and he was tumbling through the air. A splayed foot came down on his chest driving his breath out as the bristly fat mass of the thing ran over him. He rolled upright, still fighting for breath as it turned, side swiping a tree and bringing down a rain of grey nodules. Stun fire tracked along its body, steadily increasing in intensity until the air filled with the stink of burning flesh, killing pheromone input. But they had little effect on the thing.

'I don't like this! I don't like this!' he could hear Gleeson shouting.

The creature came back at him, snapping at the air as if being attacked by something invisible. He had no doubt that when it reached him it would be snapping at something wholly visible and material. A weapon cracked and he heard a meaty impact. The creature juddered sideways, shook itself, a wound welling just back from its neck. The ensuing blast took off its head and rolled it in the leaf litter before him, while its body slumped and skidded to a halt, piling up earth.

'More of them!' Arbeck yelled.

A hand reached down and wrenched him to his feet as the monsters crashed through the jungle all around. He glimpsed Armid's face grinning joyfully – expected from an erstwhile war drone. Armid dragged him aside and pushed him down by a tree where Glesson sat, knees up to her face and arms wrapped around them. Stun fire lit the air – still ineffective – then pulses of ionised aluminium and the glare of a laser carbine. That other weapon firing its explosive bullets began cracking regularly. He saw the autogun scuttling, spewing fire, then get rolled over by something large. Stinking smoke gusted across, fogging all around. He tried to penetrate it and find some reason, some negotiation, but the burning killed chemical language while the weapons killed EMR. All that remained was the horrible squealing and grunting. He tried and tried to find clarity. Gleeson pulled close to him and he wrapped an arm around her – mute communication. The sound of something thrashing, a single concussion flinging chunks of flesh into the air. The firing began to die.

'This is wrong,' said Gleeson. 'I know they're animals but...'

It seemed to key into elements in his mind. He could not communicate with the creatures around him, and that was almost irrelevant now since most of them were dead, but perhaps it was now time to go to the source. He firmly linked to his lexicon and searched for the right words, set internal transmitters to the trinary format of those Gleeson had found in the nacre.

'Don't attack,' he broadcast. *'Not danger us.'*

And then he listened.

'That's all of them,' said Arbeck, stepping out of the smoke. His envirosuit was spattered with gobbets of purplish flesh and smeared with yellow fluid like pus.

Gleeson abruptly pulled away from Perrault. To Arbeck she said, 'Was it necessary to kill them?' Then she turned and looked pointedly at Perrault.

'Stun shots didn't work. They didn't work with the spike gibbons and they didn't work with the spiders,' Arbeck replied.

Perrault, growing calmer and still listening, nodded to himself. He knew that aug com ramped up between the soldiers during a fight like this and, though he had not sampled its content, he could guess. It would be fast, military format, effect of weapons tried, vulnerable body areas, behavioural responses, tactics, logistics – a scream of com almost circumventing conscious consideration. He knew that if there had been an alternative to killing, Arbeck would have used it. But that was not what Gleeson was getting at. He stood up.

'I couldn't do anything – it was too fast and there was too much interference,' he said, then held out a hand to Gleeson. She hesitated for a moment then grabbed it and he hauled her to her feet, but nearly dropped her when the talking started.

'Don't come,' said the creature, along with a further lengthy communications. He froze as it permeated his mind, his shroud, all that he was. He picked out identifiable meaning, chemical words, intimations of danger and threat.

'I'm sorry,' said Gleeson. 'I was being unfair.'

He stared at her, hardly seeing her as his processing crunched out meaning, made connections, elucidated further words. This was almost like the gains he had made with that piece of nacre and, in a moment, he could formulate his next reply.

'We must come,' he sent.

'Are you okay?' Arbeck asked.

He held up his hand. 'It's speaking to me.'

'What's it saying?' Gleeson asked, wide eyed.

'Shush,' said Arbeck, and drew her away.

'There is danger,' was the essence of the next communication from the creature, but it came with so much more he could not, yet, parse. But his vocabulary continued expanding, turning towards an exponentially upwards curve. Levels of processing integrated and words and meaning began surfacing like bubbles from a disturbed swamp. He felt the synergistic thrill of it, knowing that the cascade would grow.

'The danger was created by you,' he sent.

'To keep you safe,' it replied, again along with so much more.

Blocks of previously unknown language began to reveal more and more meaning, slotting neatly into his lexicon. He began to get detail on the states and the natures of things. He started sending short phrases and every one had its response. A breakthrough came when he could tell it, *'We came from above.'*

It replied, *'I know,'* and the communication simply stopped no matter what he sent thereafter.

An emulation of anger seemed appropriate, just to fit in and retain a human identity with his soldiers and with the two 'experts'. And Arbeck felt he had good reason to be angry now. The AI had sent them down here with the same regard it might have had for a sub-AI probe. It had told him that to facilitate their safe transit to the surface he could destroy any orbital weapon that fired on them. It had then rescinded that, and Perrault's insight had given him the reason why. The creature had the power to destroy them and obviously wanted to keep them away. But would it actually take that step or did it have some regard for other intelligent life? Mobius Clean had tested this because the AI knew, just as Arbeck knew, that prior to every strike against their probes the creature had scanned them intensely. Clean knew it would scan the shuttle and find living intelligences inside. What would it do? Would it kill them to preserve its privacy? Apparently not. It had disabled the shuttle, which ejected its pods. Now it seemed, from a belated telemetry update he had found, it had obliterated the shuttle, perhaps in a fit of pique, but left the pods alone. And now this, now what was happening here.

Arbeck prodded the crushed remains of the mosquito autogun, then surveyed the devastation in the jungle. Six of those pig-beasts lay in mangled ruin. The creature was trying to drive them away by turning the fauna against them. Had Clean expected something like this? Of course the AI had. They were effectively in a trap now and the only way out was communication with the creature. This had been confirmed by a recent brief communication with Clean:

'It's trying to kill us and I'm not sure we can get close before that happens. I suggest you make a hole in the orbital defence and send a rescue shuttle,' he had opined.

'No – you will continue.'

'Just to see if it will kill us?'

'To get answers. Protect Perrault – he is key.'

'I think you know more than you're telling me.'

'I always do,' Clean had replied, and cut com.

Arbeck looked over at Perrault. The man had not moved since standing up and was obviously deep into something. He surveyed the ruination again, then came to a decision.

'Armid, get him moving,' he ordered.

'That such a good idea?' Armid asked. 'Gonna get nastier.'

'It takes time for it to set up its attacks on us,' Arbeck replied. 'Maybe we can get to the massif before it tries again, then set up a base we can defend easily.'

'We're still going?'

Arbeck pointed to the sky. 'No choice in the matter.'

Armid took hold of Perrault's arm, tugged him into motion and he walked with them but with his mind elsewhere, as before. Switching over to aug com Arbeck had his soldiers spread to a moving perimeter, checking the jungle all around. Gleeson came up beside him. Despite recent events she looked better now than she had in the morning. She paced beside him for a moment, saying nothing, then emitted a snort of laughter.

'What is it?' he asked.

'We're expendable, aren't we?'

Arbeck knew she was right but now, because sometimes his mind worked like that, he felt the need to defend the mission here.

'How many intelligent races have we encountered as we've expanded out into the galaxy?' he asked.

'Six or seven,' she replied.

'I mean living intelligent races, not their remains.'

'Oh.' She grimaced. 'The prador, an alien survivor of a prador genocide, then there's the gabbleducks, and whether or not they're intelligent is debateable.'

'So just a few.'

'Yes.'

'So this creature is very important and it's worth taking some risks to understand and communicate with it.'

She nodded. 'That's what the AI thinks, but it's risking our lives and not its own. This could have been done a lot slower and a lot more carefully, but the AI is careless of our lives because there are trillions of replacements for us.'

Arbeck was about to argue against that, but decided there was no point. It was all a lot more complicated than she made out, and he had no doubt Mobius Clean had incorporated immense layers of calculations to decide on its actions. But still, he felt angry too – mostly because the AI had, probably out of necessity, failed to apprise him of all it knew.

'Look,' she said, pointing.

A clear area lay in the foliage ahead where some massive plant, like a tangled fig with deep black marks on its multiple trunks that resembled fissures, had toppled sometime in the past. Through this gap they could now see the massif looming close. He calculated that it would take them only a few more hours to reach it. He then lowered his gaze to another odd looking tree in the jungle ahead. It had a trunk, then higher up this flattened and spread with nodules protruded from its perimeter. Its hue was striated pastel yellow and pink. As he stared at it a vertical slot opened below the spread area, and all around this objects like bunches of fronds protruded and retracted. Then the massive thing bowed down and surged towards them like a snake, more of its length issuing from the ground, and he realised those nodules were eyes and the slot a mouth.

'Go away! Go away! Go away!' it screamed – the chemical strength of its cry so intense he could taste it on his human tongue.

'Don't shoot,' he said – not sure if anyone was hearing.

The thing thrashed from side to side, uprooting trees. It curled down on one and folded it in its flat upper portion and then flung it away to crash in the jungle nearby. It dipped down again and scooped up a great mass of earth and rock and flung it. The stuff rained down all around and over to one side of Perrault a boulder fell into a tree, splitting it and lodging head height from the ground.

'Threat display,' he said.

The soldiers had either heard him or were under orders – stupid to come all this way to talk to a creature and then shoot it. Or rather, this small portion of the immense beast. They backed off, weapons pointed to the ground as the thing advanced and thrashed. It then seemed to single out Arbeck and side swiped him, sending him tumbling through the trees. Perrault detected restraint for it had attacked the one of them least likely to be hurt. That it hit Demarco next was only a confirmation. It then came down on Relson, drove her to the ground and pinned her there. Would it do more?

A second later the radio link opened and the scream repeated over that for just a moment, then abruptly stopped. He saw Relson struggling underneath the thing, then it abruptly lifted away and hung above her as if studying her intently, those protrusions either side of its slot mouth shooting in and out with a strange wheezy sound. It began retreating and Perrault detected a huge intense reluctance as new chemicals filled the air. In these were words involved in procreation. Had it detected that she was a woman and did it have some kind of cultural block on attacking her? He thought not, because the chemical words for urgency, need and danger also flooded the air. The radio transmission started again and he received so much more than before: the whole chemical language flooded into him, codified, linked, sequence markers in place. He studied the mass, shifted it until it slotted neatly against the trinary code the creatures used. Had the creature somehow understood him and what he needed? Because this was a large part of it.

His translation slid up the exponential curve, his components parts of brain, hardware and shroud working in perfect synergy. His lexicon expanded, reshaped and gained a logical structure so, when it spoke again over the radio link, he understood it perfectly.

Tried to stop you. Cannot without killing. Come – consequences your own,' it said. Threat and danger were implicit there, but also something else he struggled to identify, but then he did: eagerness.

'What consequences?'

'Send me your language. Will accept now,' was its reply, along with a brief transmission in binary code. This surprised him, but then surprise slid away. He had no doubt that the AI had attempted communication before.

'So that's what we've come to talk to?' said Relson, standing up and brushing herself off. 'Seems a little unstable.'

Arbeck, standing up from the remains of a tree his impact had shattered, looked over at Perrault. 'What's it saying?'

'That it cannot stop us without killing us, so it's no longer going to try and stop us,' he replied, then added, 'But it seems there might be consequences if we go there.'

'Worse than being killed?' Armid asked.

Perrault glanced at the man, or rather war drone crystal mind sitting in a human body, and thought he wasn't really one to judge on the dangers of dying, since he wouldn't. Even if something recognised that his true intelligence resided in a lump of crystal inside his skull and smashed it, he would restore from a perpetually updated backup aboard the ship.

'We keep going,' Arbeck said, and once again they set out.

Perrault now studied the recorded binary transmission. It was a piece of a Polity almanac combining written and spoken language along with a 3D image. It seemed, at some point, the AI had needed this creature to know what an apple was. His own lexicon of Anglic was much more detailed, with pictures, 3D recordings, text and audio. He considered trying to fine it down, to weed out the irrelevant, but found it difficult to know what might be irrelevant to a giant alien shellfish. He began transmitting it all. A few minutes later the creature said, *'Thank you,'* but that was all.

As they moved out Gleeson stepped up beside him. 'There's more isn't there?'

'Hard to say,' he replied. 'I'm still trying to absorb and understand an alien language and the likelihood of misunderstanding is high.'

'You're not going to tell me,' she snapped.

'Very well. Even though it has done everything to drive us away I now sense an underlying eagerness for it to have us close along with other… feelings expressed in chemical interconnections, which I cannot identify.'

'Maybe it's like the hermit, forsaking company but glad when it comes?'

'Maybe,' Perrault agreed. 'It also asked me to send it a lexicon of our language. It seems that someone tried to send one before, but it refused.'

'The AI,' she said. 'There has always been more going on here than we've been allowed to know.'

'Of course. We are essentially extensions of Mobius Clean sent to gather intelligence.'

'And what matter if we get destroyed just like the probes?'

'AIs calculate risk and gain,' he said. 'It would not have sent us here if it expected us to be killed out of hand. We do have our value.'

'Maybe you.' She glanced at him, showing some of her previous dislike of him. She then shook her head and looked down, came up and forced a smile.

He nodded acknowledgement of her self-control. 'You're right, of course. There is something here beyond establishing communications, but I've yet to understand it.'

She nodded – her concerns now social rather than scientific.

'I'm sorry about my attitude towards you,' she said.

He read her in a glance, recognising her fascination with her newly arising feelings towards him. He kept the conversation light, but sufficiently engaging, with a small part of his mind, while the rest focused on the task within. After an hour or so of tramping through the jungle the silences got longer, but companionable for all that. Finally, she moved on ahead to talk to someone else. He smiled at her back, aware that he would not have seen this change in her had she not wrecked her aug and thus been forced to further engage with the real world. This he felt was something worth remembering, and he told himself that when all this was over he would take off his shroud again, he would re-engage with normality. Then, as if it had been waiting for his full attention, the creature contacted him again.

The binary channel now engaged, feeding him back his Anglic lexicon with mating links to the information it had sent before. He altered processing to facilitate the matching of their separate languages.

'Why do we exist?' it asked in trinary.

He understood it perfectly. The linking of the two lexicons behind the trinary code almost complete even as he enquired, *'We?'*

'All intelligent creatures.' That came through clear too.

'So we have transitioned from bugger off to philosophy now?' He was immensely pleased with that. He had absorbed the grouping in science and other disciplines which, by their vast complications in this language, made his speculations about the definition of biotech seem positively infantile. He had also worked out chemical conjunctions for expletives, and felt reassured that creatures so alien would use them.

'It is an important question.'

'We are meat machines transporting slow genes into the future, while looking at the stars,' he said – a reply he had used with many others.

'Our genetic purpose is to live, to consume and to breed and there is nothing beyond that until the advent of higher mind.'

'That sums it up nicely.'

'You are male and you inject your genetic material into a female, who gestates a new human.'

'Yes.'

'I too am male, but my biology is more complicated.'

'Does your kind arise from oceans?' Despite all the complex words and meanings he had available, 'ocean' was difficult. He described water of vast extent. Almost negligently it sent him the exact word he required before replying. He located it, noting that still some links between the languages had not yet firmed.

'Yes, we come from an ocean.'

'And you are one creature alone?'

'I am.'

'Are there more of your kind anywhere else?'

'Widely scattered and hidden.'

'So all you do here is live and consume?' It was a deliberate jibe in search of revealing responses.

'My kind lived on ocean floors and males like me distributed our genetic material to the currents to be taken up by the females. We adapted ourselves to other environments where this became less feasible.'

'Easily enough solved by biotechnology as advanced as yours.'
'Supposing there is a moral inclination,' it replied.
'I don't understand that – you need to elaborate.'

The creature had no reply for him, so he replayed the conversation while running an analysis of the words used, and their meanings, to ascertain whether or not he might have misunderstood. Though he was translating to Anglic at the front end in his mind, behind that were layers of other human languages, computer code, symbolic logic and comparisons with the chemical communications of many life forms, some of them alien. There were millions of places where the whole translation system might be breaking down, even so far as giving opposite meanings to those stated. The Anglic he 'heard' and 'spoke' was like the surface thoughts of a mind, driven underneath by the much greater mass of the subconscious. Time again slid by as he lost himself in this world. He tinkered, made corrections, discoveries and streamlined elements of translation, while with a much smaller part of his mind he ran the business of walking through the jungle without falling flat on his face.

Finally, when he realised he had stopped walking, he paid more attention to his surroundings. They had left the jungle about half an hour earlier, crossing an area of churned ground free of large vegetation. He blinked, noting new red shoots scattered all across this area, a smaller worm cast over to one side revealing one of those nacre tunnels. Here lay an area the creature had fed upon – denuding it of plants and doubtless of animals. He saw that Arbeck and the others were discussing something, pointing to the surrounding terrain as they did so. He walked over to them.

'You're back with us?' Gleeson asked.

'For now,' he replied.

'Anything we need to know?' asked Arbeck.

'I may have misunderstood our last exchange and I am checking. We briefly discussed procreation and I've learned that there are others of its kind on other worlds, but then it said something I did not understand.'

'That being?'

'Its kind were sea creatures who distributed their seed in the seas before moving to the land. I said any problems with that could be solved by their biotech. It replied, "Supposing there is a moral inclination," – I think that might have translated wrong.'

They all looked thoughtful as they chewed that over, then Arbeck pointed again. 'Over on that, I reckon. We can set a fence and will have a good view all around.' He turned to a soldier who until now had remained firmly in the background. 'Dasheel?'

The man shrugged. 'Best option if we are to remain here.'

'Retreat will be more difficult,' Armid opined.

'We won't be retreating,' said Arbeck.

Perrault studied the flat-topped mound indicated – heavy boulders strewn about its lower slopes. It looked like the kind of place some medieval human might have built a fort. He supposed this made it more defensible in those terms, and would be a good place from which to drive off the kind of animal attacks they had endured. But now it seemed likely there would be no more of those, while the more likely attack would come from a creature massing thousands of tons, and residing in the nearby massif and in the ground below.

They set off towards the mound, and Perrault soon found himself scrambling up a slope over boulders. At the top the soldiers cleared some debris then set out the tents. Dasheel began hammering in small posts all around. As Perrault moved out past these and seated himself on a boulder, the man then set up a couple of inflatable tripods and on each mounted pulse rifles. Shortly after this he set out with a handful of small silvery spikes Perrault recognised as seismic detectors. It seemed evident now Dasheel's expertise, or at least one of them, lay in setting up defensive positions. Now an argument behind. Perrault only half focused on it, but knew that Gleeson finally got her way when she set out with Relson and Armid, and her equipment, towards the massif. She would continue her studies despite her lack of an aug.

'And now it's down to you,' said Arbeck, from over the other side of the new camp. Perrault held up a hand to indicate he had heard.

Gleeson felt her groping for access to her aug akin to reaching out to grasp something and finding her wrist ended at a stump, and it hurt too. Though, she had to admit, she was probably being overdramatic. In her long life she had never actually lost a limb. Her greatest injury had been a broken arm, and she soon negated the likelihood of that happening again by having her bones reinforced. As they headed towards the massif Armid abruptly halted and peered at something at the ground. He stooped and picked it up.

'What have you got?' she asked.

He held up a fragment of nacre.

'Bag it – we'll check out the intervening ground on the way back.'

He nodded, but slipped the fragment in his pocket, probably sensing her urgency to get to the massif so not prepared to take off his pack and search out a sample bag. But why, she wondered, did she feel such urgency? Perhaps it came from Perrault, his repetition of the cryptic and threatening communications from the creature, and the knowledge from him that chemical language filled the air. It was as if by being made aware of this she had somehow been sensitised to it. She was breathing words, they were landing on her skin, entering her eyes and nostrils. The air seemed telic, dangerous and they might be driven away at any moment. Or, more likely, the odd stuff she was feeling had more to do with aug withdrawal.

They finally reached the foot of the massif. Looking up she could see many more of the nacre tunnels than had been evident in the older one before. This was probably due to erosion and collapses covering those other tunnels.

'Run a grid as before,' she instructed the other two. 'Keep an eye out for anything we didn't see at the other one, even if it lies outside the grid. Move fast.'

'Will do, boss,' said Armid.

She stared at him. The guy had something odd about him she could not nail down. Again she felt this feeling had something to do with her loss of her aug. She shook her head and began climbing. She had already examined old nacre and now felt it time to look at the newest stuff she could get to. It seemed likely this would be around one of the upper tunnels, though that was really just a guess. As she headed up, she peered at some of the lower tunnels and noted spill from them – obviously new. The air here smelled of a decaying tideline, while she noted a steady background noise that itself reminded of the sea. This time there would be no spiders, she felt sure – the creature probably had an aversion to others sharing its home as it had to visitors. It also seemed likely that any that did venture here became aperitifs.

Finally she reached the tunnel she had been aiming for and, stooping down, opened up her shoulder bag. She took out the box of remotes and wondered what reaction she might get if she sent them in, then put them away again. That might be too much of an invasion and, anyway, it would take far too long to program them manually. She next took out her hand scanner and held it before her for a long moment, before realising she had been trying to key into it with her aug. She sighed and began using the controls on the handle to focus on the nacre – an action that gave her an abrupt and sharp feeling of nostalgia. The last time she had used this thing manually had been over forty years ago and, of course, before she got herself an aug.

Structure revealed itself to be much more even than before. She could see no signs of disruptions, wear, or age. She also began noticing organics. Stuff here around the contact holes actually seemed part of the nacre, while here and there lay scraps of fibrous flesh and beads of liquid that certainly were not. She abruptly turned back to her bag, removing a micro vacuum brush and began running it over the surface.

'Gleeson!' It was Armid. Perhaps he had found something exciting, but he would have to wait for her attention.

She finished brushing, then injected what the brush had drawn up into a sample bottle. The result was a few millilitres of yellow fluid. Here, she felt sure, they now had the genome of the creature. Belatedly she cursed herself for not thinking to look for samples when the creature had come out of the ground earlier. She could have used the brush on Relson's envirosuit.

'Gleeson!'

She sighed, stood up to stretch her back, then turned to look down the slope of the massif, and froze.

She simply hadn't heard anything and she should have. Now between her and the foot of the slope where Armid and Relson stood, the huge protrusions of the creature, like the one they had seen earlier, snaked through the air. Movement behind. She stepped away from the tunnel and looked back into it. The thing filled with flesh, folded like a cauliflower or a human brain. It welled up and then came out, rose up above her, its flat end opening out. She now saw much closer than she liked what she had glimpsed back in the jungle. The nodules were certainly eyes – in fact they looked like the eyes of an octopus. The slot mouth unzipped almost with obscene eagerness and revealed wet convolutions inside. And then, as if in great excitement, frondy protrusions shot out around the mouth, tasting the air she felt sure.

Gleeson just stood frozen, too scared to move. Even so her mind did not freeze and she continued to study the thing. Its flesh resembled that of an octopus or a squid and the yellows and pinks did bear some similarity to that of creatures found under one of Earth's oceans. She noted a sheen of slime – probably to aid its transit through its tunnels. What were these she wondered? Were they sensory tentacles extending from some major part of the beast deep inside this massif? Scans had been unable to penetrate deep enough to reveal a central body.

'Gleeson! We have to go back! Arbeck's orders – it doesn't want us here!'

That snapped her out of it and she looked down at the other two. She felt a brief surge of anger. *Fucking Perrault!* Then she experienced confusion about her feelings for the man. When they had talked down in the jungle, she'd realised that they were changing. She reached down and took up her bag and scanner, dropped the brush and sample bottle inside, but retained the scanner as if it might be some weapon she could use to defend herself against the massive life form here. She turned to look back at the nearest tentacle.

'I'm sorry,' she said, wondering if it now had any grasp on human words, if it could even hear them.

The thing was quivering and after she spoke it jerked back a little and its quivering increased. Stupid to read eagerness in that, or fear, she felt, but there it was. Swallowing dryly she turned away and began to make her way down the slope. Ahead of her the other tentacles reluctantly shifted out of her way. She could see that they were quivering too.

They are coming back, but of course you can see that,' said Perrault. *'Why do you not want them close to you?'*

Gleeson had reached the bottom of the slope now with Armid and Relson either side of her and walking back. They got about fifty yards out whereupon Gleeson pointed. The other two moved off and began collecting samples. She turned to look back. The tentacles there were still out, all facing towards her, slightly hooked over. The impression given was of a group of meerkats sitting on their mound.

The seas were dangerous,' said the creature.

Perrault contained his impatience – perhaps this would be an explanation of the creature's urgency to have Gleeson and the others away from it.

The seas your kind evolved in?'

'Yes.'

'I can understand that.'

Perrault thought of the dangers shelled molluscs faced in the seas of Earth. Other hunting shellfish like whelks with their hollow drills to bore holes in shells, to inject digestive fluid and suck out the contents; crabs tearing them open to feast on living contents; otters beating ormers with rocks; the hard-mouthed fish and, of course, the humans. Shelled molluscs sat some way low down on food chains, which was why they produced so many offspring. He checked references, then a section attached to his lexicon. The section on mussels he absorbed for conscious inspection was interesting. The males released sperm into the water to be siphoned up by females, who produced thousands of larvae. These drifted through the ocean as part of the plankton until attaching to the gills of specific varieties of fish. There they encysted and grew, dropping out a few weeks later to attach to some rock and continue their growth into adults.

'Getting some seismic readings,' said Dasheel. 'Maybe that thing below us is extending out to hunt?'

'Maybe,' said Arbeck. 'We don't know what's usual here.'

On an impulse Perrault sent the section on mussels in binary to the creature.

'Our cycle became similar,' it replied quickly – amazing him with its speed of apprehension. *'This was necessary because of the distances our territoriality put between each of us. In our prehistory we males released sperm as packets only, but more predators evolved to seize these. So we evolved into something similar to these mussels. The sperm packets encysted in hosts and guided those hosts to females, who took in the packets and consumed the hosts.'*

Parasites were ubiquitous both in terran and alien biology, could have vastly complex life cycles of many stages. Perrault did not need to look at data on them to know that many seized control of their host's bodies and minds.

'And then?'

'The larvae the female produced also sought out hosts, and took them to suitable locations and there fed upon them while making their first burrows.'

'So this negated the predation on your young,' he stated, starting to feel very uncomfortable with all this. He groped around for somewhere to take the conversation next. *'I suppose such a technique became difficult when you moved to the land? I expect by then you used your biotechnology for the purposes of procreation?'*

He put his hand down on the rock, yes he could feel vibrations now. Out at the massif those big tentacle things were retracting into their tunnels. Gleeson, meanwhile, was down on her knees digging at the ground with a trowel. She had revealed a short arc of nacre. He glanced across at the other two. Armid was still wandering, staring at the ground, but Relson was down on her knees too, pushing soil aside with the flat of her hand.

'*No, we continued on the land as we had in the sea,*' the creature replied. '*The hosts were land creatures you have already seen – the ones that one of you described as pigs. They were perfect for the chore. In fact we adapted some of them to return to the sea for our brethren there.*'

Perrault nodded to himself. The creature had been aware of them since they landed, but now it was evident it had also been more attentive than he had supposed and must have recorded their exchanges. How else had it known about Oaran dubbing their first attacker in the jungle a pig?

'*So you weren't so territorial then?*'

'*Creatures change – it is the nature of life. We became a society.*'

Until now Perrault's concentration had been on the intricacies of the translation, but he began applying his mind more to the content of the communication. He started to make connections and began to see part of the picture the creature was drawing for him, and it looked ugly indeed. He turned and caught Arbeck's eye.

'Tell them, via aug, to get back here,' he said quietly.

'What the hell, Perrault?' Arbeck asked.

Rather than get into detail about sperm packets and the like he said, 'It uses land animals as hosts for its children.'

Arbeck stared at him for a moment, nodded, then looked out to the three. Perrault watched them too. Armid paused in his wanderings then abruptly turned and ran back towards Gleeson. Relson stood up, peered back towards the massif, then set out at a fast walk back towards the camp. But Gleeson of course had heard nothing. She continued her digging and now it was obvious what she had found because the curve of nacre she had revealed had almost completed a circle. The mouth of one of the tunnels lay there in the ground. Relson had been revealing similar too and now Perrault felt sure they must be all around them. He next realised he had delayed too long. He needed to keep talking as if he hadn't understood the implications of the creature's story.

'Then you went to the stars,' he said. *'That must have been difficult for creatures as large as you.'*

'We built our tunnels to the sky and made our vessels, and we explored,' it told him. *'Did you take your pigs with you?'*

'We spread out to many worlds,' it continued, ignoring his question. *'But, as our technology advanced our old territoriality reasserted over time. Worlds where thousands of us resided became worlds with only hundreds and then just a few, and ultimately one.'*

'And that is the stage you are at now?'

'You wish this to be the end of the story?'

'I'm sorry, please continue.'

Armid had finally convinced Gleeson to leave her find. They too began heading back, though Gleeson kept pausing to study the ground. After a moment Armid grabbed her arm and hurried her along.

'Though we had changed much and once again become territorial,' the creature continued, *'our urge to breed remained. It in fact became stronger due to our separation.'*

'A difficult situation.'

'Yes, especially when ones' chosen hosts were incapable of travelling between stars.'

'A technological answer, surely.'

'Yes, but not the one you would wish for. Consider the mentality, the morality of a race of creatures who use other creatures for procreation. Our regard for other life was not as yours. It was the regard of predator for prey. So the answer to the dilemma of breeding when we had found but generally studied from a distance other star-faring races was obvious: here were the hosts we needed to take our seed between worlds.'

Perrault could think of no reply as the full horror of it hit him. Until this moment it had been an intellectual slotting together of facts, fragments of conversation, and intimations of danger and intent. The ground was really shaking now and this began displacing loose earth all around, revealing more nacre.

The creature continued relentlessly: *'The biotech changes were easy for us by now and our studies of those other races revealed many ways we could lure them to our worlds. There were failures at first and some necessary exterminations when we found difficulties in controlling some hosts. But soon we were thriving again, and using those other races to spread us to further worlds.'*

Something kept nagging at him – something did not feel right about this story – but right then the ground exploded behind Armid and Gleeson and one of those tentacles reared into view. Relson had by now reached the boulders. She turned to go back but doubtless Arbeck ordered her on and she scrambled up into the camp. Armid and Gleeson broke into a run, another tentacle breaking through the ground over to one side, while the one behind poured out, now snaking along the ground after them. The soldiers in the camp moved to its edge. Arbeck and Demarco held weapons he had not seen before, and which had obviously been secreted away, disassembled in their packs. These were big heavy things only the two mostly cybernetic men could carry.

'Perrault?' said Arbeck.

He was about to tell them they should all run, but still something kept nagging at him. Then, despite his fear, he saw it.

'But where are all of your kind now?' he asked.

During the ensuing long pause further tentacles exploded from the ground. Armid and Gleeson reached the rocks and began climbing up, one of the tentacles not far behind them. Arbeck moved out, pointing his weapon down.

'Perrault.'

'Don't fire.'

Arbeck glared at him and kept the weapon pointed, but he did not open fire even when the tentacle nudged Armid and sent him sprawling. A beat passed and then the thing reared up and just hung over the camp, like a question mark. Perrault could see it quivering as the two made their way up and in through the perimeter.

'Creatures change, societies change, moralities change,' said the creature. *'We began to accept that the hosts we used so badly were thinking and feeling creatures like ourselves. The females desisted from feeding on them when they delivered our seed. Both males and females chose a form of celibacy by ensuring none of the other races came to their worlds. Disgust at our base drives formed in us a new morality. Over the centuries we began dying and now few of us remain.'*

'But the desire to breed remains,' Perrault pointed out.

'It does,' said the creature. *'But like all base desires it must be controlled.'*

Perrault gazed around at the forest of tentacles surrounding them, then watched as gradually, here and there, some of them began retracting into the ground.

The creature had one last thing to say, however: *'You can tell the artificial intelligence that is watching from that ship up above that I have passed its test. I know I can control myself now, and I will talk to it.'*

Perrault grimaced, studied Gleeson and the soldiers and knew that when he told them everything, their reaction might not be good. But he would couch it in the best of terms and choose his words wisely. He was incapable of doing otherwise.

After my wife died I did plenty of research into ways to ameliorate the after-effects of that event on me: drugs, nootropics and meditation etc. This transitioned into a more general interest in health and how to optimise it. Anyone who reads my social media posts will know that. I then got into reading about longevity stuff on a site called fightaging.org. This story incorporates much of what I learned there and I even sent it in to the guy 'Reason' who runs the site to look over. He suggested a couple of changes but mostly I got it right. All of what follows is entirely possible within the life times of many reading this (though maybe I was a bit optimistic about the politics), but don't wait in expectation, do the things you can do now and maybe you'll reach LEV: knock smoking and drinking on the head, exercise, eat well, and lose the fat. First published in Analog May 2021.

LONGEVITY AVERAGING

Carlson peered down through the one-way glass of his quadcopter at streets packed with protestors. In the city centre they waved placards and chanted but, further out, the rioting had started and already plumes of smoke rose from burning cars. Probably the lower crowd density there allowed for it, not because those on the outskirts had more inclination. Police were now deploying behind shield walls, stun batons rising and falling, water cannons washing the streets and even a vehicle-mounted inducer heating up the rioters and driving them into retreat. But what was it all about? Almost certainly the latest legislation through Parliament.

'Longevity averaging' was a political hot potato that had the rioters out torching cars and coffee shops where previously they had discussed strategy. Since most protestors were college kids or the jobless youth, 'disenfranchised by increasing automation and artificial intelligence', with just a scattering of older left or right diehards, it all seemed a bit counter-intuitive to Carlson. The concerted cry, 'You're stealing my future!' concerned necessary 'pension averaging' in response to the massive proliferation of biotech companies giving them a future that might not end.

Soon the city slid behind and gazing at the roads below he wondered if he should have taken a ground cab, longevity now his aim. The

Manchester hyperloop and copters like his own and those buzzing over the city behind as if someone had poked that hive with a stick, all reduced the traffic density. But ground cabs were no safer – the reality of the figures dismissed old thinking stirred up by quadcopter crash scare stories. The chances of dying in either mode of transport were about the same. But waiting for a ground cab he did stand a chance of being flensed by a mugger drone or stabbed or acid soaked in a gang attack, especially being so 'spry'.

The copter passed over a small belt of open countryside, the new city sprawling before him. Massive warehouses, skyscrapers, enclave communities and office buildings occupied twenty square miles behind layered security fences patrolled by Darpadogs, stun drones and the private police force employed by the Biotech Alliance. His copter slowed to a halt out from the fences. Had it continued without permission, transmitted viral software would have put it down outside the fence. But he had permission. His phone beeped. He scanned through the legalese of the text message to press 'confirm' and the copter took him in. Soon over the huge circular building of Lancaster Biotech, it descended to one of the circular pads in the surrounding perfectly-manicured parkland.

'Freeland Carlson?' The security guard peered in suspiciously after Carlson pushed open the copter's door. 'If you could step clear of the vehicle please?'

'Give me a minute.' Carlson pulled on a wide-brimmed hat. 'Sarcopenia has its penalties.'

The long stretches of sitting – in the terminal, on the flight up from Stanstead, then in this copter – had left him with that stiffness and lack of impetus all too familiar in recent years. And even though it had been done weeks ago, he still felt sore from the biopsies, blood, lymph and spinal fluid sampling of the Lancaster Biotech telefactor in his doctor's office.

He finally heaved himself up and out, embarrassed by his grunts and pause for breath. He had kept himself as fit as his exercise and health regimen allowed; in fact, at seventy-seven years old, some annoyingly pointed out how he was 'good for his age'. Not as good as the surfers of course… when they failed to evade being identified. The anger stirred up against *them*, and his intention to join them, had informed his choice of a quadcopter, with its one-way glass, to get him here. He did look 'spritely' and that made him a target for the disaffected. Some mistook him for a surfer, others, knowing his wealth and fame, were sure of his intention to become one.

Finally clear of the cab he glanced back at his suitcase, then pointedly towards Logan, who had arrived here earlier. Beside his heavy, muscular bodyguard – as ever filling his suit to breaking point – stood the Chinese woman Chunhua. She wore the white and blue medical uniform of Lancaster, her black hair tied back from facial perfection owed to cosmetic surgery. Before Logan moved, she reached up and tapped a second guard on the shoulder and pointed out the case. He fetched it, while the first guard ran a scanning wand over Carlson from head to foot.

'Your phone,' the man said.

Carlson handed it over, annoyed he had not done so beforehand.

'It is necessary, unfortunately,' said Chunhua. She stepped forward and held out her hand when the scanning completed. 'I'm Chunhua.'

'Spring flower – I know.' He smiled, having researched her. She was one of the Chinese diaspora of highly-trained professionals who had found themselves places in most high-tech industries. 'Nice to meet you and yes, I know it's necessary – too many doctored video clips and edited voice recordings.' He raised an eyebrow, adding, 'They can't decide what angers them. You're either stealing their future by extending the lifespans of the elites, or making false promises.'

'Precisely,' she said. 'Welcome to my world. Let's go in now and get the induction out of the way. Your case will be waiting for you in your apartment.' Her English was of course perfect.

The security guard lugged his case away. They would open it and scan its contents before he got it back. The unending hostility towards this place even extended to a recent rocket attack from the Manchester suburbs, so they had to take precautions. He glanced at Logan, and pointed after the departing suitcase.

'Check my room, then join us unless you have something else to do?'

'They're still checking me out on the protocols,' Logan replied.

'Later, then,' Carlson replied.

Utterly professional, Logan had studied for over a year in preparation for this. Originally trained as a nurse he had been a good choice. His other skills, beside technical security, included black belts in a selection of martial arts resulting in the ability to snap an attacker's spine like a twig.

'Sir.' He nodded smartly and moved off.

'You're safe here, and no one will know you are here,' said Chunhua.

He glanced up at the sky from under his hat brim, then quickly dipped his head again. No drones up there but those this place used, since any media drones got zapped on approach. However, some media rented satellite time and watched when Biotech Alliance did not run interference. Lancaster had assured him no satcams would see his arrival, but he had mistakenly trusted assurances before, hence the hat.

Chunhua led him along a marblecrete path bordered by neatly-pruned roses. He paused to eye a spidery agrobot dead-heading a plant and eating the prunings. Soon they passed through sliding glass doors into a foyer scattered with comfortable chairs from which he knew he would struggle to rise, then through aseptic corridors to small private lounge. Social civilities ensued. He asked for coffee then made for the clearly-marked toilet door. He supposed them accustomed to visitors with weak bladder control. When he returned she gestured him to a sofa that looked manageable, and took the seat opposite. Coffee arrived on a silver tray deposited on a glass-topped table by a female nurse in Lancaster white and blue.

'Do your customers always get such private service?' he enquired.

She shook her head. 'The level of service is congruent with what is being purchased.' She smiled and, noting slight wrinkles beside her eyes, he wondered at her age. She continued, 'We are also thoroughly aware of how publicity, good or bad, affects our business.'

'Ah, I see.'

'You are, to put it bluntly, famous. People listen to you and your opinions. We would be stupid not to take that into account.'

'That people listen to me is hardly warranted. I'm famous for creating the narratives of virtual realities. That doesn't make me an expert in biotech, politics or the sexual peccadillos of the latest media upload star.'

She shrugged. 'We deal with realities.'

'So someone else might receive less personal service?' He couldn't resist the dig.

'Don't get me wrong,' she said. 'I'm here to ensure our service is precisely what it should be. Because of your media status I want everything done correctly. You are not receiving more than anyone else paying for the same procedures as you.'

'And no mistakes?'

She looked uncomfortable. 'There are few mistakes. Usually problems arise when a client has not perfectly understood the risks involved. Then falling afoul of the statistics, and their own biology, they complain loudly to the world.'

He sat back, sipped his coffee. 'So let's get to it then. Tell me about the procedures.'

His apartment consisted of a bedroom, small sitting room and a bathroom. It had a Spartan aspect to it, someway between a hospital and a hotel room. He unpacked his suitcase and hung up his clothes, took a shower and changed into the loose pyjamas and slippers provided. The living room window gave him a view into the central greenhouse of the building. He walked over, peered out into a jungle and thought about the recent meeting. Chunhua had gone through the paperwork again and told him he could have a cooling off period of a week before they began. He had already read the stuff a couple of times, and had his lawyer and an independent longevity doctor look it over, so signed a waiver instead. They could begin at once.

'Why have you chosen this now?' she had asked.

He had been able to afford such therapies since he turned fifty and most people in his league grabbed at the chance. He tried to explain what it had been like being married to a woman struggling with cancer, and who current immunotherapies had failed. Maybe she understood his aversion to 'treatments' to which he had been a spectator. Of course, he had used black market senolytics and crosslink breakers but, when his wife noticed, he felt guilty and left them alone. He tried to explain his malaise, watching someone die, the moment she did, the ensuing lengthy treatments for depression and anxiety, and the way time just seemed to get away from him. Then, one day, with the biotech revolution in full swing, he began to look at the data, and finally accepted that such a choice would not be a betrayal.

A knock at the door pulled his attention away from the jungle. He walked over and opened it to Chunhua and Logan.

'You look like a Bedlam nurse,' he said.

Logan wore hospital whites distinct from the blue and white of Lancaster.

'Bedlam?' the man enquired.

Feeling old, Carlson explained, 'A psychiatric nurse in some old lunatic asylum.'

Logan nodded, and Carlson knew he would be researching that later. He turned to Chunhua.

'How will this be?' he asked, stepping out.

She glanced at him with a raised eyebrow. 'You've already demonstrated that you have more of a grasp on this than most.'

'Humour me.'

She sighed, leading the way down the corridor, then said, 'Mild at first to allow your body to garner strength. The first will be senolytics specifically targeted to destroy senescent cells in your liver, kidneys and closely related organs. We give it a couple of days, run some scans, then, if the response has been good, upgrade to all body senolytic therapy.'

'Makes sense: get the toxin processors up to speed before hitting the rest. How does all-body senolysis relate to longevity averaging?'

'Hardly relevant to you.'

'I know but, nevertheless...'

'You'll lose your pension,' she replied bluntly. 'Pensionable age for a man is now seventy. All body senolysis gives, according to government statistics, an average life extension of fifteen years, thus your pensionable age would increase to eight-five.'

'And the risks?'

'Government figures say the risk of this therapy killing you is between one and ten per cent. The risk of other adverse effects decline below that. I can run through them but you've read the literature. I have to add that the most likely adverse effect is that the therapy will not be optimum – that your average lifespan will not increase by fifteen years but less than that. The percentage of those who come for treatment, for whom it is not optimal in this respect, is twelve.'

'Government figures,' he said. 'Inclusive of unrelated maladies in the elderly.'

'Yes.'

'And your own?'

'I am not at liberty to tell you them.'

He smiled, letting it go. 'I guess this all might be a bit mystifying for those whose grasp of mathematics is, shall we say, slippery?'

'Tell me about it.' She frowned.

She led him into a room with 'HAL1' stencilled on the door. Inside, everything gleamed, but most specifically the robot poised over the back of a surgical chair like a mechanical octopus. He eyed hands with an excess of fingers and other implements. The thing opened out two of its limbs to permit access to the chair and a head, loaded with sensors, tilted towards him.

'The personal touch?' he enquired.

'This is better – no mistakes at all.'

'This is for the socket shunts?'

'It is.'

He walked over and sat back in the chair, arms along the rests. The robot hesitated for a second, then reached down, pulled up his sleeve and firmly gripped his right forearm. Other hands moved in – shifting manipulators concealing his arm. Gas hissed and numbed him, he felt pressure, then even that faded. Something cracked like a nail gun, and when the robot hands moved away they left a square of plastic on his arm with a circular socket at its centre. He raised that arm and inspected it, even as the robot went to work on his other one. A moment later he climbed out of the chair.

'Prep for Smyth's thymus biopsy,' Chunhua said to Logan.

'More training?' Carlson enquired.

Logan nodded. 'I might as well learn what I can while I'm here.'

Carlson accepted that, but wondered if his bodyguard was in the process of being poached. He did have medical qualifications, but his other skill set might be useful to a biotech alliance increasingly under siege. Carlson grimaced, making a mental note to look at the man's salary. Chunhua led him out as Logan headed over to the robot.

'It's a shame that people like you now need people like him,' she opined as they walked down the corridor.

'It's getting worse,' Carlson replied. 'Even median and low earners are having their problems now and they can't afford Logans.'

She said no more but obviously knew about his recent problems. Being driven about in a limousine made you as much a target as apparently 'undeserved' youthfulness. He had stubbornly wanted to continue using a limo after the rioters torched his first, but his advisors, like Logan, said that was high risk now and advised he vary his transport.

First-world problems, he thought, and grimaced.

As he stepped through the next door he felt a surge of anxiety nothing to do with the madness beyond the fences here, but in reaction to the room's layout. Comfortable chairs stood in a row along one wall with complex drip feeds and monitors beside each. Open frames scattered across a screen painted wall opposite showed preferred entertainment for each patient. A man, apparently of about fifty, if it were possible to judge such things in this place, occupied one of them. Having chosen another entertainment, he wore virtual glasses while doing something frenetic on a touchpad. The other occupant, a positively ancient looking woman, grinned at Carlson crazily then returned her attention to the screen wall. Both had drip feeds running into their arms from collections of glass cylinders of variously coloured liquids, while the woman also had tubes up her nose. Chunhua glanced at him and immediately knew something was wrong.

'We can always set you up in your apartment if that is preferable,' she said.

'No, that's okay.' He grimaced. 'It'll make a change to be the recipient in a place like this rather than the spectator.'

'Oh, of course, your wife.'

'Years of treatments. As much delaying the inevitable as this. Where do I sit?'

'Wherever you like.' She gestured to the row of seats.

He considered sitting off alone, but then changed his mind and took the seat next to the woman. Chunhua set about sticking on monitoring electrodes, sampling patches and a device like a small chrome beetle that sat over his heart.

'Inevitable is not as inevitable as one would suppose,' she said. 'It is conjectured that we hit LEV three years ago... at least for some people.'

The woman in the seat beside him looked around sharply. 'LEV?' she asked.

'Longevity escape velocity,' Carlson replied, surprised that someone here did not know the acronym. 'That point when life span is increasing at the same rate as time is passing.'

'Yes, of course.' Obviously annoyed she leaned forwards pointing a finger first at the tubes in her nostrils then at further tubes plugged into sockets in the back of her neck and down her spine. 'Plaques,' she explained. 'They're dissolving but my memory's a bit hit or miss.'

Carlson stared in fascination. He hadn't done much research on the new treatments for Alzheimer's, but had read enough to recognise a cerebro wash. Tailored bacteria with CRISPR scissors were breaking up the plaques in her brain while a fluid containing these and what could only be described as a surfactant, were washing out the debris to be drained out through the cribriform bone in her nasal passages and her glymphatic vessels. If she was sensible, and had the funding, she would use other available treatments to prevent her from getting to this pass again. Perhaps she could only afford this.

Chunhua next plugged tubes into his arms. Into his right went a fluid the colour of emerald – the precise colour of the bile he had become so familiar with over the years of his wife's treatments. The other tube ran something translucent laced with microscopic glitter. Now it begins, he thought, now the clock begins to wind backwards.

'It should take two hours.' She gestured to a trolley beside his chair, on which rested virtual glasses, touchpad, a remote for the screen wall and ear plugs. 'You can summon an attendant with the remote should you need the toilet or any food and drink. I'll come back when you're done.'

The sensation was not unfamiliar. A hot flush arose as from anxiety, and with his pulse thumping in his head he responded with meditation and positive mantras. Was he actually experiencing anxiety or panic attacks? Such had been their variety in the past he couldn't tell. Work pressures and stress could induce them, as could too much exercise without rest, and fasting. He also remembered experiencing similar symptoms while mega-dosing on fisetin decades ago. The present senolytics could feasibly cause the same.

After an hour the worst passed. A low grade nausea ensued during which he called the attendant to unplug him so he could head to the toilet. He didn't vomit, but was glad of the toilet brush after the explosive diarrhoea. In the second hour, while he watched news of riots in many UK cities, the woman poked his arm. He took his ear plugs out.

'You're Freeman Carlson,' she said.

'I am.'

'The fuckers don't like you.' She stabbed a finger at the screen frame he had been watching. 'They're not bright enough to know what to do with all their free time. Come post scarcity.' She waved a hand in the air. 'We'll be fucked.'

She wasn't exactly eloquent but had a point. Automation had killed just about every factory job, mobile robots making inroads into manual jobs outside of the factories, while AIs cut into the professional classes. When he visited his personal doctor now it stuck monitors, samplers and scanners on him, asked him his problems and listened intently. It then made its diagnosis and delivered instructions, a prescription or a referral. Perhaps to its brother in that room marked 'HAL1'. It tended to be more attentive, precise and plain right than the human doctor he had long ago attended. That bored young man limited personal interaction to a hello when Carlson came through the door. Thereafter he seemed more intent on his tablet, and deaf to much of what Carlson said. And recently, during his last property purchase, his solicitor had been a chunk of hardware among twenty in a small office in the high street, plugged into printers and the internet. The one human working there kept the place clean and posted letters to those in archaic need of them.

Supposedly, all this bright new technology would provide new opportunities for employment, just like the IT boom at the end of the twentieth century. But the need for professionals could not be met because of a lack of intensive education and, frankly, intelligence. So the AIs took up the slack, leaving millions unemployed and unemployable. The most secure jobs were ones like his own: creative, and to a large extent predicated on social notoriety.

'Boredom is a problem,' he opined.

'Only if you're stupid,' the woman replied. 'They've got everything they need but for something to occupy their tiny minds.'

He nodded. Nobody was in need any more but everyone was in *want*. The welfare state covered the former, but couldn't do anything much about the latter. The disaffected received their welfare and, since the building boom of the 30s, nobody need be without a home, albeit state-owned. Taxes paid by employed individuals and industries were of course huge, but only those individuals were objecting. Industry leaders had fallen quiet because of plain economics. Simply put: if no one worked in your factories, and in fact fewer people had any kind of work year on year, who bought your goods? Welfare had transformed from safety net to a necessity to prevent economic collapse.

'You are wrong, you know,' he said.

She peered at him warily.

He gestured to the screen, now showing protestors sat on a runway at Gatwick Airport. 'They do find things to occupy their minds.'

She snorted and turned away.

Chunhua arrived later, with Logan in tow pushing a wheelchair.

'Is that necessary?' he asked.

'We will see, won't we?' she replied knowingly.

They stripped the paraphernalia from his body and unplugged the tubes, both now clear. When he tried to move he discovered that yes, he needed the chair. They pushed him back to his apartment where Logan helped him to a sitting position on the edge of his bed. He felt he had aged to a hundred rather than downwards from seventy-seven. Chunhua pointed to the beetle thing still on his chest, over his heart.

'I'll leave that on,' she said. 'It keeps a very close watch on your heart and the rest of your vascular system.' She pointed to the ceiling. 'Other monitors up there will detect if you are in distress, otherwise use the call button above your bed or simply say the word "help". Logan will be at the watch station and ready to respond. You'll need to sleep now.'

As waves of weariness rose up from his feet to pass through his body, he looked at the bedside clock. Seven in the evening was five hours before his usual bedtime and ensuing sleep of five hours, though he could see it as one of his numerous nap times. He nodded mutely. Logan helped him into bed and under the covers. Then he remembered no more.

Carlson woke and damned insomnia as he peered at the 10.30 on the clock. He felt thoroughly dopy, as if he had loaded up on Sominex or poured into a human-shaped mould in the bed and set there. Annoyingly someone had left the lights on in his small sitting room, but he felt too tired to get up and do anything about that. He drifted off, woke to a stentorian snore, drifted off again, woke again with a sore throat that told him he'd been snoring like an engine. The clock said 1.30 and he knew he wouldn't get any more sleep – had in fact slept longer than usual. He pushed the covers back and blearily swung his legs over the side of the bed. Like a hotel the apartment had the makings for coffee and he'd start with that. He stood, feeling weak and shaky, headed over and opened the door into the living room, and just stood staring dumbly.

Light beamed in from the greenhouse – the automatic blinds having opened. He walked over to the window and looked up towards the glass ceiling and could see the sun glaring in. Heading over to the screen he checked the time: 1.40PM. He had slept for fifteen and a half hours. He couldn't remember ever sleeping for so long. The shock now woke him to urgent signals from his body. Grabbing up a glass he headed into the bathroom. He filled it and gulped – plain water tasting wonderful. His urine came out the colour of strong tea and he felt like a tapped barrel. It went on and on interminably until he finally consciously stopped, because waiting a moment always produced more. Two more glasses of water went down. In the living room he set the coffee maker running, then returned for another endless session of urination. He showered, dressed and drank coffee and more water, then began to get ravenously hungry, but with such bladder activity he feared leaving the room. Briefly he considered ordering in food, but then inspected the map of the facility on his screen. After one more lengthy session in the toilet – the colour of his urine darker now if anything – he set out.

After a huge meal he felt sure would give him indigestion, but didn't, he headed back with familiar waves of weariness traversing his body. Sleep over the years having become a precious thing, he slumped on the sofa and closed his eyes. With seemingly no transition, he surfaced out of lurid nightmares of aliens chasing him through a jungle, and knew that owed more to his profession than to the scene outside the window. Leaden again, he heaved himself up and inevitably straight to the toilet. His urine dark as coffee now, he drank four glasses of water in quick succession afterwards. The time was 8.05PM and he feared the prospect of a sleepless night. He took a walk, grateful for toilets everywhere inside the facility. Darkness encroached by the time he had his bladder enough under control to do a circuit outside – after he fetched his hat. Upon his return inside he ate again, hugely again, and weariness pummelled him. His bed beckoned again before his usual time and he slept for ten hours.

Days of senolysis ensued – the treatment divided up because of his age. Two days passed much the same as the first, though with the addition of bowel movements crapping out a seeming lifetime of meals, rather than those of previous days. He slept a minimum of nine hours each night and, on the day after his last treatment, enjoyed a huge fried breakfast when Chunhua found him.

'How are you feeling?' She sat down opposite, placing a tray with a teapot and cup on the table.

'Like a small stream was diverted through me. Like the world it trying to fall out of my bottom,' he replied.

She gave a moue of distaste and poured tea. 'That's all good. The urination is your body clearing detritus and the other is due to improvements in your liver and bile system. The destruction of senescent cells there will have killed off much of the SASP.'

'Senescence associated secretory phenotype,' he said.

'We'll run further tests a little later.' She checked her watch. 'Logan will come for you at about ten?'

'Okay.' He focused on his breakfast, intent on finishing the black pudding since he was damned sure his body needed it.

They weighed him and despite all the food and literal gallons of fluids he had consumed, he had dropped five pounds. No wonder he felt light on his feet. They took samples and scanned him before sending him on his way again. 'As expected,' said Chunhua, later contacting him via his screen. Twenty minutes later he sat in the treatment room by a bald-headed and heavily-muscular man, who was reading an actual paper book.

'And the senolytics this time?' he enquired, while Logan plugged him in again.

'Everything else,' Chunhua replied.

He sat back as the fluids ran into his arms.

'First time?' the bald-headed man enquired after she headed away.

He nodded. His body seemed to be on fire.

'Third time for me,' said the man. 'Also a bit of fat conversion, white to brown. I still put the on weight if I'm not careful.'

'This time?'

'Yeah. First time was before they even built this place.'

Carlson stared at him, beginning to note the light scarring from nose and ear reduction, because as people aged their gristle kept growing, the thick finger joints, and other subtle signs. The man wore an expression of mild interest and wariness, and Carlson recognised the long confidence of one who had seen and survived much, and perhaps grown wise. He realised he was sitting with a surfer.

'If you don't mind me asking... how old?'

The man smiled amenably. 'My birthday tomorrow – I'll be a hundred and six.'

Judging by his muscles, that sounded like the number of kilos he could bench press. Even though various longevity therapies had been around for some time now, surfers of his age were rare. Many had not survived the illnesses the therapies had failed to account for. Meanwhile, the bulk of the population had been wary of the treatments, unable to afford them or unable to get to the countries that allowed them. Surfers also tended to keep their heads down, especially those in the media, like Carlson himself. He thought then of the thousand or so questions he wanted to ask a person like this.

'Have you plasticised?' he asked. The aged brain got set in its ways, but it was now possible to return to it, for however long might be required, the plasticity of youth.

'Four years ago when I started studying genetics,' the man replied. 'I won't do it again until some form of mental backup becomes available.'

'Why? Didn't it work?'

'It worked, I completed my Master's thesis, and I'm now working for Alvaron Biotech.' He shrugged. 'Everything seemed okay until I took a look at some old photo files and video clips. Only then did I discover, after much research, that I had forgotten I had a brother.'

'Ah, I see. The brain makes its new connections but dispenses with some others.'

'Exactly.'

He couldn't continue the conversation because the attendant arrived to unplug him. This time he understood why the basin sat so close to the toilet, as his body voided from both ends. Blood in both was apparently usual. The anti-emetics killed the vomiting, but the toilet visits became constant. Later, when a whole-body ache kicked in, the attendant offered unconsciousness. He refused until someone invisible began driving a screwdriver into his skull. The attendant gave him a nappy, then an injection into one of the feed lines. Unconsciousness slipped over him like a shroud. It felt like dying.

Carlson stepped off the cross-trainer thoroughly satisfied. A difficult two weeks had entailed bed rest for two days on a drip feed, a day when he had to go everywhere with a back pack feeding more fluids into his shunts, along with a regimen of pills and potions to stabilise his gut –

some containing dried-out faecal matter. Apparently his reaction was not common, but they knew how to respond. The all-body senolysis had worked too well and too fast. His body had struggled to process the waste.

'What next?' he asked, as Chunhua, standing off to one side, checked her tablet. He felt stupidly full of energy and knew it wasn't due to the latest drop in his weight of a further five pounds. He actually had a waist now and the clothing he had brought no longer fitted. But the complex provided shops precisely for this advent.

'Glycation and crosslinks – the reason for wrinkles and sagging skin,' she replied, distractedly checking her tablet. 'What too many people seem not to be aware of is that this outside appearance is also on the inside.'

'So you break the crosslinks and get rid of the AGEs?'

'Yes.' She now paid attention and eyed him carefully.

'Another twenty years added to pensionable age.'

'Quite.'

'Why would anyone care?'

'They wouldn't care because of how good they would feel, and as you feel now?'

'Damned right.'

'I would be wary of that if I were you. You've lost weight which of course has its positive effects. We've also noted that at such a juncture as this, especially after treatment so harsh, a large placebo effect can kick in.'

'You're saying it's not real?'

'No, I'm not saying that. I'm saying that you have improved markedly but this drives a kind of euphoria. You feel too good. You feel superhuman when in reality you are only human. You have returned to a physical age arguably in your forties, but in only some respects.'

'The no longer hitting myself on the head with a hammer effect?'

'You could say that. You are due a break now of a month before we recommence. Don't push yourself too hard. Remember some systems in your body are still… old. You do not want to break them.'

He cooled a little, though could not help feeling good. 'Yeah, I understand. It's like having an old car. You replace some components with new and because they work better they put pressure on others you haven't renewed. The new carburettor provides more power and knocks out the worn out big ends.'

She looked askance at him. 'Surely you're not that old?'

'Bloody cheek. I had a classic Mark IV Cortina.'

She burst into a cackling laugh and then headed away.

The wreckage extended from the ground floor all the way to the top. They wouldn't have got into his apartment if it hadn't been for the police. When building security and members of his own staff stepped in to drive the rioters out, the police had arrested them and not the rioters, and so the property damage had continued. His staff, as per his instructions, had not contacted him. When the rioters finally tired of vandalism and left with their loot, his people called in the cleaners. Now his apartment seemed more Spartan than his one at the facility. Sprawling on his new sofa he ran a search and soon saw that yes, this building had been targeted because of him. The video, obviously taken with one of the new HD meta-lenses, only caught glimpses of his face, but enough to give 70% facial recognition. But the presence of his bodyguard, fully identified, confirmed his presence at Lancaster Biotech. Stupid mistake to make.

Protests and riots continued. The health minister had recently announced that Senolytics would be available on the NHS for age-related conditions in the over sixties. The usual crowd protested this further theft of their future, but new protestors demanded to know about the necessity for a 'condition'. Why did people have to wait until they were ill before receiving treatment? The demographic of these new protestors being silver-haired their efforts were not hugely energetic.

On his return to the clinic he brought little but himself and one change of clothes. This time, should he need anything else, he intended to use the shops in the facility. He climbed easily out of the quadcopter and, after the security checks, turned to Chunhua.

'Is this usual?' He pointed at his head.

Chunhua peered at the darkening roots of his hair and shrugged. 'Some regain their previous hair colour.'

'What about baldness?' He reached up and patted hair that had receded forty years ago and thinned ever since.

'No, you won't start growing a full head of hair unless you take a separate treatment.' She led the way back to the facility. 'Is there anything else you neglected to mention in your updates?'

'Well there is something.' He felt stupidly embarrassed. 'Erm... morning wood.'

'I beg your pardon?'

'You don't know the expression?'

'Oh, oh yes – I have heard it before. Generally the morning erections are more noticeable after your next treatment. Your hormonal balance is returning to youthfulness, but it's usually the cross-link breaking that enhances vascularisation to that extent.' She glanced at him, almost smirking. 'Anything else?'

'Nothing else I didn't report.'

She settled him in the same room as before whereupon, a little while later, Logan came to fetch him.

'I heard about your apartment,' said Logan.

'Covered by insurance,' Carlson replied. 'It should be – the amount I have to pay now.'

'You should stay here until your treatments are finished. Their security is the best.'

'I'll consider it.' Carlson resented how his fame steadily locked him in a gilded cage. But as he walked, feeling energetic and thoroughly awake, he realised he had lost perspective. He now had a very good chance to live to a time when riots and the resentment would be just memory. He guessed he *was* one of the privileged.

Logan installed him in the treatment room, unblocked the shunts he had continued to wear since leaving, then plugged in the tubes. Chunhua turned up a little while later to pull up a chair.

'Are you feeling anything yet?'

'Hot anxiety again. Nauseated and tired,' he replied.

'This ablation and removal of damage is itself a form of damage your body needs to heal from. As such it is little different from some of the treatments used to renew skin in the past. Again you will feel quite rough and need nutrition and rest. However, over the next few days, the changes will be quite marked.'

He needed the wheelchair again for his trip back to his room. This time sleep evaded him because he kept waking to the thump of his heart and an all-over soreness that seemed to penetrate right to his bones. The next day he dragged himself to the restaurant and struggled through a small meal. A glance in the mirror upon his return worried him. He suddenly looked incredibly old, the crevices deep in a face that seemed to hang off his skull. He slept through most of the day, waking in the evening to increased soreness. His fingers were like sausages and his arms seemed thicker too. Incredibly thirsty again, he headed into the wash room and filled a glass four times. In the mirror his face now looked puffy, bloated and blotched with red. Should he report this? No, he just felt too enervated to bother and went back to bed.

Late morning on the next day he woke with his throat raw and a fever kicking in. He sneezed again and again and his nose began running. After his shower a dry cough and a deep earache joined these symptoms.

'I think I've got a cold,' he told the screen.

A moment later Logan appeared there.

'I'll come with medication and anything else you might require, but please do not leave your room,' he said.

'Infection control?'

'Yes. There are many vulnerable people here.'

'I'm the one you should be concerned about.' He felt like a child having a tantrum, so added, 'Sorry, that was uncalled for.'

Clad in a transparent polythene hazmat suit, Logan arrived pushing a trolley on which lay a selection of cold medications and a jug of fresh orange. The man checked Carlson over, put a chrome beetle on his chest, then unwrapped a drug patch. Carlson recognised a new antiviral and source of ire for some protestors, since deemed too expensive for general prescription.

'Stay in bed as much as you can – we'll pick up any problems on the scanners.' He pointed at the ceiling. 'Use the lozenges, drink the juice and call if you need anything else.'

Carlson noted the use of 'we'. As suspected he was losing Logan but understood why. The Biotech Alliance was the biggest thing happening in the world at the moment. Logan could have a potentially endless future here, whereas the alternative was the personal protection of a virtuality impresario who, quite likely, would soon head off to a protected enclave.

'No aspirin?' Carlson enquired – a weak attempt at a joke.

Logan took that seriously. 'Only if you want internal bleeding, which you'll get after cross-link therapy.'

Whether the antiviral worked he could not judge. He felt rough throughout the night and the next day, emptied a box of tissues and didn't really want to do more than lie in bed. The following night it seemed to be dying off but he could not sleep. As daylight penetrated the greenhouse, he sat fully dressed on his sofa, watching a serial documentary on longevity. Noting the tone of doom and general abhorrence, he wryly remembered that the presenter had visited this very clinic. Finally, at five in the morning, he called up the menu and ordered the biggest fried breakfast he could find. Then he scrubbed at his hair and face to try and wake himself up and stared in amazement at the blizzard of dandruff this released.

In the mirror he noted big flakes of dead skin in his hair and more on his face as if healing up from sunburn. He found himself scratching at his hand then saw dead skin there too. Pulling up his sleeves released another small snow storm. He kept scrubbing at one arm until he stripped away the worst of it and felt a surge of joy at what this revealed. Fine wrinkles had all but disappeared. He turned the arm over and inspected a keratinous scar on his elbow he'd had for years. It looked bigger than before and red all around. He picked at it, lifting up the edge, then pulled. The thing came out in one lump leaving clean skin underneath.

'Two more days,' Chunhua told him from the screen. 'Then you go straight in for the next treatment. Your cold, which the antiviral has dealt with, is only an illustration of the dangers you face. The previous treatments have put a strain on your already compromised immune system.'

'My thymus,' he said.

'Yes, the thymus degrades almost from the beginning as you age, essentially turning to fat.' She watched him as she spoke and he nodded. 'From our initial biopsy of it we have grown thymic organelles, their cells reverse-engineered to an earlier state. After clearing out the fat we implant those. When they have vascularised your immune system will return, some have estimated, to the state of a twenty-year-old.'

'But there are dangers...'

'If you have an auto-immune disease it will return to its previous strength. It is also the case that the regeneration process can cause such diseases. The statistics tell us —'

'No need,' he interrupted. 'I know the figures. But tell me about averaging again.'

'No,' she said. 'First you need to know that we do not confine ourselves to thymic regeneration, as do some other concerns. Because of the dangers of autoimmune disease, thymic regeneration is conducted concurrent with full immune reset.'

'Basically killing every immune cell in the body – programming the buggers back to a blank slate?'

She nodded. 'Targeted cell killers identify the gene expression patterns of immune cells. Suicide gene therapy. Hematopoietic stem cell revision.' She paused. 'I see that I'm not telling you anything you don't know.'

'Generally not,' he agreed. '

'Then you'll know that illness and the symptoms of the same will be your companions for a while. Immune reset means you will not have the resistance to diseases you had before. Broad spectrum inoculation will deal with the worst of course, but there will be those you'll have to gain resistance to the old fashioned way.'

She wasn't kidding.

After anesthetising the spot, the robot injected a thick segmented needle just above his breastbone, angling it downwards. Keeping still and fighting the need to keep swallowing, he glanced over at the screen Chunhua watched, and saw the needle moving like a worm inside him, inside his thymus – guided liposuction to extract the fat. A short while later it extracted the needle, folding it into its 'hand' then turned out another needle and injected again.

'These are vesicles containing substances to inhibit fat growth, or rather conversion, and to prepare the thymus for the later implant of the organelles,' she explained. 'But now we must clear out the old throughout.'

Knowing his history, she kindly did not say they were about to fill him with immune cell killers – they'd tried that on his wife. A short while later he found himself in one of those chairs again with tubes plugged into his arms. This time he saw no liquids but his own as blood departed from one arm and then, a short while later, entered the other. Apparently, as well as the chemo drugs being added, the blood went through a meta-material filter to take out immune cells in his blood.

'It's not so severe as it once was,' she told him. 'Much more targeted and specific.'

Later he replayed the words as he shit away his insides in a toilet and vomited in the basin. This time he walked back to his room, but felt worse than he had when he needed a wheelchair. He didn't want to eat or drink, but sipped water anyway to give himself something to throw up the next time the nausea hit. His body felt battered, and he knew he wasn't thinking straight. He noticed an antiseptic smell in the room and heard the steady thrum of air conditioning. Later, he noticed the strange light quality, and spotted ultraviolet bulbs glowing in the ceiling. Hour after hour slid by like toxic snails. He had been told not to leave his room and to order in anything he needed. He felt incapable of climbing out of the sofa, let alone leaving, and only the danger of shitting himself or throwing up on the upholstery compelled from it. Finally he slept, utterly dead to the world, then woke to an aching body and sore neck when the door opened.

Logan arrived in a Hazmat suit, even with its own air supply. He helped Carlson into similar gear but with access hatches to his shunts and another over the top of his breastbone. Again the wheelchair – probably to stop him stumbling into something and tearing the suit, but he was grateful for it. Logan brought him to the robot again where Chunhua waited. She didn't even ask him how he was, just nodded an acknowledgement and set to work. He guessed she had no need to ask.

Tubes went into his shunts and again his blood headed out and then back in again. His mind still foggy he couldn't remember why, nor did he feel any inclination to ask. She opened the hatch over his breastbone and swabbed the area. Why she did this and not the robot he didn't know. A segmented needle went in and he just did not have the energy to cough or swallow, then... nothing.

Carlson woke up in his bed, burning hot, and sore through and through. Enough coherent thought returned for him to recognise the result of multiple inoculations this time round, along with the extra immune cells they had generated from the thymic organelles prior to implanting them. He felt as sick as he had felt some years ago when suffering a dose of the latest flu. But a deep depressive hollowness also opened inside him. What was the point of all this? If he died that would be it and he would know nothing. Was it really worth all this suffering to cling onto life?

He now remembered old depression and the way he had dealt with it. He tried to meditate, but could not concentrate on his breathing because his lungs felt raw. Repeating positive mantras helped, but exercise, which he had always used before, was impossible. He stuck it for some hours then made a screen call that Logan answered.

'I need something.' He hated the admission. 'My mood is low,' he added, avoiding the 'D' word.

Logan arrived with two containers of powder and Carlson stared at them. The man mixed them into a glass of orange juice and handed it to him.

'What the hell is this?' he asked.

'Phenibut and sulbutiamine with a lipid dispersal agent.'

'You're kidding.'

'They will do the job, though you'll need to gradually withdraw from them later. We can't use any of the other drugs because they'll interfere with your later stem cell treatments and cerebral balancing.'

He gulped the stuff down and sat back. When Logan departed he started in on the positive mantras, searching for the good things in his life. The powders did their work and he started to accept the words: he was rich, talented, hard-working and, damn it, he had a chance at living well beyond the span of most mortals. Finally he got the impetus to do more than lie on the sofa and accessed media through the screen. A report on protestors who had set up camp a legal distance outside the facility threatened depression again, so he didn't watch it and looked elsewhere.

The rioting was practically non-existent now and he stared at the screen in puzzlement. The media were selling the narrative of this being due to the introduction of a 'living wage' – which scanned so much better than 'welfare'. But no, he saw the crash in rebellious fervour had occurred directly after a change of policy on senolytics. Anyone could have them above the age of forty now. On top of that the government mooted making cross-link therapy and thymic regeneration available too. These changes must have impinged even on those who thought their future being stolen. Reading between the lines he saw the policy change was due, from initial figures, to an expected massive downturn in those requiring treatment for chronic conditions and a consequent explosion in available funding. It seemed those in power were realising that treating cause of the diseases of aging, rather than their symptoms, might be worthwhile after all. Within a few hours of watching this he felt mentally a lot better, and he knew that wasn't just due to the Nootropics Logan had given him.

That day passed, then another. Logan came in to give him further inoculations and he spent the remainder of the week feeling like hell. That passed and Chunhua allowed him to leave his room. He exercised, and instead of that resulting in the usual pain and exhaustion, found himself euphoric. However, a few days of that obviously exposed him to something he had not been immunised against and he ended up with rashes all over his body and a dry cough. They never identified that malady, though they did nail down the leaking spots he acquired a few days later as a new form of chicken pox. Day after day passed and none of them without skin eruptions and aches and pains, yet they seemed a layer over an ever improving core. He spent his time watching the screen; watching the world outside change.

Good news continued: the presenters were dealing with a new paradigm in which they had to look for news other than the latest riot. Struggling to find their preference for bad news, they had to seriously twist their narratives to accomplish that. Some media presenters, however – usually the independents who had risen out of the morass of social media over previous decades – had accepted defeat and now told positive stories. For the first time ever he heard admission of the drop in world population. He saw graphs also depicting poverty rates and, even with the political adjustments for 'relative poverty', they were plummeting.

One long presentation attempted to get back to the narrative of gloom. This concerned the continuing failure of ITER to produce fusion energy, but then fell flat at the end with a piece concerning the new laser-boron and steampunk General Fusion plants in the US and China. They were online and producing power at ridiculously small costs. The much-ignored space programme even got a look in. The underground moon base was doing fine, while the manned mission to Mars out of its stall and back on the agenda. Carlson smiled at the surprise this must be to those for decades fed a diet of doom and misery.

'You're doing very well,' Chunhua told him. 'It's time for the stem cell treatments and OSKM.'

He glanced at her but kept hammering at the treadmill. She walked round to stand in front of him. He slowed, inordinately pleased to have enough breath to speak. 'OSKM – reprogramming the four master genes to take my cells back to a youthful state. As much as I read of your literature, I don't understand the necessity for stem cells now... with that.'

'OSKM tends not to be long-lasting. The reprogrammed stem cells we'll put back into you work synergetically with it.' She grimaced. 'It is of course more complicated than that, but that is an explanation that will have to do.'

'It will do – I gave up on the lengthier explanation.' He slowed further. 'And this is one of the highest risk treatments?'

'It is. Government figures give a twelve per cent chance of it killing you. A twenty-three per cent chance of cancer and a near fifty per cent chance of some autoimmune disorder.' She spoke without expression.

'Figures you must by law ensure I understand?'

'Yes.'

'But of course government figures are what the government previously used to delay the clinical application of such therapies because of cost. The figures are cumulative, mangled and incorporate the statistics over the last twenty years. They do not reflect the reality now.'

She shrugged. 'You know that I cannot by law, at present, give you our own figures. We are hopeful this may change sometime soon.' She paused for a second and looked down at her tablet. 'Logan will come for you in your room in an hour.' She headed away.

At present, he thought. Political manoeuvring had been much in the news too. He hadn't been able to get a read on it but felt sure the recent health policy changes had been driven by the Biotech Alliance. They had money and influence and their power was growing.

Carlson picked up his towel and wiped off sweat, watching her depart. He had never been a great lover of corporatism. Through legislation it tended to protect big and powerful but inefficient industries from competition. But the growing reach of the Biotech Alliance he could only see as a good thing. Sure they were out to make money, but they wanted less legislation and more personal choice. Change certainly was coming.

With Logan at his side Carlson walked to a part of the complex he did not know. Logan seemed pre-occupied as he brought him down to the double doors of a clean lock leading into a surgical theatre. Carlson peered inside at a surgical table almost concealed by equipment, including HAL1's big brother.

'You're trying to figure out the best way to tell me,' he said, and looked round at the man.

Logan frowned. 'I've been with you for a long time.'

'Just tell me.'

'I want to quit my job with you. I'm sorry but...' He gestured about himself to encompass the facility.

'But the opportunities here for someone like you, with your training, are self-evident.' He smiled. Who, given the chance, would not want to be on the fast train to the future? 'You have two months on your contract. I've written a letter of recommendation that cancels them and have forwarded it to your house AI.'

'There's no hurry.'

Carlson pointed a finger into the room beyond. 'The cancellation may not be necessary, since I might not survive what comes next. But I at least wanted the recommendation letter in place.'

'Thank you.'

Carlson patted him on the shoulder and pushed through the doors.

In the clean lock he stripped naked, pushing his paper overall into a disposal hatch. Closing his eyes and holding his arms out as instructed, he stood in vapour sprays and intense UV light. His skin prickled and in some places felt sore. He then pulled on the shorts provided and went through the next door.

'Freeman Carlson,' said Chunhua. 'Let me introduce my team.'

He studied the four others in their hazmat suits, exchanged pleasantries as they directed him to the table, and knew he would not remember their names. He lay back with tubes going into his arms, electrodes and needle patches bonding to his skin.

'See you on the other side,' said Chunhua, which were the last words he heard.

He remembered waking a couple of times. He remembered Logan's worried expression and Chunhua speaking, but no words. The experience had the slow-motion nightmare quality of a car wreck, only all bright chrome, glaring lights and aseptic white. Full consciousness at first had the quality of dream. He looked at the tubes and the monitors, at the chest bruises where they restarted his heart, and it all seemed hellishly amusing from the comfortable and highly stoned place he occupied.

'You're back with us.' Logan sat in a chair beside the bed.

It slowly impinged that the medical equipment marking out the processes of his life surrounded his bed in his Lancaster apartment. He noted an excess of tubes plugged into further shunts in his chest, belly and further down. Reaching up he touched his shaven head and found others in the back of his neck.

'I'm… alive, then,' he rasped.

Logan handed him a drink with a straw and he sucked thirstily, thawing the ceramic of his mouth. Afterwards he dozed, woken briefly by Logan removing some of the tubes, then dozed again. The next time he woke the drugs wearing off allowed his body to tell him something had happened. Discomfort came first, then soreness but none of the actual pain he expected. He felt odd – fizzing from head to foot. Logan kept feeding him the drinks and only when his bladder filled to bursting did he relent and use the catheter. He noted the container at the side of his bed half full of strong tea again. When the tubes came out of his nose Logan brought solid food. He ate it all and wanted more, but that wasn't allowed. A day passed, and then another, the number of tubes plugged into him steadily declining and some of the equipment going away.

'It went very well,' Chunhua told him.

'Apart from the bit about me dying?' he enquired, because Logan had told him about the robot massaging his heart and the paddles on his chest that left those bruises. And about how they chilled him down in a tank of icy gel to finish some procedures.

'Define death,' she said.

In the ensuing week he really hated the bed pan and, finally, when he took out the last tube, Logan allowed him to use the toilet, his body laden with wifi monitoring devices and needle patches. These too gradually spirited away and, by and by, he began wearing items of clothing. Energy returned and the need to do something. His first session in the gym left him exhausted and he slept like a corpse for two hours. But he felt ready to go again that afternoon, though Logan dismissed the idea.

'You're particularly attentive,' he said at one point, when no more medical equipment cluttered the apartment.

'Seeing things through to their conclusion,' Logan replied.

He opened up the screen after Logan departed and watched the news from various media sources. The government had made cross-link and thymus treatments available to all and in a by election Parliament had acquired three MPs who also worked for Biotech Alliance. Some die hard protesters ventured out again but, judging by their signs, were confused about what to object to. He later studied a drone view of all that remained of the protest camp outside this facility – strewn rubbish and single abandoned tent.

'Chunhua wants to see you,' Logan later informed him.

Carrying his own suitcase, because he could now do so with ease, he found her in her office, busily working at a computer screen. She looked up and gestured to the seat in front of her desk. He sat, noting the changed power dynamic in the room now with the desk separating them.

'Today marks the end of your present treatments,' she told him. 'You have had the full gamut of what we have available and your payments have been received, with thanks.'

'I am happy to have made them.'

'Do you have any further questions about your treatments?'

'The averaging, what is it at now?' he asked.

'I find your interest in how your state pension is affected quite curious, Mr Carlson.' She seemed quite amused.

'It's a reference point for me.'

She shrugged, then steepled her fingers. 'Well, I can pretend to be unhappy about this but I am not: you no longer have a reference point. Each treatment puts on a decade here or there, but their cumulative effect is still open to debate in Parliament, while the effect of the stem cell and OSKM regeneration has not, and cannot, be measured. Under new legislation your pension has been deferred indefinitely. They are presently trying to determine if the markers of biological age can be used in that respect.'

The answer to the perennial question, 'How long have I got' in his case, now seemed to be, 'Maybe forever'.

'Are you satisfied with your treatments?' she enquired – back to the rote questions on the company script.

He thought about the toilets he no longer visited and the grunts he no longer made when standing up. His joints no longer ached and his skin no longer hung like over-stretched linen, delicate and wrinkled. He thought about his times on the cross-trainer and the deep ache from lifting weights that swiftly departed, and the euphoria of exercise he now experienced, every time. He scrubbed at the dark fuzz of hair on his head, remembered seeing a man in his room he could not place but felt sure he remembered from somewhere, then realising he was looking at the mirror. And he thought about huge vista now opening out ahead of him.

'Yes, I am satisfied,' he replied.

AND THAT'S YOUR LOT! FOR NOW...

Also from NewCon Press

Night, Rain, and Neon edited by Michael Cobley

All new cyberpunk stories from the likes of Gary Gibson, Jon Courtenay Grimwood, Justina Robson, Louise Carey, Ian MacDonald, Simon Morden, DA Xiaolin Spires ++. "Three hundred pages of thought-provoking cyberpunk that will give many hours of pleasure." – *SF Crowsnest*

Wergen: The Alien Love War – Mercurio D. Rivera

Shortlisted for the 2022 Arthur C. Clarke Award. The Wergens: a highly sophisticated alien race biochemically infatuated with humans. They crave us, they need us, while we need their technology. Humanity exploits them. Until, that is, the Wergens find a way to fight back.

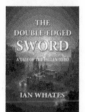

The Double-Edged Sword – Ian Whates

A disgraced swordsman leaves town one step ahead of justice. His past, however, soon catches up with him in the form of Julia, a notorious thief and sometimes assassin. Against his better judgement he undertakes an impossible mission, knowing that his life is on the line.

Vital Signals: Virtual Futures

Short sharp stories that present alternative visions of the future, drawing attention to the impact of cutting-edge science and technology on society and humanity. Established SF authors join civil servants, artists, etc, to provide a broader view of what the future might hold.

The Wild Hunt – Garry Kilworth

When Gods meddle in the affairs of mortals, it never ends well... for the mortals, at any rate. Steeped in ancient law, history and imagination, Garry Kilworth serves up an epic Anglo-Saxon saga of revenge, featuring warriors, witches, giants, dwarfs, light elves and more.

www.newconpress.co.uk

CPSIA information can be obtained
at www.ICGtesting.com
Printed in the USA
BVHW070933310123
657510BV00001B/27